Secrets in the Dark

Would you tell your best friend your darkest
secret - if it could change your life?

Written by

Ceril Campbell

Text copyright @ July 2020

Ceril Campbell

All Rights Reserved by

Ceril Campbell

Published by SatinPublishing

ISBN No: 9798674805793

Author Biography

Ceril has always been passionate about fashion and 'Secrets in the Dark' - her debut novel - is not autobiographical in any way, but is based on her insider knowledge of the world of celebrity. In her early twenties, with a fashion design and merchandising degree, she was given the opportunity by the Jean Machine brand to create and design for two FU's flagship stores in London's Knightsbridge and Bond Street.

Ceril subsequently opened her own kids emporium, 'Kids on the Green' on the Kings Road, whilst also styling for magazines, TV commercials, pop promos.

For the last thirty years she has worked as a celebrity stylist, fashion commentator and expert on TV and radio with her own magazine columns and features. She is now a broadcaster and inspirational speaker, helping clients with lifestyle, image, life change, self-esteem, positive body confidence and mental wellness. Ceril has written self-help books - the most recent being 'Discover the New You, celebrity stylist secrets to transform your life and style' available on Amazon. Ceril lives in London and has two adult children.

You can follow Ceril on;
Instagram @cerilcampbell
Twitter @cerilcampbell

Dedication

For the inspirational people in my life - my late parents and my favourite aunty Sylvia - who all lived with joy and irreverence into their mid-nineties - and for those who are always there for me now; my son Rory, my daughter Bella and my cousin Fran. Love you ❤

Acknowledgements

With thanks to:

Nicky Fitzmaurice who accepted the challenge of publishing this novel and whose inspirational editorial advice helped Secrets in the Dark become the version it is now.

Mary Alexander who gave me the confidence and tools as a first time fiction writer to improve my story telling, actually finish the book and not get depressed at the thought of re-editing 400 pages multiple times.

Jacq Burns for the insight into the world of writers, agents and getting published at her London Writers Club talks.

And a big thank you to those brave enough to read my early drafts and offer feedback - Bella Campbell, Irene Taylor, Teresa Graham.

AUTHOR LINKS:

consultancy: www.cerilcampbell.com
Instagram: @cerilcampbell

LinkedIn: Ceril Campbell
Twitter: @cerilcampbell
Facebook: Ceril Campbell style your life
Facebook: www.facebook.com/ceril.campbell
Pinterest: Ceril Campbell
Blog: Styleyourlifeblog.co.uk

Transgender consultancy: TRANS.style
Email: ceril@cerilstyle.com

Satin Publishing:

https://www.satinpublishing.co.uk
https://twitter.com/SatinPaperbacks
https://www.facebook.com/Satinpaperbacks.com

Email: nicky.fitzmaurice@satinpublishing.co.uk

Table of Contents:

Prologue

Cannes, France. 15th May, 1980

It had been an exceptional party; the standout party of the week that everyone would be talking about for a long time afterwards - but maybe not for the same reasons as he would have wanted, it was the night where lives were forever changed.

The early morning heat from the French Riviera sun was already shimmering off the marble floor of the palatial terrace. Bowls of Russian Caviar had been scraped clean and empty bottles of vintage Krug left floating in the melted ice of the silver champagne buckets. The master bedroom was steamy, even with the air-conditioning on high but it was a different heat that had been building in there. A hundred dollar note lay rolled up beside powdery coke residues smeared across the dark brown wood coffee table and a silky slip of an evening dress lay in a crumpled heap, exactly where a beautiful young woman had stepped out of it by the French windows.

He had been enjoying their private after-party for some hours now with her, but he could suddenly feel beads of sweat gathering on his forehead, running onto the silk Hermes tie she'd used to blindfold him. He'd never sweated before, why would he have started now? His chest felt as if it were about to explode, as though someone had cut off the oxygen supply to his lungs. His senses seemed heightened and extreme, causing him to feel disorientated and dizzy. He was finding himself unable to focus on anything but the incredible sensations coming from the erotic massaging, licking and stroking movements of her finger and tongue actions. An overwhelming exhaustion seemed to be

1

overtaking him, even with all the lines of coke he'd done. He pushed her head down further onto his cock. He could still manage that. 'Oh God...' Was that his own voice he could hear moaning uncontrollably? He'd always liked to dominate and be in control – being submissive was a revelation. How could she possibly understand how to have made his body feel such intense sensations? Every single touch stimulated and aroused his senses to levels he didn't know were possible. This was sex like he'd never before experienced.

'Lie still and don't do anything, this is just for you. Try this... breathe in... now.'

He heard her whisper softly, yet decisively, close to his face and then there was a sharp snap of something breaking under his nostrils before he smelt the pungent fumes of what he recognised to be amyl nitrate. He had no choice but to inhale. His heart was racing so fast now that he wondered if he was having an out of body experience. Why was his chest being squeezed so tightly and becoming increasingly painful.

'Babe... can't breathe... so much pain... my chest... my heart pills...'

Marcus Lean was a man who until now, had always been in control, but the one thing he had no control over was his own demise. Death had come unexpectedly early to him with a final heart-stopping climax. The best he'd ever had. She felt his pulse but there was nothing to feel. Karma was a bigger bitch than she could ever be. She calmly and methodically removed the blindfold tie from his eyes and hung it back in his wardrobe. She found her discarded evening dress and scrunched it up into a tiny ball into her evening bag.

How could she leave the suite and blend in unnoticed if she were to come across any hotel staff or early-rising guests?

She looked quickly around the room for inspiration. An oversized white, fluffy hotel bathrobe hanging in the bathroom and slip-on slippers were perfect. Exactly what any girl would throw on for an early morning dip. Enveloped in white towelling and sunglasses, she slipped anonymously out of the first floor suite down to the deserted Boulevard de la Croisette and across the road to the beach.

Chapter 1. Phoebe. London, 1967–1970

Phoebe hated being thirteen. It was so hard to fit in with the girls at school, particularly with her bossy mother wielding her own agenda on how her only daughter should behave and dress.

'Dahling,' her mother began, at least fifteen times a day. Phoebe knew she wasn't important enough to her mother's egocentric life to actually be called by her own name. It was always dahling, her father was dahling too.

'Dahling, it's so important to always be properly turned out. People will make assumptions about you, based on what you wear. You wouldn't want them getting the wrong idea, would you?' What wrong idea might that be, Phoebe wondered, but she didn't stop her mother to ask and let her carry on without drawing breath. It was better that way as she never needed or wanted a reply. 'You never know who you might run into. Remember that story I told you of how your father and I first met, when I was a young fashion model back in the Fifties?' How could Phoebe forget? It was a story her mother liked to tell at every opportunity. 'As the Hon. Mrs Michael Clarke it's so important to keep up appearances. You know, I'm always in the society pages - Tatler's Jennifer's Diary, The Daily Express's William Hickey. You will be too when you're older, dahling. People will judge you.'

The cool girls in her year group already had, Phoebe thought despondently. They'd already formed a judgement about her and it wasn't a positive one. She dreaded the start of each new term, when classroom desk positions needed to be bagsied. She always wondered where she'd end up, as the cool girl group shot-gunned the back rows. She didn't want to always be the front row goody-two-shoes girl lumped together with the geeks and the swots.

She stared at herself in her bedroom mirror. Curly red hair and a freckly round face stared back at her. It seemed to lack potential. How could she make herself popular and interesting? If only she could have just one proper friend at school. As an only child, she was used to her own company at home, but at school she knew it just made her seem like a weirdo. Maybe if she transformed the way she wore her pristine, new, slightly too big school uniform she could win some new friends. She rolled the waistband of her grey school pleated skirt over and over, until it no longer ended at her knees but sat around mid-thigh. She then clinched the snake clasp of the grey elasticated purse belt over the rolls of skirt fabric at her waist. She stared at her reflection again. It was definitely an improvement.

She'd always felt 'less than'. Not good enough, lacking. Maybe it was because she had such a perfect looking mother. When she'd been really young, she could remember standing in her mother's dressing room. It was like a special, magical Aladdin's-cave world, smelling of musky perfumes and mothballs. She'd loved it in there. She would drape glittering diamond necklaces from her mother's jewel box around her then-small-stubby fingers and stroke all the silky fabrics and furs which felt so beautiful to touch. She'd slide her little feet into her mother's Ferragamo evening shoes. She couldn't quite reach the hangers to try on dresses, so she'd just hold a handbag and imagine her favourite dress. She always hoped she'd see a mini version of her tall, blonde, beautiful, slim mother looking back at her in the mirror. The only reflection she saw was a short, chubby, red haired child, with overcrowded teeth (at least she now had braces) and

5

tortoiseshell spectacles (recently swapped for painful contact lenses), and a navy velvet hairband losing the battle to hold back her curls. The trouble was, apart from the braces and the lenses, nothing much had changed over the years. She wasn't that much taller and still on the plump side. Her hair was still red and impossibly curly.

Phoebe forced it into two wonky plaits and surveyed herself one last time. This new look would have to do or she was going to be late for school. She picked up her stiff, shiny brand new brown leather satchel and ran downstairs to the family's chauffeur James, who was patiently waiting in the hall to take her to school.

'Can you drop me round the corner please, James? I'd prefer the girls not to see me in the Bentley with you.' Phoebe leant forward over the driver's seat back and added anxiously, 'please? Promise you won't tell my parents?' James caught her eye in the rear view mirror. He had soft brown eyes and a rolling Scottish accent.

'Don't you worry, Miss Phoebe, I won't. Good luck at school today.' He was always kind to her.

'Thank you,' she said, sounding relieved as she trusted him. She had deliberately planned to get to school early to try to bag a desk right in the middle of the cool girl group, not the back row as she wasn't that brave. A middle row would do. She took a deep breath and walked into the classroom but the popular group she longed to be part of were already there.

'Hi girls, is it okay if I sit here?'

'Oh, hi Phoebe.' The girls had said hello back to her. Her hopes briefly rose. 'Sorry Phoebe. I've bagged this place for Kate.'

'What about here?'

6

'Sorry, Louisa's there.'

Phoebe moved further along the row. 'Here?'

'Sorry Phoebe, Susie and Emma are there.'

She tried one more time.

'No, that's Joanna's place.'

So it was back to the front row again. She'd so wanted to be part of the cool girl gang. Inside her, something turned over and formed into a thought of steel.

She wasn't sure how, but one day she'd be so cool, famous and successful that they'd regret not including Phoebe Clarke.

At break time, her classmates didn't exclude her but they didn't welcome her either. She sat on the edge of the small group, trying to overhear their weekend gossip. She had no idea what they were talking about. So she just listened and smiled when they laughed. Most of their gossip was about sex. She only knew the very basics of what her mother called "the birds and the bees". The girls seemed to be learning more advanced stuff from their parents' paperback books. They pored over their illicit adult contraband in the playground.

'Let's find all the naughty bits.'

'Okay, my book's The Delta of Venus.'

'Mine's The Prime of Miss Jean Brodie. See, in the book it says, "My girls are the crème de la crème". We could be the crème de la crème too, couldn't we?'

But the cool girls knew they were already. Phoebe watched them huddled around their biblical tomes of sexual information as they proceeded to read the juiciest bits out to each other. She'd never heard of anything they were discussing, it was like another language. She knew more words in French than the ones they were using. If all this was to do with "the birds and the bees", her mother had never mentioned it. The girls shared so much that Phoebe just didn't understand. It all sounded strange to her. Her class-mates didn't enlighten her either. They thought she was way too babyish, she didn't even wear a bra yet. Maybe that was another way forward – she could ask Abby, Mrs Abbott, the housekeeper to buy her a bra; Abby was *always* there for her, unlike her mother. Mrs Abbott triumphantly produced a Woolworth's nylon Ladybird brand bra - 32A cup with a rosebud print all over it. Phoebe excitedly tried the bra on in her bedroom, and although she didn't yet fill it out, she felt properly grown up, just like the rest of the girls. She experimented with padding the cups out with cotton wool and discovered that this was the final part of the no-boob-to-boobs conundrum. She knew that no boy was going to be putting his hand inside her bra any time soon, so the cotton wool felt a pretty safe option. It just needed not to fall out, especially in front of any class mates. So she made sure she always undressed for gym, facing the lockers and never added the padding unless she knew it was completely safe. When it came to swimming she told the sports teacher she had the curse. She'd heard the other girls using that word as an excuse, but she hadn't got hers yet, so it was just another fib to add to the ever growing list.

Another school year passed and nothing much really changed in Phoebe's world. The cool girls still huddled together in the playground, sitting in the only sunny corner. Phoebe sat in her usual position, on the fringes of the group, saying nothing. The girls just acted as though she wasn't there. Like an annoying fly that didn't go away, even after it had been repeatedly swatted. The girls chattered on, oblivious to her presence.

'Wasn't Way In at Harrods groovy last weekend? It was so fun there with all the pop music and flashing lights. What are you going to wear next time? Tell you what, I'll phone your home to see what you're wearing before we leave and then we can wear the same. Shall we go to the Chelsea Drugstore afterwards for a milkshake on the way home?' The girls' cycle of group chats continued, whilst Phoebe remained always on the outside, looking in. She spent a long time considering what she could do to join in as she so wanted to go to these places too, and then do more than just sit and listen. One day, suddenly, it came to her. She'd create a pretend life that would mirror theirs - an alter ego - with a boyfriend. She'd pretend to be somebody she wanted to be until she finally became that person. She chose her moment carefully, selecting Louisa to tell as she'd always been a little kinder to her than the others.

'Louisa, don't tell anyone but I've got a boyfriend I've been seeing.' Phoebe tentatively whispered to her at the end of one break-time. Louisa looked at her, mouth open, gobsmacked.

'Really? You? I don't believe you!' Louisa abruptly walked off, immediately catching up with her girlfriends, who were a few yards ahead.

'Hey, girls, guess what...'

Phoebe walked meekly behind them, already prepared for the fact that Louisa had been likely to run back to convey this extraordinary news as soon as she was able. The girls would then digest it and come and ask more. Phoebe knew exactly how these girls worked together - she'd watched them for long enough. When they came, she'd be ready. She felt sure she'd hit on the way into the sacred inner sanctum of the cool girls. Now she just needed to make up stories about what she'd been doing with this imaginary boyfriend. But if she was going to make it all up she needed to know what she was talking about and how could she do that if she'd never done anything at all? She knew she needed to be convincing and to have as much knowledge as possible for when they started quizzing her. Phoebe's alter-ego was everything she wished she herself could actually be - sexy, sassy, outgoing, confident and popular with everybody.

After lunch the cool girls sat in the playground in their usual sunny corner and for the first time ever Phoebe was in the circle too and it felt good that she was learning how to assert herself as Phoebe Version Two. It seemed that the difference between try and triumph was just a fib or two. She didn't really like lying but look where it was getting her.

'So, Phoebe, tell us... *everything*.'

'Well...'did she really have all six girls' attention? It seemed she did. 'I met this boy Paul in the holidays.' Giving this fictional character a name seemed to make him more real. The probing questions came fast and furious.

'How old is he?'

'Think the same age as me, fourteen.' Phoebe answered with confidence.

'Blonde?'

'Dark?'

'Tall or short?'

'Good looking?' The girls couldn't get their probing questions out quick enough, but so far these were all easy questions for Phoebe.

'Blonde, good-looking, taller than me but that's not difficult as I'm only five foot two.' Phoebe attempted to make a joke and giggled self-consciously. Gosh, this was working, the girls were laughing with her too.

'Where did you meet Paul?' The girls were now relentless in their interrogation and there was no letting up.

'The ballroom dancing classes at my parents' club. Paul asked me to go with him to the Teenage Ball there.' This was all nearly true. She'd gone to holiday dance classes and there had been boys there too. However, they hadn't talked or danced with her and she'd stood on the side of the room with no partner and had to dance with the teacher. Her alter-ego would never have suffered such indignity. 'Paul and I danced for ages in the disco and when we were too sweaty, we escaped to the fresh air outside, walking to the jetty by the river. It was sooo romantic. That's where we had a quick snog and he offered me a cigarette.' Phoebe hoped she was using the correct terminology and that it all sounded realistic. She must be, the girls were looking impressed. Gosh, she was surprisingly good at telling these stories.

'Wow, Phoebe, you had a snog? How was it with your braces, didn't he mind... didn't he say it hurt his tongue?'

Phoebe now found herself with a dilemma in how to answer with authority as she still hadn't kissed anyone yet. However, she was on a roll and she wasn't going to stop now. 'No, he didn't say anything... but it was really brill,' then she had a sudden moment of inspiration, 'but while we were out there, some parents came past us just as he was about to put his hand inside my bra,' she paused for optimum effect.

'Wow Phoebe...' the girls were now hanging on to her every word, 'what happened then?'

Phoebe realised she might have nailed the story now. 'They told us we weren't allowed to be outside and to go back inside the party rooms immediately.' She thought this sounded plausible but maybe less exciting. The girls however seemed suitably impressed.

'Wow, Phoebe and you were smoking!'

'Yes Consulate Menthol.' She knew that was the brand that some of the girls smoked. All her listening was paying off.

'Phoebe, you've really changed this hols. Come and sit with us in the playground next break so we can hear more, absolutely everything... *all* the gory details.'

She'd cracked the cool-girl code; now she just had to keep going but she became obsessed with wanting to experience everything that she was describing. She wanted to know more about sex - whether it was all that it was cracked up to be by the girls. She wanted to come to school hiding love bites. She wanted to know what the girls meant by "soixante–neuf" and finger screwing. She wanted to transform into her alter-ego.

Phoebe's subsequent plan of action was to buy Honey and Jackie teen mags and avidly devour them from cover to cover in search of the important details that would add gravitas to her stories. Any little nuggets of detail that she could find out about sex were her way forward to improve and embellish her stories. She forensically examined every single teen magazine problem page so she could sound like she really knew her stuff.

She also learnt the names of pop singer crushes that she'd heard the girls say they'd stuck up on their bedroom walls, then scrutinised all the makeup, hair styles and High Street fashion pages which seemed to be nothing like the styles she'd seen in her mother's magazines. She'd often snuck downstairs at night and borrowed copies of her mother's Vogues which lay next to perfectly aligned stacks of expensive glossy coffee table books. She read them under her duvet cover with a torch so Mrs Abbott wouldn't see a light coming from under her bedroom door. Phoebe always returned them to the exact position they'd come from as she knew her mother would notice anything out of place in her carefully curated perfect rooms.

Phoebe cut up all her teen magazine pages; mixing, matching and pasting outfits into fashion scrapbooks. She added styling changes and notes about fabrics and colours with little sketches of her own. No one would ever see them, they were her secret. She didn't want to be laughed at, she just wanted to be liked.

Halfway through the term a new girl unexpectedly appeared.

'Girls, please meet your new classmate, Paula. She'll be joining your class from today.' The teacher introduced a tall and skinny, moody-looking girl standing beside her in the doorway of the classroom. The girl looked sulkily back at her new classmates. Phoebe watched her sweep her blonde, very straight, thick long hair back with one seemingly well-practiced single movement, so that it fell back off her face for a short time and then heavily down over her shoulders. In that fleeting moment, Phoebe noticed over-plucked eyebrows framing the bluest but saddest eyes she'd ever seen. The new girl stood with her arms crossed sullenly across her generous bosom. Her sourness and disengagement detracted from her prettiness.

'Please go and sit there in the front row next to Phoebe,' directed the teacher in a kindly tone. The girl didn't bother to acknowledge the teacher or her neighbour as she sat down. Phoebe decided she had nothing to lose by being friendly. The cool girls had already dropped her from their inner circle again once they'd realised that she had no more personal gossip to feed them, side-lining her as quickly as they'd picked her up. Loyalty wasn't big on their teenage agenda.

Phoebe overheard them discussing the new girl immediately after lessons ended. They didn't hold back in their immediate and negative assessment of this unknown girl.

'Have you chatted to that strange new girl Paula yet?'

'Where do you think she comes from?'

'What school was she at before this, a state school?'

'She won't say, maybe she got a scholarship... but what's she good at?'

'Dunno - she doesn't talk to anyone.'

'Boring.' That was the girls' summary of Paula before they completely wrote her off.

Phoebe could understand how Paula's "don't care, don't mess with me" attitude had stopped anyone engaging with her. Phoebe didn't care where Paula came from, or how she talked and that maybe she wasn't posh. She knew what it was like to be an outsider looking in and to always be on your own.

'Hi Paula, I wondered if you'd like to walk down the Kings Road with me after school tomorrow on your way home?' Phoebe tried asking using her braver alter-ego persona, hoping to break though Paula's icy demeanour. Paula looked surprised at the unexpected approach and swept back her hair before she started to speak. Phoebe wondered whether it was a studied and contrived affectation or a nervous habit.

Paula took a few minutes to consider the question before she answered. 'Why me? I thought you was mates with that cool gang.'

'No, not anymore.' Phoebe's own reply was immediate.

She could see Paula's hesitation before she allowed a flicker of a smile. 'Okay tomorrow then, Phee.'

No-one had ever shortened Phoebe's name to Phee before. *Maybe Paula could become her friend, a proper friend, the first one she'd ever had. A friend who wouldn't judge her, would keep her secrets who would always be there for her.*

Their friendship started from that afternoon. They walked together after school down the Kings Road to the bus stop by the Chelsea Drugstore, where Paula caught a bus to go to her home which Phoebe thought she'd mentioned was in Fulham, but Phoebe had no clue where Fulham was, though. The girls never phoned each other or invited each other to their respective homes and their friendship seemed to work well like that. Phoebe knew her mother's small mindedness about anyone whom she deemed common or 'vulgar', but knew nothing about Paula's reasons as she'd offered so little insight into her life. Their social arrangements were always made in the school playground at break-times.

'I know where we can go after school today, Kensington Gardens.' Phoebe gabbled excitedly.

Paula, more measured, stared expectantly at her new friend, shielding the sun from her eyes as they sat together in the corner of the playground.

'Why?' she asked, loading her myriad of questions into the one single word. She was the master of less is more when it came to their conversations.

Phoebe didn't lose her enthusiasm for her jaunt idea even with her new friend's response. 'It's a park. I used to go there a lot when I was a little girl, and we would feed the ducks at the Round Pond at the top of the hill there.'

'Who's we, Phee?' Paula was now looking confused.

'Whoever was looking after me then.' Phoebe decided not to elaborate as she didn't yet know Paula well enough to tell

15

her everything, and she didn't want Paula to judge her like everyone else had done. So she simply continued. 'Sometimes I was allowed to take my bicycle and I'd bicycle all around the pond and then freewheel back down the hill.'

Paula uncharacteristically interrupted her. 'Blimey our lives were so different. Me and my bruv just played in the street.'

Phoebe momentarily became silent with amazement that Paula had actually made a comment about her own life, then she took up her story again.

'I so looked forward to those afternoons with the ducks at the Round Pond as my life was so sheltered that it was exciting to leave the house for anything. I didn't even mind if it was raining as that meant I could splash around in the puddles, but I knew that doing so would have made my mother angry as it would have dirtied my smart White House wool coat with its velvet collar.'

Paula looked at Phoebe incredulously. 'Never heard of your White House place, but a coat with a velvet collar sounds proper posh. You must've been a right little madam." She smiled as she said it, hoping that Phoebe would realise she was teasing.

'Maybe I was a little madam but if so, it was unintentional. I am trying to change now.' Phoebe secretly crossed her fingers hoping that Paula would agree that she'd noticed changes.

'Mmm, maybe you have, just a bit.' Paula was now looking away as she spoke, so Phoebe couldn't see Paula's expression but she guessed that "just a bit" probably meant "quite a lot" in Paula's vocabulary. Phoebe could feel a warm glow of happiness inside her, realising that her new friend had just paid her a compliment.

The following Saturday was the girls' next planned trip, taking a number fourteen bus to the Harrods Way In. A thought suddenly came upon Phoebe as she gazed out of the window from the top deck. 'This is only the second time I've ever been on a bus.'

'You're joking, aren't you?' Paula looked back at her in shock.

'No, I'm serious. That's how my childhood was and the first time was with Abby.' Phoebe decided to drip feed a little more information about her home-life.

'Abby?' Paula was starting to wonder how many people lived in Phoebe's house with her.

'Abby's always looked after me and her real name is Mrs Abbott. I think I was about six then.' Phoebe wondered whether she should sound apologetic as she continued, 'Usually, I was driven everywhere in Daddy's car by James - you know I told you about him, the one who dropped me off round the corner from school.'

Paula gawked at Phoebe and raised her eyebrows. 'Yeah, I did spot you once in that flash Bentley car. You didn't get away with that, Phee.'

That's annoying, Phoebe thought to herself as she'd tried so hard to be discreet, but now that she'd started explaining about her life, she wanted to continue. 'The thing is, everything I tell you may shock you but please understand that however wonderful it sounds, it wasn't. It was like living in a gilded cage. Do you know I'd much rather have been you.'

'Nah, trust me, you wouldn't.' Paula responded definitively.'

'Yes, I would. I know you don't believe me. Anyway, back to how I ended up on the bus. Abby took me on the bus to

Marble Arch to the Lyons Corner House, The Maison Lyons I think she called it. It was so exciting.'

'Going on the bus was exciting? That's mental.' Paula was now looking at her friend as though she was completely mad.

'No, the Corner House, duh. It was so big, a bit like Harrods. It was a huge building with lots of restaurants in it, with names like The Grill and Cheese, the Bacon & Egg and the Wimpy Bar all linked together by one central kitchen. We could even look through the glass wall into the kitchens where chefs were cooking eggs in every way possible, served up with fried potato chips. I'd never seen anything like this sort of food before and was mesmerised by the kitchen staff stirring, flipping and tossing eggs around. I had never seen anyone cooking, even in my own house as I wasn't allowed in the kitchen by Cook. My mother never went into the kitchen either unless it was to check a dinner party menu or talk with Cook about the week's meals.'

'Phee, your life is mad. How can you never have been in your kitchen and what's a dinner party, or whatever you called it? I have tea when I come home from school on a tray in front of the telly and sometimes cook a roast dinner on a Sunday for me, my bruv and my dad. Your life's like a whole other world.'

'Paula, I know, your life shocks me too.'

The two girls looked at each other equally stunned and bemused by the information they'd just swapped about their lives.

The bus slowed down at a bus stop. The pale pink Harrods building loomed into view.

'Phee, we're here. Quick, come on down the stairs, otherwise we'll miss the stop. I've already rung the bell.' Paula grabbed Phoebe's hand and scrambled with her down the stairs, but the bus lurched forward again into the traffic. 'Oh no, we've missed it now, never mind, we'll get off when the bus next stops in the traffic...quick... now...jump!'

Phoebe was finally doing all the same things she'd listened to the other girls in class doing. She was seeing all the cool shops in Chelsea and Knightsbridge, and all the fashions that were so far removed from what her mother wore. She and Paula had managed to sample milk shakes in Harrods Way In and found Laura Ashley on the Fulham Road where they'd tried on the Victoriana-style print smock dresses and maxi skirts. Phoebe suddenly felt so grown-up, it must have been the Paula effect rubbing off.

Phoebe had never questioned paying for both of them on their outings together; she knew Paula had no money. She'd pushed away the tiny flicker of worry that her best friend might only be with her because she funded everything. She hoped she wasn't just buying her friendship... no, that could never be possible and she quickly dismissed the thought.

One day Paula unexpectedly came up with an invitation of her own. 'Fancy a pop concert at that posh Albert Hall gaff? A friend's just given me two tickets for Deep Purple playing with the Royal Phil... ham... something band... orchestra... dunno. Didn't ask how he got them, what do you think?'

Phoebe tried not to show how excited she was. This was her first ever concert, but she had absolutely nothing suitable to wear as her wardrobe had always been chosen by her mother. She now wanted to channel the "groovy hippy chick" vibe she'd seen photographed in all her magazines. Kensington Market was exactly the place to find the perfect outfit. She knew Mrs Abbott would definitely say no to her going there and Phoebe had no idea how to get there on her own - maybe James could take her and pretend it was an errand for a school homework project.

He swallowed her story, she was getting really adept now at fibbing. James waited for her at the side of Barkers Department store where she entered through the nearest side door, and snuck out again at the front onto Kensington High Street to the Kensington Market. She had to stop outside to literally breathe it all in for a minute. She could smell the market before she'd even walked in. If she could have bottled the smells, she would have mixed together old musty leather, Indian spices, wet dog, maybe a bit of horse manure and pot pourri. It wasn't just the smells that were so amazing, it was the random arrangement and colour of the stalls, narrow passageways leading deeper into this heady other-world and an eclectic mix of fashions as she'd never seen before. Once inside, she realised the mix of smells had very precise origins. The furry Afghan coats stunk of dung, Patchouli oil and incense sticks were everywhere and random mouldy old clothes being sold as vintage added to the musty smell.

She couldn't decide where to start as she only had a short time whilst James waited for her. She pushed past stall holders and browsing shoppers who all seemed to be functioning at a slow thirty three rpm LP speed, unlike her speedy forty five rpm fourteen year old self. There were so many nooks and crannies and hidden stalls to navigate around. It was so exciting but she wished she was sharing the experience with Paula. Phoebe fell upon a perfect turquoise three-button granny t-shirt, costing a pound and to go with them a purple pair of loons - that's what the stall holder had called the wide bottomed trousers. Phoebe guessed the size she needed as there was no way she was going to try them behind a poorly-draped sheet. She found a patchwork leather belt that did up with tassels and a small silky Indian patterned scarf that smelt of Patchouli incense.

Next she needed shoes, maybe boots. Her Harrods Start-Rite school shoes or her black patent party shoes weren't going to pass muster with this new hippy-style look. She thought back to how different this was to when she'd been shopping for her childhood shoes with her mother; Harrods had been the only place her mother had felt to be a suitable shopping destination. She remembered standing inside a wooden, four foot high x-ray fitting machine which showed whether any intended shoes would be a perfect fit for her slowly-growing small but still perfectly formed feet that did weekly ballet classes. The sales assistant had peered through the viewing porthole at the top of the machine at the spectacle of the wiggling toes. "These fit lovely, Madam, plenty of room for growth." These memories were so vivid and not so long ago. Phoebe suddenly really appreciated her new found freedom of choice and re-focused on the amazing metallic brown platform boots. No need for any toe wiggling or growth room in these. A very quick try on and her shopping spree was complete. Her heart flipped with excitement. She just had to smuggle all the stuff home. She hoped the car wasn't going to be stunk out with the market smells, even now clinging to her own clothes.

She rushed back out and round to the side street where she'd left James. She climbed in the car with her purchases hidden in a large Barkers bag she'd picked up on the way out. She noticed James wrinkling his nose but he said nothing. She understood his place was never to comment, to be invisible. This seemed similar to how she saw her own role in her parents' lives.

The moment she arrived back at the house, she rushed up to her bedroom to experiment with the whole outfit. She finished it off with the Indian scarf tied bandana-style around her head leaving a mass of red curls flowing loose - just like the girls in the market posters. She looked back at herself in the mirror and smiled. Somehow the t-shirt, loon pants and boots made her look taller and more sophisticated. For the first time in her life, Phoebe considered that she might even look passable.

But Phoebe's positivity about her own transformed grown-up appearance quickly dissipated on seeing Paula, who was now unrecognisable. Paula was wearing the tiniest pair of hot pants and a short cross-over rainbow striped coloured sweater accentuating her bosoms. Phoebe was gob-smacked but it wasn't just the outfit, her friend now looked about twenty years old, not fifteen.

'Gosh, you look like one of the models out of Honey magazine,' she stammered in shock, 'and you've even done eyeliner and false lashes. Doesn't your mother mind you wearing lots of make-up?'

'Nah,' just for a moment Phoebe thought she saw Paula show some emotion. 'My mum's dead and no one's at home to see what I do. My dad's always out and my bruv wouldn't ever notice.'

'That's so sad. Did she die... umm... recently?' Phoebe hesitated in asking.

'She died when I was eleven. She was the only person who'd ever looked out for me. One day she was well and the next day she went to bed feeling really ill and the following morning, dead – gone - just like that. I was at school. My dad said it was a heart attack but I dunno. It was all so quick. No one talks to no one in my family and my dad's angry all the time, worse when he's had a drink or three.' Paula suddenly looked like the lost young girl she really was, despite all the outward appearances of make-up and sexy clothes.

'Phee, sometimes my dad really frightens me with his scary Irish temper so I try and keep away from him as much as I can.'

Phoebe looked at her friend, not sure what to say. They both had their problems but right then, Paula's seemed far worse than her own. Phoebe put out her hand to touch Paula's arm and comfort her. She could see that her usually fearless friend was now biting her bottom lip and had tears in her eyes, but as quickly as she'd let her guard down, she'd pulled herself together and fixed her smile, reverting back to being the unemotional Paula, the only version Phoebe had so far got to know. Phoebe quickly dropped her hand and decided to say nothing more. She'd never yet asked Paula anything about her life and time would tell whether she'd ever want to tell her more, like all best friends did.

The girls had a bird's eye view of the stage from their seats in the uppermost tier, where there were loads of other teenagers too. Phoebe was desperately trying to look cool and not appear naïve by asking any questions but finally she gave in. She attempted to shout over the impossibly loud music.

'Paula, what's that funny smell? It smells the same as the incense and joss sticks I smelt in the Kensington Market.'

'Nah, Phee. Not incense, it's hash.' Paula didn't bother to look at Phoebe as she replied, as she was now peering down over the edge of the rail at the pinprick-sized figures performing on the stage far beneath them.

'Hash?' Phoebe had no clue what her friend was talking about.

'How can you have managed to stay so innocent living in Chelsea? Welcome to real life; hash, pot, weed, marijuana, it's all the same sort of thing; you smoke it and get stoned.' Paula didn't feel like engaging in any more of an explanation as it might have opened a can of worms about her own life. Phoebe was still none the wiser, but she didn't want to look as though she really knew nothing more than her own little world, so she nodded as if it all made perfect sense. She'd begun to feel slightly spacey by the end of the concert, but she wasn't sure why, maybe it was from breathing in all that funny smelling hash stuff around them. She suddenly realised that Paula was chivvying her to move quickly from their seats at the very highest tier of the Albert Hall and leave.

'Phee, come on, we're going to a party.'

'A party?' with confusion now added to her spacey feelings, Phoebe looked back at Paula wondering at what part of the concert she'd missed this conversation.

'Yeah, a party in Bayswater.' Paula practically yawned with boredom as she replied, as if she'd already repeated this a hundred times before. Phoebe didn't remember any chat about a party, maybe that smelly-hash stuff had made her forgetful, but no-one at home would ever notice if she was in much later, as long as she was back before Mrs Abbott locked the front door around midnight. Her parents were definitely too wrapped up in their own lives to care. It then struck her, at that moment, that she and Paula were so different but yet the same; both neglected by parents who – in Paula's own words – didn't give a fuck. Yes, she was definitely learning more about life hanging around with her best friend.

'Okay, let me pay.' Phoebe offered as she hailed a black taxi.

'Bayswater, please driver - Cleveland Square.' It was Paula who confidently instructed the driver as if she'd always been used to taking cabs. Phoebe never stopped being amazed at Paula's outward bravado. She wiped the condensation from the inside of the cab's window so she could see where they were going, but she was none the wiser as it certainly didn't look like Chelsea. She felt shocked as they drew up, as although they'd arrived in a pretty London garden square, the outsides of the surrounding tall buildings looked tired and dilapidated. They all seemed to have been divided into flats or student hostels. Others looked as though they were the cheapest sort of budget hotel accommodation. She could see paint peeling off the front of the buildings and torn nets and half-draped pieces of faded fabric masquerading as curtains on the windows. Everything looked so run down and so far removed from her own previously limited views of the world. She wasn't yet sure whether she felt shocked or frightened to be going to a stranger's party in such an alien environment, but she was sure Paula would look after her so it would all be okay.

Music was blaring out into the street as Phoebe followed Paula down the steep cracked concrete stairs to the basement flat. The insistent driving beat of the music grew louder as the girls drew closer, and Phoebe braced herself, wanting to put her hands over her ears as they were still ringing from the concert's decibel levels.

'What's that song playing – love it.' Phoebe absolutely knew Paula would know.

'Canned Heat On the Road Again.' There was no hesitation from Paula with her definitive answer, adding impatiently; 'Come on, do hurry up Phee.'

Phoebe followed her in like an obedient puppy dog. It was difficult to focus at first as the small room was intensely smoky and crowded. Everything seemed to be dirty, from the furniture to the people, who all looked unlike anyone she'd ever met before, even in the Kensington Market. The boys had long dirty hair and everyone had hippy-style clothing that looked like they'd never been taken off or washed. Phoebe tried discretely to hold her breath as the smoke was acrid and heavy – like at the concert but ten times worse.

'Hey guys, come in. We've got great sounds and just had some fab gear delivered.' One of the party goers shouted over to them where they were still standing in the doorway. Fab gear, what was that? Phoebe had no idea.

Paula took Phoebe's hand and pulled her further into the room.

'Here, try one of these.' she said as she handed her a can of beer. Another first, Phoebe thought to herself, as she'd never tried alcohol before. She held the can nonchalantly, not knowing whether she should drink straight from it or find a glass, but the can seemed marginally preferable in light of the filthy surroundings. She was beginning to feel overwhelmed by the strangeness of everything and suddenly wanted to go home quite badly. She knew she'd experienced enough new things for one day. She turned round to speak to Paula but she'd disappeared.

Phoebe scanned the room and spotted her entwined with a boy. Now Phoebe really didn't know what to do - sit, stand or leave - everyone seemed to be snogging, all in various stages of what the cool girls at school may have described as heavy petting; bodies tangled in clinches on the floor. This meant she would have had to step over bodies if she were to move anywhere in the room so she decided to stay standing exactly where she was, leaning against a wall as it seemed to be the safest place. A scruffy boy with acne and greasy shoulder length hair suddenly grabbed her and Phoebe jumped, startled.

'It's a gas in here, isn't it? You digging the sounds?'

Did this yukky boy actually need a reply? Phoebe's horrified expression must have exuded all her negativity and more, due to her increasing anxiety. The boy leapt back as though he'd been electrocuted. 'Hey, don't get so uptight man, I was just being friendly.'

This unattractive teenage specimen of male adolescence was not the one whom Phoebe had been dreaming of having her first kiss with, from as long ago as when she'd been making up in her stories at school. *She wanted to remember her first kiss as being something special.* She looked round for Paula again, who seemed now to have detangled herself from the boy she'd been snogging and was looking even more dishevelled. Her cross-over sweater had become more uncrossed and there was a glimpse of a dirty looking, off-white bra. Phoebe stared at her and Paula stared back with what Phoebe decided was funny-looking eyes, pupils bigger than usual. Paula was coming over and Phoebe, even more desperate now to go home, decided now was the time to make her stand.

'Do you mind if we leave now, Paula?'

'Umm, I was going to stay around for a bit.' But then Paula seemed to refocus and reconsider as she peered at her anxious friend who was shuffling her feet from side to side in anticipation of the possibility at leaving. 'Nah, Phee, you can't go home on your own. Give me five minutes.'

Phoebe felt a sense of overwhelming relief and went to sit outside on the crumbling concrete step, gulping in the fresh night air. Her anxiety was already subsiding. Eventually Paula re-appeared, looking even more worse for wear and the girls made their way down the Bayswater Road together, clutching onto each other, until they managed to hail another passing taxi. Once in, they both sat slumped against each other.

'You didn't enjoy yourself.' Paula mumbled with her eyes shut.

Phoebe knew she didn't want to admit she'd actually hated it and sound ungrateful to her best friend, so she simply referenced only the first part of the evening. 'I loved the concert, thank you so much for taking me.'

Paula looked satisfied with the Phoebe's response and kept her eyes closed until they'd arrived back into the familiar territory of the Kings Road, where they both got out of the cab to make their separate ways home.

The party was never mentioned again. Paula continued to keep her home life to herself, but sometimes during their weekly Saturday shopping excursions new small bite-sized snapshots of her life would slip out. 'I'm feeling a bit hungover today, bad mistake, should have known better.'

Phoebe always waited for Paula to say more, but she never did.

Chapter 2. Paula, London

Paula loved hanging around with Phoebe. Their worlds were so far apart but yet so close together. It was surprising how she could have so much in common with someone so different from her. She recognised the same lonely girl in Phoebe as in herself, but realised that Phoebe dealt with her anxieties in different ways from the way she did. Phoebe, little Miss Innocent, had no idea how naughty her friend really was and how often she put out with boys, but all that side of her life was best kept in the dark.

She aspired to living in Phoebe's privileged world and envied the fact that Phoebe didn't think anything of spending twenty or even fifty pounds just like that, whereas she had to scrimp and save, or buy and sell some dope to have even five pounds in her purse. Her dad had never given her any allowance, as she'd heard Phoebe call it, or pocket money. When her mum had been alive, she'd give her a few shillings saved from housekeeping money, but that was a few years ago. Her life was now spent mostly on her own and sometimes with her dad. She rarely saw her only brother, who was six years older, as he'd joined the Navy when she was still a little girl and now rarely came home. They'd never had much of relationship even though her mum had tried to make them appreciate their few family times together with her home-cooked meals. She now tried to emulate her mum's Sunday roast dinners to make her dad happy and see him smile, but it seemed that nothing she could ever do was good enough for him, even when she'd worked really hard and managed to get the scholarship. Even then, he hadn't ever said well done. She had no idea what else she could do to make him happy.

Even when her dad came home drunk and happy from a day at the dogs, or drunk and angry from losing all his winnings again, she'd always try to make a nice cooked tea for them both, straight after school and serve it up properly on their avocado-coloured Formica table in their tiny kitchen. She wanted to make their tea-time special so that he'd chat to her, ask her about her day at school, instead of sitting silent and comatose on their old, worn-out and lumpy sofa, staring at the telly. She was proud that she now knew how to lay a table and hold her knife and fork properly from carefully watching Phoebe, even though she knew her dad would never notice these minutiae, he would only think she'd got above herself if he saw her doing anything differently.

All Paula wanted was to hear her dad say 'thank you' and 'I love you' just occasionally – it didn't matter when. It could be when she'd put all her daughterly love for him into baking a macaroni cheese she'd laboured for ages over, or the slow-cooked Irish stew made with the cheapest cuts of meat she'd managed to buy. How difficult could it be for a father to cuddle his daughter and show her that he loved her? She was sure he did love her, but since her mum's death he'd changed and was drunk more often than not, but he was her dad and all she had in the world. His acknowledgement of her actual presence in the house and anything she did, however small, would have meant the world to her, but it seemed that she would be waiting forever, as the harder she tried, the more he withdrew and his alcohol dependency became more evident. The more he drank, the more moments he had of uncontrollable anger where Paula often felt safer hiding away in her bedroom. Maybe, she wondered, she reminded her dad too much of her late mum? Paula knew, when she looked at the few old photos she still had of her, that when her mum had been her age now, there was a distinct resemblance.

Paula wasn't in the slightest bit jealous of Phoebe, she'd seen that money hadn't made her any happier. She also appreciated her friend's generosity but sometimes felt embarrassed accepting it. She'd learnt that it was prudent for a girl to never turn down anything on offer; money, a compliment or an opportunity. She didn't really want to take advantage of the only girlfriend she'd ever had, but sometimes a girl just had to do what a girl had to do, especially when it came with no expectations of a favour in return. That was unusual in her book.

She'd learned from Phoebe how to talk 'proper', taking care not to drop her 'aitches', although she wasn't sure if Phoebe had noticed anything yet. She'd heard Phoebe use the words sitting room and drawing room, but she wasn't sure if they were the same as a lounge, she definitely knew though that asking for the loo instead of the toilet was how posh people spoke. There was a lot to remember; all the new words she could never use at home as her dad would think she'd turned into some fancy girl with airs and graces above her station.

Paula had also concluded that she'd never be able to style her outfits in the clever way that Phoebe did, but she could definitely rock a good mini, wearing it as short as she could, just covering her bum cheeks – even if she had to pull it down every so often as she walked - so her panties didn't show. So when Phoebe suggested a new shopping adventure, planned as usual from their social office in the school playground; she found the tightest Mickey Mouse child's t-shirt in a charity shop, which barely reached her waist and accentuated her boobs as it was pulled so tightly across them. She teamed this with a t-shirt and mini-skirt with a pair of platform sandals which made her appear about ten foot tall. She didn't know why she felt compelled to compete with her best friend. She was sure that it had never crossed Phoebe's mind that her best friend could be just a teensy bit jealous of her.

The girls window-shopped up and down Carnaby Street together, both proudly wearing their latest outfits.

'Golly, Paula, these dresses are only eight guineas. I've got to have one... And maybe one of these coats to go over it.'

Paula could feel Phoebe's excitement as she drooled over the dresses. She had no clue why she should hanker after one of these dresses so specifically, but knew whatever her friend chose, it would look good.

Phoebe was on a roll, 'Which bag do you like? They're only four guineas. I'll treat you, don't worry, it's daddy's money. He won't know, he never checks his bank statements.' Paula didn't get a chance to reply. 'Go on, try on these trousers, they're so way out and these ones are your size. You're so much skinnier than me.' Phoebe handed the trousers over into the tiny changing room and Paula wriggled into them. The legs fit fine but the zip wouldn't do up, nor would the button at the waist.

'Nah, Phee, I'm coming out. They don't look proper good.'

'No, hang on Paula, wait. I want to see what they look like.'

'Nah, I'm done.' Paula was annoyed that the trousers didn't fit and didn't want Phoebe to see. Strange that she couldn't get them done up, she must have put on weight. That was odd, as she often made herself sick after a meal when she'd eaten too much, just so she could stay skinny. Skinny was good, but Phoebe had quickly put her head round the changing room curtain and managed to catch a glimpse of the zip not meeting.

'That's weird, they must have come up really small.'

'Yeah, they must do, didn't like them anyway.' Paula decided there and then that she wasn't going to have anything else to eat that day and if she did, it would be straight off to the toilet – no loo.

Shopping trip over, the girls sat having a coffee back in the familiarity of their local café, the Picasso on the Kings Road. It was like their second home, their go-to place. Suddenly Phoebe thought of something that made her exclaim excitedly out of the blue. 'I've been invited to a party. You can be my plus one and we'll have so much fun. It's a Charity Ball.'

'You're having a laugh, aren't you, me going to a posh charity ball? Nah, not happening.' Paula instantly rejected the suggestion.

'No, it's not like that,' Phoebe quickly intervened, 'it's the Feathers Ball, a teenage charity party at the Hammersmith Palais, it can be my Christmas present to you.'

'Fanks but dunno. Would I have to act all posh and behave myself?'

'No, you can just be yourself. You could come to me to get ready first and borrow something to wear. No, that's not going to work, is it? You're so tall and slim and I'm so short and dumpy. Tell you what, I'll treat you to something to wear. I spotted the perfect outfit just now in that shop across the road. I'm going to quickly dash across to get it now, wait here.'

Paula suddenly felt a bit awkward. 'You're always buying stuff for me. One day I promise I'll repay everything you've done for me but if you really mean it, then possibly in a bigger size than usual, I seem to be a bit fat at the moment.'

Phoebe frowned at her friend. She couldn't believe her ears as Paula could never be called fat in a million years.

Paula sat at their table on the pavement at the front of the little coffee shop and watched the world go by as she waited for Phoebe. She stirred her cappuccino and thought how Phoebe had truly changed her life. She felt happy every day now when she got up for school. She could even cope when she went home for tea and faced her surly drunken dad, as she knew she now had a best friend who was there for her.

This party of Phoebe's would be a good test of putting into practice everything she'd secretly watched Phoebe doing over the last two years; how she'd talked, walked and behaved, especially if she was likely to meet Phoebe's mum at her house before the party. That would be proper scary. Phoebe was back really quickly with a large carrier bag. Paula didn't want to open it yet as she didn't want to show how excited she was. She still liked to hide her feelings.

But Phoebe was bursting with excitement. 'Go on, please look now.' Inside was the most fantastic outfit Paula had ever seen, it was so her. It was a silky white pair of trousers and top. The plunge-necked top tied under the bust, leaving the wide ties hanging down. The sleeves were tight to the elbow and then became swooshy and full to the wrist. The wide bell-bottomed trousers were cut to sit on the hips. Paula had never seen anything like it, she was speechless and overwhelmed by her friend's generosity.

'Don't you like it?' Phoebe was looking anxiously at her. Paula realised that Phoebe had expected a more positive and emotional response but it was the first time in Paula's life that anyone had ever done anything like this for her and she didn't want to show how much it had really meant to her. When she eventually spoke, her voice quavered and was unusually quiet.

'It's proper beautiful. I've never owned anything like it and I can't wait to wear it and come to your house next week to get ready.' She hugged her friend, trying to hide her rising tide of emotions.

Phoebe smiled at her friend with pleasure, realising that another issue now needed to be addressed. 'Don't worry about taking it home. I'll keep it at mine till then.'

Paula looked at her friend gratefully, realising that Phoebe was so much more thoughtful than she'd ever be.

On her way home, Paula sat on the top of the bus staring out of the window, but not seeing anything. She was lost in her thoughts. She'd almost cried when she'd seen the dress. Why was she so over-emotional all the time now, maybe it was just what happened when you got to be sixteen, maybe it was because no one had ever been as kind to her as Phoebe since her mum had died - still, it was strange. She knew she was always more emotional when she was due her period, but come to think of it, she must be due. Hmmm, she was late, but then she often was.

The day of the Feathers Ball arrived and both girls found it hard to focus on any school work that day. Paula found it even harder than Phoebe as she knew there was a strong possibility that she could meet Phoebe's mother. The thought terrified her and her heart was beating doubly fast as she walked up to the house. Blimey, Phoebe's house was as big as Buckingham Palace. It was lucky Phoebe had never seen where she lived. She knew Phoebe was never judgemental but their lives were literally worlds apart.

Paula rang the bell, stepped back down a stair and looked back up at the huge house and waited. The door opened and a tidily dressed, matronly older woman stood staring down at her from her elevated position in the doorway. Paula decided that the woman looked all sort of upright, buttoned up and proper, like she'd starched and ironed herself as well as her clothes. The woman had short tidy grey hair and a rosy complexion. Although her body language was stiff and formal, her face was open and friendly, with crinkly smile lines around her eyes. It wasn't quite how Paula had imagined Phoebe's mother to look but then again, she knew to never judge a book by its cover. She knew she had to do her best manners and voice and stepped back up the stair and put out her hand.

'Good afternoon, Mrs Clarke. Lovely to meet…'

'Hello, Paula. Phoebe told me that you were coming. I'm Mrs Abbott. Mrs Clarke is out.'

Paula breathed an audible sigh of relief.

Mrs Abbott smiled, just a fleeting half-smile that showed Paula she'd understood her anxiety. 'Come on in my dear, Phoebe will be down in a minute.'

There was a flurry of footsteps down the stairs and there was Phoebe, flushed and excited. 'Paula, this is so exciting, come on, let's go up to my room, mummy isn't here.'

Paula tried not to appear nosey as she followed Phoebe up the stairs. She drank in the thick carpet, the paintings on the walls and the beautiful antique furniture. She knew when something smelt like money and this house was reeking of it. This was how her life would be one day too.

The girls started their beauty, hair and makeup preparations, these were even more important to them than the actual party.

'You look so fab!' Phoebe was thrilled that the white outfit she'd chosen looked so good on her friend.

Paula looked at herself in the full-length mirror of Phoebe's very pink girly bedroom. Yes, she did look good, in fact better than ever before, but curvier. Her boobs looked even bigger and she definitely now had a bit of a belly. She'd really have to watch what she ate more carefully. She looked appreciatively at Phoebe, 'you look so grown up this evening, I love your mini dress. You're so clever choosing your clothes.'

'Aw, thanks Paula, but however well I style myself, I'll never look as beautiful as you.' Phoebe still wasn't good at the whole compliment thing and always tried to shrug one off. 'Are we ready now, James is taking us there. Mummy liked me going to a charity party as it was such a good cause, so she told him to take and collect us.'

'Blimey… in the Bentley?' Paula tried to contain her excitement.

James was waiting by the car with the engine already switched on and gently purring. 'Good evening young ladies.' He doffed his cap. He'd never seen Phoebe with any girlfriends before. It made him so happy to see how this lonely young girl who he had driven around since she was a baby, had slowly come out of her shell, blossoming into a pretty and confident young woman. He exchanged a look across the girls' heads with Mrs Abbott. He could see she was feeling the same.

'Enjoy yourselves, girls.' Mrs Abbott waved them off standing on the house steps, her eyes filled with happy tears.

Paula sat in the back of the car; tall, self-possessed and elegant. She would make Phoebe proud. No one would ever guess she was the girl who'd grown up on a council estate. She almost belonged into this privileged world now. No-one could ever take it away from her again.

* * * *

But in the same week of being on such a high of going to the amazing party with Phoebe, and feeling that she'd finally fitted in, she hit an all-time low. She suddenly felt so much older than sixteen - a whole lifetime older. How ironic it was that Phoebe had tried to be more like her, whilst she'd tried to be more like Phoebe. But then Phoebe had known so little about her and her life, the life she'd kept so well hidden. Taking drugs and selling them and sleeping with boys since the age of fourteen was what she'd always done. She'd enjoyed the look of lust in boys' eyes when she offered herself to them as she was the one in control, not them. The dope she smoked made her feel sexier and the dope sold gave her a small emergency stash of cash.

How could everything have gone so utterly tits up? She'd always remembered to take the Pill since she was thirteen. All her action with the boys off the local estate had blended into one vague collective blur of sexual encounters. How could she ever have got herself into such a mess? She'd been invincible until now, the girl who'd managed to sort anything. Should she run away or tell her dad? She'd even considered returning to the Process, a strange place she'd hung out at ages ago with some random stoner she'd scored dope from and fucked a while ago. But she didn't want to escape life, she wanted to embrace it. This was one of the times she missed her mum so much it was like a physical ache. She knew she could never tell Phoebe she was pregnant, she'd be so shocked. Maybe her dad would help her if she caught him before he'd had his first drink of the day. Yes, this had to be her best option but she didn't hold out much hope.

'Dad, can we talk for a minute?'

'Now?'

She knew immediately by his tone this wasn't going to have a good outcome.

'What would you be wishing to say to me then. You skint or got yourself up the duff?'

Paula looked up at him for the first time since she'd started talking to him, as she'd been staring down at her toes until then.

'Yes dad. That's bang on.'

There was a pause, whilst the silence hung in the air between them like an explosion waiting to happen, and then it came.

'How could you do this to your family, Paula? How could you fuck up your life and now mine as well? Your mam, God rest her soul, would be turning in her grave now, so she would, if she could see what you've done after everything I've done for you. No man's ever going to want you, an unmarried mother. You've brought shame on us, a good Catholic family. You're an eejit, so you are.' Her father continued to rant on, seemingly not needing to pause for breath.

At the mention of her mother, Paula started crying.

Her dad ignored her tears. 'How far gone are you?'

'Dunno. Maybe three months, as you can see, I don't really look pregnant, do I dad?' Paula pleaded quietly, with desperation sounding in her voice.

'Well, you've got no choices girl. You can't be staying here and you can't be getting rid of the bastard. So I'll be taking you to a mother and baby home. They can sort you and the baby out and then you can find your own bloody way in life. Don't think I'll ever be helping you again. You're no longer any daughter of mine.'

Paula wiped her eyes on her sleeve. This was the man whom she'd called dad for sixteen years.

'You'll not be going back to that fancy school of yours either that you apparently got a scholarship to. Was that the truth or did you have to fuck someone to get that too?'

Paula recoiled at the cruelty and unfairness of his words. Was that what her own dad really thought about her? She felt sick from her emotional turmoil.

'You can forget too about any friends you made there, those toffee-nosed girls won't care if they never see you again, they only look after their own kind. You may have learnt to talk posh now but it hasn't changed you from being a whoring slut.'

Paula felt like she'd been punched in the stomach at her dad's harsh words, but she was used to his mood swings and mean words. Phoebe was the one person who would have cared, but how could she ever tell her she was pregnant? How would she judge her? Maybe it was for the best that she was going to disappear completely.

Her father made the arrangements and two days of icy silence later, he told her to get her things together. Paula tearfully packed a bag full of anything she thought she might need for her immediate future. A few of her favourite clothes, some trinkets which her mum had given her and her old tin savings box which contained some photos and about ten pounds of savings.

Once she was packed and ready, she stood outside what had been her home, with her small suitcase and waited for her dad to start up his battered Ford Cortina. She climbed in, with a thick wall of silence between them as they drove away from the only life she'd known until now. She felt sick, not from her pregnancy, she'd never felt ill once over the last few months, but from the thought that the life she'd known until now was over, and how different this car journey was from her last one with Phoebe in the Bentley.

They soon left London behind and she saw sign posts mentioning places she'd never ever heard of. She had no idea where they were going as they drove through one suburban village after another until they finally turned into a driveway behind a high hedge. In front of her loomed a very large unfriendly-looking old-fashioned house with wide steps leading up to the entrance. It reminded Paula of pictures that she'd seen of Victorian mental asylums or institutions where they incarcerated mad women who were never to be seen again. Was that going to be her fate too?

'Bye Paula, your mam always said, "as you make your bed, so you lie on it" and indeed you have. She'd be turning in her grave now with disappointment.'

Her father uttered his parting words to her as coldly as any stranger and drove away without a backward glance at her and out of her life for ever. Paula stood in the driveway, clutching her small suitcase, trembling from fear of the unknown and shock. She felt more alone at that moment than she'd ever felt in her life before and wished she were dead. No-one would care as she felt completely abandoned and her one and only friend had no idea where she was. She now had no one in the whole world that would notice or care if she was gone.

How could she have ended up here like this with just one small suitcase containing the few items that reminded her of the home she'd once had. She'd always been a fighter, but the fight had finally been sucked out of her. She stood there for a moment unable to move, watching the small blue car until it was a tiny dot in the distance. Her shoulders slumped in despair and a wave of longing for Phoebe washed over her.

Chapter 3. Phoebe. London, 1970

One day towards the end of the school term, Paula didn't turn up at school. Phoebe ran so many scenarios of what might have happened through her head, but none made sense. Paula didn't turn up the next day, or even the following week and no one in the class knew what had happened, it was as though she'd disappeared off the earth. It was really strange. The school teachers remained silent too, it was as if she'd never existed.

Phoebe didn't have Paula's home phone number and the only time Paula had ever been to her house was before the Feathers Ball. The rest of the time, the girls' plans had always been made in the school break times or on their way home from school, so she was now at a total loss as to what she could do; she felt like she'd lost a limb. Phoebe tried going down the King's Road, checking in at all their favourite places, just in case she came across her. But weeks passed and nothing. She simply couldn't understand what could have happened to her and really missed her. Paula had been her first real friend and real in all senses of the word; a friend who had opened a whole new world to her over the two years that they'd hung out together, showing her what life was like outside her comfortable Chelsea bubble. Phoebe wondered if she'd ever be brave enough to do any of the things that they'd discussed together now on her own.

She didn't want to go back to her solitary world of being on the outside looking in. She had no one to talk to any longer at school, and it wasn't any fun going to all the old haunts that Paula and she had frequented on her own. She tried sitting at the Picasso one Saturday morning and ordered the same Cappuccino and toasted ham and cheese sandwich that she'd always ordered, but this time the usually frothy coffee seemed flat and the yummy slightly burnt cheesy crispy edges of the toasted sandwich tasted like cardboard. Life just wasn't worth living like this, Paula had to be out there somewhere, and it was up to Phoebe to find her. Maybe she could even go and ask at one of the places that Paula had mentioned she'd been to: there was one particular weird sounding place in particular called the Process. She'd never really understood what the place was when Paula had described it to her but yes, that was where she would start, although maybe she should run it past Mrs Abbott just in case the place was really, really weird and the people from the Process really had kidnapped her friend.

Phoebe spoke really quickly, trying to get everything she wanted to say to Mrs Abbott out in just one breath.

'Abby, you know Paula has disappeared and that she's no longer at school and no one at school knows what's happened to her? Well, I want to go and search for her as I'm really worried about her and if James could take me to this place near Park Lane, could you come us too and wait whilst I go in just in case they've kidnapped her and then they try to kidnap me too?' Phoebe finally stopped for breath. Good she'd said it now. She hoped Mrs Abbott wasn't going to think she was silly.

'Dear girl, kidnapped her? Whatever sort of place do you want to go to? We're in Chelsea not the East End of London, your imagination is running away with you. I'm sure there's some logical reason why she's no longer at school, perhaps her family moved at short notice.' Mrs Abbott stood with her arms crossed over her ample bosom looking at Phoebe with a bemused expression on her face, as though Phoebe had suddenly gone mad. Mrs Abbott was a stoic woman, used to containing her feelings, it was rare for any emotions to be seen that might cause her to raise one of her unplucked eyebrows.

'No, Abby, I've got a bad feeling about this. The school have said she's not coming back but they won't say why.'

Mrs Abbott shook her head of thick curly grey hair and pursed her lips in slight disapproval. 'Well, I must say this all sounds very strange dear, but I'll come with you and then wait nearby. You'll have to show me where you're going and if you haven't come out within fifteen minutes, I'll come in together with James to find you.'

'Thank you Abby, you always come to my rescue, I do love you.'

Mrs Abbott crossed her arms protectively, tighter across her bosoms, seemingly flustered at Phoebe's unexpected show of feelings. 'You know James and I will always be there for you. It'll all be alright in the end, you'll see.'

Phoebe wrapped her arms around Mrs Abbott's matronly body in a huge emotional bear hug. Mrs Abbott unused to such public displays of affection, stood stiffly and patted Phoebe gently on her back as though she was winding a baby.

Phoebe discovered the Process Church of the Final Judgement was in Mayfair, which was a smart neighbourhood, so the Process, despite its name, couldn't be all that weird. James parked the Bentley away from the entrance, just as he'd done when dropping Phoebe off to school – except this time there was the addition of Mrs Abbott in the car with them.

Phoebe braced her shoulders and took a deep breath as though she were going into battle. 'Right, I'm going in.'

Mrs Abbott opened her car window and peered suspiciously at the building. 'I don't like the look of this place

Phoebe. Why would they have a Swastika-like symbol with four P's around it. What could it mean?'

'Abby, I don't know but I'm going in to have a look and I'll be back very quickly. I'll find you back at the car.' Phoebe had just noticed a small group of men wearing black hooded robes, standing together with a large Alsatian at the entrance.

Phoebe, I don't like this.' Mrs Abbott's normally calm tone of voice had changed to a slightly higher pitch, full of anxiety.

'Abby, I'll be fine, stop your worrying, I just want to ask if they've seen Paula.' Phoebe attempted to sound more confident than she felt, as her heart was now beating way faster than usual. She got out of the car and tentatively walked inside to find a surprisingly normal-looking entrance hall that had a small book stall area and a coffee shop where there were more black-robed people milling around. Phoebe picked up one of the magazines lying around, it was called The Process. She flicked through it and came across a photo and an interview with Mick Jagger.

'Can I help you?'

Phoebe jumped and turned around startled, finding that it had been one of the black robed people talking to her.

'Welcome to the Process, come on through. Have you come to visit our Church?' The hooded man was standing very close to her, even though he was speaking quite loudly. This whole place was already creeping her out.

'Umm, I'm looking for a friend actually.'

'We've got all sorts of people, famous ones too like Marianne Faithfull, who've joined the Process... Marianne's not your friend, is she?'

Phoebe had no idea who Marianne Faithfull was. 'No, my friend's called Paula. She's tall and very pretty.'

'I'd remember a tall pretty girl and there's been none here recently.' The hooded man winked at Phoebe as though he was sharing his secrets with her before he went back to sounding more business-like. 'Come with me and I'll introduce you to our founders -Robert de Grimston and Mary Ann MacLean - they might be able to help you.'

Phoebe followed him into a church-like area that was so dark she couldn't see that much, but she could hear people chanting. The strong smell of incense was overpowering and Phoebe knew it would have seeped into her clothes, her hair and her very being long before she left. A new older man with long hair and a droopy moustache materialised in front of her, together with a slight woman with equally long lank hair and a blank expression.

The woman spoke first in dull monotones. 'I believe you're looking for someone? I'm Mary Ann and this is Robert, together we founded the Process Church based on Scientology. All our members go through processing or therapy on their arrival, which we find is helpful for them; it could be that your friend has already done this.'

Phoebe was starting to feel physically sick at the woman's words; she was hearing her worst possible fears spoken out loud.

The woman, although drab and grey in appearance, spoke with a quiet intensity.

'We believe there are four gods who exist within each of our personalities; Jehovah is the strength, Lucifer is the light, Satan is the separation and Christ is the unification. Our members can choose which god or gods to follow, as their personalities and future relationships will be defined by their choices. Come with us now and we'll show you around.'

Phoebe suddenly felt that the longer she stood close to this weird couple, the more likely she was to be sucked deeper into the dark vortex of their religious beliefs. She took a step backwards away from them and towards the safety of the brightly lit café near the front entrance. She was beginning to feel a magnetic force pulling her further into the depths of this place and the further she went in, the less she'd be able to leave. She now wanted to escape as quickly as she could.

The woman was still speaking, persuasive in the way she enunciated, making every word meaningful. 'The real "devil" is humanity, so we limit drugs and alcohol and sex. Our work is spiritual as we want you to love your enemies.'

Phoebe had started trying to shut her voice out so that her words would simply become a meaningless noise, but her husband was taking his turn to speak as though he'd been programmed to finish the whole sales pitch.

'You're welcome to join us, you're just the sort of girl who would enjoy and benefit from our teachings. We have Sabbath services each week and lots of events you can join in with, or you could even come and live with us here in our commune. Why don't you go and have a cup of tea with one of our members in the Coffee Bar so they can tell you more about us.'

Phoebe could feel the panic bubbling up in her chest. She had, by now, decided that this couple were really odd, almost robotic but she'd come here to find Paula and they still hadn't answered her original question properly. She knew now she wasn't going to get any more answers from them. She'd been looking around them all the time to see if she could spot anyone who looked at all like Paula, but it was so dark in there and everyone dressed in black blended into the background.

'Thank you so much but I really have to go now and maybe come back another day.' Phoebe spoke quietly and politely as she never forgot her manners, even in difficult circumstances. She tried to look calm and collected, even though inside she was in turmoil. She turned with one last backward glance, just in case Paula should miraculously appear, then did a cross between a walk and a run towards the coffee shop, daylight and the welcoming sanity that she would find again with Mrs Abbott and James. As she approached the car, she broke into a proper sprint and climbed in as quickly as she could, her words tumbling out on top of each other.

'Oh Abby, that was so weird in there... it's a sort of a Church place with hymns and chanting and people all dressed in black. Paula hadn't ever described it to me like that. I really don't think she's there. James please can we get away from this place as quickly as we can? It was freaky.' Phoebe could feel herself still shaking and finding it hard to breathe and speak in her panic.

Mrs Abbott turned round to look at Phoebe from the front seat of the car with concern written all over her kindly face. 'Phoebe, please don't ever go back there.'

James, who rarely offered his opinion or even spoke, chimed in too. 'I think it sounds like what they call a Cult. They like young girls like you, especially ones with money or celebrities who can spread the word. You're lucky you got away.'

'I can safely say that I won't ever be going back,' Phoebe spoke with conviction, 'but how am I ever going to find Paula now?'

Mrs Abbott, always the voice of reason, offered Phoebe some of her Yorkshire voice of pragmatism for reassurance. 'She'll turn up when the times right, dear. You mark my words.'

Chapter 4. Paula. London, 1970-1971

A woman in a nurse's uniform appeared from the inside of the building and surveyed her new arrival with cold uncaring eyes - eyes that had seen so many unmarried pregnant girls like Paula arrive and leave from her establishment for years now.

'Good morning, Paula, I'm Matron Mary.' Paula looked at the woman and didn't feel a single kindly vibe emanating from her, only cold, clinical efficiency. 'Follow me please and I'll give you a quick tour. You'll need to know where everything is as you'll be living with us for the next few months until the birth.'

The Matron's words echoed around the dark wood-panelled hall interior which smelt strongly of fresh furniture polish. Paula instantly knew that this particular smell would always remind her of the moment she'd walked in here, for the rest of her life. She followed uncharacteristically meekly after the woman, climbing the steps of the grand sweeping mahogany staircase to her new future. She felt like she'd time-travelled and was no longer in the nineteen seventies, but somewhere back in Victorian times. The Matron strode purposefully on ahead, her sensible flat lace-up shoes squeaking on the shiny polished parquet floors. She finally stopped at huge double doors and with some effort, pushed one slightly ajar.

'This is our recreation room.' The Matron waited for Paula to step forward and have a better look. Paula peered over the woman's shoulder through the half-open doorway where she could see a group of girls in various stages of pregnancy, sitting around a long trestle table strewn with magazines and coffee mugs. Some girls were smoking and others knitting, but they all had the same distracted and disengaged look in their sad eyes. They all looked up as one and glanced towards Paula at the open door. Paula tried smiling in their direction, but they all looked back down as quickly as they'd looked up and returned their attention back to whatever they'd been doing. Maybe friendliness wasn't allowed here Paula thought to herself, but she'd just become one of those women now and they didn't look as though they were filled with too much joy, laughter or hope. Suddenly she felt properly scared of what her future may hold.

Meanwhile Matron had marched on ahead of her on a mission to finish this newest inmate's tour as quickly as possible. 'This is the dormitory and this is your bed.'

Paula looked aghast at the narrow cot bed with two worn blankets folded in a pile on the end of it. She thought back to her lovely comfy double bed in her own bedroom at home, with all her pop posters on the wall. She wondered how her life could have suddenly been so quickly reduced to this, all from one stupid pill not working.

'Right, now you've seen everything, you need to come with me for a medical check for any venereal diseases.' Matron's instructions were delivered in a voice so devoid of any warmth or feeling that Paula wondered if she'd been born this way, or had this grim and grey foreboding building moulded her into this grim and grey, cold and heartless person.

Paula looked at the woman in horror; why would she have anything wrong with her -she was simply pregnant, girls like her didn't get diseases down there. How much worse could this get? She had learnt how to be resilient and keep the peace from living with her dad and his drunken mood swings, so she was prepared for whatever was thrown at her in this dismal and depressing place. She knew that it would be easier to keep doing exactly as she was told until it was the right time to re-assess the situation, and now wasn't the time. She needed to have the baby first. She decided there and then she wouldn't argue or be combative and if it meant someone checking her girly bits, then she'd have to suffer it.

She quickly learned how to survive there. No one bothered to talk to her, even though she'd tried to talk to them. Maybe it was because all the girls knew that this place was simply a transitory moment in their life, a miserable memory to be discarded as soon as possible. So by trial and error she quickly discovered that she needed to get up every day at seven O'clock for breakfast, after a quick wash at communal basins separated only by modesty partition screens. To keep her sanity Paula quickly realised that she needed alone time to think, so she regularly tried to book a weekly bath in the one and only tub; it was the one time she could ever get away from the other girls.

The Matron made it very clear that Paula's daily chores were both her penance and payment for being looked after there, together with Sunday Church visits. As a Catholic girl, she'd been happy going to Church when her mum was alive, but then had stopped soon afterwards. She'd wondered why God could have been so cruel to have taken away the person she'd loved most. Paula wasn't sure God was doing much to look after her now as the chores given to her were all really hard, but she was strong and healthy and hardly showing even at seven months, so she set to work without grumbling.

She scrubbed floors and stairwells and fetched buckets of coal or water with others doing the same, even on the day they went into labour. Paula had read enough books to wonder if she'd returned to Dickensian times and had to pinch herself every so often as a reality check, but she kept reminding herself it wasn't forever; the moment her baby was born, she'd be gone. She tried to imagine how she could escape, to go and live somewhere with her baby, using her meagre savings to start off with. She was sure that she'd managed to squirrel away enough to keep them going for a few weeks until she could find a job of some sort. She had to keep positive and keep her dream alive.

As one week rolled into another, with the same continuing drudgery and monotony, Paula occasionally managed to have monosyllabic moments of verbal interaction with the other girls. It seemed that most of them, just like her, had been abandoned and banished from their families and their previous lives. As unmarried mothers-to-be, they had all become social outcasts, pariahs - the lowest of the low.

She lay in the dark each night, unable to sleep, whilst her baby kicked away inside her. She tried to convince herself that one day Phoebe would appear out of the blue, so she could tell her what had happened and everything would be okay again, but she knew this could never happen. She was positive that Phoebe would never be able to understand her situation. Nevertheless, Paula constantly checked and re-checked any magazines that had been left lying around in case she saw photos of Phoebe or even of her mother, Mrs Clarke. She knew she would never give up or stop looking, just in case.

One morning whilst she was in the middle of her daily chores, Matron appeared suddenly accompanied by a woman that Paula hadn't seen before, and her first impressions of this visitor's body language and demeanour was that she was a harbinger of gloom and doom.

'It's time to see your social worker and have your health check now Paula.'

So this was the woman who was to decide her future. Paula shivered inwardly with fear and felt as though she could have been ordered to the executioner by the icy cold chill of mean-spiritedness that was emanating from both women. Paula quickly assessed her social worker and wondered how she would have described her to Phoebe afterwards. She decided that it would have been as a mean-lipped, age-indeterminate spinster, dressed in mismatched drab coloured charity shop finds. She peered over her wire-rimmed spectacles at Paula with disdain. She had an attitude that made Paula believe that she too had given up on life ever treating her well. She had a manner and a way of speaking to her that made Paula feel evil and dirty.

Paula stared back at the woman's angular face framed by wiry, dry grey hair, she faced her silently but defiantly across the large oak desk that now separated them in the interview room. Rays of sunlight shining through the dusty windows accentuated the woman's fine dark hairs growing across her moustached narrow upper lip and more sparsely and randomly on her chin. Paula couldn't help staring even more. She wondered how any woman could ever take so little care of themselves - she knew that could never be her.

She realised that the social worker was already mid-flow in her conversation, but speaking as though she had a personal vendetta with Paula, even though they'd never met before. How could that be? She tuned back into the long and angry tirade that was in full flow.

'Paula, if you truly loved your child you would give her up to parents who could give her a better life. What have you got to offer her?' Paula tried to answer but wasn't given a chance.

'No, you're right, absolutely nothing.' The social worker spat her next words out at her. 'Girls like you are just a blot on society.'

Paula wondered whether this woman spoke to every unmarried mother in this way, but tried to rise above her mean words, not take them to heart and to hold herself together. She was determined not show any weakness or cry. Paula knew a bully when she came across one and this woman was the worst sort as the girls were in no position to ever stand up to her.

'Your only option, Paula, will be to have your baby adopted; you will never find any financial or social help with a baby in tow.'

Paula thought back to her nightly dreams of how she would set up home with her baby; just the two of them. How could this woman be so unempathetic and cold, offering her no sympathy or understanding with options for her and her baby's future. Paula decided that it would be better not to say anything now but to fight for her child once she'd given birth. She would be in a stronger position then and maybe she could simply disappear. The social worker stared at Paula, waiting for the young woman's acquiescence, or at least some show of compliance, but she realised when none was forthcoming that maybe she'd finally met her match in this feisty new girl who wasn't crumbling under pressure.

After her encounter with the social worker, Paula became even more determined to survive her incarceration in this depressing place and carried on as she had before, mostly left alone by the Matron, the social worker and the ever changing cycle of pregnant young women. Until one day, as she was sweeping the snow off a side path in the garden, trying to ignore a mild cramping in her lower belly, a gush of water ran down her leg. Her waters had finally broken. Paula realised that the baby was actually coming now and the fear and panic swirled within her as she dropped the broom and rushed inside to find Matron.

No-one had prepared her mentally or physically for what was to come and, after hours of what seemed unrelenting and agonising pain during her hours of labour, she gave birth to a baby daughter in the nearby hospital local to the unmarried mothers' home. She immediately named her Phoebe-Jane; Phoebe after her best friend and Jane after her late mother.

Ten days later she collected her few belongings from the home for the last time. She sobbed all the way on the bus to the Church of England Adoption Society in central London. She would never forget standing afterwards, shivering at the bus stop, empty and alone, with heavy aching breasts full of milk. She'd just been told that her baby would be placed in a foster home in North London and she'd be allowed to visit just once a week.

Paula tried to think clearly through her hormonal mood-swings of highs and lows and decided her priority would be to look for somewhere to live. She needed to conserve her small amount of saved-up money as she didn't know how long it would take to find some sort of job, but now she was beginning to wonder who would really want to employ her? She still had her fantasy of living somewhere with her beautiful little baby and making a life together, but she couldn't yet rationalise how she was going to manage this.

She finally found a shabby run down hostel in her old stomping ground of Bayswater and started looking for jobs to do literally anything and for places to live that would accept an unmarried mother and baby. Once a week, she walked to save money, from the hostel all the way to the North London foster home to visit her baby, but when she was there she felt too scared to pick her little girl up and cuddle her, because she knew a mother-daughter bond would be forged between and then she wouldn't want to hand her back. She tried imagining running away with her but she had nowhere to run to and no money.

After a month of trying everywhere for both jobs and places to live, Paula realised that she'd reached a dead end. So, finally accepting defeat, which had never before been in her DNA, she reluctantly signed the adoption papers that had been so regularly pressed upon her, and gave up her baby, Phoebe-Jane. She felt emotionally dead as though her life as she had known it had now ended; it had lost all its colour and vibrancy and she could only see it now in grey tones. She'd lost her best friend Phoebe, her dad had abandoned her, and now she'd lost her baby. Her sadness was extreme and nearly unbearable.

She couldn't bear to look at any pregnant women as the sight bought all the painful memories flooding back. She had an overwhelming sense of unfairness that they'd been allowed to keep their babies, and she hadn't been allowed, just because they had a husband and a ring on their finger, simply because *they were the property of a man.* Paula wondered why she should have to belong to a man to have any rights. It all seemed so wrong, but she would somehow get back on her feet again and build her own independence. Every day she woke up with the same dull ache of sadness and loss in the pit of her tummy and wondered whether life was even worth living any more, but it was only a short time since she'd given up her baby.

She had no idea how to grieve for the loss of her daughter, and no-one to grieve with. She'd grieved for her mother's death and had had time for closure but as her daughter wasn't dead, this was different and she needed to deal with the pain. She eventually concluded that her only coping solution would be to make a ritual of lighting a candle each year on her daughter's birthday, so she'd never forget her then, she would bring out the few photos of her baby, passed onto her by the adoption agency that had been taken by the new adoptive parents. Paula told herself that only then would she allow herself to cry and send her daughter telepathic messages to tell her how much she loved her. Maybe, one day she'd be able to be re-united with her Phoebe-Jane.

She would never give up hope. So for now, she'd stay on in the same room in this cheap and run-down hostel to restart her job search – no longer a single mother but as a young woman looking to the future.

Chapter 5. Phoebe. London, 1971

By the time she was seventeen, Phoebe had finally grown a bit taller. She was still only about five foot two inches, but at least she'd graduated from glasses to contact lenses and from a cotton wool-filled bra to a bra filled with properly and, even one could say, generously sized bosoms. Her braces were gone too. She liked to practice smiling in the mirror now that her teeth were really straight, unlike her hair which still had a mind of its own.

Her mother had decided that she would have one last attempt to help Phoebe look better and took her off to Vidal Sassoon, her very smart hairdressers. Phoebe knew Vidal was "the" hairdresser that all the famous people and models went to, and who'd recently done Twiggy's elfin haircut. Phoebe felt that she could now safely call herself a font of all fashion and high street knowledge, having become such an avid magazine reader. So one Saturday morning, Phoebe found herself standing together with her mother, in the Vidal Sassoon salon, reverting back to her childhood. Her mother had instantly taken control and spoken for her, as though she was unable to speak for herself. Had her mother forgotten she was actually now seventeen?

'Vidal, dahling, please can you do something with this child's hair for me, it's always such a mess. There must be *something* clever you can do.'

'Let me see...' Vidal stared intently into the mirror at Phoebe's mad curls for what seemed an eternity. Phoebe still really hated being stared at; it made her feel so uncomfortable. Vidal, however, managed to work his magic and she emerged from the salon a few hours later, an improved version of herself. She still had long thick curly hair but the red had now been dyed to a deep auburn colour and the curls had been cut and layered to frame her face. She supposed she looked like the modern seventies version of a pre-Raphaelite girl. Even though she appeared to be a glossier version of herself, she still felt the same emptiness inside. She'd forgotten all about her alter-ego Phoebe as she hadn't needed her when she'd hung out with Paula. Paula had always made her feel confident and cool, perhaps this alter-ego needed to revisited... but not yet, maybe in a few days' time.

Later in the week, when Phoebe was still lying in bed reading one of her teen magazines before it was time to get up, her bedroom door burst open. Phoebe panicked as Mrs Abbott always knocked first and no one else ever came up to her bedroom floor at the top of the house, apart from the cleaner. Was the house being burgled in broad daylight?

No, it wasn't a burglar, it was her mother. Phoebe glanced at her watch - maybe it had stopped - it was far too early for her mother to even be awake, let alone up and about. Something dramatic must have happened, maybe someone had died. She looked more closely at her mother, trying to assess the situation. Her mother had giant rollers still in her blonde hair and no makeup. This was a revelation, especially as she wasn't dressed yet either, but still in her designer silk nightie/négligée set and fluffy stiletto heeled slippers. Phoebe had never seen her mother like this and looked at her expectantly. It must be something really serious for her mother to be seen in this state, outside her own bedroom suite and even more so, to be standing in Phoebe's teenage messy; clothes everywhere, poster-covered bedroom.

Her mother was quivering with excitement. 'Dahling, this is just so exciting. I've just received an invitation in the post from Peter Townend of the Tatler Magazine. It reads like this;

Phoebe Clarke is invited to be one of our 1972 Debutantes.

You're going to be a debutante and presented to royalty dahling.' As she spoke, her intensely and regularly well-moisturised face lit up with pleasure, or at least as much as her usually-static and expressionless features allowed. Phoebe knew this was already a done-deal; the perfect culmination of her mother's upwardly mobile aspirations. She'd have to go with the flow.

'What's a Debutante, mama? What will I have to do?'

'Well, it will be a lovely opportunity for you to make new friends and meet eligible young men. It will get you out of the house and mixing with *proper* sorts of people. There will be lunches and teas, drinks parties, dances and private balls in castles and stately homes, charity balls and country house party weekends. Also, Summer Season events like Royal Ascot and Henley Regatta and then of course your own drinks party or dance.' Mrs Clarke finally paused for breath.

Phoebe was silent. This was a world that filled her with horror, all those ghastly horsey twin-set and pearls girls and mothers possibly even worse than her own. She realised that whilst she'd been considering this whole new social world she was about to be launched into, she clearly hadn't emoted enough for her mother. Her mother's voice had changed from her initial higher tone of excitement to one with a subtle hint of annoyance and even bewilderment.

'How could you not want to do all these things, most girls would dream of having such opportunities, you're a very lucky girl. You could even find a husband, maybe an old

Etonian with a country estate or a stately home and you could become the future chatelaine and it wouldn't matter a jot if he were spectacularly stupid or even unattractive as long as he's rich or titled. Think, dahling, of the life you could then have.'

Phoebe stared back at her mother, ashamed at her shallowness. So this was her mother's ultimate aim in life to find her an eligible husband. She'd often overheard her mother's vapid conversations as she gossiped with female friends in the drawing room. She'd definitely heard her say 'For a marriage to be successful, it combined money with title, title with title or beauty with wealth'.

Well, thought Phoebe, her parents had money and she certainly wasn't beautiful, so it was obviously the money with title scenario her mother was pitching for. However, what she did know for sure was that whatever her mother's personal vision, her own wasn't kissing endless posh frogs to find her prince. Phoebe had already shut off her mother's endless chatter as she pondered all this, then suddenly she was jolted back to the present when she heard the unexpected word sex in her mother's monologue.

'Good girls don't have sex. Some of the young men you may meet are only seeking sexual adventures and may take unfair advantage of the good girls like you, who are too young and inexperienced to recognise what the young men's intentions are. Remember, you aren't that sort of girl Phoebe, and there are some young men around who aren't very nice.'

'Yes Mama.' Phoebe knew this was the only reply she should give, but what her mother didn't know was that she already had a packet of birth control pills hidden in her bathroom cupboard.

Phoebe thought back to the day that Paula had asked her to go to her doctor's surgery with her. 'Why are we going together to the doctor's, Paula?'

'My mam told me never to trust any boys and that it should be our responsibility to look after ourselves and make sure we never get pregnant, so I take the pill every day,' and then Paula added, 'just in case.' Playing down the fact that she'd already slept with about five boys. 'Maybe you should get some too whilst we are there, you can always keep them hidden until you have a boyfriend.' Paula had thought that this was the best way of putting it to her friend. She knew Phoebe would have no one else to go to when the time came. This might be one step too far, even for the kind and sympathetic Mrs Abbott. Paula's doctor had written prescriptions for both girls. Phoebe was sure that she was supposed to have had parental consent or to have been over a certain age, but Paula had obviously found an obliging doctor who didn't ask questions.

So Phoebe's supply of pills still lay hidden in her bathroom cabinet but maybe she should consider starting to take them now, just in case, what with all these new young men she was about to meet. She focused back to her mother's lecture.

'By the way, dahling, your father has now opened a Coutts bank account for you and has given you a generous allowance for additional clothes shopping, so you can dress appropriately for all these parties you'll be going to. You can't keep wearing all those ghastly garish coloured clothes you insist upon. No one will ever speak to you or invite you to anything. They'll think you're some sort of hippy druggy person.'

'No, mummy, I understand you wouldn't want that to happen. Please thank daddy for opening the bank account for me.' Phoebe had always felt her parents expected this stiff formality, especially as they seemed like strangers to her.

Mrs Clarke hadn't finished yet, 'Dahling, we will have to arrange a tea together with Peter Townend. He will want to meet and get to know us more but you can let me talk, not you. I can tell him all about Daddy's family ancestry but he probably knows already, it is how you were invited as he only ever invites girls he feels are the *right ones.* Daddy's family is already in Debretts, so you'll be in perfect company with the other girls.'

Once again, no answer was required, Mrs Clarke was on a mission to sell her dream to her daughter.

'I've heard Peter has a little black book. Everyone who's anyone has their details in it. Peter is like a walking encyclopaedia of personal information. You'd better behave, Phoebe, so he doesn't write anything too ghastly about us. We will also have to let him know the prospective date for your eighteenth birthday party, as it can't be on a night that could clash with any of the other girls' parties; that would simply be a disaster. So, dahling, to start with, you and I will be invited together to mother and daughter tea parties, where I can network and mingle and make certain that you aren't missing out on meeting all the right people and going to the best parties – it's going to be such a marvellous opportunity.'

Phoebe was underwhelmed by all this information, especially as she was in the middle of her A-levels, but this news seemed to have made her mother the happiest and most vibrant she'd ever seen her. She'd become her mother's latest project; her mother always had one, scheming and planning like Becky Sharpe in Vanity Fair. Gosh, she hoped she would never become like her mother. Was it actually possible to dislike one's own mother? That couldn't be right, she'd have to try really hard to look just for her good points, especially as she was going to be spending so much time with her over the next year.

By the time the start of the debutante season had come upon them, Phoebe had spent more time with her mother than she'd ever done in her whole life. She'd shopped for day dresses, cocktail dresses and handbags and shoes to go with every outfit and of course ball gowns. Her wardrobe was now overflowing. However, Phoebe knew that she was going to have to put her own styling touches on every single dress to modernise and customise them to become her own unique style. The one dress she'd managed to get past her mother's strict fashion guidelines and etiquette barometer was her Queen Charlotte's Ball dress. She wasn't sure how she'd managed it but here she was, now standing at the Grosvenor House Hotel ballroom in a *backless* Valerie Goad white silk dress. The dress code had simply stated *long white dress, worn with long white gloves.*

She looked round at the other girls standing together with her on the ballroom floor and realised that her dress was distinctly more daring than any of the other girls' dresses. Phoebe wanted to be her own person and not look like the other girls. She had her own ideas of how she should look and had hung out long enough with Paula to now have the self-belief in her own unique style and own it. The other girls' dresses were all from established designers such as Bellville Sassoon or made to measure by their mother's dressmakers; nothing too modern or out of the norm. These girls were all younger duplicates of their mothers, some even wearing their mothers' original coming out dresses. They were all standing in a semi-circle, grouped around a large white wedding-style tiered cake that had been wheeled out onto the dance floor. This was the big moment where they'd all curtsey together and be presented to a Royal person. They'd all had curtseying lessons in the St James's Church, Piccadilly, the week previously. Phoebe silently thanked her mother for all her ballet lessons which had enabled her to be graceful, curtseying low to the ground without stumbling. It was good to feel that she'd done something well and had found it hard not to giggle at some of the girl's clumsy efforts.

It seemed that Phoebe's choice of dress had been causing a bit of a stir whilst they were standing waiting for the royal person to appear.

'We love your dress Phoebe, it's so brill and different and you're so brave to wear a backless one!'

She was surprised that the girls liked it. Her own mother had just about managed to turn a blind eye to it but now she could hear the other mothers' whispers.

'What is that rather odd Phoebe Clarke girl wearing? It's a bit risqué, isn't it?'

'Isn't she showing a rather a lot of flesh?'

'Not sure it's altogether appropriate, how on earth could her mother have allowed her to dress in such a provocative way!'

Phoebe didn't understand provocative, but she did know that wearing certain clothes gave her joy. It was also the first time any of the girls had ever come up and chatted to her. It seemed that dressing in her own immutable style was helping her to be more popular. Strange... well, she'd tried story telling at school which hadn't worked, maybe clothes were now her way forward. At least she knew loads about fashions and trends, whereas she hadn't progressed any further in her sexual knowledge or actual "action" as the girls at school had called it.

'Have you had any action?' they'd ask each other.

'None,' was Phoebe's silent reply.

The girls' fashion queries escalated as the weeks passed. 'Where's your fab trouser suit from?'

'I found it in a shop called Annacat on the Brompton Road.' Phoebe was ready and confident for full disclosure on where she'd sourced all her fashion finds.

'We love your fabulous chiffon print dress.' They'd chorused.

'Thank you, it's an Ossie Clark with the print by Celia Birtwell, it's so pretty, isn't it?' Phoebe wished Paula could have seen it. This dress was her pride and joy.

'You're so "with it" and trendy, do you think you could take us shopping with you? We'd love your help.' A small group of girls clamoured around her.

Phoebe was thrilled to be asked. She hoped that this enthusiasm for her to be wanted would last longer than she'd managed with the cool girls at school.

So she began helping the girls find granny button-through t-shirts and wide legged loon trousers, just like her own, in the incense filled basement stalls of the Kensington market. She also found herself amazing wedge-heeled snakeskin Terry de Havilland shoes and appliqued platform boots. They took pride of place in her now quite eclectic wardrobe. The stall holders in the market all knew Phoebe by name now as she went in there so often. She was like the market tour guide for her friends. She knew everyone everywhere and all the best stalls for all the patchwork leather and suede and the smelly Afghan coats. The girls with pearls from the country had never seen anywhere like it before in their lives and went around open mouthed, just as Phoebe had done her first time.

Roger and Freddie were two guys who sold old Edwardian clothes and scarves; items that Phoebe knew her mother would have called exotic or tat, their stall was one of Phoebe's regular destinations. She'd discovered that Freddie found his stock, unique vintage pieces in her opinion, in random places from dodgy dealers. Phoebe loved Freddie's flamboyance - he wasn't like anyone else she'd ever met.

She'd chat to these two young men for ages every time she went there. They always greeted her warmly as though she were their best friend, 'Babe, cool to see you today. Thanks for bringing your friends with you yesterday.'

Phoebe hadn't considered that all the girls were actually proper friends yet, but now she understood that they were; maybe not yet close friends like Paula but nevertheless, friends.

'Babe, stay here and hang out with us for a while. It's quiet at the moment with no customers.'

Phoebe felt flattered that the two young men wanted to spend any time with her chatting.

Freddie was always the more outgoing of the two. 'Did you know that this is only what we do some of the time?. Roger's been in the band 'Smile' with a guy called Brian and now I've joined him in a new renamed band called Queen.'

Phoebe had heard of Queen. She now knew all her pop music too, from all the magazines she'd avidly devoured each week. 'Queen! Gosh I've heard of you. Oh wow, and I'd thought you both just did this stall here. I'd love to come to see you play one day.'

Phoebe suddenly realised that some of the alter-ego Phoebe must have stuck, as she would never have dreamt a few years ago that she'd ever be saying this to two members of the band Queen. She definitely loved this whole fashion and music world, it was so much more exciting than the debs and their stuffy mothers.

'Sure, babe, we'd love you to. Keep dropping by the Market and we'll let you know our next gig date.'

Phoebe was thrilled, but she was even more thrilled when she was able to hear Freddie's gossip when he was standing at the stall on his own. He was particularly forthcoming some days, it was however, mood-dependent.

'Did you know that last week David Bowie came in looking to buy some boots.'

'Bowie? Gosh.' Phoebe was fully engaged. Bowie's Ziggy posters been glued up on her bedroom walls for ever.

'Yes. I fitted and sold him a pair but he didn't seem to remember me from when we were at Ealing College together. Although, I remembered him but then I suppose he's famous and I'm not.'

Phoebe was quick to pipe up, 'But you will be, I know you will.' But now what she was wanted even more was gossip. 'Anyone else famous Freddie?" She wanted to immerse herself in his world.

'Dunno, don't really notice who they are that often. There was a guy called Noddy who bought his mirrored top hat he wore with his band Slade.'

Phoebe had heard of them but they weren't really her thing. 'I don't think I like their music that much, Freddie.'

'I don't think Noddy liked me very much either. I told him I was going to be a big pop star like him and he told me to fuck off!' Phoebe and Freddie laughed together at this recollection. Phoebe always liked to try to say something nice back to him.

'Oh, dear, maybe he was just having a bad day? Anything is possible though, isn't it? You and I may both be famous one day but I think it'll be you first though.' Phoebe wondered if one day she could regularly dress pop stars for their gigs. This thought sowed a small seed of hope for her future, one where she could work and hang out with people like Freddie all the time.

The next big event of the Season was the Berkeley Dress show. Phoebe was dreading the selection day for the models as she knew she'd never be picked. It would be like being back at school during team sports selection. She sat quietly in the background, pretending she was invisible, but then she realised one of one of the mothers was talking to her.

'How would you like to be on our Junior Committee, Phoebe? You can help with the styling of the Christian Dior dresses that will be modelled by the other girls. My daughter Araminta says you're really rather good at putting fashion together.'

Was Lady Cooper actually talking to her? Asking her to do something more than just observe from the side lines and properly style dresses.

'Oh, yes please, that would be super, Lady Cooper. Are you sure?'

'I always listen to my daughter, she's a clever girl. Actually, if I might say, while she's out of earshot, I know you've been helping her quite a bit with her wardrobe and I have to admit, you've done a rather good job.' Lady Cooper guffawed. Her laugh reminded Phoebe of a whinnying horse.

For the next few weeks Phoebe assisted in the Maddox Street Christian Dior boutique and the catwalk show rehearsals at the Berkeley Hotel. She was in seventh heaven, touching all the beautiful Dior gowns and having the run of the store. It was the grown up version of being that small child in her mother's dressing room. Phoebe finally felt that life was treating her well.

She even felt brave enough now to check out all the latest Chelsea boutiques all on her own, but she hadn't as yet got around to seeing a brand new one called the Universal Witness on the Fulham Road. She'd read this boutique had links to the pop world too as Robert Plant of Led Zeppelin owned it. Maybe if she offered to work there on Saturdays, just for fun, perhaps even for free as she didn't really need the money, she would have the chance to immerse herself in fashion all day. She was beginning to believe in her own ability to style-up a girl's "look" and wanted to put it into practice.

But she'd need a new outfit to impress the shop owner or manager when he first met her, and she knew that it had to come from Biba. Phoebe had avidly watched Ready Steady Go a pop music show that was on every Friday night, presented by a girl called Cathy Mcgowan. Whatever Biba outfit Cathy wore on TV was available to buy in-store the very next day. The dresses had always been available from the previous tiny boutique behind Kensington High Street, but now that the new bigger one had just opened on the High Street, Phoebe couldn't wait to see it. She'd heard everything sold out within hours of a new delivery so she arrived there really early and joined the queue of girls waiting outside for the store to open. As soon as the doors opened, they all rushed in and Phoebe was swept forward in the wave of excited girls to the back of the shop.

'Why's everyone run immediately to the back of the shop?' Phoebe realised she was speaking out loud to no-one in particular, as she stood there in the midst of the scrum of pushing and shoving teenagers who all knew exactly what they were looking for.

'The new colours of the suede boots came in today! They sell out straight away, so you've got to be quick,' shouted a random girl. Phoebe immediately understood and pushed through the other seemingly desperate girls and grabbed a box in her size; she was now holding a pair of the most beautiful teal colour boots in the softest suede. She leant against a wall, trying to balance as girls jostled past her. She managed get just one boot on to see if it fit and as she pulled the zip up she fell in love with everything about the gorgeousness of these boots. She'd never owned anything quite like them before. The boot came to just over her knee; their fit was a tiny bit tight on her chunky calves so the zip didn't quite do right up to the top, but these were absolutely her dream boots and were now about to have a new home in her wardrobe.

Once she'd managed to queue up and pay for the boots, she decided her shopping adventure should continue with a trip to the Mr Freedom boutique on the New Kings Road.

'Alright, luv?' A short tubby man shouted from the back of the shop as she stood in the entrance admiring the satin-appliqued Disney themed t-shirts.

'I'd like to try these on, please?' Phoebe held out the purple velvet dungaree hot pants and Mickey Mouse t-shirt she had hung over her arm.

'Ere luv, behind this curtain,' and he pulled it aside so she could walk into the tiny changing space. She pulled the curtain tightly back along its rail, trying to leave no space between the edge of the curtain and the wall. The curtain didn't shut properly and she was convinced she could be seen through the gap in the curtain, but maybe it was her imagination. She dressed again quickly, unable to look the man in the eye as she paid for her new outfit, in case he'd seen too much.

The following Saturday, Phoebe dressed herself in all her new clothes purchases. Wearing this new outfit gave her confidence in the same way her alter-ego had at school. She found the shop easily on the corner of Fulham Road right next to the Laura Ashley that she and Paula had once visited together back in the day. She walked in and the first person she saw was an intimidatingly beautiful tall black girl behind the counter.

'Are you looking for anything in particular?' the girl asked disinterestedly, as though she didn't really want to help at all.

'Erm, yes please. I'm looking for a Saturday girl job, do you know if there might be one here?' Phoebe didn't get as far as saying she'd even work there for nothing as the girl was quick to reply.

'No, sorry. No jobs here, luv. There's only me who works here every day and Paul who owns it.' She turned her back on Phoebe and strode off dismissively. Phoebe felt deflated and started to walk out but as she was leaving the shop, she heard someone call out to her;

'Hang on young lady, wait a minute!' Phoebe turned round. Maybe it was the manager or shop owner talking to her. 'Did I hear you ask if you could work here on Saturdays? It would be great to have another girl here; Chanelle can't hold the fort on her own all the time.'

'No, suppose not.' Chanelle sighed. Phoebe noticed that Chanelle wasn't too keen at being contradicted.

'I'm Paul. Could you do a trial day next Saturday? We pay three pounds fifteen pence a day'

Phoebe decided to forget that she'd been prepared to work for free. 'I'd love to and thank you so much for giving me a chance. I'll be here then at 10 O'clock next Saturday.

'Perfect, what's your name again?' Phoebe decided that she liked Paul; he had kind eyes and seemed gentle.

'Phoebe Clarke.'

'Well then, Miss Phoebe Clarke, we'll see you next week. Oh and by the way, we'll lend you clothes from the shop to wear when you're here as we find it helps to sell them. I like what you wearing, it's from Mr Freedom isn't it - Tommy, a friend of mine owns it, did you meet him?'

Phoebe felt herself blushing at this question, as this was probably the tubby man who'd served her. Anyway, she was too excited to worry as she'd got her first job and it was in a trendy boutique. The following Saturday, she took great care in getting ready for work. She turned up at five to ten to find the shop not yet open and no sign of Chanelle, which she soon discovered was the norm as the weeks went on, but she also soon realised that Paul did appreciate his new Saturday girl.

'You're great at styling and putting outfits together for our customers, Phoebe. You've definitely got an eye, would you like to work here sometimes in your school holidays too?' Phoebe was so chuffed that Paul was asking her. There was a silence whilst Chanelle looked at Paul and then at Phoebe. Phoebe wondered what she was going to say as initially there had seemed to be no love lost between Chanelle and herself, but then Chanelle surprised her.

'Yes, great idea. Phoebe's really good, in fact she's brilliant. Robert came in with some of his friends last week and the fashion choices she made were inspired. I didn't need to help her at all and the girls all spent a fortune. Phoebe's the best girl we've ever had in here.'

Phoebe was amazed by Chanelle's praise and got so hot from blushing and embarrassment that she thought she was going to pass out. When she went to leave, she realised she hadn't stopped smiling all day and was still smiling as she walked back into her house. Her confidence was building again, even without the Paula effect.

Chapter 6. Paula. London, 1971

Paula lay on a single bed that had long ago seen better days. She hadn't dared untuck the sheets as she didn't want to find out what might be underneath. Stains, wear and tear were apparent everywhere and on all the shabby pieces of furniture that just about fitted in her tiny room. She stared up at the peeling paint and the damp patches on the ceiling. She had just enough cash to pay for this hostel for another few days.

She walked down the stairs and out of the run down building to a greasy spoon café a few yards away. She'd found that the husband and wife team who ran it were friendly enough, she'd had a cup of tea there a few times before and they hadn't minded that she'd sat there cradling the same cup for over two hours. She sat down at a window table with an Evening News from the previous day still left on it. The wife came over to take her order.

'Cup of tea, luv? Toast and Jam?'

'Ta.' That was exactly what Paula fancied, something that was cheap, hot and comforting. She sat there with a chipped mug of steaming tea and the newspaper in front of her. She savoured and prolonged every single bite and chew of the toast, as regular meals were not a financial priority. She wasn't yet sure what she was going to do but she knew she quickly needed to find a job, otherwise she would be on the streets by the end of the week and that wasn't in her future life plans. One major setback at a time was enough.

She opened the paper at the Classifieds and scanned down the ads. Well, it was never going to be an office job for her, so no point looking at situations vacant. What else could she do? There wasn't much and she'd left school without taking any exams. Then she saw it. Just a small box ad, right at the bottom of the page.

Do you have the right attributes to be a working girl in Paris?
Call Pierre to find out more.
Tel: 331-06-66

She gulped down the rest of her mug of tea and gobbled the last bite of toast. Clutching the newspaper open at the ad page and grabbing her holdall, which she hadn't trusted to leave in her Hostel room, she hurried to the nearest public phone box down the street. She opened the door of the phone box and the stench of men's wee hit her; blimey, did they have to? She tried not to breathe too deeply, jamming the door open with her holdall, and looked for coins to feed into the pay box. She'd never called abroad before but knew that a non-local call was a "trunk call". Maybe she could reverse the charges via the operator, she had the name of the person to ask for - Pierre. Her heart was beating so fast that she thought passers-by would hear it. She dialled 0 for the operator.

'Hello Caller.'

'Erm...' Paula had never had to search for what to say but this time she did. She put on her best posh voice, the voice that she'd learnt from Phoebe. It still wasn't perfect but it was the best it had ever been. 'Please can I have a reverse charge person to person call to Paris, France.'

'Yes, Miss. What's the phone box number you're calling from, the number in Paris and the person you'd like to speak to please?'

'My number is 688 1600 and I'd like to speak to Pierre in Paris please on 331 06-66. Thank you very much.' Paula almost said "ta" but she bit it back just in time.

'Will this person know you, Caller?'

'Nah. Um, no he doesn't but he said to ask for him.'

She could hear the tapping of the connecting British dial tones, and then a brr - brr… brr - brr … a different sounding foreign ring tone but the phone just rang and rang and she began to think the operator was going to hang up until she heard her say: 'Is that Pierre? I've a London call for you. Will you accept the charges, please?'

Paula could just hear, 'Oui, yes.'

'You are now connected, Caller,' said the operator and rang off, with Paula and the man in Paris now connected. Paula suddenly realised that this was all just so strange. There she was standing all alone in a disgustingly dirty and smelly red telephone box in the middle of Bayswater, talking to a random unknown man in Paris.

'Bonjour, who is zees please phoning from London?'

'Bonjour, Pierre. I saw your ad in the newspaper here for working girls in Paris and I'm replying.'

'So, you'd like to come to work in Paris for me. How old are you?'

She thought quickly on her feet, in case she was too young. 'Eighteen.'

'D'accord and are you already working for anyone in London?'

Paula didn't really understand this question, why should she be calling if she already had a job but a no seemed to be the obvious answer. 'No, Pierre.'

'Then you will meet my friend Benjamin at 63e Lexham Gardens, Earls Court, at midday tomorrow. If he like you and find you suitable, we pay for you to come to Paris to stay at my apartment by the end of next week. Have you a pen to write the address?'

'Yes, yes, I've already got it, 63e Lexham Gardens. Merci, Pierre, I'll see Benjamin tomorrow.' She slowly replaced the receiver, picked up her holdall and stepped out of the phone box. As she stood in the weak spring sunshine, she felt a little bit hopeful for the first time in a long time. Something, she sensed, something major, might just be about to change for her, and for the better.

Paula woke up early the next morning, looking forward to her interview. She'd spent a little of her savings yesterday on a cheap new bra and knickers set. It was the first underwear she'd bought since before she was pregnant and it had immediately made her feel better, even though it would only be she who was seeing it.

Today, she resolved, was going to be the first day of the rest of her life. She nipped into the shared shower on her landing before any of the other transitory guests in the hostel left their pubes behind in the grubby shower tray. She tried not to let the grimy plastic shower curtain touch her body as she soaped herself clean. Her stomach just wasn't quite as flat or firm yet as it had been before, but no one would ever have guessed she'd just had a baby. Back in her room, she put on her new undies, with an old but clean sweater and a pair of tight jeans that showed off her long legs. Her hair hung shiny, straight and blonde now way down her back, as she'd had no money to get it cut.

She looked at her London A-Z map in her diary and found Lexham Gardens. Her first thought was that it wasn't far from Phoebe's house, and then she stopped and thought for a moment. As she was as smart as she could look in her current circumstances, maybe she could just drop past Phoebe's house on the way. She could see if Phoebe was there or at least leave a message for her.

Her heart was beating so fast as she stood outside Phoebe's front door that she thought she was going to pass out. The last time she'd been there was the afternoon they'd got ready for the Feather's Ball. She rang the bell. It felt like a lifetime before she could even hear any footsteps walking to the front door, across the marble front hall that she remembered so clearly. The door opened. Thank fuck it wasn't Mrs Clarke. It was the housekeeper again, who looked astonished to see her.

'Paula?' Mrs Abbott's expression changed from one of confusion to a brief glimpse of something that resembled joy.

Paula breathed again. She didn't know how to start and now that she was here what to say. 'Erm… Hullo again Mrs… err…'

'Abbott, dear.' Mrs Abbott smiled kindly back at Paula.

'Oh, I'm so sorry, that's so rude of me. I should have remembered.'

'It's quite alright, Paula dear.' She spoke reassuringly, but her facial expression asked a million questions.

'Umm… I wondered whether Phoebe might be here?'

'No, dear, she's out at the moment.'

'Do you know… umm… when she might be back?' Paula stumbled over her words.

'I'm afraid I don't, dear. Can I give her a message? I know she'll be so happy to hear from you. She's been quite worried about you.'

When Paula heard Mrs Abbott say that Phoebe had been worried about her, it was as though someone had opened the flood gates and everything she'd been wanting to say rushed out. 'Please, can you tell her that I came around today and also, that I'm so sorry that I've not contacted her this year, but, erm… I suddenly had to go away for a while, family stuff,

81

but I'm back here now in London and… maybe when Phoebe comes back, you could please tell her I'll meet her tomorrow at the Picasso at midday?'

Paula suddenly had an overwhelming urge to burst into tears and become a child again; to feel the reassuring warmth and comfort of a cuddle with this kindly older mother-figure. She could feel Mrs Abbott looking at her with a worried expression.

'Are you sure you're alright, you're very pale. Don't you worry, I'll pass on the message as soon as I see her.'

'Thank you so much, Mrs Abbott.' Paula breathed a huge sigh of relief and tried to pull herself together as she left Phoebe's house with a mixture of emotions tumbling around in her brain, but a lighter spring in her step on her way to her meeting in Earls Court. At five to twelve she stood outside the Lexham Gardens address; a tired looking building, several storeys high with white stucco peeling on its front. She rang the bell and waited. The door buzzed open.

'Come in, fifth floor.' A voice crackled through the intercom.

Glancing around the hall which was full of old letters and leaflets, it was immediately apparent there was no lift and five floors was going to be a long walk up. Paula could see this was one of those faceless, unloved buildings, with ever-changing tenants, whose mail continued to be sent there even though the recipients had moved on long ago. She climbed to the fifth floor and there standing at an open door was a sun-tanned man, maybe, Paula thought, of North African origin. He smiled at her, exposing a mouthful of yellow teeth which, Paula instantly observed to herself, hadn't ever seen much in the way of dental attention.

'Salut, Paula. Thank you for coming. I'm Benjamin. Come in.'

Although Paula had always had a certain amount of street savvy and self-preservation about her, as she'd grown up having to survive and look after herself, she instantly felt uncomfortable with this stranger. He was so clearly sizing her up like a prize animal about to be sold at the market.

'Bien, Paula. What do you know about zees job you apply for?'

'I thought working in Paris sounded interesting.' Paula decided to revert to her "less is more" strategy of information and anyway his English didn't seem to be too fluent.

'D'accord. So, I explain. We pay for you to work in Paris with other girls in our apartment in the thirteenth arrondisement. We look after you and protect you.'

'Protect me?' Now, Paula was not just feeling uncomfortable but increasingly confused. She was beginning to wonder what she had got herself into.

'Paula. Do you not know what eez working girl business men visit and you are –how you say - très sympat with them, you've done this before? Did Pierre not ask you zees when he spoke wiz you on ze phone from Paris?'

Paula was slowly starting to understand and the realisation was making her feel slightly queasy from what he was saying and as the saying went, "beggars can't be choosers". She now needed the money so badly that she was about to say yes to almost anything.

'Yes.' She hesitatingly replied.

'Well, Paula, I send you to Pierre but first I have to make small test with you, so please déshabilles.'

Paula recoiled as she hadn't been expecting that. Her school French was enough to know that he wanted her to undress. She tried to keep a neutral expression on her face as though it was what she was asked to do every day. However she couldn't help herself hesitating and he must have noticed it in her body language.

'Now, please.' He was sounding impatient.

She very slowly pulled her sweater up over her head and pushed her jeans down with as much attitude as she could manage. Thank fuck she had new underwear but it seemed that the underwear was merely incidental in the scheme of things.

'Nu, naked please, Pierre like to know ze body all good; he only have best girls.'

So Paula stood in front of the man holding her hands protectively in front of her. She felt so vulnerable and she'd never had such a feeling before. A multitude of fears were now racing around her head and the primary fear was that he would notice she'd had a baby just a couple of months ago.

He continued to scrutinise her and she could sense his eyes boring into her naked body.

'Put your hands either side of you and turn around. You have good body, Paula. Clients will like. Now, agenouilles, kneel.' With that he undid his trousers and pulled out one of the biggest cocks that Paula had ever seen and pulled her towards him. She tried not to recoil. 'Suce sur elle Paula, do you understand... suck! Show me how good ze English girls do it.'

This wasn't the interview that Paula had been expecting, but it wasn't the first time she'd been asked to suck a dick and this time the reward was a paid future in Paris, not just some teenage boy's spunk over her face. She put as much of his cock as she could in her mouth, trying not gag. The more she gagged the more he pulled her head towards him. His size was choking her but she tried to relax and do her best and then she knew he was about to come, but she couldn't swallow, she just couldn't... and then it was all over.

Paula could see that Benjamin looked less than happy as he wiped himself with a handful of tissues from the box of tissues on the table next to him. She suddenly felt sullied and dirty and wondered how could she have ended up giving a blow job to this unknown man with disgusting yellow teeth and a huge cock in a dirty room simply so she could afford to live? This wasn't how she'd ever envisaged her life just last year when she'd been so happy go-lucky, hanging out with Phoebe on the King's Road. She felt angry and disgusted at herself and then defeated. Waves of sadness washed over her as she remembered her baby that had been cruelly taken away from her, and why she had just done this. Grief bubbled up within her but she tried to suppress it and looked up at him defiantly, whilst still naked and on her knees, waiting for his verdict or score of what she supposed she might call "her performance".

'Good, Paula, you have some experience. You will leave for Paris wiz me tomorrow. Put your clothes on now as I take photo of you for special passport we arrange - I think you don't have one? D'accord, I see you tomorrow here, twelve O'clock.'

Paula quickly threw on her clothes, the ones she'd put on, so full of hope this morning; the ones that had given her the confidence to visit Phoebe's house. What would Phoebe think if she'd known what she'd just done? Paula had never felt dirty before, even when she was fucking random boys who'd taken her fancy on one night stands, but now everything had changed. She realised that she'd do anything now to survive.

85

Suddenly she remembered that Benjamin had said that they were to leave tomorrow at midday and she'd just left the message for Phoebe to meet her then. Oh fuck, fuck, fuck! She was going to have to go back to Phoebe's house. Paula ran practically all the way back to Phoebe's house and then stood for a moment to breathe normally and compose her thoughts, before ringing the doorbell once again. She waited to hear footsteps echo on the marble hall floor towards the front door, but everything seemed very silent. She rang again and waited, but still nothing. She rang once more and heard footsteps. Paula breathed, everything would be okay. The door opened and she found herself looking into the steely cold eyes of a very skinny, immaculately dressed and groomed blonde woman.

'Yes? Who are you, do I know you? No, I think not, you don't look like someone whom my daughter would know.' The woman spoke in clipped, staccato tones, whilst peering dismissively at Paula.

Fuck. It was Mrs Clarke. God, what an absolute bitch she was, poor Phoebe, now Paula had an insight into what her life must have been like. Mrs Clarke had instantly made Paula feel awkward, gauche and insignificant, just like the low-life she'd been described as by her social worker. Maybe that's how everyone saw her now. She knew that if she'd been an ant, Mrs Clarke would happily have squashed her underfoot with one of her expensive designer heels.

Paula hesitatingly spoke, 'I just wanted to leave a message for Phoebe, please.'

'I simply don't know if or when I will see her,' Mrs Clarke answered curtly, 'what is your message?' she added as an afterthought.

'I'd be most grateful, Mrs Clarke, if you could just say her meeting needs to be at ten in the morning tomorrow, not midday.' Paula didn't want to say the meeting was with her as she was positive that Mrs Clarke wouldn't pass on a message from someone who appeared to be such an unsuitable choice of friend.

'I will see what I can do. Phoebe is a very busy girl, as I am too.' Phoebe's mother decisively closed down any further communication, slamming the heavy front door firmly in Paula's face. Paula never prayed but for one of the only times in her life, she hoped that God, whoever and wherever he was, would be looking down on her. All her hope from this morning had drained away and she turned to set off on foot back to the hostel. She desperately wanted to see Phoebe before she left for Paris, it was as if she just needed to touch, however briefly, that old happy period of her life, before setting off into the unknown. As she walked with a heavy heart, dragging her feet up Kensington Church Street towards Bayswater, she knew undoubtedly that Mrs Abbott would pass on her message to Phoebe, but there was a stronger chance that Mrs Clarke wouldn't.

'Please God,' she prayed silently, 'please let Phoebe come.'

Paula didn't sleep well all that night and as she lay in the narrow uncomfortable bed for the last time, she looked around the small, cramped room with distaste. Even in the half-light, the brown water stains down one wall from the leaking roof seemed bigger. She didn't want to stay a moment longer than she had to, in this miserable dirty hostel room. She sprang out of bed and began to pack her few belongings, all the while planning her morning. She would walk to the King's Road through the park, saving money so she could afford a coffee whilst she waited for Phoebe. She didn't want to rely on Phoebe's generosity ever again. She thought of her friend as she walked through the park, past the Round pond and the ducks they'd once fed. She remembered that this was the park, Kensington Gardens that Phoebe had once mentioned she'd spent her childhood playing in. Her life with Phoebe now felt like another life a million years ago when she was just a girl. Now she was a woman and a mother, although no-one knew that. Would she look the same to Phoebe? She had no idea. She certainly didn't feel the same, but she didn't know what she felt - excited, nervous or scared - or all these emotions mixed together. Her tummy had now tangled itself into knots.

She arrived way too early at the King's Road and the Picasso wasn't even open yet, so she decided to have a walk down the road to Peter Jones and back. The whole morning felt like she was time-travelling back to the past, even though it was only rolling back one year and every shop she passed reminded her of Phoebe. Then finally by the time she'd walked the length of the Kings Road and back, the Picasso was open. The grumpy waiters and waitresses were all smiley this morning as it was still early and no one was waiting impatiently for their cappuccinos.

Paula sat at one of the two pavement tables and decided to treat herself to a cappuccino and also a toasted cheese and ham sandwich as she was soon going to be earning money again. She remembered how yummy those toasted sarnies had been. Behind her, the café was filling up with customers and one of the grumpy waitresses was now looking busy and still shouting "cino" orders at the Barista behind the counter every few minutes. Paula smiled. It had taken her and Phoebe ages to realize that "cino" was the shorthand for the

88

customers' cappuccino orders. She sat back and enjoyed watching the King's Road once again coming alive as the shops opened up and people passed by on their way to work, it was like old times. She sipped her frothy coffee and appreciated the layers of flavours and textures in every single measured bite she took of her toasted sandwich. Ten O'clock came and went and then ten-thirty with still no sign of Phoebe. The knots in her tummy tightened, as her certainty grew that Mrs Clarke hadn't delivered her message. Eleven O'clock came and went and now she really, really needed to leave.

'Can I get you anything else Signorina, another coffee?'

'No thanks, I'm just waiting for my friend.' Paula remembered this particular waitress from all the past times she'd sat there with Phoebe for their after-school coffees. She attempted to smile at the waitress but tears seemed easier to come by than a smile. Her feelings of excitement had now changed to a dull empty ache in the pit of her stomach. She knew that eleven-thirty was the latest she could be with Benjamin as he was her future and Phoebe was her past... unless she arrived now.

The friendly waitress was still hovering attentively in case Paula had wanted anything else.

Paula came to a decision. It was now or never. 'Have you got a biro and some paper please? I'd like to leave a note for my friend. Do you remember my friend with all the curly red hair?'

'Si, Signorina, certainly I do. I'll give her the note for you.'

Paula paid her bill and gratefully gave the waitress her folded note. She slowly picked up her small suitcase and handbag with a heavy heart and turned down the King's Road again to wait for the forty-nine bus to take her towards her new life where she resolved to grab every opportunity firmly by the balls.

Phoebe had had a brilliant time. She'd spent all day with the debutante girls rehearsing the fashion show at the Berkeley Hotel and the evening show itself had been a huge success. The mothers had praised her on how well she'd put together the Dior outfits and how perfectly she'd chosen their daughters' outfits to suit their personalities, whilst the girls themselves had loved her styling too. Even the staff from Christian Dior had congratulated her, and most surprisingly her mother and father had both turned up together to watch her for the first time in her life; but she was realistic and realised that it had probably been more of a social networking opportunity than to support their only daughter. She wished Mrs Abbott could have been there as she would have been there for no other reason but to support her.

Phoebe finally flopped onto her bed, happy but exhausted and lay staring blankly at the ceiling for a moment. It had probably been the best day of her life so far, the planets were finally aligning. Suddenly she noticed a note that had been slipped under her bedroom door, no-one had ever done that before.

Phoebe,
While you were out today, Paula your friend from school came round. She asked me to leave a note for you. She would like you to meet her at midday tomorrow at the Picasso, she said it was important.
Mrs Abbott.

Phoebe suddenly felt physically sick that she'd missed Paula's visit - it was one of the few days she'd been out in ages. She'd literally been aching to see Paula but now, tomorrow, she actually would and then she would finally know what had happened to her and finally have a best friend in her life again. Although she was exhausted and it was now so late, her brain was buzzing and when she finally fell asleep, her sleep was broken and restless.

The house was silent when she left in the morning, her mother still asleep as usual, her father at work and it was Mrs Abbott's day off. Phoebe shut the front door quietly behind her and walked down the side street just off the King's Road. Although she was tired, she felt energised with the thought that her life seemed to have a meaning and purpose again; she'd made some new friends but now her best friend was actually coming back into her life.

She arrived at the Picasso early, to be precise, eleven thirty-five. Her mother had drilled punctuality into her and Phoebe was always early. There was an empty table outside which was unusual. The outside tables were always taken by the same group of men, they obviously hadn't arrived yet. The table hadn't been cleared, though with the remains of a cappuccino left on the table and an empty plate with not a single crumb left on it. In fact the plate appeared to be so clean, that Phoebe decided that the person who had eaten something off it must have been so hungry they'd nearly licked it clean.

A waitress came out from the café ready to take Phoebe's order.

'Bongiorno signorina, how are you today?'

'Good thanks. I'm waiting for my friend but I'm early as usual. Please can I have a hot chocolate whilst I wait?'

The waitress stopped writing the order on her notepad and chewed momentarily at her biro end, looking thoughtful.

'Is your friend a very tall girl?'

'Yes, she's very tall, blonde and very pretty.'

'Alora, I think I have a little note for you from her.' The waitress looked rather pleased with herself at the news she was now giving to her customer whom she'd recognised as a regular.

Phoebe's heart stopped, 'She's been here?'

'Yes, signorina, she just left. You're sitting where she was sitting. She went that way.' The waitress waved her hand towards the traffic lights junction in the direction of the Fulham Road.

Phoebe couldn't understand how this could have happened. The note had clearly said midday and she was even early.

'One moment, I'll be back.' Phoebe stood up so she could see better down the street towards the town hall but she couldn't see anyone that looked like her friend, nor at the traffic lights either but she couldn't see properly round the corner where a number forty-nine bus was turning into Sydney Street.

She walked back to the table, her heart pounding; she'd believed that today would have been the rekindling of her friendship with Paula. She was positive the message had said midday. She sat down again, deciding she'd have her hot chocolate order anyway while she worked out what to do next. She tentatively opened the note that the waitress had just left tucked under her plate and she started to read.

Dearest Phee,
I don't know how to start this and I don't even know if you'll get to read it. I've missed you. You're the only friend who has ever understood me. So sorry I disappeared. No choice - Family problems. Yesterday I left a message with Mrs Abbott

to meet you today but I then had to change the time to earlier, 10 O'clock. I returned to your house and gave your mother the 2nd message. Maybe she didn't see you to tell you?

Phoebe stopped reading and couldn't have hated her mother more at that moment. She then continued reading through the tears that were welling up in her eyes.

I'm leaving London again today. I don't know when I'll be back.
Hope you will become that brilliant fashion stylist you always wanted to be.
Miss you so much.
Love you
Hugs.
Paula xxxx

Phoebe could hardly see to finish reading the whole note as her vision was now completely blurred with tears; she also missed Paula just getting on the number forty-nine bus.

Chapter 7. Paula. Paris, 1971

Paula didn't remember much about her journey to Paris together with Benjamin and two other girls; she still felt numb, like something had died inside her. She didn't even feel any excitement on her first ever aeroplane trip. The two girls were older than her, but already seemed to know each other and she wasn't sure yet whether she needed to make friends with them or to keep herself to herself to survive this new life.

When they finally arrived at Paris Orly airport, standing there in arrivals waiting to greet them was a dark swarthy man similar to Benjamin, but a better looking version. The girls all trooped out behind the two men to a small Renault Four car.

'Salut les filles, please get in the car, I'm Pierre. You spoke wiz me on ze phone.'

Although he'd greeted them politely, Paula instantly read menace and intimidation in the depths of his dark eyes. She knew she needed to stay on-side with this man; he definitely looked as though he could turn nasty at any moment, but she'd lived with a dad like that, so she was confident she could handle him. The Parisian suburbs passed them by in a blur. She didn't really notice their surroundings until they'd stopped in front of a modern high rise block of flats and driven straight into the underground car park. Pierre got out first and then Benjamin swapped into the driver's seat, waiting until everyone had got out before he drove off again, tyres squealing on the shiny car park floor as he did a three-point manoeuvre towards the exit.

'We're here now girls, allez-y. I show you around your new home before I leave you to wash and to get ready for work. It may not be all of you tonight, as it depend who arrive and request you.' Pierre spoke quietly in a strange mixture of French and English, but whatever his language, there was no doubt in Paula's mind that he wasn't someone to be messed with.

The girls obediently followed him into the large living room which was clean and minimally furnished, with square chunky modern furniture. Paula could see that there were three bedrooms further down the long hallway and a master bedroom at the end, which she assumed must be Pierre's.

Pierre pointed Paula towards the first bedroom they'd come to and waved the girls to continue down the hall.

'This eez your bedroom and Tracey and Gina, the bedrooms down the hall are yours.'

Paula slumped down on her double bed, surveying her new surroundings. If she stretched out her arms she could touch both walls on either side of the bed as her room was so small. There was a partitioned-off area at one end with a shower cubicle and toilet. The basin was in the actual bedroom, set into a small and very basic melamine vanity unit, which was squeezed in beside the single door wardrobe but everything was clean. At least now she'd not have to worry where her next meal was coming from and soon there would be money coming in. However, she still hadn't connected properly with the other two girls, but she was sure there'd be ample time.

Pierre suddenly appeared back into her room. Paula realised that he was never going to knock and privacy just wasn't going to be a thing there.

'Your first client tonight is a regular and he like, how you say... girl together, so I give you easy first night with one of ze girls. Tracey and Gina have done zees before.'

95

Paula felt a sense of relief that there were to be no huge cocks to start with. To be fair, she'd always quite fancied seeing what it would be like with a girl, maybe it could even be fun and she was getting paid too. She followed Pierre back into the lounge where the other girls were now sitting.

'Les filles, if you wish any white powder tonight, I give you later. You'll find new work lingerie in each of your bedroom and this I deduct from your first week monnaie. Compris? I expect you to be sympat and do what is ask. In each bedroom eez panic button for any problème, but I know you will not need zees.'

The three girls looked at each other. Paula looked at Tracey and Gina and they looked back at her. She tried to decide which girl she fancied more but maybe they were deciding too. Tracey broke the silence first.

'Have you done this before Paula?'

'Paula decided to be truthful. 'Nah, never.'

Paula realised she'd inadvertently gone back to not trying to be posh any more. It was hardly going to matter anyway, as she could see that conversation wasn't going to be high on the agenda.

'Gina and I decided that it's you and me and you'll just do what I tell you. Girl on girl is the easiest request.'

So it was going to be her and Tracey then. Tracey was really pretty so this wasn't going to be too hard to fake.

'Okey dokey, see you in a bit.' Paula returned to her room and lay down on her bed and shut her eyes. It had been a long day and it wasn't nearly over yet. It felt like a lifetime ago she'd been waiting in the Picasso for Phoebe.

The next thing she knew, Tracey was banging on her door, sounding agitated. 'Paula, you were supposed be ready for seven and it's already ten to, quick, hurry!'

Paula felt panic rising as she realised she must have fallen into a deep sleep for the last few hours. She quickly got up and hurriedly washed every nook and cranny of her body and shaved her bikini line so everything was tidy with no stubbly bits. She looked at the selection of underwear that Pierre had left in her room but they all screamed "cheap slut" at her. She reluctantly picked up a red bra and pants made of thin scratchy see-through nylon lace and put them on. They felt cheap and nasty and she couldn't have felt less sexy if she'd tried, but her life was going to be a performance from now on and she'd always been a good actress.

Wearing a little silky kimono-style robe that she'd found hanging behind her bedroom door, tied loosely around her waist leaving a glimpse of cleavage, red lace undies and leg to tease the client, she walked into the lounge. She'd brushed her thick blonde hair until it shone and added just a touch of lip gloss to draw attention to her full lips. Once she'd committed to something she always faced it full-on. She looked across at Tracey who was equally transformed from earlier. No, this wasn't going to be too hard to act out. Pierre was waiting by the bar area with a man who looked older than her dad. He wore an ill-fitting shiny suit which was closed with one straining button over his large belly. As he stood there, Paula watched him take out a crumpled cotton hanky from his pocket to mop some sweat which was trickling from his bald head down his forehead. The longer she stood there, waiting to be thrown to the metaphorical lions, the quicker any positivity she'd already built up was ebbing away.

'Girls this is Serge, he speak no Engleesh, so I tell you myself he like to watch ze girls pleasure each other, allez-y – go now with him.' Pierre waved the girls to take Serge with them, quickly adding some additional information for Serge's ears only, under his breath.

'Serge, Paula est ma nouvelle fille, elle a seize ans - une vierge. Tracee est très expérimenté.' Pierre had reverted to speaking completely in French to his client to impart this news. Paula realised that Pierre probably didn't know that she spoke or understood a little French but she'd got the gist that he was selling her to Serge as a young inexperienced virgin. Well she could play act that role, no probs.

Tracey took Paula and Serge by the hand and led them slowly towards her bedroom. Paula's heart was already beating faster as this wasn't the same as a quickie with the boys back on the estate. This time she was being paid and she wasn't even stoned or drunk, maybe she should have accepted some of the white stuff Pierre had offered - it wouldn't have been the first time she'd tried some cocaine.

Serge, still sweating, sat down on the chair by the bed, legs spread, fat fingers already busy down inside his flies. The girls lay down and Tracey gently cupped Paula's boobs, tracing their curve lightly with her fingers, kissing them softly through the nylon mesh of the bra. She then pulled down the bra straps and started to lick her nipples. Paula decided that Tracey's touch felt much nicer than when the boys had done this to her - so much gentler.

Maybe the best way to play this would be to mirror every move that Tracey did. Paula was very much aware that Serge's hand was extremely active down his trousers whilst his piggy eyes eagerly followed the girls' every move. Paula tried to imagine her role a bit like a pas-de-deux ballet performance where each girl took a turn to be in the spotlight and then hand over for their solo so when Tracey's hands wandered all over her body, hers now did the same. Paula decided that she was probably doing okay by the look in Tracey's eyes and was aware that Tracey's fingers were now creeping slowly down her body... and then they were in her knickers. She felt her lips being parted and then a finger inside her; gentle, probing and persistent. Paula inadvertently gasped with pleasure and Serge groaned simultaneously. Tracey stepped up the action and whispered in Paula's ear to turn round and get on her hands and knees, facing away from Serge so he could get a better full-on view. Paula clumsily repositioned herself over Tracey's face. No-one had ever had been this close up and personal to her pussy before. She could hear Serge breathing more and more heavily as she felt the pace increase of her own breathing. Tracey's tongue was darting away like a lizard's as her fingers never stopped exploring everywhere - pressing, squeezing, stroking, wiggling, caressing, flicking, tapping and rubbing.

Paula shut her eyes and tried to block out the image that she was trying to un-see of the sweaty masturbating man in the room. She relaxed into the moment and suddenly felt an overwhelming sensation of the most amazing orgasm she'd ever had about to take over her body. She felt that she might possibly pass out as wave upon wave of pleasure hit her. This, she realised was the first time in her life she hadn't faked it. However she then made doubly sure that it was noisy enough for Serge to appreciate the moment and kissed Tracey passionately back.

Lost in their moment, the girls suddenly noticed that Serge had managed to quickly undress himself and was now climbing onto the bed to join them. His extraordinarily hairy body and stiff cock was rubbing up against the girls' thighs as he placed himself between them. The girls exchanged a look of horror as they'd not been expecting this. He then quickly and deftly manoeuvred himself on top of Paula and forced himself inside her. She was still wet from Tracey's efforts but she hadn't been ready for this. She gasped in pain - it had only been a few months after giving birth. Serge continued, oblivious to anything but his own lust.

Paula knew that this was what she'd signed up for - he was the punter. She desperately tried to pretend that she was enjoying it and to block out the pain. Then she managed to briefly catch Tracey's attention. Tracey, being an old pro at this, quickly realised Paula was having a problem and steamed in with all the tricks in her book to make him come as quickly as possible. The magic instantly worked and Serge rapidly pulled out, and promptly came all over Paula's breasts. Tracey looked at Paula in horror, realising too late, that this man hadn't bothered to wear a condom. Paula felt physically sick but grateful he hadn't come inside her. She was back on the pill again, so no chances of pregnancy but she'd have to be more vigilant next time and sex without a condom would be an absolute no-no. She'd always have to have one ready in her hand from now on.

The girls quickly pretended to look satisfied and pay lip service to Serge whom they knew would immediately be reporting back to Pierre. Paula reached out for a tissue to wipe away the wetness now between her legs, but found blood instead. Serge noticed, but misunderstood what he saw and grinned at Paula lasciviously.

'Pour la première fois une vraie vierge ici.'

He then happily strutted, peacock-like to the shower room, only to return dressed again in the shiny suit clutching a handful of French franc notes.

'Merci les filles. I say to Pierre très très bon.'

Paula and Tracey both stood up still naked. They gave the small sweaty man a cuddle, making him feel extra special before he returned to the lounge where Pierre had been waiting.

'Well done girl, you did good for the first time.' Tracey was smiling kindly at Paula.

'Nah, it was all down to you,' Paula then continued a bit sheepishly, 'I'd never come with a bloke before, I'd always faked it. That was a first… and with a girl.'

'Any time luv; happy to oblige.'

Tracey winked and patted Paula playfully on her bottom as they went back to their rooms. Paula stood under the shower and let the hot water soap away the emotional and physical traces of her first paid-for fuck. Perhaps in time she'd become as chilled about it as Tracey obviously was. She then sat cross-legged on her bed with a towel wrapped round her and counted up the money she'd just earned: over three hundred francs, equal to about one hundred pounds, crikey. That was more than she'd ever saved before she got pregnant. She could definitely do this, but she'd need to make sure that she would become Pierre's favourite girl and make as much money out of her tricks as she could before she escaped to start a new life somewhere.

Chapter 8. Phoebe. London, 1971-1972

Phoebe now appreciated every single invitation she received to spend time with any of her new deb girlfriends after so many years of being an outsider. These personal invites meant so much to her, as all the party ones simply had guest lists taken from Peter Townend's little black book of socially desirable aristocrats.

Jane, one of her new friends since the Berkeley Dress show, had joined her for a coffee on the Kings Road to enjoy a post-mortem on the dinner party they'd both stayed at until late the previous night. Phoebe loved a good catch-up, hearing what she may have missed out on, as her own actual love-life action, or extreme lack of, hadn't evolved. Jane had just finished systematically working through who had fancied who at the dinner and if anything had gone further. It seemed that even Jane had already snogged someone. Things would have to change. Phoebe was lost in a world of her own for a moment, wondering how and when this might happen when Jane suddenly grabbed her arm with excitement.

'Phoebe, my parents are away at the moment so their country cottage in Sussex is empty this weekend. I think I'm going to get friends down, would you like to come for the day?'

Phoebe didn't have to think twice. 'Ooh yes please, what a great idea, I'd love to.'

Saturday turned out to be a hot and sunny, perfect for a road trip in her new MG Midget sports car, which she'd christened Millie. Phoebe drove to Sussex with the roof down and arrived feeling windswept at a chocolate-box pretty cottage. She shielded the sun from her eyes as she looked up at the roses that climbed over the front of the house and up to the thatched roof. It was exactly how she'd imagined a perfect country cottage to be. She parked her car next to a few others at the back of the cottage but then had no absolutely no idea where to walk to next.

'Hi... Jane?'

No answer. Phoebe tried the back door which happened to be open and walked hesitantly through what she realised was the boot room, through to the kitchen, finally arriving in a light and airy drawing room which led though French windows onto the garden. She now realised why no-one had heard her calling as the music from the record player in the floral and chintz-fabric filled drawing room, where she was standing, was so loud. She recognised the album as Pink Floyd's Atom Heart Mother; the perfect music for a hot and sunny Summer's day. Phoebe could now see Jane and her friends sitting in a small group on the lawn. Jane had seen Phoebe too and ran over, greeting her with a huge hug.

'So pleased you could come. Hey everyone, this is Phoebe.'

Phoebe smiled shyly at everyone and did a tiny self-conscious wave.

'Here, come and sit down. How about a drink? We're on Pimms.'

Phoebe sat herself down at the edge of the group feeling all eyes on her. She still hated being the centre of attention and there was nowhere to blend into in the middle of the lawn.

'Don't worry, we won't bite. I'm Simon by the way.' One of the boys in the group was the first to greet her. Phoebe looked over to him and smiled but then did a double take as he was so good looking. He had delicate feminine features and long curly blonde hair resting on his shoulders; he was the spitting image of the beautiful boy from the movie Death in Venice. 'Here, come a bit closer so I can pass you this spliff, I can't quite reach you from here.' Simon was holding out a roll-up cigarette out to her, so Phoebe shuffled herself further into the group. She looked at it and then back at Simon quizzically.

He answered her unspoken question, 'It's just grass in case you're wondering – nothing strong.'

Phoebe wanted to fit in, so took a puff but was immediately wracked with a coughing fit which she tried desperately to disguise with her hand over her mouth. She then had a second attempt which made everything worse. It was beyond yukky.

'Eurgggh,' she muttered involuntarily in the midst of her coughing and spluttering, 'I think that might be enough for me,' passing the joint quickly on. She could feel herself blushing as she felt so silly and embarrassed but everyone seemed to be laughing, but *with* her. She looked around and decided to join in too and at that moment she felt totally included.

She didn't want the beautiful boy to catch her staring, her mother had always drummed into her that it was rude to do so, but he was just so good looking. Phoebe even noticed that his hands were beautiful, elegant and slender. She continued to stare wondering why his hands were now fascinating her so much; maybe it was the effects of the grass that made everything she looked at so mesmerising. She linked her hands behind her head as a pillow and lay back on the grass, changing her focus from his hands to the sky, watching an occasional cotton woolly cloud move slowly across the blue expanse. She was feeling strangely happy and serene, nothing seemed to matter anymore and everyone was so friendly... it was a perfect day.

She was interrupted by a voice in her ear. 'It's okay, you can keep your head there, it's nice.' It was Simon who had laughter in his voice.

'Oh? Okay thanks,' Phoebe felt awkward. How had it happened that her head was now resting on Simon's chest? There seemed to be a whole inner dialogue running around in her brain. Was he just being polite? He had his eyes shut now. She lifted her head slightly to look round at him. He opened his eyes at the same time, smiled back at her and then his mouth seemed to be coming extremely close and then their lips touched. His mouth was slightly open and she could feel the tip of his tongue. What she actually *finally* kissing a boy? She silently panicked. This was her first ever kiss, should she kiss back, should her tongue be doing something too? Then suddenly it all seemed so natural and easy. She stopped over-thinking what to do, melting into the moment and into Simon's arms; it seemed so gentle and romantic. After a few minutes he stopped, looked at her and spoke softly.

'That was lovely and unexpected, just like you.' Phoebe felt time stand still at that moment and that they were both in their own time-warp bubble and no-one else mattered. She'd just fallen in love with a boy she'd only just met and she wanted to see him again. They sat close together holding hands for the rest of the afternoon. She could only hope with all her heart that he would ask for her phone number.

Simon phoned her the very next day and over the next month they constantly met up, but always together with Jane or this new group of friends, never on their own. Phoebe was becoming frustrated that they were never alone and that he had still attempted no more than a kiss. Then finally her prayers were answered as he invited her over to his little flat in the basement of his parent's house.

'Phoebes, fancy coming over for supper?' Simon hadn't said "sleep-over" in so many words, but Phoebe decided that it's probably what he'd meant but was maybe too shy to actually articulate it. Her expectations were now running high as this could be her moment to no longer be a virgin, she was sure she was the only one of her friends who still was. She'd been conscientiously taking her pill since she'd met Simon so she was totally ready for all this.

'That's so cool, I can't wait.' Phoebe could just about make a cup of tea and toast, so anything more than that was impressive. Her anticipation grew as the evening drew closer. She spent hours in a bubble bath, surreptitiously borrowing some of her mother's expensive bath treats and perfumed oils. She tamed her hair and experimented with her Biba make-up and false lashes. She tried every dress in her wardrobe until she finally found one that she decided showed enough cleavage, but not too much and turned up at his door at the dot of seven.

'Phoebes, you look so pretty tonight; come in.'

Simon's words filled her with confidence that tonight would be the night. There was music playing and he had laid his tiny kitchen table for supper for two and a small vase of one yellow rose. There was a bottle of champagne already opened with two glasses poured and waiting.

'Cheers. Here's to our first supper together and many more.' Simon smiled at Phoebe affectionately as he raised his champagne glass in his toast.

'Thank you so much for cooking, it looks yummy,' but Phoebe now had a warm fuzzy feeling in her tummy and could hardly eat a mouthful of the lasagne he'd cooked as her excitement had become overwhelming. She pushed the food around her plate.

'Don't you like it?' Simon looked worried.

'It's absolutely delicious but I seem to not be very hungry, thank you though.' Phoebe tried to sound outwardly calm whilst her tummy was now turning somersaults.

Simon took her hand and led her to the sofa. She cuddled closer to him and he put his arm around her, this seemed promising to Phoebe, so she moved her face closer to him and he kissed her back, things were definitely on the up, tiny steps so she slowly undid his first few shirt buttons and gently stroked his hairless chest. He went on kissing her and then he put his hand inside her bra. Alleluia! Result! What was he going to do next?

Simon suddenly broke away, sat right up again and shuffled towards the front of the sofa poised to stand up.

'It's getting late, shall we go to bed?'

Phoebe's heart was racing. This was finally it. 'Sure.' She answered sounding more confident than she felt and waited for him to lead them both towards the bedroom.

There was a bedside light already on in there, giving a dim red glow through the shade. Phoebe lay down on the bed next to him and waited to see what he was going to do next. Simon undressed her slowly and appreciatively, stopping every so often to look at her, kiss her and stroke her all over but then stopped abruptly at her bra and panties. He proceeded to then undress himself in a swift and business-like manner, pulling back the duvet for Phoebe to get under the covers with him. He reached out and switched off the bedside light, leaving them in total darkness.

'Turn over so we can spoon,' he whispered.

Phoebe turned her back to him and Simon wrapped his arms around her and she felt her body melt back into his, clam-like. She wasn't sure if she felt something hard pressing against her back or not...could it have been his willy? She didn't know as she hadn't been brave enough to know what it could feel like as she hadn't put her hands down his pants yet. She lay there quietly feeling his breath on her neck, waiting for something more to happen – anything, even another kiss - but there was nothing and his breathing turned gradually into a gentle snore.

What was wrong with her? Didn't he fancy her? Didn't he find her sexy?

It was the elephant in the room as months passed and Simon never did any more than kiss, stroke and fumble, occasionally play with her breasts but never ventured into her knickers. As a result she held back and never tried to touch him below either. His constant subliminal rejection caused her to pull away from him, feeling lonely, confused and depressed. She loved him, he said he loved her – so she must be doing something wrong. She turned for help to Jackie magazine's Cathy and Claire problem page to search for any similar questions and solutions.

How do I know if I'm kissing properly? How do I know if my boyfriend fancies me? When is the right time to have sex with my boyfriend?

She didn't want to bring the question up with Simon and she didn't want to discuss it with any of her girlfriends as she was embarrassed. Maybe it would have been different if Paula had been around; she would have known what to do. So Phoebe just accepted the situation as she loved him. Maybe Simon simply respected her too much and wanted to wait for sex until they got married...yes that must be the answer.

She loved hanging out every weekend at Simon's little flat. It was Saturday morning and Cat Stevens's 'Father and Son' from the Tea for the Tiller-man album was playing as she lay with Simon along the length of his brown and orange paisley-patterned sofa. Phoebe extracted herself from his cuddle to change the record. Simon had so many albums to choose from. She spent time flicking through the album covers, settling on Simon and Garfunkel's 'Bridge over Troubled Water'. The song reminded her of Paula and all their times together in the Kings Road record shops. Phoebe still thought about Paula all the time -she'd have loved her to have met Simon and wondered what she would have thought of him.

Simon looked over at her.

'Good choice, Phoebes. Come back over here again, I was enjoying that cuddle.'

She snuggled back down with him and as she lay there, she looked around his funky sitting room. It demonstrated his artistic personality, with all his blu-tacked posters of bands, psychedelic art and black and white photos completely covering the walls. Simon was creative and so very different from his father. She'd often been upstairs to the main house where his parents' rooms were full of large brown antique furniture and amazing valuable artworks hanging on the walls. She'd always considered that she could talk about most things to him, except the unspoken topic of no sex. Simon was absolutely her best friend but what she was about to say felt like a grown up conversation and needed to be said sitting up properly. She pulled away from their snuggled position and he looked surprised. She hoped she now had her serious voice on.

'I know you said you don't want to work in insurance like your father but doesn't he want you to follow him into the City as a broker too? You're so artistic, I can't imagine you ever as a City boy.'

Simon suddenly looked crushed and Phoebe felt the mood in the room change. She began to wish she hadn't opened her mouth.

'Phoebes, I can't think of anything worse. Pa's given me this year to do anything I wish before I join him in his business. So I've enrolled in as many courses and evening classes as I can manage - acting, modelling, photography, art, design... I'm trying them all but when the year is up, I have no idea what I'm going to do. My father's hopes are all on me as his only son to run his company one day.'

Phoebe immediately understood how he felt, so torn between pleasing his father and going down his own career path, but now she was completely stumped at what she could say next to cheer him up. She was beginning to wish she hadn't opened up the conversation. It was Simon who lightened the mood.

'Come on, shall we go out now and try the new 'Great American Disaster' on the Fulham road?'

'Ooh that sounds fun, ready when you are then.' Phoebe silently breathed a sigh of relief. The awkward moment had passed. She leapt enthusiastically onto her feet and pulled him up from the sofa. 'Love trying new places with you, Si.'

They stood on the pavement outside the restaurant and waited patiently in an interminable queue of other excited teenagers. When they finally reached the door, they were shown inside to a small round table in the window. As they sat down on the Bentwood chairs, Phoebe immediately fell in love with the place - it was young, fun, busy and buzzy - in fact everything was busy, even the walls which were decorated with vintage New York Times newspaper disaster stories such as the assassination of JFK and the Wall Street Crash. The delicious chargrilled beef smell together with the sight of overflowing wooden platters of juicy burgers and chips was making Phoebe feel increasingly hungry. She'd never seen anything like this before. She kept looking around at the other diners' meals to decide what she should order.

'Do you know I've never had a proper burger before, Si.' She wondered if it was only her who hadn't had this whole American burger experience.

'No, I haven't either.' Simon echoed. Good, she wasn't the only one. By the time the waiter finally came over, she was sure he could hear her tummy rumbling too.

'Hi guys. How are you both today, good? So have you decided how you'd like your burgers?' He then fired a series of multiple choice questions that needed focused concentration.

'Quarter-pounder or double; well done, medium or rare; cheese and or bacon; onion or relish toppings; Blue Cheese or Thousand Island dressing; fries or baked potato?'

Simon and Phoebe looked at each other, bemused as they'd already forgotten what the waiter's original question was and he was still on a roll.

'And what flavour milkshakes would you both like?'

They had absolutely no idea as the choices were just too many. 'Shall we both have different flavours and then we can see which one we like most?' Simon, being always the problem solver decided this was the easiest solution.

'Chocolate for me please and strawberry for my girlfriend here,' Simon made the decision and finally their order was successfully completed. Phoebe smiled happily, not only was she about to get food but she also loved it when Simon called her his girlfriend.

The waiter thanked them with a flourish of his pen and order pad and rushed off to place the order to the busy kitchen. The shakes arrived before the burgers.

'Can I try yours, you can try mine.' Phoebe tried to sip his chocolate milk shake up through her straw. 'It won't suck! It's so thick!'

Simon attempted to suck unsuccessfully too. 'Do you think we should be using a spoon?'

They started laughing and couldn't stop. Simon always saw the funny side of everything, Phoebe felt flushed with joy that they were now having the best day together, all the earlier awkwardness forgotten.

Simon suddenly stopped laughing. Phoebe followed his gaze and noticed he was looking towards the door. A group of boys and girls had just walked in, but no one that *she* knew. Why did Simon suddenly seem so uncomfortable and fidgety? She didn't understand what had happened and why his mood had changed from relaxed to on-edge. She looked back again in the direction he was staring. A chiselled featured boy with a mop of spiky jet-black hair was heading towards their table, and to her surprise, kissed Simon right on the lips.

Phoebe wasn't sure whether she was shocked or confused. She'd never seen two boys kiss before. She felt strangely awkward, as if she were suddenly an interloper. Was she imagining some invisible connection, a current of energy between the two boys; something that now seemed to be missing in her own relationship with Simon. She looked backwards and forwards between the two boys, waiting for someone to break the awkward silence.

'Phoebes this is Jake.' Simon spoke hesitatingly. Phoebe wasn't sure why and looked at Jake, wondering whether she should shake hands or kiss him but she wanted to hear how

Simon knew him. Before she had begun to ask the question, she could see Simon gathering his thoughts before he spoke again.

'I met Jake at a life drawing art class.'

As Simon answered Phoebe's unasked question, he made quick eye contact with Jake as though he was sending him a silent message. Phoebe didn't remember Simon telling her about any such classes until earlier that day, and he certainly never mentioned Jake.

'Jake was our model at the art class. He's saving up to travel over to California where he wants to do an acting course.'

Jake now found his voice.

'Yes, I've just applied for Cal Arts, a cool university campus just outside Los Angeles that was founded a few years ago by Walt Disney for young actors with only eight students to each teacher. There's nothing like that here in England.'

Phoebe really had no idea what she felt yet about this handsome stranger who seemed to know Simon well, although as she'd listened to him speak, she realised that his voice lured her in; it was rich, warm and inviting with multiple layers. She could understand why he wanted to be an actor, he would be a super successful one, of that she was sure.

She could see Simon was still looking tense. She didn't know why but it seemed to her that the two boys were more than just good friends and she knew she should always trust her gut feelings. The initial awkwardness had now passed but she still felt confused.

'Why don't you come and join our big table?' Jake pointed to the back of the room. 'It's that one over there in the corner.'

Simon took Phoebe's hand and squeezed it tightly, as though he was reassuring her it was okay to go and he was still there for her. Phoebe looked at him. She didn't really want to sit with the new people but she could see he did, so she followed the two boys feeling strangely uneasy. Something subtle had just changed between her and Simon and she wasn't sure what yet.

Once she'd sat down, she looked round the table and then nudged Simon.

'Is that George, the Earl of Dudley, who lives all on his own now that his parents are dead, in a huge pile Chorley Hall in Gloucestershire?'

'Yes,' Simon whispered back, 'and all the deb mothers disapprove of him.' She wanted to ask why but didn't, as she felt now was definitely not the moment. She looked closely at George whilst he was chatting to everyone. He wasn't at all good looking but he was the sort of person who was the life and soul of a party. He must have sensed her gaze, because he looked straight across at her.

Hi, I'm George and great to see you again Simon.' Phoebe wondered how he already knew Simon. 'And this is Caroline Stanhope,' he pointed to the girl on his left, 'and Mary Fitzgibbon-Percy,' he pointed to the girl on his right.

Phoebe smiled at them nervously. She'd come across them occasionally during the deb season, but hadn't been part of their elite group. She remembered seeing the girls' photos regularly in Tatler magazine's Jennifer's Diary pages and in the Daily Mail Nigel Dempster gossip columns. They had been seen as two of the most eligible debs of the Season.

'We briefly met when Phoebe was styling the Berkeley Dress show,' Caroline explained to George, smiling back at Phoebe, 'and she did the most brilliant job.'

Phoebe broadened her smile in acknowledgement of the compliment.

'But we didn't really get a proper chance to chat to each other as she was so busy behind the scenes.'

'Yes, you were so good, Phoebe, everyone said so.' Mary chipped in. Phoebe was now beaming and relaxed just a little. George suddenly clapped his hands with glee as though he were congratulating himself with an idea that he'd just thought of.

'I know, you should all come to stay with me next weekend at Chorley. We're having a shoot on the estate and a black tie dinner on the Saturday night. Is that a yes from everyone?'

Phoebe couldn't believe he'd just included her, was he really sure? The table erupted with whoops and cheers. Phoebe had never before been to a pheasant shoot. There weren't too many live pheasants around Chelsea; only the Pheasantry night club on the King's Road, but she did have all the proper country kit - Hunter wellies and a Barbour. She wasn't sure the weekend was exactly Simon's thing either, but he too was nodding enthusiastically together with everyone at the table. Maybe, Phoebe thought hopefully as she watched Simon, this next weekend could finally be the moment that Simon might actually have sex with her as they were overnighting together for the first time in a country house far away from his parents.

Chapter 9. Phoebe. Gloucestershire, 1972

The following weekend Phoebe drove Simon down to George's house in her little two seater car, with Jake squeezed, knees to chin, in what pretended to be a small back seat. As she turned through the wrought iron gates into the in-out drive, she slowed down almost to a complete halt; looming up ahead of them was a not a country house, but a stately home, as big as Blenheim Palace. It was seriously impressive and she hadn't been expecting anything quite so grand or imposing.

'Ohmygosh!' was all Phoebe could manage.

Jake's mouth hung open too, as he tried to climb out of the car, stretching his limbs again trying to get the circulation back. 'Wow!'

'Ssssh,' Simon shushed, 'come on both of you, pull yourselves together. We're not going to look impressed now are we? We're going to act as though it's what we've always been used to on a daily basis.'

'Of course we are.' Phoebe laughed. This weekend was going to be fun.

On the front steps a uniformed butler was already waiting to take their bags. He did a small head nod as he greeted them formally.

'Good afternoon, Sirs and Madam. If you'd like to follow me please, I'll show you to your rooms as I'm sure you would like to freshen up.' As the three friends followed him, he announced the afternoon and evening's schedule. 'Tea is being served now in the conservatory for the next hour and dinner will be served at eight O'clock with drinks in the drawing room from seven O'clock. I'm sure Lord Dudley had already let you know that Saturday's dinner will be black tie.'

'Thank you, yes.' They all chorused.

Jake was shown to his room first which was at one end of a long gallery corridor, filled full of ancestral portraits from centuries past, which overlooked a Great Hall also with huge family portraits and men on horseback with large dogs.

'Do you think any of them look like George?" Phoebe whispered to Simon as they walked past.

'Not sure, but look at that one, definitely not a looker was he?'

They stopped for a minute, staring up at the huge oil painting, trying to contain their laughter before Simon and Phoebe continued to follow the butler along the galleried balcony. The butler finally paused in front of a large, polished wooden door and opened it and inside was the most beautiful room Phoebe had ever seen.

'Gosh!' Phoebe couldn't help herself, had she really said that out loud? Simon gave her a withering look.

'Is everything all right, Madam?' The Butler asked sounding concerned. Phoebe realised that her mouth was still wide open, fish-like and she snapped it quickly shut.

'Yes, thank you, lovely. Absolutely perfect, thank you so much. Sorry, what was your name again, I missed it when we first arrived.'

'Henderson, Madame. Please don't hesitate to ring down if you require anything at all.'

Phoebe couldn't wait to shut the door and to climb up onto the largest, most fabulous, antique mahogany four-poster bed she'd ever seen. The mattress was very high off the ground and she wasn't very tall so she realised it was going to be extremely difficult to get up on and down off the bed.

'Simon, you're going to have to help me up. They must have had bedside steps in the olden days; they were even shorter than me then.'

'Not that much shorter,' Simon immediately reposted.

Phoebe looked back at him with daggers in her eyes. She'd always been sensitive about her lack of height.

'Silly billy, I'm joking but yes, I think they did have steps then, hang on though, I'll come and be your steps.' Simon crouched down, ready for Phoebe to climb onto his back and onto the bed.

'Thank you, kind sir.' She laughed and daintily stepped up, sinking straight into the depths of the softest goose-down duvet and comfiest mattress she'd ever lain on. As she starfished on her back, she looked above her at the inside of the beautifully ruched frills hanging from around the top of the canopy and the generous drapes which puddled onto the Aubusson rug.

'Si, this is the most romantic bed I'm ever going to sleep on, aren't you excited to be in such a beautiful room with a bed which must have known so many romantic trysts? We can be part of its history as well now, can't we?'

Simon didn't look up or reply, which seemed strange to Phoebe. After she'd stared at Simon focusing intently on unpacking his bag and hanging his clothes systematically in the large dark wood antique French armoire, her eyes travelled around the rest of the room, taking in the floral wallpaper, maybe it was a William Morris print, and all the framed watercolours on the walls. Everything was simply beautiful in this room - the weekend would be perfect as well – how could it possibly not be?

The next day began early. After a full English breakfast all the guests piled into Land Rovers for the morning shoot, returning to the house for a late lunch, leaving their muddy wellies outside. When they'd finished lunch, ready for an afternoon walk with all the guest dogs, Phoebe realised that she couldn't find her wellies anywhere.

'Have you seen my wellies?' Phoebe questioned Simon.

'No, can't find mine either.'

Welly-less, they decided to walk around to the back of the house, staying on the gravel paths instead, stopping every so often to take in the country views and the extensive gardens. As they rounded the corner, they came into a courtyard.

'Phoebes, I think we might have solved the welly-gate mystery.' Simon pointed to a line of shiny clean wellies drying in the sunshine.

Si, they've all been washed and polished. That's so funny.'

'Hilarious,' Simon whispered back, 'I thought all country clothes were supposed to look old and used.'

They both burst out laughing as they always got the same jokes. Sometimes they laughed so much that Phoebe had to stand with her legs crossed as she was frightened she might wee in her pants and then Simon would realise why she was standing like that and try to make her laugh even more to see what would happen.

'I do love you, Si.' Phoebe spontaneously declared, catching his hand. He was just so easy to be with, her soul mate, in every way. She'd never had to try to be anything other than her true self with him. Simon simply acknowledged her comment with a peck on her cheek and a squeeze of her hand. A sense of total bewilderment of Simon's real feelings about her washed over her, and Phoebe suddenly felt drained.

Her mood picked up again as the time to get dressed for the evening's black tie dinner grew closer. Both she and

Simon took ages to get ready; their preparations interspersed with the topping up of their glasses of champagne from the bottle that had generously been put in their room. Phoebe looked admiringly over at Simon.

'I do love a man in a dinner suit.'

'You look beautiful too, Phoebes. Where did you find that beaded twenties dress? It's so perfect for tonight; they don't make dresses like that anymore do they?'

'I found it down the Portobello Road market on one of my Friday crack-of-dawn forays and it was such a bargain too. It's so satisfying isn't it when you find something fabulous.'

'You're really clever at it too, Phoebes.'

'Do you think we make a glamorous couple tonight?' Phoebe actually liked what she saw for a change as she stared at their joint reflections in the antique mahogany mirror, especially as it included Simon.

'We do,' he agreed and gave her another quick peck on the cheek. 'Let's go down and knock them dead.'

Phoebe wished it had been less of a brotherly kiss and more passionate. It was still preying on her mind why he hadn't tried to do anything more with her. She was sure most of her girlfriends' boyfriends would have already leapt on them as soon as they'd arrived in their rooms. There had been absolutely no action last night in their bed apart from a platonic cuddle. She was beginning to feel short-changed.

Simon held her hand as they walked down the grand staircase and Phoebe felt all eyes on them as they walked into the drawing room and she was proud to be on Simon's arm.

'You both look so glam.' Jake was quick to come over and pay them a compliment. Other house guests gradually appeared; a mix of George's London friends and locals that they'd never met before.

'Everyone seems to be on their best behaviour tonight, don't they?' Jake commented quietly, trying to be discrete, with his hand in front of his mouth.

'It's true, why are we all talking in whispers?' Phoebe reasonably questioned.

'No idea!' Simon replied and once again the three friends tried not to laugh, but the more they suppressed their giggles, the harder it became. Phoebe realised guests who didn't know them were now glaring at them, were they about to be sent to the naughty step? They were saved by the appearance of the Butler carrying the dinner gong.

'Dinner is served, my Lords, Ladies and Gentleman. This way please.'

Phoebe, Simon and Jake followed everyone through into the huge dining room. Waiting to be seated, Phoebe stood admiring the long table, which was laid with George's family-crested china and the most beautiful crystal glasses.

'Looks like a State Banquet,' Phoebe whispered into Simon's ear, 'oh and it's all place-named and I don't think we're next to each other.' Simon was now wandering around the table staring at the place cards.

'Will you be okay?' he looked at her expectantly.

'Of course, see you after dins... good luck at your end of the table.' Phoebe was good in formal situations, especially after all the years of her mother's stringent etiquette instructions. Dinner was going to be a breeze, however boring her neighbours were. She'd learnt how to make small talk when she had to.

After dinner the boys all stayed at the dinner table to smoke cigars and drink port, offering the girls no option to stay behind and Phoebe felt like she'd returned to the olden days, when women "withdrew" to the drawing room to play the piano or make polite small talk. However, Phoebe was now feeling more comfortable with all the girls, especially Caroline and Mary.

When the boys rejoined them, cigars were replaced by joints. Phoebe was getting used to the idea of joints being rolled up in unexpected places, even in the smartest of surroundings, with a butler on hand to clear the ash trays at the end of the night. In fact, she realised, she was actually getting used to all sorts of experiences outside her familiar comfort zones. After a while, she pretended she was exhausted and excused herself, hoping that Simon would notice and soon follow her to the bedroom too where they could finally consummate their relationship.

Simon was sitting chatting to Jake, together with some of the other boys. She caught his eye.

'I'll be up in a minute,' he responded and blew her a kiss.

She lay in the huge bed, hopeful but minutes passed and turned into hours and Phoebe could no longer keep her eyes open and fell into a deep sleep. A few hours later she suddenly woke up thirsty and realised there was still no Simon in the bed next to her. Maybe he'd been persuaded to stay up really late getting stoned with everyone downstairs, so she stopped worrying and fell back to sleep.

When she woke up in the morning, Simon was there beside her but up and out of bed really quickly, and he seemed to be on edge.

'Afraid I've got a really bad hangover, Phoebes. Just going for a quick walk in the grounds and I'll see you soon at breakfast.' He spoke apologetically.

Phoebe smiled back at him but once again started feeling that same upset queasy feeling she'd had the other day, as usually they'd always have a long lie-in at the weekends with a morning cuddle.

By the time she came down to a full English breakfast, laid out buffet style in the sunny morning room overlooking the sloping manicured lawns, she found that most guests had already left, including Jake. She politely helped herself to some kedgeree and a coffee and sat quietly together with George and Simon and another couple who were all nursing their apparent hangovers. There was little chat, just the occasional scraping noise of a knife buttering toast and the chink of bone china cups placed back down on saucers. Phoebe also felt self-conscious to make conversation whilst George's staff were still serving in the dining room, so she focused on her breakfast.

On the drive home, Phoebe sensed Simon just wasn't himself. She finally couldn't contain herself any longer.

'Are you okay?' she blurted out, keeping her eyes on the road. She could see out of the corner of her eye that he looked upset. At first he said nothing, then he began to mumble very fast.

'I just don't know how to even start or articulate this. For the last few months, I've tried to make you and me work as a proper relationship. I've tried not to listen to my inner feelings and be a proper boyfriend to you. It's not your fault or anything you've done. I'm so confused right now as to who or what I am; queer or homosexual, or whatever you choose to call it – it's all the same.'

Phoebe could feel her heart beating faster and faster as she listened to what Simon was saying, but not totally comprehending the implications.

'Phoebes, I hadn't felt I could open up to you or anyone else either. I know you've always listened to me and wanted to be there for me, but it was impossible to make you understand something I didn't even understand myself. The truth is, I really do love you – and always have - but as a sister. Meeting Jake has made me realise this.'

Phoebe suddenly understood why she'd had those gut feelings when she'd first met Jake; she should have listened to them but she loved Simon and could feel the utter despair that was emanating from his whole being. She took one of her hands off the steering wheel and reached out to him. Simon took it and started squeezing her hand so tightly that it was beginning to hurt, but she didn't say anything and let him continue speaking.

'So I've decided that the honest thing to do now is to be true to myself and walk away from you so you can find someone who'll truly love you in every way, the way you deserve to be loved. I'm so sorry. I'll always, always love you and I promise I'll always be there for you whatever.'

Phoebe realised she was now sobbing her heart out too, not just for the end of their relationship, but for Simon's obvious pain. It had now become too hard to continue driving on through her tears, so she pulled over to the side of the road. Simon pulled her close and hugged her tightly, his face buried into her shoulder.

'I don't completely understand my feelings towards Jake, but I do know I just can't keep on trying to be something I'm not. You know I'd never hurt you deliberately, so please don't hate me. Please can we still be friends?'

Phoebe knew he was desperate for her to say yes. She felt torn as she didn't know how she'd feel seeing him regularly on this new version of their friendship, but she knew she had to make him feel better. She'd deal with her own feelings later.

'Of course, we'll always be friends. I love you too, but you always knew that.' She spoke compassionately, stroking his hand softly.

'Phoebes, staying friends means so much to me and remember my promise that I'll *always* be there for you.'

Phoebe drove the rest of the journey home through a blur of tears and a wall of miserable silence in the car between them. She felt like her heart was broken, but she was stronger now than she'd ever been and had new friends to support her. Life would carry on.

Chapter 10. Phoebe. Yorkshire, 1972

Phoebe's new friends immediately rallied around her when they heard the news of her break up and tried to keep her busy with a social whirl of activities and invites, with Caroline Stanhope being the most supportive and generous out of all her new girlfriends.

Phoebe questioned whether she could be morphing into her mother, but right now this was helping to get her mind off Simon. She never confided in any of the girls about her personal life, simply hung out with them and listened to their stories. Each time they met up, they'd always quiz her on where she'd bought her clothes and how and where they could find similar styles. Phoebe was thrilled to be able to help as she loved feeling useful and it gave her purpose to each day. The more outrageously she dressed the more the girls loved it and wanted to copy. She systematically worked out each day's outfit, rotating ever-changing combinations from her extensive and eclectic wardrobe with Mrs Abbott designated chief fashion consultant.

Abby, what do you think?' Phoebe asked as she gave Mrs Abbott a twirl.

'Brave,' responded a poker-faced Mrs Abbott.

With every brave acknowledgement offered up by Mrs Abbott, Phoebe knew she'd cracked it. She'd never wanted to play safe.

'How do you do it?' the girls all asked her. 'You can't have a totally unlimited budget, no one does, yet you manage to wear a different outfit every time we meet up.'

Phoebe was confident in her response; fashion was easy, it was life that was hard.

'You're so clever, Phoebe.' The girls seemed really impressed.

'Mrs Abbott, my parent's housekeeper would say brave.' Phoebe laughed as she spoke.

'That's so funny, sounds like we all need a Mrs Abbott.' The girls were all nodding at each other in agreement.

'You don't know how true that is.' Phoebe sighed.

Slowly, with the support of these new girlfriends, Phoebe adjusted to her new life without Simon. Long Saturday lunches at Italian restaurants in and around Chelsea was where their plans were made, relationships began and ended and the world put to right over wine, champagne and liqueurs that never stopped flowing with lunches that never began before 2pm or finished before 6pm.

'Ciao, beautiful ladies.' Mara and Lorenzo, the owners of San Lorenzo always came over independently to greet each of the girls with double air kisses. 'How many are you today, eight? Here we are, the best table for you.'

Phoebe knew that Mara liked to have prominent tables of pretty girls and celebrities in her trendy Knightsbridge restaurant. It was like an elite private club which Phoebe was now a fully-fledged member of, together with a jet set group of Greek ship owners, French and Italian bankers and British playboys who loved the aristocratic blonde-haired girls. Phoebe realised that she was the only non-blonde, short curvy red-haired girl with a style more boho than Belgravia- how had she managed to sneak into this group, accepted and included, although never flirted with, or taken on, a one to one date. She was simply part of the gang. Then Phoebe realised that these wealthy young men with whom she was now mixing, simply wanted girls who put out when invited onto their yachts for weekends to the Monaco Grand Prix or

St Tropez. Jet set life came with an unspoken caveat: sex. Phoebe would have given her right arm for sex, if only anyone would ask; she wondered if she was destined to be the only virgin left in Chelsea.

It was the end of yet another long Saturday lunch. Phoebe stood up and Caroline, who'd been sitting the other side of the table suddenly materialised next to her.

'Phoebe, I've been meaning to ask you something, as I know you've been invited too. Would you like to come and stay with my family for the weekend of Mary Fitzgibbon-Percy's eighteenth birthday dance in Yorkshire?'

'That would be so much fun I'd really love to.' Phoebe's enthusiastic response was instant.

'Goodee, we'd love to have you. I've been telling my mother all about you and she can't wait to meet you.'

'Oh dear, hope all good things?' Phoebe joked suddenly feeling anxious.

'Of course.' Caroline answered emphatically, wanting to sound reassuring to her new friend.

'Phew! I've never been to Yorkshire before either, so I'm really looking forward to this.' Phoebe was nearly dancing up and down with joy at the table with the excitement of the invitation mixed with the after-effects of the many glasses of Pinot Grigio and flaming Sambucas she'd finished with.

'Mary's dance is going to be "the" party of the season and it's at her family's castle, so now that you're staying we can get ready together and my twin brother Jonathon and his best friend Giles can be our escorts. Mummy will send you a letter with the directions to our house; it's not really that far if you'd like to drive, or we can collect you from the station.'

Phoebe considered this for a minute before she decided that it would be better to have her own transport. 'I think I'll come in my little car, if that's okay?'

Caroline and Phoebe had now arrived outside the Beauchamp Place restaurant, and were standing next to a gaggle of predatory Paparazzi photographers hoping that one of their tip offs might materialise from inside.

'Of course, whatever works best for you – can't wait to see you in Yorkshire.' The girls hugged each other, with double air-kisses and went their separate ways. Phoebe suddenly felt life was worth living after all, even without Simon, and immediately started planning what she might wear for the ball, even though it was still a few weeks away.

Phoebe instantly loved Lady Stanhope, Caroline's mother. She was homely, down to earth, warm, welcoming and inclusive, so very different from Phoebe's own mother, with no pretensions, airs or graces. Caroline's mother didn't just greet her but clasped her to her bosom like a long lost family member.

'How wonderful to meet you Phoebe, I've heard so much about you from Caroline.'

Phoebe looked back at Caroline and laughed.

'Thank you so much for having me to stay with you, Lady Stanhope.'

'Absolutely delighted, now we don't *ever* do the "Lady Stanhope" thing here. Please call me Fiona, Caroline's mummy, or anything else you like. Anyone staying with us is family too. Now come on in.' She waved Phoebe on in front of her towards the kitchen, flapping her arms like she was shooing birds. 'I know you've just had a long journey so you must be dying for a cup of tea. How about a slice of my homemade banana cake too, just out of the Aga? Can't guarantee how good it is, but it's still warm.'

Phoebe's mouth started to water at the thought of warm banana cake, it was her favourite.

'Oh yes, please. That would be lovely.' She also realised that her tummy was rumbling as she'd not actually eaten since she'd left London that morning. She looked back at Caroline, hoping that was okay in case Caroline had wanted to do something else but Caroline was nodding as she followed behind.

'Mummy's cakes are always yummy. She's a brilliant cook but doesn't think she is. That's right, isn't it mummy?' Mother and daughter laughed and hugged each other as they walked together into the kitchen. Phoebe felt a tiny pang of sadness. She couldn't ever remember having any moments like that with her own mother. She followed them into the flag-stoned floored farmhouse kitchen. It was exactly how Phoebe had always imagined her perfect family kitchen to be; two large black Labradors lying in front of the Aga, an old pine table in the centre of the room, crowded with books, bowls of fruit, the aforementioned newly baked cake and anything else that any of the family had been doing there together. This table was obviously the central hub of the whole house, where everyone congregated.

'So this is my son Jonathon and Caroline's father Oliver and my son's friend, Giles. Oh, I forgot to add; Fred and Barney the Labradors.' Caroline's mother introduced Phoebe to her family sitting around the table, who all greeted her with enthusiasm, even Fred who'd immediately lolloped over and promptly sat on her foot, giving her his paw. 'Fred will lick you to death given half a chance; best not encourage him.'

Phoebe loved all this family familiarity and interaction. She would have let Fred sit on her foot all day too, if he'd wanted. She'd always imagined how it would be to be part of a close-knit family like this and now she knew she didn't want it to ever end.

The following day, after a quiet country walk with the dogs ending in a pub lunch, the two girls began their party-glam preparations in Caroline's bedroom. Phoebe realised that the last time she'd got ready for a party with a girlfriend was with Paula on the night of the Feathers Ball. This felt so different, as this time they weren't hiding in her bedroom away from her own mother. Caroline's mother seemed to be fully embracing the whole experience of her teenage daughter and friend beautifying themselves ready for a ball and kept coming upstairs to see how they were doing, eventually appearing clutching an armful of evening dresses.

'Phoebe, I've heard from Caroline how good you are at fashion advice so I hope you don't mind me asking but which dress do you think I should wear?' She held up two evening dresses in each hand, putting one after the other in front of her body to demonstrate its possibilities to Phoebe. Phoebe looked back at her in amazement, she couldn't believe that even Caroline's mother was asking her for advice. Then she thought back to when she was a child standing in her mother's dressing room, when own mother had often asked her which dress and which accessories to wear. Phoebe now knew that her mother had never really listened to her reply, maybe she'd only wanted an audience, not an opinion, whereas Lady Stanhope – Fiona - Caroline's mother, Phoebe still couldn't get used to calling her by her first name, actually wanted and even valued her opinion. Phoebe was gobsmacked.

She pointed to the pale blue silk dress in Fiona's right hand. 'I love that one, Fiona. It's beautiful and the colour really suits you.'

'I knew you'd be able to help me. Much appreciated, thank you. See you girls downstairs later.' She waltzed out of the room holding the favoured dress high.

Phoebe was beyond thrilled that she'd been listened to. The theme of the ball was Midsummer Night's dream. The girls spent hours on their makeup and hair. Getting ready was as important as the actual party.

'You're just so talented at creating looks and always getting it spot on.' Caroline was watching Phoebe get ready. 'Tonight you look just like an ethereal fairy queen with your floaty dress and whole hippy boho vibe. You know, I'd really like to look like you with wild ringletty hair and big boobs. Look, see? Mine are tiny, it's not fair.' Caroline was critiquing her boobs in the long mirror as she spoke.

Phoebe blushed. She was putting on her make-up, looking in the mirror that hung over the bedroom fireplace. She could see Caroline attempting to make more cleavage, pushing her boobs together and wondered whether she was brave enough to divulge this info, yes she would, as it might make Caroline feel better. 'You know when I was at school and still a flat chested teenager, I stuffed my bra with cotton wool.' She looked back at Caroline to see how she was going to react.

Caroline had creased up with laughter. 'Well, that's certainly not necessary now is it.' Then she pulled herself together as she continued, 'I know you don't see how pretty and sexy you are, but you are. I overheard Giles, my brother's friend, saying how sexy he thought you were.'

Phoebe paused, her blue mascara wand in mid-air. Had Giles really said that? How strange, good-looking boys like him just didn't notice girls like her. She continued on with her make-up, adding some blue glitter eyeshadow. 'Well, I love your family, Caro, your home is full of happiness, love and laughter and slobbery Labradors. You've also got a *proper* mummy who cooks amazing family dinners on the Aga for you all.' Phoebe spoke with her emotion showing all over her newly made-up face.

'I know I'm so lucky.' Caroline stopped her own boob appraisal and came over to hug Phoebe, who felt the love and just wanted to hold on to this moment for ever and even more so when Caroline made a quick resolution. 'Do you know, I've just decided from this second on, I've decided that I'm going to call you Bea, yes definitely, it's much better than Phoebe. So Bea, please can you wave your magic wand and transform me to go to the ball?'

The only other person who'd ever nicknamed her was Paula. This clearly meant that Caroline had become her new best friend and Phoebe felt overjoyed.

'I love Bea, yes, so much better than Phoebe. So, Miss Stanhope, your wish is now my command, let's see what my invisible magic wand can do!' Phoebe stood back and scrutinized her friend intently for a moment. 'I think you actually already look fab, but let's see...maybe, we could still add a little something extra.' Phoebe picked up some strings of pearls and held them up in front of her, shutting one eye, imagining how she could use them creatively. 'Maybe we could put these pearls in your hair. Yes, I really like that, it works. Mmm... maybe tie a knot in the bottom of your dress so it becomes asymmetrical.'

Pearls secured and dress knotted, Phoebe surveyed her handy work. Caroline rushed back over to the mirror to see how her friend had transformed her dress.

'That's so good, thank you so much.'

Phoebe loved making her friends happy; maybe one day she really could do this whole styling thing as her proper job. No, styling wasn't working with charities like some of her debutante friends were going to be doing, but if she could simply make people happy, feeling and looking good just from the clothes they wore, then why not? She wished that her clothes could always do just that for her too.

The girls went downstairs together arm in arm, like sisters. They were greeted with appreciative wolf whistles from Giles and Jonathon. Giles was straight in there.

'Wow! Stunning, a sexy Titiana! Hot chick!' Caroline's brother threw his friend a friendly warning look. He wasn't sure he trusted his friend anywhere near his sister's new best friend, he knew his reputation.

They all piled into Caroline's parents' Land Rover which had been washed and polished inside and out especially for the occasion. They drove down the narrow country lanes to the ball which was just a few minutes away.

'It's so beautiful,' Caroline exclaimed as they approached the floodlit home, 'it looks just like a fairy tale castle.'

'And romantic,' added Phoebe.

Even Caroline's parents and Jonathon, who'd all seen it before, stared up at the imposing sight from the long driveway lit with flaming torches. The girls hugged each other with excitement whilst Giles just looked disinterested, itching to get stuck into the party. The entrance to the ball was through the castle's Great Hall. They were all handed glasses of champagne whilst they stood in the long snaking queue of guests waiting to be greeted by the birthday girl and her parents. When the Stanhope group finally reached the party hosts they were warmly greeted by Lady Fitzgibbon-Percy.

'How lovely to see all the family together and you too, Phoebe,' she gushed, giving each of them large hugs, one after the other.

'It's so lovely to be here Lady Fitzgibbon-Percy, and Mary you look so pretty tonight.' Phoebe always liked to say something nice rather than nothing at all.

'Phoebe that's kind, thank you and so do you. Have a super evening.' The party girl looked thrilled at Phoebe's compliment.

Phoebe suddenly noticed that Caroline was staring long and hard at Mary's cousin, The Honourable Charlie Cameron who was standing together with the Fitzgibbon-Percy family. Phoebe spotted him staring equally intensely back at Caroline and smiled to herself conspiratorially, they'd be so perfect together. She could see Charlie was now grinning at Caroline and mouthing 'Dance later?' Caroline's expression screamed yes back whilst she was nodding so hard that her head nearly fell off.'

'I think you may have made a bit of a hit there!' Phoebe whispered to her friend. Caroline grinned back at her, eyes sparkling. The girls walked on into the huge marquee.

'This is definitely the biggest party of the year.' Caroline surveyed the scene and knocked back her glass of champagne in one go, whilst Phoebe attempted to be more restrained with hers. 'There are so many people here.' Caroline continued to do a quick scan of the guests. 'Oh there's a gaggle of girls from Heathfield, my old school and loads of my brother's Eton school friends.'

Several photographers had been discreetly working the room, taking photographs of groups of people who were standing together.

'Oh Bea, that photographer just took a few sneaky photos of the two of us. Did you smile? He's the one from Tatler and over there that one's from Harpers and Queen, and to your right Tom Hustler who did the "the Girls in Pearls" photo of me in last month's Tatler.'

Phoebe was starting to feel nervous. Caroline obviously knew loads of people here and how things worked at this kind of ball. She'd grown up in the system and somehow seemed to breeze happily through it all. Phoebe could see a few familiar faces, but otherwise she was just looking at a sea of well-dressed strangers. All the photographers were now in front of them, how had that happened, they were all elsewhere a few minutes ago. She felt Caroline link arms with her and with that gesture she gained courage and managed to pose and smile confidently together with her new best friend as the photographers snapped away.

'Names please.' The photographers all crowded round the two girls asking the same question.

'Phoebe Clarke.'

'Caroline Stanhope.'

The photographers scribbled on their pads and thanked the girls, immediately sauntering off amongst the guests to look for their next photo opportunity.

'Ooh look! There's Simon and Jake!' Caroline squealed, waving madly at them. The boys waved back and Phoebe gulped. This was the first time she'd seen Simon since the end of their relationship. She started to feel anxious, maybe another drink would help before she had to speak to him; it would calm her butterflies.

'Caro, I think I may need another drink quite quickly.'

'Shall we head over to the bar then and see who else we bump into on the way? I think the party's spread out all over the ground floor of the castle and into the gardens and the rest of the house is closed off.'

'I'm happy to do whatever you say, Caro, as long as I can pick up a glass of champagne or wine first.'

'I wouldn't mind finding Charlie again.' Caroline said in her very British understated manner. 'He did say "see you later for a dance" didn't he, Bea?' Caroline was sounding worried.

'Yes, he did. Listen, I'll be fine. You go and find him and I'm just going to stand here and people watch for a bit now I've got another drink.'

'I'll be back soon. I'll get my bro to look after you whilst I'm not here.'

'It's really okay, honestly.' Phoebe tried to reassure her friend, who had already started to walk over to her brother.

'Hey, Phoebe,' a voice came from behind her. Phoebe knew that voice so well, it was Simon and now her heart was suddenly racing. She turned round to see both him and Jake. She stared at Simon. Every time she saw him, she was blown away by how good looking he was. How could any boy look that perfect? She took a deep breath and tried to look calm on the outside, even though her tummy was now doing triple somersaults. She took a large swig of her champagne hoping it would give her Dutch courage. Simon immediately spoke, leaving no time for an awkward silence.

'You look stunning, Phoebe. I'm so glad you're here and it's so lovely to see you again. Didn't we see Caroline with you? We're on our way to the other bar where there's less of a queue, do you want to come with us, or do you want to wait here and we'll bring you back another glass of champagne and then keep you company.'

'Thanks boys that would be really nice. I'll wait here until you're back.' Phoebe's heart was starting to calm down now that she'd actually spoken again to Simon. The boys had only been gone for a moment when Giles appeared.

'Hi Phoebe, you gorgeous young filly. Lucky me finding you again, super party, eh? Enjoying yourself are you?' Giles spoke to Phoebe in a loud overbearing tone, although his words could have initially sounded flattering.

'I'm having a lovely time, thank you.'

'You should be, you look fucking hot tonight.' He barked.

Phoebe pretended she hadn't heard him use a swear word but secretly she thought it was pretty cool to throw in one here and there as nonchalantly as he did, no one else posh that she knew peppered their sentences with such rude words. She'd already noticed Giles' eyes, which were the darkest, mesmerising eyes glinting in the candlelight as he stared at her with an intense and penetrating gaze, whilst he brushed his floppy-fringed jet-black hair off his forehead. She felt his gaze boring into her very soul, unsure whether it made her feel frightened or excited. She dared herself to look up at him and stare for just for a minute. He was so much taller than her but then everyone was.

He reminded her of some fairy tale character. Well, she was already in a castle but wasn't sure whether Giles was more vampire or wicked prince, but she knew he definitely wasn't Prince Charming.

'I think we should find somewhere a little quieter,' Giles decided, without waiting for Phoebe's answer and grabbed her hand towing her along after him. They bumped into

Simon and Jake bringing back the promised glass of champagne.

'Phoebes, here's your champagne.' Simon proffered and then stared at Giles. 'I don't believe we've met? I'm Simon and this is Jake.'

Giles was curt and dismissive. 'We've never met. Thanks for the champers mate but unnecessary as Phoebe and I are off for a bit of a wander.' He didn't bother to introduce himself and instead muttered under his breath, just low enough for no one to hear, 'Bloody poofters, don't know how they got invited.'

He grabbed Phoebe's arm again and possessively whisked her abruptly away. Phoebe looked helplessly back at the boys not knowing how to deal with this situation. She felt so rude but she also felt she had no choice than to keep following Giles as he was now holding her arm so tightly. It felt good to be desired, especially by someone who seemed to be so cool and grown up. The noise of the party diminished as they moved further away from the central areas of the festivities.

Giles leaned against a wall and took something out of his pocket. 'Hey, beautiful, try this with the champers, everything will be so much more fun.' He handed Phoebe half a tiny pill. Just as she'd done with the joint when she'd first met Simon, she didn't want to seem childish, so she didn't ask anything but just looked at it hesitantly. A quick look of scorn passed over Giles's face.

'It won't hurt it'll just make you feel more relaxed.'

Phoebe suddenly felt silly questioning it, she could feel his impatience but still wasn't sure.

'Don't be such a baby, it'll just loosen you up a bit.

Phoebe recoiled at his sudden abruptness. Maybe it was okay, it was only half a tiny pill so she swallowed it quickly with a large sip of champagne, ignoring her inner voice of reason. It seemed no sooner than she'd swallowed the pill Giles was kissing her; his kisses at first felt nice but odd, not the same as Simon's gentle and tentative ones. At least with all her extensive and prolonged kissing experience with Simon she felt she now knew better how to respond and maybe she wouldn't seem so young and inexperienced.

Giles surveyed his innocent prey. 'You're so fucking beautiful... and such great tits.'

His arrogant self-importance and lewd language had begun to seem normal to Phoebe and she felt strangely fuzzy and happy. She decided to go with the flow, wherever it was taking her and to stay with him for the rest of the party; the possibility of her becoming his girlfriend even briefly passed through her mind. She followed him deeper into the house which he seemed to know quite well, finding his way through the rabbit warren of corridors. Her balance seemed to be becoming a bit wonky and the walls a bit wavy, like those crazy fun fair mirrors... how strange.

Giles pulled her though an open door into a small room, shutting the door quickly behind him. Phoebe realised that they were now in a downstairs study that was being used as some sort of cloakroom where coats were hanging on rails and the overflow heaped on a sofa. Giles grabbed her and she lost her balance, falling backwards with him on top of all the piles of coats. Feeling all the furs against her skin suddenly reminded Phoebe of her mother's dressing room, but the memory quickly disappeared as his hands seemed to be everywhere all over her body. She knew she shouldn't be letting him do this but why should it be wrong when it felt good, her muddled and foggy brain couldn't engage any proper thoughts. His body-weight on top of her and overbearing male physical proximity was beginning to frighten her, she felt like she was suffocating and his hands were now cupping her face. She felt so disorientated, it was as if she'd entered someone else's nightmare, maybe she'd wake up soon and find herself back in the castle's Great Hall. Why had that tiny pill and the champagne made her so totally incapable of movement and speech?

She now felt she was being swallowed up by Giles's giant slobbery tongue that was licking everywhere; her eyelids, her cheeks, her earlobes, her neck. Now her breasts, her nipples – nooo - this just couldn't be happening. She felt powerless, as though she was having an out of body experience where she was watching a slow motion movie with herself as the heroine or victim, she wasn't sure which. His voice seemed to be somewhere in the distance.

'Fucking gorgeous, babe. I knew you'd have fabulous tits.'

As much as she'd wanted him to stop, her body's nerve endings felt like they were on fire with her body responding in ways that she'd never felt before. He pinned her hands behind her head with one of his hands and with the other pulled her dress up and shoved his hand into her knickers.

She struggled to articulate her desperate need for Giles to stop there and then.

'Please, stop,' she tried again to get the words out; 'please stop, no more. I don't want to do this!'

She tried to keep her legs tightly closed together to keep his insistent fingers away but her leg muscles seemed to have a mind of their own and the more he probed and rubbed, the more her thighs opened to welcome him. Suddenly it wasn't his hands between her legs anymore but something hard pushing inside her and oh God, it hurt so much.

'Nooo!' She could hear someone screaming, but it was her own voice she could hear resonating within the small room.

'Shut the fuck up.' Giles muttered under his breath as he clamped his sweaty hand over her mouth. She understood then, even in her drugged state that he just didn't care; she could have been any girl as long as he could fuck her. When would this end? It was hurting so much, she struggled to move again but he'd pinned her down. She was just aware of the continuous painful pounding that was happening to her insides that felt like she was being torn in two. The pain was becoming greater and greater until she could bear it no more, everything was fading into darkness, the pain was going away... then she passed out.

When Phoebe came round, she saw through her strangely distorted and foggy vision that Giles was leaving the room without a second glance. He was tucking his pin-tucked evening shirt back into his dinner suit trousers and straightening his dinner jacket before he opened the door a little, peering outside as if to check the corridor was clear, before he swiftly stepped out and closed the door firmly and decisively behind him and then he was gone.

Phoebe lay curled up in a foetal-position on the coats, still hazy and disorientated from the pill he'd given her. At least she knew she couldn't be pregnant as she'd started taking the pill when she'd been going out with Simon - as Paula would have said; just in case. She would never be able to tell Caroline or her brother as she felt so much shame; how could she have let this happen? She was sure that no boy should ever treat a girl like this.

She tried to get herself together and crawl into the adjoining bathroom and once there, she locked the door. She slumped down against the cold tiled wall, legs splayed out in front of her. She looked down and could see trickles of blood and the beginning of huge bruises down her inner thighs. She struggled to adjust her dress and cover herself up again, but the effort was more than she could manage and she promptly passed out again on the bathroom floor. Voices outside the door woke her up once again and she wondered why would anyone need to talk so loudly outside her bedroom door, it was the middle of the night, wasn't it? As she came round again and focused she realised she wasn't in her own bed, she was curled up in a corner on a cold flagstone bathroom floor. Nor had it been a dream; it had been a real life nightmare. She ached all over and now she was shivering and couldn't stop her teeth chattering.

There was a knocking on the door and she could hear Simon's voice sounding anxious and agitated.

'Phoebes are you in there? We've been looking for you everywhere and no one's seen you for ages. We were the last people to have seen you when that rude boy was rushing you away from us and we've been worrying about you ever since. Are you okay? We can't open this door. Why's it locked? Phoebes? Please open the door.'

She could hear the door handle being repeatedly rattled. Grasping anything she could, she crawled over and managed to unlock it to find both Simon and Jake falling into the room as the door opened. As she leaned on the edge of the door to support herself she could see that they both looked really shocked. The boys quickly locked the door once again behind them and sat on the floor next to her.

'What happened to you, Phoebes?'

Phoebe burst into hysterical tears at seeing her friends and collapsed once again in a crumpled heap. The boys crouched down to hug her but she couldn't bear the thought of anyone touching her and made herself into an even smaller curled–up ball.

'Phoebes what happened?' They asked again. All she could do was rock backwards and forwards with huge sobs still racking her whole body. Simon looked at Jake, really shocked at the state of his best friend.

'We need to take her back to Caroline's house and get her into bed as soon as we can.'

'Nooo,' Phoebe wailed, 'please don't make me go back there.'

'Why not?' Simon looked at her confused.

'I just can't, please? Don't make me explain,' she sobbed.

'Phoebes, we haven't got anywhere else we can take you. How about we take you back and put you to bed, then return to the party and let Caroline know that you'd gone home as you weren't feeling well?'

'You can't tell her that anything's happened to me, promise?' Phoebe pleaded. The boys heard the desperation in her voice and immediately promised.

They found a back door used only by the party organisers, and managed to escape without anyone seeing them. Simon had left his car nearby in one of the designated car park fields to which they half-carried Phoebe, with both their jackets round her to keep her warm. Phoebe drifted in and out of consciousness and in her moments of clarity could hear the bass of the music from the disco in a seemingly parallel universe.

Once safely back in the house they carried her up to her room. Luckily everyone was still at the party, so no one saw them.

'Let us put you to bed, Phoebes.'

'No, no,' Phoebe protested, 'I can undress myself.' She tried to wrap her arms around her body to stop the boys helping her but she couldn't manage and collapsed again with pain. The boys lifted her gently onto her bed where her nightie had already been laid out on the pillow. She tried to stop them pulling off her dress but too late - they'd seen the bruising down her thighs and arms.

'Oh, Phoebes,' both boys murmured completely shocked, 'who on earth did this to you?'

Phoebe had never before seen such murderous anger flash in Simon's eyes. Even in her haze of pain, she knew she hadn't imagined the look she'd just seen.

'Please don't ask.'

'But whoever it was just can't get away with this.' Simon's voice was full of anger and dismay.

'Please forget it... it was my fault. I'm going to leave here as soon as I can in the morning; I can't face Caroline.'

'I just can't bear the thought of anyone hurting you." Simon was sounding more and more distraught. Phoebe gazed at both of them with a sad, empty kind of smile. Was this the same bedroom where she'd got ready with so much excitement only a few hours ago?

'You're such good friends,' she mumbled, 'I love you both so much but don't worry, I'll be fine.' And she shut her eyes again.

'You remember I promised you that I'd always be there for you, well I'll *never* let anyone hurt you ever again.' With that vow, Simon kissed her gently on the cheek, switched off her lights and left the room together with Jake.

'What do you think happened to her, Si?' Jake couldn't believe what he'd just seen.

'I think that pompous Hoorah Henry arsehole that we saw grabbing and walking off with her, took advantage of her and we should've stopped him before it got out of control.'

'Do you think he raped her?' Jake asked the question they'd both been thinking.

'I don't know but she's in such a state and clearly doesn't remember that much. Is she so traumatised that she's wiped the memory, or did he drug her? I guess Phoebe will tell us when she's ready and then we can decide how to help her. I'd like to kill that guy if he did rape her. At the moment all we can do is be as supportive to her as possible, and make sure Mrs Abbott keeps an eye on her without us telling her too much. We definitely can't tell Caroline now as we promised not to.'

Jake and Simon walked slowly back to the car, both deep in thought. They knew that although they were returning to the party, their night had really ended the moment they'd found Phoebe.

Phoebe slept fitfully until dawn. Her badly bruised body, both internally and externally, told her more about what had happened at the party than her memory did.

She tried closing her eyes again, hoping all the pain might have gone away when she re-opened her eyes, it didn't. She wondered how her life could so suddenly have turned around like this. One thing was for sure, she couldn't ever face the Stanhope family again. She struggled to sit up in bed. She could see dried blood on her nightie - thank goodness not over the sheets. She now needed to leave as soon as she could. It was only five thirty in the morning, so she still had some time.

It was impossible to dress quickly, everything ached as she moved and the bruises all over her body seemed to be spreading. She felt both mentally and physically beaten.

She packed her small weekend case once more and tiptoed slowly down the corridor, praying she wouldn't bump into anyone. Every movement she made jarred her body as she tiptoed down the main staircase into the entrance hall and out by the back door to where she'd parked Millie. She switched on the engine, gave the car a tiny rev and drove slowly down the drive to make as little noise as possible.

Only one person noticed the little red MG leaving. It was Giles, who was only just now coming back from the party. He didn't care, he'd had a great night; drugs, champagne and fucking that pretty young thing Phoebe – she'd been so clearly up for it. All girls wanted to fuck him, didn't they? They just all said *no* when they really meant *yes*.'

Phoebe drove back to London, burning with humiliation. She resolved that this shameful secret was one she'd never share with anyone. She would write thank-you notes to Caroline and her parents, hoping that they'd accept her explanation and then she could push the memory away deep down inside her and try to do the impossible; forget it had ever happened.

Later that day, once again at home, Phoebe sat in her bedroom, her notepaper resting on top of one of her hardback fashion books and began to write.

Dear Lady Stanhope,
Thank you so much for having me to stay. It was so kind of you to include me in your family on the weekend of the ball and I very much appreciated it. I am so sorry that I had to leave so abruptly straight after the ball. I was not feeling very

well and I did not want to bother you if I was ill. I thought it would be better to go home again.

Thank you for your kind and generous hospitality.

Once again, please forgive my rapid departure.

Please send my love to Caroline.

With best wishes

Phoebe Clarke x

Then she had to write to Caroline;

Dear Caroline,

I am so sorry I never got to say goodbye to you after Chloe's ball. I had to leave suddenly as I suddenly felt quite ill. I am so embarrassed that I had to leave without saying goodbye either to you or your lovely parents. You welcomed me with such warmth into your family.

Please don't try to call my home as I am going away for a little while.

Thanks again for your friendship,

Phoebe x

Over the next few days Phoebe was aware of Mrs Abbott's regular presence outside the bedroom door. She heard her gently knocking, trying to speak to her through the door that she'd had numerous phone calls from Caroline. Notes were slipped under her door too. Phoebe believed that given time, Caroline would eventually give up. However it seemed that Mrs Abbott wasn't going to give up and was becoming increasingly persistent in her efforts to feed Phoebe.

She knocked three times a day; leaving breakfasts, lunches and suppers outside her bedroom, with a note simultaneously passed under her door letting her know what was on each tray. The trays were full of Phoebe's favourite home-cooked dishes, but when she tried a tiny taste of the usually delicious

Mrs Abbott-special-recipe macaroni cheese, she felt no pleasure at all. The crispy crust and unctuous creamy, cheesy sauce now just made her feel nauseous. She no longer had any appetite or interest in eating. Soon, she was the thinnest she'd ever been. No one noticed as she hadn't yet left the confines of her bedroom.

After more than two weeks of this with no sign of any change, Mrs Abbott decided to take matters into her own hands. She phoned Caroline Stanhope's home and suggested that she should come over unannounced to see Phoebe.

Chapter 11. Phoebe. London, 1972

Phoebe's world was no longer full of light and joy, but plunged into darkness. The orange and white bold floral print curtains had been pulled tightly closed to keep out any chinks of light, as she lay curled up amongst all the cushions on her bed with her eyes squeezed tightly shut; shutting out her favourite waking view of the fashion collages she'd painstakingly spent hours tearing from magazines, blu-tacking them all over her bedroom walls, together with her prized psychedelic Fab Four Beatles and Bowie Ziggy Stardust posters.

Her new world had shrunk to existing within her bedroom which now felt even smaller and more isolated than the nursery suite she'd grown up in when she'd only had her dolls and Mrs Abbott for company. She no longer knew what to do with herself as she was wracked with guilt and shame. She didn't want to see anyone or anyone to see her and she didn't want to eat or to live. She wasn't quite sure if she actually wanted to die, but she was sure her mother wouldn't miss her. Would anyone miss her though? Maybe Mrs Abbott just might. She pulled her knees to her chest and hugged her Kensington market cushions in close to her. Why were her sewing scissors on her bedside table? She hadn't altered or made any clothes for a while now. She suddenly felt a compulsion to pick them up and to run the sharp blade of one scissor side lightly across her wrist.

She watched, fascinated as the blade parted her thin skin and blood began to trickle. It hurt but the pain was numbing her inner emotional pain and feelings of self-loathing, guilt and sadness. She cut once again, it felt good although she didn't know why. A black hole of emptiness was weighing down inside her. The physical pain she was now feeling was an improvement on feeling nothing at all; nothing actually mattered any more. The blood slowly dripped drop by drop onto her White House Egyptian cotton white nightie. Just one more cut...

Why was Mrs Abbott shouting at her? She never raised her voice.

'Phoebe, you have to open the door, I'm not taking no for an answer any longer.' Mrs Abbott was now banging on the door with all her curvy size eighteen force. 'Phoebe, if you don't open the door I'll break it down. Your mother won't be best pleased with me if I have to do that.'

Distracted, Phoebe half-opened the door and stood there unaware that she was still clutching the scissors in her hand with blood still dripping down her. Mrs Abbott and Caroline had been totally unprepared for what they saw.

'Oh Lordy, what are you doing child?' Mrs Abbott shrieked with more emotion than she'd shown in the whole of Phoebe's eighteen years, and grabbed the scissors. Phoebe looked like death; her normally glossy curls were matted and dull, her face pale and drawn and a mix of congealed and fresh blood still oozing from her cuts. Caroline was really shocked, she'd had a sheltered upbringing and had never seen anything like this. She felt queasy at the sight of all the blood, especially on her friend. Being a practical country girl, especially when dealing with emergencies, she pulled herself together and immediately hugged Phoebe as tightly as she could, stroking her lank hair in smooth continuous calming movements back from her forehead, as a mother would do for her child.

'Bea, what's the matter, what happened and why aren't you speaking to anyone? I got your note but you haven't answered any of my calls or my messages. I've been so worried about you.' Caroline tried to sound as composed as she possibly could in the circumstances.

Phoebe felt utterly incapable of answering and started to cry again. Caroline and Mrs Abbott were blurred in her teary and unfocused vision. Why were her wrists and the inside of her arms stinging so badly? She looked down and saw blood, how could there be so much from those few cuts she'd made?

'Phoebe, put out your arm,' Mrs Abbott took control, 'we need to stop the bleeding. Here, hold this towel tightly whilst I go downstairs and get proper dressings.'

Phoebe did as she was told. She always did when it was Mrs Abbott doing the telling.

'What happened that night at the party?' Caroline looked into Phoebe's eyes as she continued to hug her.

'Why did you leave so suddenly? I knew you weren't ill and Mummy knew too. We both knew something significant had taken place. I asked Jonathon, but he didn't know although he hasn't seen or spoken to his friend Giles since that weekend. Giles was still drunk and stoned the following morning and Jonathon had an argument with him about it. Mummy doesn't want him to ever come and stay with us again. We don't know where he disappeared to during most of the party, we couldn't even find him to give him a lift home.'

Caroline finally stopped to take a breath as all her introspections from the last few weeks finally tumbled out.

Phoebe could hear Caroline's words but they made no sense, nothing made any sense. Mrs Abbott had now returned with a first aid kit and started to bandage Phoebe's arm whilst Phoebe sat there as meekly as a child.

'Please tell me what's happened Bea, so I can help you?' Caroline looked at her friend imploringly. Phoebe knew she simply couldn't tell her; maybe Paula might have understood, she was sure Caroline wouldn't.

'I just can't tell you... but thank you for coming round.' Phoebe spoke really quietly, eyes cast down.

Caroline wasn't to be fobbed off that easily. 'I'm not leaving you like this. I'm waiting here until you've had a bath and washed your hair then I'm taking you out for a hot meal and some daylight.'

Mrs Abbott gave Caroline a grateful look, hoping that her stubborn stance would make the difference to Phoebe's attitude, as she swept open the curtains letting the sunlight flood in. Phoebe's room looked worse in the bright light, more like a student squat than an interior-designed Chelsea bedroom.

Phoebe sobbed and exhaled a long and drawn out sigh, 'I can't face going out. I just want to be on my own.'

'Sorry Bea, I'm not taking no for an answer and I'll just sit on your bed and wait until you're ready. I'm simply not going anywhere until you get dressed and nor is Mrs Abbott.'

Phoebe realised when she was beaten. She looked down at her wrist, now tightly bandaged. Maybe she could have a coffee with Caroline if she didn't make her talk.

Mrs Abbott meanwhile had been pulling various items of clothes from Phoebe's wardrobe handing them over to Caroline to keep hold of, until Phoebe was ready to put them on. 'Here's her favourite pair of jeans and a nice printed shirt, dear. They'll do nicely. Now I'll just go and run a bath for her.'

Phoebe was just doing as she was told now, going through the motions was all she could manage. Soon she was sitting on her bed, clean and washed, getting dressed robotically in the outfit Caroline was handing to her.

'Could we go somewhere we won't bump into anyone we know?' Phoebe pleaded so quietly that Caroline strained to hear.

'Sure, let's just get you out of your house, into my car and then we'll find somewhere really quiet.' Caroline tried to keep her own tone upbeat and as buoyant as she could manage, hoping it might rub off on Phoebe.

Mrs Abbott shut the front door after the girls and uncharacteristically slumped down for a moment on the hall sofa, waiting for her normal inscrutable self to come back. She breathed an audible sigh of relief. She constantly worried about Phoebe, even though she would never have let anyone know.

The girls ended up sitting at a small deserted nondescript café around the corner from Phoebe's house that no friends of theirs would ever have gone to. It seemed just a coffee wasn't on Caroline's exact agenda, soon two steaming hot bowls of pasta with tomato sauce arrived as well as the coffees. Phoebe was sure that she wouldn't be able to eat a single bite but the strong aromas of garlicky tomato, basil and parmesan cheese hit her nostrils and she realised she might actually want to try a tiny taste, even though she still had no real desire for food. She didn't remember when she'd last eaten. She focused on her bowl of pasta, using her fork to repeatedly twirl and play around with it so she didn't have to make proper eye contact with her friend.

Caroline thought she'd try once more to get her friend to talk. 'Do you want to talk about the night of the ball, Bea?'

'Not really,' Phoebe replied in a gloomy and slightly sullen monotone, wanting to close down further questioning, 'sorry.'

'Okay,' Caroline quickly acquiesced, 'just remember though, that you can always phone me whenever you want or need someone to talk to. I'm going home again to mummy in Yorkshire after today and I'll be back down in London every so often. I'll phone Mrs Abbott every time I'm coming down so she can let you know.'

'Thanks, Caro.' Phoebe's voice remained flat with no tonal light and shade creating any life or vibrancy.

Caroline could feel the heavy dark cloud of depression that was weighing there in her voice, but carried on regardless. 'By the way, probably not the best time to tell you this, though might cheer you up a bit, I've been seeing Charlie ever since the ball and it's really going rather well. In fact, I'm actually going to stay with his family up in Gloucestershire next weekend, it's all rather exciting.'

Phoebe tried to muster up the enthusiasm she knew she should be feeling for her friend and attempted to make it resonate in her voice, 'Oh Caro, that's wonderful. I so hope it works out for you.'

By now she'd managed a bite or two of her pasta and was now sipping at a coke which had miraculously appeared out of nowhere. She did feel a bit better for eating and was slowly making eye contact again across the table with her friend. In fact, she was now looking straight into Caroline's eyes which she could see were only radiating kindness and caring back at her. Caroline started to speak again.

'Bea, listen, if Charlie and I ever get married and have babies, we'd love you to be god-mummy.'

Phoebe promptly burst into tears again. Caroline reached out to hold her hand across the table. Phoebe shook her head. 'No, it's fine Caro, these are happy tears now, not sad ones,' she managed to speak between sobs, '... I'd be honoured and thank you again for coming round. I do feel a bit better and don't worry, I'm not going to do anything stupid again. Everything had just become too much for me and I'll be okay now.'

Hoping to alleviate Caroline's worries about her, Phoebe knew that her own positivity about her mental wellbeing was far from the actual truth.

As the weeks went on, Phoebe still had flashbacks especially when she lay in bed at night. Sleep was difficult to come by so she tried keeping the light on. When that didn't work, she tried writing a diary putting her feelings down on paper. She wasn't sure this helped either and she was frightened that Mrs Abbott would find it.

Then there were the issues with her body shape that she'd never liked: she'd always felt short and dumpy compared to her tall elegant mother, and those negative feelings about her body had escalated even though she was really quite skinny now. Phoebe only saw a distorted fat version of herself on the few occasions she'd looked in the mirror. The only way she felt she could take back some control of her life was by restricting her food intake.

As she knew Mrs Abbott was keeping a very keen eye on her, Phoebe became quite adept at pretending to eat her carefully and lovingly prepared meals cooked especially for her. She pushed the food around on the plate, ate a tiny morsel of it and then flushed the rest of it down the loo. She did feel guilty about the waste as she knew there were those who couldn't afford to eat, and she also felt guilty about all

Mrs Abbott's efforts. Even with all this introspection, she still couldn't break her self-destruct patterns. Mrs Abbott wasn't sure what had happened to Phoebe to cause her so much distress but she was going to make very sure that Phoebe was no longer self-harming. She wasn't sure how she could monitor the situation but she knew that talking to Phoebe as much as she could would help. She also planned to get Phoebe out of the house, seeing friends and doing things. Caroline was fully on board with Mrs Abbott's plans, although being stuck in the country she could do little on a regular basis to help.

Inventiveness had become Mrs Abbott's middle name. 'Phoebe dear, now that the Debutante year has finished and you've finished school, what would you like to do?'

'I'd always wanted to do something with fashion, Abby.' Phoebe answered, still sounding depressed and pessimistic.

'I'm sure we can sort something. I'll look into it.' Mrs Abbott radiated positivity from every pore.

'Thank you, Abby, I do love you, you're always there for me.' Phoebe tried to sound grateful.

'Don't be such a silly goose, young lady, of course I am.' Mrs Abbott pursed her lips and crossed her arms across her ample bosoms, not wanting to display her continued silent annoyance at how little Phoebe's own parents actually cared for their only daughter.

The next morning Mrs Abbott was once again knocking on Phoebe's bedroom door. Phoebe opened the door to a particularly smiley-faced Mrs Abbott.

'Morning, Abby.' Phoebe liked to see her each day now, she seemed to bring some light into her constantly dark world.

'Phoebe I've bought you up your favourite soft boiled egg and soldiers for breakfast and I've something else for you too.' Mrs Abbott was looking extremely pleased with herself as she handed over a very large Green and Stone plastic bag. Phoebe knew what Green and Stone was – it was her favourite art supplies shop which she'd passed by on the way to school on the King's Road. She opened the bag and inside was the most amazing assortment of pencils, pens, art pads, brushes and watercolours. Phoebe stared at them, not believing how Mrs Abbott had managed to buy her so much. She suddenly felt a tiny flicker of joy, a new sensation that she hadn't felt for quite a while.

'Ooh Abby, thank you.' Phoebe really meant it this time.

'Now you can spend time drawing and painting whilst you get better.' Mrs Abbott knew more about Phoebe than Phoebe had ever realised. Having worked for the Clarke family for eighteen years, Mrs Abbott knew exactly how disinterested Mr and Mrs Clarke were about their daughter and did her best to plug the gap. She'd written down in her old leather address book all the home phone numbers of Phoebe's closest friends. There were so many extensions in the Clarke home it was easy to monitor calls as it had always been she who'd answered all phone calls transferring the calls to the appropriate member of the house. She'd collected the home numbers of Simon, Jake and Caroline, but not Paula as she'd never phoned Phoebe.

Mrs Abbott understood her place and would never have called anyone unless it was an emergency and if the need arose again, she knew she wouldn't hesitate. She'd done it once before with success and now that Phoebe still wouldn't leave her room and she could see her slowly wasting away before her very eyes, the time had come again. She knew

Caroline rang Phoebe several times a week and tried her best to jolly Phoebe along over the phone. It obviously wasn't enough, so she decided that Simon was next to be included in her Phoebe-rehab plan. He'd already been calling regularly but Phoebe was consistently adamant she wouldn't take his calls.

Mrs Abbott knew all the art materials had helped slightly as Phoebe had happily showed her a few of her paintings. Not enough though, so something dramatic needed to be done to get Phoebe up and out again with a purpose in life. Mrs Abbott was a stoic, resilient Northern woman who faced adversity head on and would sort this for once and for all.

Chapter 12. Mrs Abbott. London, 1972

It was Sunday morning and Simon and Jake were in Jake's tiny Hampstead flat where they had a Sunday morning ritual of reading the papers together in bed over croissants, freshly squeezed orange juice and a cafetiere of freshly ground coffee, all with the Sunday papers delivered from the local Belsize Village paper shop; they always had one proper newspaper like the Times and one trashy one like the News of the World, their Sunday guilty pleasure. They took it in turns to make the coffee and freshly squeezed orange juice bringing the breakfast tray back to the bedroom. The two young men were like an old married couple.

However, they both knew their domestic bliss was soon to end. Jake had mixed feelings about his future, he was excited but knew how much his life was about to change.

'In a few months' time I'll be in LA for my four year acting course. That's such a long time and I'll miss you so much.' Jake sipped at his orange juice absentmindedly as he spoke.

'I'll miss you too, Jakey, although I'll come as often as I can. I've still got to work out what I'm doing with my life and it's got to be something that earns money, as my father's so unhappy that I'm refusing to train to be a banker. Can you imagine what would happen if I told him next that I'm queer? He'd disown me. Maybe one day I might be able to tell my mother, but right now it's going to be bad enough for him to discover that my future work might be something more artistic than he'd ever envisioned.'

Jake stretched his hand out to Simon, wanting him to know that he'd be there for him, whatever happened, even from across the ocean. He carefully moved the breakfast tray off the bed onto the side table and rolled over onto his elbow so he could look at him properly. 'Okay, let's make a pact. We'll see each other as often as we can and then when we're both successful, we can share an apartment in L.A and live there together.'

'I love you so much and I can't wait for that to happen; whilst I still have an allowance from my father it's easier, except it may not be for that much longer.' Simon's mood swings were always unpredictable, so Jake realised he needed to rapidly act and chose to shut him up with a passionate kiss until the ringing of the house phone broke up the moment. Jake sighed and picked up the phone.

'Hullo, who's speaking please?'

'Morning Jake, Mrs Abbott here. Sorry to bother you but I thought you might be with Simon and I need to speak to him rather urgently.'

'No problem, Mrs Abbott. Are you well and is Phoebe alright?' Jake decided that Mrs Abbott sounded unlike her usual calm self, almost agitated.

'Yes, thank you dear, I'm fine. You know I wouldn't call you though unless it was absolutely necessary... and now I believe it is.' She sounded apologetic now.

'No problem, I'll pass you over to Simon. Bye for now.' Jake handed the phone to Simon, putting his hand over the mouthpiece. 'It's Mrs Abbott. Think all is not well with Phoebe.'

Simon was instantly on full alert and grabbed the phone to hear Mrs Abbott reiterating that it was she on the phone.

'Simon dear, it's Mrs Abbott.'

Simon decided to not waste time with pleasantries. He was already deeply worried as it was so unusual for Mrs Abbott to call, especially on a Sunday morning. 'Mrs Abbs, what's happened to Phoebe?'

'She won't leave her room; I've tried everything and so has Caroline. I think if anyone can work their magic, it might now be you. Could you come round to take her out, take her anywhere fun that might give her a reason to embrace life again. If anyone can do it you can, dear.'

'Mrs Abbs...' Simon was quickly processing Mrs Abbott's request before he spoke again. Mrs Abbott was already smiling to herself at her end of the phone line, she loved Simon and especially his abbreviated version of her name. Meanwhile, Simon had already gathered his thoughts, 'Of course I can. Jake and I will find something really fun things to do with Phoebe before Jake goes off to LA.'

Simon had only visited twice during the time he and Phoebe had dated, but he and Mrs Abbott had loved each other immediately. He also realised that she'd concluded why he and Phoebe's relationship hadn't worked out.

'Mrs Abbs, I'll call you back in a few minutes when I've come up with a plan.' Simon put down the phone and looked thoughtfully at Jake. A plan was brewing in his mind, so he ran it past Jake and five minutes later he called her back.

She must have been sitting poised by the phone as she answered straight away, 'Hello young man, that was quick. What have you come up with?'

'We will collect her on Friday night after dinner, which means it may be quite late – would ten thirty still be okay? See if you can persuade her to dress up in a disco outfit, actually tell her we won't take no for an answer. We will literally kidnap her and carry her out with us if she won't come.'

'Simon dear, consider it done. She'll be dressed and ready no matter what.'

'You're a star, Mrs Abbs. Please tell Phoebe that Jake and I will be taking her on a magical mystery tour.'

'Thank you, dear. I won't let her back out even if I have to help you drag her screaming down the stairs.' Mrs Abbott replaced the phone receiver feeling slightly happier now about the situation. She knew she'd done the right thing calling Simon.

Friday night arrived and Simon waited outside Phoebe's house for Mrs Abbott to let him in. He'd left Jake waiting in the car in case Mrs Clarke happened to open the door.

'Evening Mrs Abbs.' He went in for a hug and Mrs Abbott yielded her body stiffly into his. Simon realised she obviously wasn't used to public shows of affection. He released her taut body from his embrace. 'Have you managed to get Phoebe up and about for our outing?'

'Well, dear, she wasn't keen but I gave her a bit of my straight talking and she's on her way down.' Mrs Abbott looked quite proud of her success so far.

'You know I haven't seen her since we all went to that ball in Yorkshire.' Simon owned up to the housekeeper, feeling ashamed that he'd failed his friend.

'Well, whatever happened that night she won't talk to me or Caroline about it and retreated straight back into herself, not seeing anyone since Caroline first came round; so I called you because if anyone can help her it's you, dear.' Mrs Abbott stared at Simon with expectancy written all over her face; he was her last hope to save Phoebe from herself.

Chapter 13. Simon. London, 1972

From the moment Simon appeared to take her out, Phoebe could sense him scrutinising her from top to toe and felt self-conscious under his gaze, unsettled by the concern that clearly showed in his expression. He knew her so well that he'd appreciate how much effort she'd made with her outfit; however, he would also notice how her usually tight black Spandex disco leggings were now baggy and that her big boobs had disappeared. Regrettably, "fat Phoebe" still remained as her perceived image whenever she'd looked in the mirror.

'Simon,' Phoebe spoke softly and hesitantly, 'Abby wouldn't allow me to not see you and literally stood over me as I got dressed; it was like being a child again getting ready for school.' Phoebe squeezed Mrs Abbott's hand tightly as she spoke.

Mrs Abbott, always one to shrug off any shows of affection butted in, 'And you look a picture of loveliness. Enjoy your evening dears, I'll see you in the morning Phoebe, maybe I'll bring you some breakfast up on a tray so you can lie in? I have a feeling Simon might have a big night planned for you.'

Simon took over the supportive role of hand-holding from Mrs Abbott and started walking with Phoebe back to the car, turning back to speak to the kind housekeeper.

Thanks Mrs Abbs, you're a star. Come on, Phoebes, Jake's in the car. We're going somewhere you've never been before where, I promise you, you won't bump into anyone you know.'

Phoebe followed Simon slowly to the car. She'd felt anxious before leaving the house even though she trusted

Simon, and knew Simon wouldn't ask her any difficult questions, it didn't stop her wanting to ask questions.

'Where are we going, Si?'

'Not telling, it's a surprise. Wait and see Miss Impatient.'

'Hi, Phoebes.' A deep voice suddenly sounded from the back of the car.

Phoebe had already forgotten that Simon had said Jake was in the car.

'Oh Jake, I'm so sorry, hi!' She turned round and blew him two air kisses. She was trying really hard to put on a show of energy and still be the old fun Phoebe, although she felt robotic and drained. 'Sorry, can't reach you in the back, we'll have a proper hug when we get out again.' She then sat very quietly immersed in her own world as Simon drove and the boys let her be.

Soon Simon was pulling the car to a halt. 'We're here, Phoebes.'

'That wasn't far to go, Simon. Are you sure I'm not going to see any of the old crowd?' Anxiety was starting to overwhelm her again. She couldn't see out of the car windows as they'd misted up, so she wiped a clear patch with her long sleeved top, sleeveless had been out of the question, as the cuts on her arms still hadn't healed up. She peered out of the car window, seeing she was in familiar territory just off Kensington High Street, near the Kensington Market. 'We're in Kensington?'

'I promised you that you won't bump into anyone you know here, and I always keep my promises. This is mine and Jake's favourite new place to go. We'll both look after you. Stop worrying.' Simon helped her out of the car, giving her a confidence boosting hug at the same time. 'Trust me.' And somehow Phoebe did.

All Phoebe could now see in front of her was an enormous sombrero over a doorway under an El Sombrero restaurant sign.

'Why are so many men hanging around outside a random Mexican restaurant on Kensington High Street... what is this place?' Phoebe's brain already felt foggy, now it was really confused.

'Phoebes, please stop asking questions.' The boys chorused and each grabbed one of her hands. She could hear the sounds of disco music coming from inside the building, as she was immediately confronted by a giant sized bouncer at the entrance who looked at her with raised eyebrows and a 'why are you here?' attitude.

'She's with us.' Simon and Jake quickly responded to his unspoken question, handing over already-counted pound notes for the entrance fee. The bouncer looking slightly happier waved them in. The trio went down a rather grand sweeping staircase into the basement.

'Phoebes, welcome to the Sombrero, a gay club. It's really called, 'Yours or Mine' but everyone just calls it the Sombrero - what do you think?' Simon looked expectantly at Phoebe hoping for a positive response.

'Gay club... what's that?'

'A club only for men like me and Jake. A safe place where we can hang out and dance; no straight couples or girls allowed on their own.' Simon hoped that explained enough.

Phoebe looked around the tiny club with an even smaller dance floor, surrounded by tables covered with red paper table cloths. The atmosphere there felt different from anywhere she'd ever been before. For the first time since the night of the ball, she realised that maybe life was still there to be enjoyed and her feet started tapping involuntarily to the music with a life all of their own. It was impossible to stay still with the loud upbeat music and she'd forgotten how much she loved being with Simon and Jake.

She realised that she must be feeling better as she'd also suddenly started comparing what she was wearing to what everyone else's outfits were; even her own version of disco seemed tame as everyone else was dressed so outrageously. Had she always been that boring, she'd always believed that she was quite adventurous, even avant-garde. At that moment, Phoebe came to the conclusion that anything she might wear now, wherever she went with the boys, could never be too over-the-top.

'We're sitting here.' Simon shouted to her over the music as they sat down at one of the little round tables by the side of the dance floor. Phoebe looked around her, wondering why all the girls in there were so tall. She'd have to ask Simon about this when there was a break in the music and she could hear herself think. Before she could ask the question, she realised that a stranger was now standing at their table with his hand firmly on Simon's shoulder.

Simon looked round and immediately stood up, a good couple of heads taller than his friend. 'Phoebe, this is Rudy, our brilliant Italian DJ in here. See over there, that's where he does his DJing.'

Phoebe looked at Rudy and was thrilled to see someone who was actually the same height as her, and then over to the floral decorated arch over his DJ booth.

'Ciao, Phoebe, welcome. Is it your first time here? I then play something for you, perhaps Timmy Thomas, "Why can we not live together" I always make everyone happy with my music.' His smile and bubbly energy was infectious and although Phoebe didn't know the song, it didn't matter - she was finally beginning to relax.

'Come on, we're going to dance.' Simon grabbed her by the hand and Jake followed onto a tiny raised multi-coloured perspex dance floor which reminded her of a crowded boxing ring. As she stared around her, at the most extraordinary mix of men that she'd ever seen, she knew undoubtedly she was never going to bump into any of her original friendship groups here. These men were an eclectic ethnic mix of Oriental, Middle Eastern and black; with big lacquered-hair, gold chains and little handbags being a common theme. Young men were together with old and she was sure she'd spotted some famous pop stars; even David Bowie over on the other side of the dance floor with a woman, maybe his wife Angie.

Having ended up right in the middle of the crowded dance floor, Phoebe was beginning to feel increasingly vertically challenged, similar to Alice in Wonderland after finding and drinking the 'shrink me' bottle.

'Simon...' She tried to whisper in his ear but the music was so loud she had to shout. 'Why are so many of the girls in here so tall?'

Simon immediately roared with laughter. 'They're men! Drag Queens, trannies - *all* of them men, dressed as women.' He continued to chuckle.

Phoebe looked at Simon now even more confused. 'But some of them are so beautiful, they could be women and I can't tell any difference.'

'Darling, that's the whole point.' Simon acknowledged Phoebe's innocence in a kindly way.

Phoebe suddenly understood that a whole new world was now waiting for her out there to discover, one that she'd never before known about.

The three of them returned hot and sweaty to their table. Phoebe had always loved people watching, especially when everyone was as interesting as they were in here. It was as though she'd been given an intravenous shot of adrenalin and a re-affirming conviction of why she should keep on staying alive.

'I love it in here, it's so much fun.' How could she have forgotten how to enjoy herself?

The waiter had just placed a plate of unappetising looking food on their table. Phoebe looked at what was on the plate and then back at the waiter, she was sure they hadn't ordered anything and definitely not this – yuk!

'Here we go, ham and potato salad for you.' Phoebe politely tried not to make a face and Simon noticed.

'Phoebes, you don't have to eat it. They just have to serve something that passes as *supper* to keep their licence.' Phoebe breathed a sigh of relief as she didn't want to appear rude or ungrateful. 'Come on, back to the dance floor.' The boys pulled her up again. Gosh, it felt like she'd never danced so much in her life.

'Phoebes, this is the Hustle.' The boys seemed to be fully committed to demonstrating the disco moves for Phoebe to copy, so she started following tentatively, growing bolder as she got the hang of it, then finally letting herself go. The song suddenly stopped and she realised that everyone was standing around cheering, how come? She looked incredulously at Simon and Jake.

'They're cheering *you*, Phoebes. You were really good!'

Phoebe was shocked, how could that have happened? In that moment she recognized that her life had turned around once more and why Mrs Abbott, Caroline, Simon and Jake had all tried so hard to get her out of the house. She also

169

realised that she must have actually looked good dancing just now.

Phoebe sounded surprised at what she was saying as she shouted over the music. 'Si, you know how it's very unusual that I should ever have my mother to thank for anything she's ever done for me? Well, when I was a child, she sent me to Madame Vacani's where I learnt all sorts of dance there from ballet to modern…'The boys interrupted before Phoebe could finish her sentence, they were so happy their plan had worked.

'Your dance expertise certainly came to the fore just then.'

'No, it wasn't ever just about learning to dance. It was my mother's greatest wish for me to mix with royals, dancing with Prince Charles in these ballroom classes and one day to marry him. She even took me to a class herself, it was only once, when she strategically sat herself right next to the Royal Nannies.'

The boys looked at each other and started to laugh. Phoebe couldn't understand what she'd just said that was so funny – her mother's aspirations were more sad than funny.

Simon managed to get his words out between his peals of laughter. 'Well, it's safe to say, it probably hadn't been in her mind that you'd now be dancing all night with a load of queens - definitely not the sort of queen though that she'd envisaged.'

Phoebe could now see what both Jake and Simon were doubled up laughing at, and started laughing too. Laughter was something she'd long forgotten about, although once she started she couldn't stop until tears ran down her face and her tummy ached.

When they could all catch their breath again, Simon and Jake looked at each other and then back at Phoebe with seriousness expressions for a moment.

'We've just made a decision. We're going to take you out as much as we can, before Jake leaves for LA, to get you back on your feet again and back to the old Phoebe we love.' Phoebe realised that she had missed this version of herself too. This new world that Simon and Jake were introducing her to, where men preferred men, seemed to be somewhere that she realised she could take small safe baby steps to finding herself again.

So over the next few months Phoebe found herself coming down to meet Simon who would be standing at her front door, whilst Jake remained in the car, as he was still terrified of Mrs Clarke and determined not to risk meeting her. As usual, Mrs Abbott answered the door.

Phoebe could hear her talking to Simon. 'Hullo Simon dear, lovely to see you as always. I don't know what you've done to give Phoebe her spark back but she's started to eat a bit more and even gets up every morning to draw and sketch all day. She still won't go out unless it's with you two, however, it's a start and she's seems so much better. Well done.'

'It's a pleasure Mrs Abbs. I'd do *anything* for my best friend in the whole world. We're off to the Rainbow Rooms tonight - dress code twenties glam.' Simon always liked to have a doorstep chat with Mrs Abbott, he was beginning to feel quite attached to her.

Mrs Abbott unexpectedly beamed with the realisation she'd heard of where they were going. 'Aren't the Rainbow Rooms the very ritzy new Art Deco restaurant on the top floor of the old Derry and Toms where the new Biba store is?'

Simon looked at her in astonishment. 'Yes, Mrs Abbs, how on earth did you know that?'

Phoebe was now standing next to them and completely fascinated by the exchange. Mrs Abbott constantly amazed her.

'Simon dear, you'd be surprised at where I go and what I do. I'm not decrepit just yet.'

Simon stared at her and wondered how old she actually was, probably only in her early fifties; she'd just always seemed ancient to him, maybe it was how she dressed and her upright old fashioned demeanour.

'To answer your question dear, no I haven't yet been to the Rainbow Rooms, but I have been to Biba.'

'Really, Abby?' Now Phoebe couldn't contain her astonishment. 'Gosh, did you enjoy it?'

'Bit dark in there, dear.' Mrs Abbott wrinkled her forehead and bushy eyebrows in a brief frown.

'You're so funny Abby, did you go to buy a dress?'

'No, Phoebe dear, don't be daft. I would hardly be able to fit my big toe into a Biba dress. I went to the food halls to buy some of their special continental bread. I'd heard there was a huge variety to choose from and I thought it would be a lovely treat, but it was all sold out by the time I'd got there - even by eleven in the morning.' Mrs Abbott realised from Simon and Phoebe's expressions, that she'd gained a new found respect.

'Si, could we go there this evening before the Rainbow Rooms? The last Biba boutique was where I bought my first pair of teal suede knee high boots when I was still at school. Gosh that feels so long ago now.'

'Yes, we can drop in downstairs quickly on our way up to dinner and oh, you're perfectly dressed, just like an Agatha Christie book character.'

Phoebe was completely in her element; she loved dressing up in costume and was wearing the most beautiful vintage dévore-cut black velvet dress with a nineteen twenties handkerchief-style hem together with a silver fox fur bolero. Simon couldn't believe how stunning Phoebe looked that evening.

'Wow, where did you find such a fabulous dress?'

Phoebe put a finger up to her lips, warning him to be quiet. 'I borrowed it from mummy's wardrobe; she won't notice as she's got so many dresses. I'll put it straight back tomorrow when she's out. We never see each other as she's always asleep in the mornings, or out with her charity ladies for lunch, or with daddy. Her husband-finding mission for me didn't work, so she's now given up on me and moved on with her life.

'Well, you're nearly as skinny as your mother now. There's no way you'd ever have fitted that dress a few months ago, please don't lose any more weight though, I hope Mrs Abbs is feeding you up. Maybe she'll manage to buy that fancy bread for you next time she's in Biba.'

Phoebe categorically didn't want to discuss her body or her weight, and remained silent and closed off again until they arrived at the Biba store. As her eyes grew accustomed to the dim light inside the store, she felt overwhelmed by the glamour and theatricality of the place.

'Oh wow, this is more like a film set than a department store and everyone in here is so beautiful.'

'Ha-ha Si, you're no longer the most beautiful person in the room now,' Jake immediately quipped.

Everything in there was beautiful like an exotic wonderland full of mystery with potted palms and Bentwood hat stands draped with feather boas, sequins, silks and crushed velvets. It was full of Art Nouveau, pre-Raphaelite and retro twenties glam mixed with Moroccan Kasbah. Phoebe now understood what Mrs Abbott had meant about dark; it was very, very dark in there. Everything was dark even the clothes; all in purples, plums, blacks and browns and the music so loud. Phoebe tried unsuccessfully to imagine Mrs Abbott in the store - she failed. The sales girls all looked like top models and stood around, bored and aloof, no offers of help clearly ever to be on their agenda. Phoebe realised Simon was gently prodding her in the ribs.

'What's the matter?' She was enjoying wandering around soaking up the novelty of the atmosphere.

'We've a dinner table waiting in the Rainbow Room upstairs.' As Simon sounded so anxious and impatient not to be late, Phoebe realised she'd have to come back another day on her own to browse properly. She walked across the shiny marble floor towards the ground floor escalators, all lit by bronze statues of women holding lamps, waiting for him to tell her where to go next.

'Hey, this way Phoebes, we're taking the lift, not the escalators upstairs.' Simon was fully in charge of everything.

They arrived at the fifth floor in the ornate Art Deco mirrored lift and walked out into a huge space that evoked a Busby Berkeley film set more than a restaurant. Phoebe, Simon and Jake all just stopped dead and stared, over-awed; they didn't know what to look at first, the glamour of their surroundings, the amazing coloured rainbow lit ceiling or the sexy cigarette girls wearing more attitude than clothes who were offering Biba own-brand and rainbow-coloured Sobranie cocktail cigarettes from their equally stylish trays.

Simon continued to stay in the evening's driving seat, quickly ordering from the three course menu. 'We'll have the roast beef and three vegs and a carafe of red house wine please.'

Phoebe looked down at both her menus, food and wine, checking out the price of the wine that seemed expensive at £1.50 a litre. Then the dessert section of the menu caught her eye.

'Boys, look at the puds section of the menu; syllabub and pouff's pudding - only twenty five pence, cheap at the price, how many shall we order? We've two already!'

The three of them screamed with laughter.

Simon felt full of satisfaction that Phoebe was laughing and enjoying life again.

'Phoebes don't you think it's completely fabulous here, is it making you feel like a Hollywood movie star?'

'With both you and Jake as my leading men and Jake, you do realise that you may well really be my leading man when you've finished your acting course in a few years, but be so famous that you won't talk to me.'

'Don't be so silly, not talking to you will never happen. Anyway, you could be a very famous fashion stylist by then.' Phoebe felt unconvinced about her own future, wondering what Simon would say.

'So, Si, what are you going to be famous for?'

'I've decided to train as a makeup artist, then one day the three of us could work together.' He looked filled with positivity as he announced his career intentions and put out his hands so they could all link their little fingers to wish for their futures, just as the Manhattan Transfer Band live cabaret began their set singing cappella.

Phoebe's face was lit up with a beaming smile and she clapped hands with pleasure.

'This is such fun here, thank you so much boys. I love this place and this whole Palm Court orchestra vibe from the band.'

A fleeting thought passed through Phoebe's mind; how wonderful life would be if only every evening could seem as perfect as this one.

Chapter 14. London, 1973

Mrs Abbott was thrilled that Phoebe seemed to be much more herself again and decided to eat her meals as regularly as she could together with Phoebe in the breakfast room. She still didn't trust her to eat properly; she also tried to discretely peer at Phoebe's arms in case she was dressing to hide any self-harm cuts. Phoebe was definitely on the mend with the help of Caroline's regular phone calls and the boys' social outings, although Mrs Abbott knew these would soon be ending as Jake was about to go off to LA and Simon to start his makeup course. She worried how Phoebe would then cope without the reassuring presence of these two young men as her constant support system.

Phoebe had already left the house to meet the boys for a coffee in a local café.

'Phoebes, this next evening out will be our last with Jake.' Phoebe could hear the sadness in Simon's voice.

'What are you going to do without him?' Phoebe wondered how *she* could help him now.

'Jake and I have made a pact to meet up as much as we can. I'll fly out to LA as often as I can afford with what's left of my allowance that strangely hasn't yet been stopped. Phoebes, you could come with me too.'

Phoebe looked thoughtful. 'Actually Si, you know what I'd like to do?'

'No?'

Phoebe started fiddling with some of her long curly strands of hair as she spoke, feeling increasingly nervous at how what she was about to say would be received. 'I'd like to go and live somewhere abroad for a bit - somewhere I can feel as safe as I do when I'm with you and Jake.'

Simon gazed at her, considering her statement whilst both Jake and Phoebe wondered what he was going to say. Phoebe knew that Simon, being Simon, would immediately come up with something now she'd spoken her thoughts; he was that sort of person.

Two minutes later he did. 'Phoebes, I think I may have the perfect person to help you. Do you remember George whose house we stayed at for the shoot? Well, he lives in Paris most of the time, and he knows everyone who's anyone so he might also be able to help you with your whole fashion dream too. And take it from me, he definitely isn't interested in girls at all. Would you like me to ask him for you? I'm sure he'll say yes, he'd love to have a house guest like you to stay.'

Phoebe didn't know George well but if Simon said George was to be trusted, then she would believe him. 'Gosh, that would be so brilliant, thank you.' She moved swiftly onto the subject of their final big night out.

'So, boys, where's this big finale night going to be?' she was excited.

'Sorry, can't tell you, Phoebes. It's a surprise and you'll need to dress up again. Definitely don't hold back, be as wild and outrageous as you like. See you later, don't forget, no holding back.' As they left the café, Simon turned round laughing and turned his pretty face into a distorted grimace of shock and horror - eyes as wide as saucers – demonstrating his expression of what could happen later when Phoebe appeared in whatever mad creation she might have chosen to put together.

Phoebe stood in her bedroom and once again stared reluctantly at herself in the mirror. Who could she transform herself into? She didn't want to become a "femme fatale", she still wasn't ready for the possibility of any straight men hitting on her. She needed some inspiration, continuing to stare at herself imagining all possibilities. Then it came to her. She had red hair, so why not become androgynous like Bowie, her pin-up poster idol - yes, that was the perfect solution.

She quickly scanned her latest magazines and it appeared that Keith at Smile hairdressers in Knightsbridge was "the" man to go to for this transformation. She picked up the phone and began to dial, her fingers initially misdialling with excitement. One hour later, Phoebe was firmly installed in a chair by the salon windows overlooking Knightsbridge as Keith ran his fingers through her long thick curls, whilst they both stared at her hair in the mirror. It was so different from the time when she'd been with her mother for her haircut at Sassoon's – this time she was in control.

'So what have you got in mind, young lady?' Keith kept playing with her hair as he spoke.

'A complete change please; short, spiky and dyed a deep red please just like Bowie.'

Keith removed his hands from her long thick hair as though he'd been given an electric shock and horrified, took a step back.

'I always love to do a great haircut but it would be such a crime to cut off all your beautiful hair, most girls dream to have long hair like yours.'

'I'm not most girls and it'll grow again, please Keith?' Phoebe looked back at him in the mirror with beseeching eyes.

He looked at her again to check she was really being serious and caved in. 'Alright, although the deal is that I'll cut it in the style you'd like but not as short as Bowie's.'

Phoebe flushed with joy at the excitement of her new image.

After the hair wash, the junior returned her back to Keith's chair. She squeezed her eyes tightly shut as the snip-snip-snip of his scissors sent her wet curls tumbling to the floor forming a red carpet of hair. It took ages. Then she heard Keith say, 'You can open your eyes now.'

She slowly opened one eye at a time frightened to look. She didn't recognise the girl that was now staring back at her in the mirror.

'Wow. I don't look like me anymore.'

Keith, who wasn't much taller than Phoebe, rested his hands in a fatherly way on her shoulders as they both looked at his handiwork. Phoebe was finding it hard to speak as she felt overwhelmed with all sorts of emotions.

'That's so perfect, exactly what I wanted.'

She wanted to hug him but wasn't sure it was the thing to do. She could see that Keith was looking as happy as she now felt; he'd succeeded in creating exactly the look she'd envisioned. On the way home from Knightsbridge, she stopped and smiled at her new reflection in every single shop window, starting each step with a renewed and bouncy spring ready for her new life-journey and then she came across the perfect outfit to wear for this big night out – one that wasn't just brave as Mrs Abbott would have said, but fearless. This new style Phoebe, with a brittle and thin veneer of bravado, was now willing to step outside her longstanding comfort zones, although the old version was still there deep inside, struggling to suppress her anxieties.

Phoebe took special trouble over her makeup to make it strong and vibrant contrasting with her now flaming red spiky straightened hair. She managed to wiggle into a pair of her highest heels and the skin-tight leopard print cat suit that had screamed "buy me" to her from one of the boutique windows on her way home from Knightsbridge. This new version of Phoebe was now ready for them.

The doorbell rang. She knew Mrs Abbott would answer it, so she waited until she could hear all their voices and then went downstairs to make a maximum impact. There was complete silence as though time stood still. Then the boys both spoke at once.

'Phoebes! Wow! That's dramatic!'

Mrs Abbott didn't say anything.

Phoebe couldn't tell from their expressions whether they were shocked, amazed or impressed. She was beginning to feel a little less confident, maybe even slightly crushed and deflated.

'Phoebe dear, all your lovely curls have gone.' Mrs Abbott was now looking positively shell-shocked. Phoebe had been expecting a more positive response. Simon broke the awkward silence.

'Phoebes, you look totally fabulous and your makeup is wonderful, couldn't have done it better myself, you look just like Bowie.'

Jake simply added, 'Stunning.'

Even Mrs Abbott managed to collect herself again, 'Very brave,' she said quietly, in her immutable fashion. With Mrs Abbott's final endorsement, Phoebe now knew that she did indeed look good and regained some of her confidence and equilibrium. 'So where are we going?'

'We're off to Andrew Logan's event, an 'Alternative Miss World.' Simon finally filled her in.

'Alternative Miss World and...' Phoebe suddenly lost her train of thought as she focused more closely back on the two young men standing in front of her.

'Why have you *both* got actual make up on if we're going to see girls in a beauty contest?' Phoebe was confused, although she had to admit Simon really was rather pretty with full make-up. Jake simply looked more handsome.

'You'll just have to wait and see.' Simon tapped his finger on one side of his nostrils as he spoke.

The drive took forever with Phoebe seeing parts of London she didn't know existed.

'Where on earth are we going, Si?'

'Hackney, in East London.'

'Hackney... are you sure we're still in London? It's so rough and run down round here, is it safe?' Phoebe was already stressing.

'Of course it's safe and Jake and I are here with you. We'd never put you in harm's way and there'll be lots of gay men there to protect you too; although if they're all in drag - I've no idea how fast they'd be able to run in their heels.' Jake and Simon were both already giggling together at Simon's comment which had gone right over Phoebe's head.

'Drag? What's that?' Phoebe felt she was discovering new things daily.

'Drag is when men wear women's clothes. I think the word "drag" started when men played female roles in the olden days when their costume dresses would "drag" across the floor, would you agree Jake?' Jake was nodding.

'How did you know that, Si?' she wondered how Simon was so knowledgeable about everything.

'You know I love reading, especially old newspapers archived in the library. I've been reading up all about the history of costume and makeup, so obviously Jake has been part of my learning too.'

'When did you find time?' Phoebe sounded surprised.

'When it's your passion, as you know, you find time... so whilst we're on the subject of drag, would you like to know more?' Phoebe hadn't replied, so Simon carried on anyway.

'So, whilst I was doing my research the other day, I discovered the first famous drag queen was a man called Julian Eltinge in the early 1900's.'

'Just a tad before your time, Si.' Phoebe joked but Simon ignored her.

'Julian opened the door for future generations of drag and was so good at his transformations that most audiences didn't even realise he was a man until he removed his wig at the end of his act. He created such magical illusions that he became a huge star, one of the highest-paid male actors in the world, earning more than Charlie Chaplin at that time. He even had his own magazine in which he gave women makeup advice and promoted his own cosmetics range which was best known for its cold cream.'

'Oh golly, if you're going to be a makeup artist, you could follow in his footsteps and have your own makeup range too.'

Simon gave a tiny smile, more to himself than to Phoebe, and replied, 'maybe, you never know...'

Phoebe and the boys finally arrived at their destination, parking in a side street near a warehouse type of building. Phoebe had never been anywhere as gritty and urban before and looked up to see if there were any road signs, spotting one; Downham Road, Hackney on the corner of their street. However, they could have been in Outer Mongolia for all Phoebe knew as she was so far away from her South-West London post code.

The friends walked into a large concrete floored, brick-walled warehouse. Phoebe was finding it hard to take everything in all at once; the artworks all over every wall and shop mannequins stood everywhere in mad outfits that made hers look boring. Madder still were the guests, Phoebe couldn't believe her eyes and kept blinking in case she was imagining things.

'Boys, I thought the Sombrero was quite far out but this is way more so. What are we doing here?' Phoebe suddenly felt she needed some clarity, otherwise it was all too surreal especially as both Simon and Jake were in full makeup.

'It's a fancy dress contest which a friend of ours called Andrew Logan, just started holding last year. Jake and I met him at an art show we went to when Andrew told us he'd had this idea for a party; not a beauty pageant like in America but a party that celebrated transformation. He was going to christen it "The Alternative Miss World" where men or women could enter, participating on an equal footing, whatever their ethnicity or sexuality and be judged using the same criteria - poise, personality and originality.'

'So that's why I can't tell who's who or what's what here. Some people do look quite bizarre.' Phoebe hoped she was being polite and understated in her critique.

'Phoebes, there's loads of famous artists and creative people here – so totally up your alley. It's an amazing place for inspiration, especially for makeup and costume. See? Over there is Zandra Rhodes, the designer with her pink hair and oh, Ossie Clark too.'

'Gosh, Ossie Clark? I've got one of his beautiful dresses and wore it when I was a deb.' Phoebe was bowled over that these Designers were actually here too.

Simon continued pointing out who was there, 'And there's Derek Jarman and David Hockney with Grayson Perry. the artist, and see that really tall girl over there? That's David

Bowie's wife, Angie.' Phoebe realised that maybe it had been Angie at the Sombrero when she'd gone there the first time.

'Oh and see that man over there, surrounded by beautiful girls, that's David Bailey, the photographer.' Simon was now nearly squealing with as much excitement as Phoebe while he pointed out all the starry and eccentric characters.

'Everyone everywhere will look so dull and boring after tonight.' Phoebe breathed.

Simon had now stopped the name-dropping. 'Oh hang on, they're about to announce and crown the winner.' A hush momentarily fell over the assembled crowd.

'... And the winner is... Eric Roberts, Miss Holland Park Walk.'

Everyone whooped and cheered as they watched Andrew Logan walk down the makeshift runway and place his homemade UHU glued-together cardboard crown on the actor winner's head.

'Jake, are you just imagining that this could be you in Hollywood winning an Oscar?'

'If I ever do, Phoebes, you and Simon will definitely be up there with me.'

But the moment passed too quickly for Simon and Phoebe to comment as Simon was back on his people spotting mission.

'See over there? That's Divine, a really famous American drag queen. She's just been in the movie, Pink Flamingos by John Waters, filmed to shock in the worst possible taste. I don't even want to tell you what she did in it, it was so disgusting. Jake and I saw it together and I had to look through my fingers at the end it was so gross.'

Phoebe didn't know what to say. She stared over at Divine and wondered what she could possibly have done that was so disgusting.

'Divine and all of John's movies have a huge cult following, and not just from gay boys like us.' Jake explained whilst Phoebe continued staring.

'Hmm… Divine isn't exactly pretty or slim or glam, is she, um, he or she? Not what you'd imagine a drag artist to be. I would always want to make people look as beautiful as they could be. You know you'd make a beautiful drag queen, Si, you're so good looking and now you've got some makeup on tonight you're easily the best looking in here, maybe you should have entered!'

Simon looked a bit sheepish. 'Thanks Phoebes but I think I'll stick to just being me at the moment, life is complicated enough as it is, my father still doesn't know I'm queer and my mother who may just have a slight inkling now, still can't tell him as he just wouldn't understand.'

'That's so hard Si and I know how difficult it is for you. Well, I love you whatever, and you too Jake. You've both always been there for me especially over the last few months; you've helped me so much and I'm beyond grateful.'

Simon eyed Phoebe thoughtfully. He wondered if she was ready to talk yet about what had happened to her, maybe he'd just test the water.

'Both Jake and I know something bad happened to you in Yorkshire. Remember, we were the ones that found you. We all have our secrets which we have to live with, just look at me and Jake, but some are better shared.'

Phoebe suddenly looked serious again. 'Sorry but I'm just not ready to talk to anyone, and I'm not sure I ever will be either.'

'Phoebes, I do understand. Look, I'll try to come and see you whilst you're at George's in Paris. I'm starting a makeup course in September here in London so I won't have that much time off.'

Phoebe smiled, the mood lightening once again. 'I'm so happy for you, it's what you'd always wanted to do, how were your parents about it?'

'My father's just about living with it as I've said I'm going to art school.'

'Why is life so difficult? I wish everything could be simpler for all of us. Let's toast to all our dreams coming true. Jake, you go first.'

'To... becoming a famous and successful Hollywood actor.'

'You *will* be,' Phoebe answered with emphasis, 'Si, you next.'

'To...'Simon thought for a minute, 'being a top make-up artist booked for amazing editorial fashion shoots in Vogue and the fashion capitals of the world *and* working with both of my favourite people Jake and Phoebe.'

'I absolutely know you will be...' Phoebe again added with even more positivity and conviction.

'And you, Phoebes?' the boys asked together.

'Err, a fashion stylist?' Phoebes replied hesitatingly.

'Phoebes you will be. What will you be known as? I know; *"Phoebe Clarke, Stylist to the stars. The only stylist who can make you look and feel a million dollars".*'

'I wish!'

'Phoebes, imagine it, believe it and it will happen.' Simon liked to believe in the power of positivity and always attempted to spread the word.

Phoebe just wanted to believe but she had to just stop her night-time terrors first. As the three best friends clinked glasses and wished, Phoebe suddenly wanted to be like Dorothy in the Wizard of Oz so she could click her sparkly red heels together three times and all her own wishes would come true.

Chapter 15. Phoebe. Paris, 1973

Phoebe quickly appreciated the brilliance of Simon's Paris suggestion. Living with George Dudley in his very grand apartment in the coolest part of Paris was absolutely perfect, he put no pressure on her to socialise with his continuous stream of visiting friends, simply leaving her to choose where and when she joined in.

Mrs Abbott was the only other person apart from Simon, Jake and Caroline who knew where she'd gone to stay. Phoebe felt that she now always owed it to Mrs Abbott to let her know her whereabouts as she'd realised how worried she'd been about her.

The news that one of Simon's friends would now be looking after her in Paris had filled Mrs Abbott with renewed confidence. 'Any friend of Simon's I know will be alright too, Simon's such a kind young man. It will be good for you to be away,' then she added with a catch in her voice after a long pause, 'but a postcard from Paris would be lovely.'

Phoebe remembered how Mrs Abbott was the master of understatement. Phoebe promised she'd keep in touch and noticed as she said goodbye, Mrs Abbott's eyes looked a little misty, whilst her mother's eyes stayed as cold and dry as they had always been. Her father simply shook her hand and Phoebe couldn't remember if he'd ever hugged her.

George though, couldn't have been more welcoming. 'Phoebe, I'm so happy to have you come and stay with me. I'm rattling around like some old queen in this huge apartment on my own, it's so lovely to have company. My little Parisian bolt-hole is your home for as long as you want, you know that saying, "la mia casa e la tua casa". Hardly a little bolt-hole thought Phoebe to herself, maybe it was to George after living most of his life in his huge ancestral pile.

George took Phoebe under his wing like a wounded bird and asked nothing in exchange; no sex - girls simply weren't his thing; no money - as he was so rich it became an irrelevance; no questions asked - he wasn't really interested, although Simon had made him promise not to ask Phoebe anything. He introduced Paris to Phoebe and Phoebe to Paris and also to his nocturnal life of European aristocrats and cool clubs. One of the nocturnal regulars in George's life was an exceptionally good looking gay British Lord, the Marquis of Langley, heir to a fortune and a huge estate back in England.

Phoebe supposed one day he'd have to bite the bullet and marry to produce at least an heir and a spare, she understood how it all worked, she'd been told often enough by her mother. She could even hear her mother's voice loudly in her head. 'Well, dahling, of course it would be a lovely arrangement for some girl. All she'll have to do is produce some babies and then live a life of luxury for ever more. How difficult could that be dahling? You could be that woman and even have a little discreet fun on the side.'

But Phoebe didn't want to be that woman and anyway, she was definitely no longer interested in men. The thought of any man touching her again made her feel quite nauseous. Maybe one day, far in the distant future, a knight on a white charger might just fall in love with her and make her feel healed and whole again; a meaningless and loveless marriage, like a business transaction, was never going to be her way forward. Ever.

Life with George was more than enough. He took her to all the ready-to-wear and couture shows as he knew she loved fashion. He also knew absolutely everyone, whilst his title and wealth opened doors to everything. In fact, there was nothing he couldn't get a ticket for. The security guards and the Designers' PRs all waved them through to the front row seats, past all the pushing and heaving wannabe fashionistas. Phoebe felt so important when she was with him as George just didn't do queues, they weren't in his DNA.

One afternoon as they shown to their seats in the front row of the Givenchy Couture show, Phoebe found herself sitting next to a fabulously glamorous woman. George tried to give Phoebe a gentle poke in the ribs to grab her attention, whispering in her ear.

'Phoebe, don't look round straight away, but next to you is a friend of mine called Bettina who was the Prince Aly Kahn's fiancée. She'd been a model until the nineteen fifties when they met.'

Phoebe hearing this was now desperate to look round but kept her eyes fixed straight ahead, listening intently to George's story.

'It was so sad, apparently she was pregnant when she survived the car crash that killed him and then lost the baby. Okay, you could quickly look now, don't you think she's still so beautiful?'

Phoebe tried to glance subtly in Bettina's direction and caught a glimpse of her high cheekbones and cat-like eyes. Yes, George was right, she was stunning. Phoebe hoped that Bettina didn't realise they were discussing her as she leant in closer to George who was continuing to fill her in on the back story.

'She was a fashion icon, modelling for everyone you can think of; Chanel, Valentino and Grès couture houses and also on the covers of all the top fashion magazines. You know, like Vogue, Elle Mode du Jour...'

'Wow, George, I bet she's got some good stories she could tell.' Phoebe was now really excited to hear all about this fascinating woman's life.

'Let's say that her love life has been, shall we call it, colourful?' Phoebe was even more enraptured now. George had opened the flood gates of insight into her personal history as he continued, 'She was married to a French photographer Gilbert Graziani, became the lover of the American screenwriter Peter Viertel, was engaged to Prince Aly Khan, the socialite son of the Aga Khan, who was killed in the car accident. See what I mean? There's a lot to tell.'

'Gosh.' Phoebe could only begin to imagine the rest.

'Anyway, she's so much fun and I know she would be really useful for you to meet as her whole life has been fashion - you'll love her. I'll introduce you, hang on though until she turns around.'

And then she did and George took his chance. 'Bonjour, Bettina.'

As Bettina swivelled round more to see who was talking to her, Phoebe could now see a woman, maybe thirty years older than herself, who was still incredibly beautiful and elegant. Phoebe suddenly realised that George was doing his intro bit.

'Je voudrais vous présenter ma chère amie Phoebe, elle vient de Londres.'

Bettina immediately kissed Phoebe on both sides of her cheeks, European style. 'Lovely to meet you, Phoebe. I'll drop round to have un petit café chez George this week. George, I'll call you to arrange.'

Phoebe was excited and took great care with her outfit choice when she found out which morning Bettina was going to be visiting. They sat together in the courtyard of George's apartment over a cup of very British tea and biscuits. Phoebe could feel Bettina evaluating her, whilst daintily sipping her tea out of George's beautiful bone china cup.

'Votre style est certainement unique, Phoebe.'

Phoebe wondered if this was a similar statement to Mrs Abbott describing her style choices as "brave". Phoebe realised that she must have looked very Chelsea compared to Bettina's own understated Parisian chic.

'I think we could work together on making you a little more Parisienne ma cherie. You'll then look très cool. Next week I'll take you to meet my fashion friends - the lovely Azzedine Alaia and also Ungaro, two designers from my modelling days and we'll see what we can do with you.'

Phoebe couldn't believe her luck, all this was beyond her wildest dreams. Being Bettina's new fashion pupil seemed to be a huge improvement on when she was her mother's get-Phoebe-married project. 'Merci Bettina. That would be so fantastic.'

'It's good to look and be different, Phoebe. You know when I was very young and had just started modelling, I wore no make-up and I had red hair, just like you, so I always looked a little different from the other models. Maybe that's why I was successful, it certainly wasn't because I was the most beautiful.'

Phoebe found herself opening up and telling Bettina how she'd ended up in Paris; not the full version, an edited one, focused on the breakup of her relationship with Simon. Bettina listened closely to Phoebe's story, empathetically and once Phoebe had finished she started to open up about her own life adding a new chapter each time they met up. Phoebe was surprised that someone so famous bothered to take the time to chat to her and be so open about their life story.

'You know life's experiences make us who we are, and my life was much less privileged than yours to start with. I was brought up from a young age by my mother after my father left. I then lived in Angers with my grandmother during the war and had to cycle to school every day across frozen cabbage fields. When I left school after the liberation in 1944, I moved to Paris as I'd always wanted to be a fashion designer just like you do, I even bravely went to see the costume designer Jacques Costet with some of my sketches, who then made me his house mannequin.'

Listening to Bettina, Phoebe realised she'd never yet had the guts to show her own sketch books to anyone. Maybe people wouldn't laugh after all if she did...

'I then worked briefly with the couturier Lucien Lelong, but I think we will leave this part of my life out as it was such a dull and colourless period; so when Dior asked me to work for him I did consider it but chose Fath instead.'

Phoebe loved how Bettina nonchalantly reeled off all these big Designer names as complete throwaways, one after the other. Then Bettina opened up even more and Phoebe was really flattered that she would want to.

'You know my real name isn't Bettina, it was Simone until I started to work for Jaques Fath, when he decided to rename me for his catwalk shows. "We already have a Simone," he'd said, "you look much more like a Bettina" and I became the face of Fath. He liked that I was *different* and maybe that I was so young then. He introduced me to everyone in high society at the Château de Corbeville costume balls, where all the best buyers, stars, writers, and even designers like Balenciaga and Balmain came. These parties in the middle of the countryside were extravagant and fantastically themed - imagination was everything then.'

194

Phoebe was completely captivated by Bettina's stories and sat there entranced, visualising some of the scenes that Bettina was describing and sounded wistful as she added, 'I'd have loved to have gone to one of those parties, it was all so glamorous in those days.'

'They were, Phoebe, though everything changes with time doesn't it, especially fashion. You know there was no ready-to-wear fashion shows then, only couture and collections were shown to select clients in salons, like a trunk show where you could actually reach out and touch all the clothes.'

'Oh, that's just how it was when I was a child in my mother's dressing room, reaching out and touching all her beautiful dresses; it's so important to touch and feel ,isn't it?' Phoebe spoke tentatively, hoping that Bettina would agree.

'C'est la vérité, Phoebe.'

Phoebe was surprised that Bettina continued, happy to continue reminiscing with her as the days turned into weeks and into months.

'You know, New York was never for me, I tried it as it was so different from my modelling life in Paris. I discovered that spontaneity and improvisation didn't work in New York as they didn't have the same laid back attitude to work.'

Phoebe loved listening to Bettina ramble on as she was utterly in awe of her.

'But Hollywood wasn't for me either - I even turned down a movie contract.'

Suddenly Phoebe felt brave enough to interrupt, 'That's where I'd really like to work.'

Bettina looked at her with surprise and immediately answered.

'Well, then you must, Cherie. You know you can do anything you want to do, if you want it enough. It just wasn't for me, so I returned to Paris and started working for Givenchy where I modelled, took on PR duties and acted as his house 'directrice'. He even produced a "Bettina Blouse."

'Gosh, a blouse that's actually named after you… you're such an inspiration. I hope one day I might be as glamorous, stylish and successful as you.'

'Listen, Phoebe, we both have red hair, don't we, so you're halfway there already; just believe in yourself.'

Phoebe was absorbing every single word that Bettina said as they sat having one of their morning cafés aux laits in George's sunny courtyard garden.

'Now remember these words, ma cherie. Never let anyone tell you to lose weight, you're perfect just as you are with your curves.' Phoebe knew she had filled out a little bit again since she'd been living with George, she was beginning to enjoy food again but only in very small portions. 'When I returned to modelling for the final time in nineteen sixty seven, my first job was for Coco Chanel's summer collection and it wasn't a happy experience. "You need to lose a little weight", Coco told me, "follow my example and don't eat at weekends". That was never going to be an option for me, so I chose there and then to never work for her again and instead became director of haute couture for Emanuel Ungaro. So, always remember exactly who *you* are Phoebe and don't let anyone ever change you. 'Phoebe wondered how much of Bettina's valuable life-lessons she would manage to retain as time went on.

Phoebe loved being George's resident plus one for all his very smart invitations and always offered to pay her way but George would never let her. The latest invitation was to a fundraiser at the Palace of Versailles for the restoration of the palace, billed as the "Battle of Versailles". She was so excited about this event, not because they were dressing up and going somewhere so completely fabulous but this was the first ever proper Paris Fashion week, 'La Semaine de la Mode' to be held.

'I can't believe I'm actually going to haute couture, ready to wear and men's fashion shows all in the same evening. I can't wait, this is what I've always wanted.'

'Just see me as your fairy godmother, Phoebe.' George stood on his tiptoes and waved his imaginary wand in big sweeping movements at her. Phoebe's imagination went instantly into overdrive as she visualised George as the Panto fairy godmother granting her, as Cinderella, all her wishes.

'Then we shall now go to the ball, Fairy Godmother George? Does our carriage await outside?'

Their carriage was indeed waiting, in the shape of a chauffeur driven Mercedes. George and Phoebe were dropped off in front of the Palace entrance and Phoebe wasn't expecting anything quite so stunning. She hugged George as she stood there for a moment taking in the view, watching all the glamorous guests arrived. 'This is just gorgeous, George. I can just imagine what it was like in the days of Marie Antoinette to come to a ball here.' Before George could reply, an immaculately dressed man in black tie had come up to him.

'Bonsoir, Lord Dudley, I'm the Versailles curator, Gerald van der Kemp. I hope you and Mademoiselle Clarke will have a wonderful evening tonight. Your extremely generous donation will help raise money for the restoration and renovation for Marie Antoinette's dressing room, Louis XV's children's play room and the staircase which began construction in the beginning for the Eighteenth Century and was sadly never finished. By the way, Mademoiselle Clarke, I believe you're interested in pursuing a fashion career? Tonight is a first as American and Parisian designers have never before shown together and we will have five American designers; Oscar de la Renta, Bill Blass, Anne Klein, Halston and Stephen Burrows together with five French ones; Pierre Cardin, Emanuel Ungaro, Marc Bohan, Hubert de Givenchy and Yves Saint Laurent. An impressive collection I'm sure you will agree?'

Phoebe was beaming and her eyes sparkling at the prospect of the evening ahead. 'Mr Van der Kamp, it's the first time I've ever been to anything like this, so even one or two of them would have been an amazing treat.'

The evening turned out to be better than any fairy tale for Phoebe. Saint Laurent sent a Bugatti limo down the runway, Dior had a Cinderella pumpkin coach, Ungaro had a rhinoceros pulling a gypsy caravan, whilst Liza Minelli sang show tunes for the Americans, Josephine Baker flapped twenties-style and sang for the French. Phoebe looked around the starry celebrity packed audience as the evening unfolded. Anyone who was anyone was there, including Bettina and even Princess Grace of Monaco and Elizabeth Taylor who, Phoebe decided, was even more beautiful in real life than in the movies. It was without doubt the best night of Phoebe's life so far; she decided that every girl should have a gay best friend like George.

George and Phoebe gradually fell into a routine in which they mostly slept in late and then walked round to Café de Flore, Bulevard Saint Germain, Phoebe's Parisian version of the King's Road Picasso. It had seemed not so long ago to Phoebe that the Picasso's cheese and ham toasties and cappuccinos were the height of sophistication, so she now overlooked the French waiters' arrogance and rudeness, as this was one of the oldest cafés in Paris – "the" place to be seen and people watch. She and George ate out more than they ate in, in fact, Phoebe wasn't sure she'd ever seen George cook anything. Brasserie Lipp and La Coupole felt like their home-from-home dining rooms and Chez Regine their personal after-dinner drawing room/nightclub; wherever they went, they were given the best tables to sit at. Regine, the Queen Bee of the Nightclub scene liked to place her most loyal or famous "courtiers" at her number one table and Phoebe realised that they were actually seated at that particular table quite often.

She still really missed her London friends, especially Simon and of course Paula, it had been a while now since they'd last seen each other. Phoebe still wondered where Paula had disappeared to and if she'd ever see her again. Maybe she would magically reappear one day if George could just conjure her up with another dramatic wave of his imaginary magic wand. She felt so spoilt with George; he was so kind and so generous in every way, including sharing his evening's cocaine lines with her.

'Why do you need to do this before you go out at night?' Phoebe was watching fascinated, as George focused on chopping neat symmetrical, parallel lines of cocaine with his gold American Express credit card on a small mirror placed carefully on his antique walnut dining room table.

'I do it because it makes life so much more fun. Go on, do you want to try some? It won't hurt you, it's not addictive and you'll be able to party all night!'

All of Phoebe's being ached to say no. His one sentence had sounded so familiar that it had triggered a flashback, causing her to wonder whether she was about to have a panic attack. She hadn't experienced any for a while now, so she tried to shut down her mounting anxiety. Anyway, she totally trusted George after all the time she'd now lived with him, so why shouldn't she try? Struggling with her inner judgement and her rational self, she reached out for the rolled-up note he was handing her.

'Okay, so what do I do now?' She stood poised, head bent over the lines of white powder, as she waved around the rolled up note, unsure what she was supposed to be doing with it.

'Use it as a straw to sniff along one of these lines I've made.' George instructed.

She did as he suggested and immediately spoke her thoughts out loud as to how she was feeling.

'Ooh, it's going past the back of my nose and down my throat too - it tastes metallic, strange even.' Then she felt a bit of a buzz and gradually she became more chatty and extrovert; a sparkier, more alive and confident version of herself. So this was George's secret source of energy and what it felt like. She could understand the draw now and decided to accept his offer of a line or two each night before they went out. She also figured she could also have more fun if she was high, and it couldn't be worse than a drink or two, could it?

As time passed, she realised that she wanted more hits than George offered her and decided she should find her own additional supply as a back-up. She needed to find a dealer and couldn't ask George for his, so she started hanging around the quirkier, edgy fashion boutiques in Saint Germain making friendly chat to all the shop girls.

Finally, she hit the jackpot with the owner's wife of La Vie en Rose, a tiny vintage clothes boutique that she loved to browse in, it reminded her of the Kensington Market. The owner, Sacha and his wife Martine, travelled all over Europe buying eclectic fashions for their shop and had just come back from Ibiza. As they chatted, it transpired that when they were last there, they'd met a group of French–Moroccan guys when they were all partying one night in the Pacha nightclub. They'd continued their friendship back in Paris and still all went clubbing together. One of the men was a doctor whom, Martine divulged quietly to Phoebe when they were on their own in the boutique, she visited regularly to secretly buy slimming pills for herself. She knew he also dealt cocaine, so if Phoebe would like to buy some, she should come with her next time she went to visit him at his apartment.

Phoebe jumped at the chance and discovered that this Doctor worked from an apartment in Avenue d'Italie in the thirteenth arrondissement, which wasn't too many stops away by the metro subway. So after her first introduction together with Martine, she'd regularly book her appointment with the Docteur Levy once a week; announce herself to the monosyllabic receptionist, wait in his lounge with other girls who never spoke to each other; see him in his office, pay him cash for one or two grams and then come away as quickly as she could, armed with her small stash of cocaine. She simply told George she was going shopping each time. Well, she wasn't fibbing, she was shopping, just not for clothes.

She carried her gram of coke with her in a tiny folded white paper packet in her purse, whenever she went out at night, just in case she wanted a further pick-me-up without asking George. She told herself she could stop whenever she needed to, of course she could, George had already told her with absolute certainty, it wasn't addictive.

Chapter 16. Paula. Paris, 1973

Paula was looking forward to Madjid's weekly visit. He was a good looking Algerian in his mid-thirties and he treated her more respectfully than all the other men who only saw her as a paid-for fuck. After a few sessions Madjid had become more chatty, beginning with the words she'd heard so many times before.

'My wife is no longer interested in sex.' Paula listened politely, shutting off briefly whilst she thought to herself, *that old chestnut of a story again.* However, Madjid slowly redeemed himself as he opened up about his personal life, 'After we'd had our two children, everything changed as my wife was always tired or had a headache, or an excuse and her legs remained firmly and determinedly closed to me.'

Paula was immediately pro-active to console him, after all she was being paid to respond to his needs and he was an attractive man and she enjoyed his company. He was funny and well-educated and he'd begun chat with her, so as paid sex went, he was undoubtedly the best of the bunch. Months passed and they struck up a regular relationship of sorts where Madjid booked her a few times a week and paid Pierre for the extra time with her.

One evening Madjid arrived and gave her an unusually intense and passionate kiss. 'Paula, I've something to tell you, come and sit here.' He patted the bed next him where he was now perched, as that was really the only place to sit in her small bedroom. Paula wondered if he was going to say he was no longer coming to see her. 'I've told Pierre I'm paying you extra to spend the whole night with you, so... we're going into Paris and staying the night at a Hotel.' Madjid was now looking like a cat that had eaten the cream. Paula looked at him, amazed. No one had ever suggested this with her before or indeed with any of the girls, Pierre didn't run that sort of an establishment. She decided that Madjid must have paid Pierre a lot of dosh to allow this.

Madjid elaborated about his plan; 'My wife is out of Paris with her family, so I'm free to spend time with you and pretend we're a proper couple. All the men who see us together will be jealous of me as you're so beautiful. Look, I've even bought you something to wear.'

He handed Paula a stiff, shiny carrier bag. She stared at it as she'd never seen such a smart carrier bag even when she'd been shopping with Phoebe. She'd never heard of the name Pierre Cardin that was emblazoned over the front of the bag, but guessed he must be some posh French Designer. Paula tore at layers of immaculate white tissue paper to reveal a perfectly folded little black shift dress. She looked up at Madjid who was watching her unwrap his present with hugely satisfied expression, similar to a father watching his child open a Christmas present. 'Keep going Paula, there's more inside the bag.'

She put her hand right to the bottom of the cavernous bag, where she discovered tissue-wrapped heels and a small evening purse. Paula looked at Madjid, overwhelmed, she'd never had gifts from a man before, just the work clothes from Pierre but those didn't count. This was different because a man had wanted her to look beautiful for his own pleasure. Yes, this was how she wanted to be treated from now on. No, she would clarify her statement of intent; this was how she'd make sure she would always be treated from now on. She remembered once reading a quote, "You may not always end up where you thought you were going but you will always end up where you are meant to be." This epitomised her life at the moment as she knew it wouldn't simply end here at Pierre's, that was for sure, she was worth more than that.

She slipped on the dress which fitted perfectly, as did the shoes. Madjid took her arm protectively as they left the apartment. The two girls left behind couldn't believe Paula's luck and wolf-whistled after her.

'Lucky cow, enjoy yourself, don't do anything we wouldn't do!' The girls cackled like two old witches and Paula could hear them still laughing as she waited for the lift to arrive to go the six floors down into the basement car park.

'Here we are.' Madjid led her to a shiny little silver Alpha Romeo sports car.

Standing there in her expensive new clothes in front of this smart new car, suddenly made Paula realise the power she could use to enjoy and take advantage of wealthy men who desired her. If the price was right, she'd be theirs, until a higher bidder appeared.

Paula and Madjid's date nights became more frequent as did his gifts to her. Each time they spent the night together, they played make-believe of how they could live an imaginary perfect life, creating plans of ways to escape from Pierre. Paula had never built any expectations of a future with Madjid, although she always happy to play along with his "imagine if" games. Sometimes she would add in some experimental thoughts, angling for a specific response.

'Pierre scares me sometimes, I saw him beat up one of the other girls when she hid some of her money.' Paula didn't add that she'd also secreted away most of her tips as she'd made a lot of money as Pierre's favourite young girl, beautiful and clever enough to know exactly how to play her tricks. She could convincingly fake multiple orgasms, making each and every one of her punters feel special and with her now bilingual French and English, she exuded a significantly classier persona than any of his other girls. In fact, she absolutely knew she was Pierre's main cash cow.

'I'd look after you, Paula, if you're ever in trouble.' That was the answer she'd been hoping for and she immediately filed it in her extremely retentive memory.

Since she'd worked with Pierre, Paula had remained on full alert, watching and learning how he operated and who his punters were; she knew that knowledge was power. Most of the "Pieds-Noirs" as the French Algerians were called, lived in the area around Avenue d'Italie. Many of the wealthier families had settled there and worked as successful doctors and professionals, well-integrated into Parisian society. Pierre had passed himself off as a bona-fide doctor too, with a shiny brass plaque on his front door naming him as the Docteur Pierre Levy.

Paula, however, still hadn't got her brain around why so many young women patients should be queuing in his lounge every lunch-time to see him. She wanted to find out if they were actual patients and if so, what sort of doctor was he, or were they fresh "working girls" waiting to be interviewed?

She, Tracey and Gina all knew, unequivocally, that they should never come out of their bedrooms during Pierre's lunch-time surgery hours. Paula had tried to listen at her door, as her bedroom was nearest to the lounge and reception desk. She gradually discovered after putting together tiny snippets of Pierre's louder overheard conversations, when his tongue had loosened after a night of drugs or drink, that he wasn't only was a pimp for her and the other two girls in this apartment, but also for other girls working elsewhere too.

She also discovered by chance that he was dealing slimming pills, prescription drugs and cocaine. Her suspicions were confirmed when one of his "patients" was speaking more loudly than usual to one of the receptionist. It seemed that Pierre was running late and the girl sounded anxious that she'd already waited half an hour.

'J'avais rendez-vous avec le médecin à treize heures trente. C'est quatorze heures maintenant.'

Paula's ears were quite well-tuned by now to the nuances of accent, especially as she'd spent all that time with Phoebe listening to how to improve her own spoken English pronunciation. As Paula listened more intently it seemed clear to her that the French currently being spoken out in the reception area was strongly accented with English.

Paula was now fascinated by the exchange, she could just hear and knew she was living dangerously if she even opened her door a smidgen. Nevertheless, she was too invested in the conversation not to take a peek. She pushed her door open a crack and had a quick look. She decided she must be imagining things as the girl she could see out there looked like a version of Phoebe. She shut the door again with her heart pounding. How could that have been Phoebe, it was impossible. This girl had sounded a bit like her but was speaking French and also, even with such a quick glance, although she'd seen that the girl had had red hair, she was very thin. She didn't remember her best friend ever being that thin. No, it must have been her imagination, her mind playing tricks, just because she'd wanted to see her so much again.

Maybe she'd risk opening her door once again. Paula looked round the corner quickly but there was no longer anyone waiting in the lounge or at the reception desk.

Everything was silent and empty except for the receptionist speaking on the phone. Paula couldn't ask her anything as she knew she wasn't allowed any interaction with her. Everything she had just seen and heard must have been her imagination playing strange tricks, so she told herself to forget it and move on.

In Paula's regular clandestine military style reconnaissance, she also noted that Pierre went out late every night once the girls' working hours had finished. She and the other two girls were never allowed out, even though Pierre knew there was little possibility for them to escape as he had their passports and continuously held back their earnings, telling them they were still working off their debts to him; he would give them money when they needed it. Paula, however, was keeping her eyes and ears open all the time for any opportunities that could benefit her and if the chance to escape ever happened, she would seize it with both hands.

Then it happened. She was suddenly woken up with loud banging and shouting in the middle of the night. She thought she was dreaming at first, then she realised the noise was coming from outside the front door, so she hurriedly threw a robe around her, shouting to wake up the other girls in case she needed help. They quickly followed behind her to the front door where over the frantic banging noises she could just hear Pierre shouting, sounding desperate as the strength of his cries became weaker. 'Paula, Laissez-moi entrer, ouvrez la porte - je suis tellement malade.'

Paula opened the door as far as the internal chain would allow and found him slumped on the floor outside the door, sweating and mostly incoherent. She took charge and as she directed the girls, 'Quick, help me get him inside,' she wondered why she was springing into action to help him.

She opened the door properly and they all dragged his dead weight into the entrance hall, closing the door and replacing the safety chain. Paula stood and stared at him lying there with no idea what was wrong. The other two girls took one glance at him and then looked at each other with knowing looks.

'Well, what's the matter with him?' Paula demanded impatiently. Pierre was now gasping for air and his skin had turned pale and his lips bluish. He was alternating between delirium and disorientation before he passed out again. Paula still had absolutely no idea what to do as she'd never seen anyone in a state like this. Tracey peered at him more closely, then pulled one of his top and bottom eyelids apart and saw his pupil had become a tiny pinprick. 'He's overdosing but we can't let him die here like this.' She looked up at Paula for support.

Paula suddenly had a moment of clarity of where she could find help in the middle of the night.

'Girls, hang on, I'll back in a minute... I've had an idea.' On the way to rushing to the front door to open it, she'd noticed that somehow Pierre's office door was ajar; he must have forgotten to lock it when he'd gone out earlier. The girls looked gratefully at Paula for taking the situation in hand. She entered Pierre's office and immediately saw a phone on his desk.

She dialled the private line number she'd memorised from when Madjid had first given it to her, from Pierre's phone, but it just rang and rang. Paula wondered whether he would even hear it if he was asleep and was beginning to give up hope, when finally he answered sounding groggy.

'Alo. C'est Madjid.'

'Madjid, it's me, Paula. You know I'd never call you except in an emergency. Well, we're having one as we think Pierre's taken an overdose and he's not in a good way. I've managed to get into Pierre's office to call you. Please, please, could you come and help us?'

Madjid now sounded fully alert and efficient. 'Paula, I'm on my way. Pack a bag quickly and then see if you can find where your passport and money could be kept whilst I drive over. Leave the girls to tend to Pierre.'

Paula rushed back over to the girls who had been trying to make Pierre vomit during his moments of consciousness. She barely gave the man a second glance as she quickly reeled off the two options for the girls. 'Girls, here's your choice. I'm about to leave with Madjid, you remember that trick who took me out on the town a while ago, as soon as he arrives. You can come with us or stay here.'

Both girls gawped, 'But Paula, we've nowhere else to go. You go on your own with him, it's okay.' Paula shrugged. She couldn't help them if they wouldn't help themselves.

Madjid arrived quicker than Paula had expected and he straight away enveloped her in his strong arms. She suddenly felt over-emotional from the warmth and security of his hug, with feelings of overwhelming sadness and exhaustion bubbling up after they'd been repressed for so long since giving away her baby. She tried to still keep herself together and look strong.

'I've looked everywhere but just can't find my passport or where Pierre may have hidden all our money. The girls want to stay as they have nothing better to go to as it would be back to the streets for them if they left.'

Madjid listened and without acknowledging Paula's comment about the girls, moved on quickly in his plan of action. 'So, we'll look again together. The passports must be somewhere.'

Madjid and Paula left the girls and the fast-fading Pierre in the hall and returned back to the office search, shutting the door behind them.

'There isn't a safe so he must keep the money and passports somewhere else.' Paula was trying to think logically as she spoke.

Madjid was meanwhile scanning the room; 'Paula, quick pull out each of the drawers of that chest over there and tip the contents out while I'll start pulling up the carpet edges.'

Paula quickly did as she was told. She emptied out the first three drawers and then as she pulled out the fourth and final one and turned it upside down, she suddenly saw passports taped to the underside of the drawer. 'Madjid look! My passport and both the girls' ones too. Come on, let's go, I can live without the money. I don't care, I've got a little I've managed to save.' Paula was now feeling desperate to get out of the place while they still had a chance.

Paula concluded that maybe Madjid might know more than he was letting on about Pierre's finances as he was adamant not to give up on their search for any money.

'No, come on, one last go at pulling back the carpet.' They both tore away at the carpet edges. Paula felt all her beautifully filed and painted nails break off as she pulled frantically at the cheap carpet. Once more floorboards became visible, Madjid suddenly came across a loose board right under Pierre's desk. He started prising it up and Paula knelt down too, peering over his shoulders.

'Fucking hell!' Paula forgot to put on any pretence of any previous ladylike behaviour, as in the gap under the floorboards she could see wads and wads of French franc notes and small plastic see-through bags of white powder. She sat back on her heels and stared. 'Fuck me, Madjid, I've never seen so much dosh or cocaine.'

'Paula, stop staring and get moving. Grab as much money as you can.' Madjid spoke slowly and calmly, as though this is what he'd been expecting. Paula didn't need to be asked twice. She stuffed as much as she could of the money into the same small holdall that she'd arrived with a year ago and left all the cocaine untouched; drugs had never really been her thing.

They returned to the hallway where the girls were now sitting by Pierre who was no longer vomiting but lying quite still face down on the wooden floor. The girls were sobbing, hardly able to speak as they realised the implications of the situation.

'He's not breathing now, we think he's dead... what shall we do?' Tracey sounded desperate as it seemed to always fall on her shoulders to make the decisions and speak for the second girl.

'Girls, listen, this is your one chance. We've found your passports and if you go into Pierre's office you'll find an escape route to freedom. You may find you want to disappear too as quickly as possible. You should be able to, no one in Paris knows you were ever here or your real names.

'Escape route? What do you mean?' Tracey sounded as though she was no longer able to process any information.

'Girls I'm sorry but I've no time to explain... just trust me and go in there and take what you can. Don't hang around for the police to arrive, his receptionist can deal with it when she arrives and sort out covering up any signs of prostitution. None of your punters will ever want to come forward to say they met you, nor anyone who ever bought drugs from him. You're safe now as long as you get out as quickly as you can. I'm sure it'll simply be put down as an unfortunate drug overdose.'

The girls hugged Paula gratefully, still not fully understanding what she'd just told them. She and Madjid then rushed out of the apartment, where she'd arrived a year ago, down in the lift to the underground car park where they climbed into his little sporty Alfa Romeo and drove out through the electric gates.

Paula now had a significant amount of money in her holdall and the couple of dresses, bags and shoes that Madjid had bought her over the last few months. She suddenly realised that for the first time in her life, a wealthy man had actually wanted to do more for her than just use her, he'd actually taken care of her and helped to rescue her. This was a new experience: no-one had ever helped her before and not asked for anything in return.

Chapter 17. Phoebe. Paris, 1975

Phoebe never knew what new places or people George would have up his sleeve for her, making it an exciting rollercoaster experience living with him. If he wasn't taking her to a fashion show, an art exhibition or a new restaurant, it was to a nightclub or a music gig.

'Phoebes darling, we're going out tonight to meet Joe, an American friend of mine who's a fashion stylist and working with some singer at the moment on his tour - what was his name- oh I remember Leon Jaks.' George sounded unimpressed by the name Leon Jaks, Phoebe wondered if George realised exactly who Leon Jaks was; he was a huge rock star.

'Leon Jaks... did you *actually* just say that name... ohmygosh! He's my most fave singer in the whole world I love, love, love him!' Phoebe was trying to look cool and not hop up and down with excitement.

George was still sounding as though everything he was saying was quite a normal and a mundane daily occurrence, even as he told Phoebe his next bit of news. 'Joe's given me two VIP passes for Leon's one-off secret gig tonight at the Club Sept.'

Phoebe could hardly speak, her excitement had reached fever pitch. 'Club Sept? Have we been there before?'

'No, it's on Rue St Anne and it's "the" gay club of the moment - you'll love it – it's a sort of sexier Parisian version of the Sombrero. Everyone who's anyone now goes there, from Iggy Pop to Grace Jones and they all have special tables reserved at the restaurant on the ground floor. Downstairs, there's a tiny disco with lots of flashing lights.'

This suddenly made Phoebe remember her times with Simon and Jake, dancing the night away at the Sombrero's tiny dance floor. At the mention of Simon's name she felt so sad she hadn't seen him for so long. Although they'd chatted on the phone occasionally, she hadn't actually seen him now for months. He'd filled her in on how his make-up career was going and she'd fed him back snippets of her Parisian life, but it wasn't the same as actually hanging out with him, so he'd promised he would visit her in Paris but he still hadn't been. Maybe he would soon.

'We won't be going there till late as it doesn't really get going until well after eleven and Leon isn't playing until one in the morning.' George was still sounding so matter-of fact, even blasé about their night.

Phoebe just couldn't understand how he could be so contained.

'I'm really not sure I'll be able to wait that long and how I'm going to do concentrate on anything for the rest of the day now?'

She decided to sit in George's little courtyard with her mid-morning coffee and croissant, together with a small sketch pad and pencils; her mind full of images of Leon Jaks. His wild, raunchy rock star style was so completely different from Bowie's theatrical androgyny. Phoebe started to doodle how she imagined Leon's "look" for a new album cover. Inspired at the thought of seeing him perform that night, her pencil flew across the tiny pad faster than it had ever drawn before.

From the moment they arrived at the Club Sept, George seemed to know everyone there.

'Phoebe darling, this is Guy, all the way from Cuba, the best disc jockey you'll ever meet and he knows everyone who's anyone in fashion."

Phoebe double-air-kissed him as she'd learnt to do after all this time in Paris, then stood with George at the edge of the tiny dance floor, watching the eclectic crowd of people posing and posturing under the vaulted ceiling, although the way they were all dressed seemed quite tame to her after experiencing the Andrew Logan's Alternative Miss World night. She wished that Simon and Jake could have been here with her, they would have loved it and would definitely be dancing to their own reflections in the mirrored walls - she smiled to herself as she remembered back to the moment at the Sombrero when everyone had clapped at their dancing.

The music pounded and she was already on a high from the first line of coke she'd just done earlier at the apartment. She shut her eyes for a moment and let the beat of the disco funk and soul music take over until she opened her eyes again and re-focused through the smoke and flashing lights. Did that guy dancing at the other side of the dance floor look like Simon? She started to push forward to see the guy closer up until the disco music and the flashing coloured lights over the dance floor suddenly stopped, leaving everyone briefly in darkness.

'Mesdames et Monsieurs, s'il vous plait applaudissez Leon Jaks.'

Phoebe then heard Leon's sexy husky tones over the club's sound system, as a single spotlight lit the rock star. All thoughts instantly forgotten of wanting to see her Simon-look-a-like, she pushed as close as she could to the front of the small sweaty crowd of VIP guests. She was now at touching distance from the singer and could see every bead

215

of sweat on his rugged face. She'd never been so close to a performing rock god before and he was as sexy in real life as he was when she'd seen him on TV's Top of the Pops - she was completely enthralled. His set ended all too quickly for Phoebe and the dance music and lights all started up again.

She looked round for George in the sweaty crowd and there he was standing just behind her, shouting over the music.

'Did you enjoy that? Come on, follow me, we're going back upstairs to the restaurant to meet up with Joe and Leon.'

Phoebe was still bubbling over with excitement and the earlier lines of coke, so she stayed glued to him, clutching onto the back of his shirt so as not to lose him through the tightly packed crowd. Already sitting upstairs at the restaurant table was a super-trendy black guy, looking cool in every sense of the word. Phoebe immediately wondered how he wasn't sweating like everyone else as it was so hot in there. She tried not to stare too hard at him but it wasn't often she met beautiful-looking black men with huge Hendrix style hair. He was wearing top-to-toe black leather; jacket and jeans together with a tight black t-shirt.

So this was Joe, George's friend. She knew straight away that he was gay as well, her "gaydar" antenna was working really well now living with George for the last year and hanging around with all his gay friends had fine-tuned it to perfection.

'Hey, Phoebe? I'm Joe and I know exactly who you are as George has told me all about you.' As he greeted her, he stood up to his full six foot three inches, which Phoebe had not been expecting. He clasped George in a manly hug, together with a macho-style pat on his back and then bent down a little to kiss Phoebe on both cheeks.

'Hi, it's lovely to meet you, Joe.' She hoped she hadn't felt too sweaty as he'd kissed her and suddenly felt shy again.

'Hey, come and sit down both of you, we've just ordered a bottle of Vodka to mix with Coca Cola, is that okay for you?'

Phoebe knew she would have said yes to anything he'd ordered. 'Perfect, thanks.'

Then suddenly, larger than life was a sweaty Leon who went round kissing everyone at the table. When he reached Phoebe she thought she was going to die and go to heaven and went mute. How could she be so dumb and star struck - that's how kids were not grown up twenty-one year olds. She felt completely overwhelmed by his hugely charismatic presence together with the heady lingering strong smells of Gauloises cigarettes and earthy male sweat.

Phoebe had barely got over the shock of being kissed by her rock idol, when she found herself suddenly enveloped in a bear hug from behind her. Why did the aftershave she could smell seem so familiar? What was it… Eau Sauvage? That's what it was, the same one that Simon had always worn. She extricated herself from the enveloping hug and turned round to find herself staring straight at Simon. She threw her arms around him again as though her life depended on it.

'I can't believe you're here, I've missed you so much and was actually just thinking about you. I'd even thought I'd seen you! Well, obviously I had.' Phoebe then went back to hugging him tightly as though he might disappear again.

'Missed you too, Phoebes.' Simon hugged her affectionately back, resting his head temporarily on her shoulder. For a moment, both of them forgot the table behind them of Joe and Leon who were watching the two of them, not really knowing what was going on. George just sat there grinning as he knew the part he'd played in fixing this surprise meeting. He loved both Simon and Phoebe and had taken ages to engineer it as Simon had been so busy.

Simon finally broke away from the long hug, feeling it was time to give George all the credit. 'Phoebes, it's George you should be thanking for getting me here - you know how good he is at organising anything, including surprises.'

'He certainly is.' Phoebe grinned broadly at George.

Simon continued, 'We've got so much to catch up on and it's too loud here to chat properly and anyway, we're lucky enough to be with Leon and Joe tonight. Let's start tomorrow morning over a coffee at café des Flores.'

'Si, it's a date.' Phoebe's evening was just getting better and better.

The two best friends rejoined the group at the tiny table and George was now trying to have a conversation over the loud music with Leon, leaning in closer so Leon could hear him. 'I loved every single song tonight, are they all the new ones on your upcoming album, Shadows Talk?'

'Thanks man, that's right, it's out this week.' Then Leon raised his gravelly voice above the pumping music and spoke to the whole table. 'Thanks guys for coming, I had a blast doing the gig here – It's such a cool place. Next stop is London, why don't you all come see me and the band there too?'

'Phoebe, you could go,' George always the facilitator, suddenly intervened, 'and you could stay in my studio flat as there's no one there at the moment, it's just off the King's Road at the Worlds End.'

Gosh, was she actually dreaming? Not only had Leon Jaks himself just included her to come to watch his London gig but George had just offered her his studio flat to stay in London. This had to be the best night of her life ever, and even Simon was here too. Phoebe was suddenly overwhelmed with happiness. She felt tearful but she couldn't let them see her crying, as she was happy not sad. How would she feel being back in London? She wasn't sure she ever wanted to see the old crowd again as it might ignite all her memories she'd managed to lock away, but Simon still lived in London so that would help. The table's attention suddenly seemed to be spotlighted on her.

'So what do you do for a job?' Joe was asking.

'I'm not doing anything at the moment, just staying with George who's been the perfect host looking after me here in Paris. I'd always wanted to go to fashion college but I was too young... then, stuff happened and I ended up here.' Phoebe suddenly found her brave and confident alter-ego voice, spurred on by the cocaine and the presence of her two friends. 'I did some doodles today for how I imagined Leon might dress on his next tour, would you like to see?'

She pulled her little sketch pad out of her handbag and put it on the table leaving it open for anyone to view. It was dark in the club restaurant, so Leon thoughtfully pulled out his silver Dunhill cigarette lighter and her doodles were now clearly illuminated for everyone to properly see. As Joe turned the pad's pages, Phoebe realised that there now seemed to be some sort of strange silent communication going on between him and Leon but couldn't read what it was. What was wrong, why had they all gone so quiet? Were her sketches so bad that they were deciding how to let her down gently. She was starting to feel queasy that she'd been foolish enough to put them on the table and show them. She wished she could turn back time and shrunk back into her chair.

George was first to break the table's silence. 'Guys, this girl has been living with me for nearly two years now and I had no idea how truly talented she was until this moment.' George sounded astonished.

'I saw how talented Phoebe was when I first met her, although I knew she didn't believe it herself.' Simon now added, stretching out his hand to give Phoebe's hand a little squeeze to confirm his thoughts.

'These drawings are incredible and completely evoke the mood of the songs that Leon's just been playing.' Joe shouted as loudly as he could to make sure everyone heard exactly what he was saying, and then looked straight at Phoebe; 'Sweetie, I think you should be coming to work with me and Leon in London, especially if you can now stay at George's.'

Phoebe couldn't believe her ears or her luck, her drawings weren't dreadful after all.

'Really? Actually work for you? Oh wow, yes please!' She then turned round to George and took his hand. 'I can't ever thank you enough for everything you've done for me, you've helped me so much.' She was beyond happy.

George smiled his funny lop-sided smile that she now knew so well. 'It's been my pleasure, I love helping my friends. You can stay as long as you like in my studio, I'm not coming back to London for the moment. So, I think we should all make a toast... to Phoebe, my favourite girl and to all her dreams coming true; to Phoebe.'

Everyone raised their glasses and Phoebe just wanted to freeze-frame that moment and hold on to it for ever. It wasn't often that she enjoyed being the focus of attention, this time it meant everything to her. She was about to do what she'd always dreamed of, to be a proper bona-fide stylist.

It was hard to wake up the next morning as she had such a bad hangover, it must have been all the Vodka. She'd had vivid and continuous dreams all night long; nice dreams though about Simon, Joe and Leon, with no nightmare flashbacks. Phoebe did, however, conveniently choose to forget that she'd also done a whole gram of coke.

So what day was it today and what was she supposed to be doing? She couldn't remember as weekdays in Paris were much the same as weekends - then it came back to her - Simon was in town and she was going to meet him at the café. She needed to pull herself together quickly and look good, she knew Simon would scrutinise her, maybe too closely, he knew her too well so, maybe just one line would get her up and about? She never did coke in the mornings but this was an exceptional day and she wanted to be on her best form for him.

Simon was already waiting at the café, seated right in the front at the best people–watching spot. Of course he was, Phoebe thought to herself, he would have charmed the bad-tempered waiters and dazzled them with his extraordinary good looks to claim the table. Simon jumped up the moment he saw her, once again giving her one of his speciality bear-like brotherly hugs.

'It's so good to see you again and you do look fabulous, a très chic version of the Phoebe I knew in London. Yes, edgy, but now with Parisian chic, love this whole new look.'

Now that Phoebe could see him better in the sunlight than in the last night's nightclub gloom, she gave him a quick visual appraisal too. 'Si, how can you be even more good looking than before? It's not fair that any man can be so ridiculously handsome.' Phoebe still never tired of staring at Simon's perfect features.

He laughed it off: 'Don't be such a silly billy, I'm nothing special.'

Phoebe felt inclined to say that he actually was, when the waiter arrived and stood there expectantly, tapping his pencil impatiently on his small order pad.

'Quick, the waiters don't hang around here. If you don't order when they're here, they don't come back again for ages. What are you having?'

Simon made a snap decision. 'Coffee and croissant, I think.'

'Un café, un orange presse, un café au lait et deux croissants s'il vous plait, merci.' Phoebe had confidently taken over giving their order in perfect French to the impatient waiter.

Simon sat there silent and impressed, his mouth open with amazement. He then spoke with admiration in his voice. 'You've changed Phoebes and you're so much more confident now. Paris has done wonders for you.' Then his tone changed to one of excitement. 'I couldn't wait to tell you but I'm now a fully-fledged makeup artist. I've always practiced on myself as well as my clients, maybe that's why you think I look so good today. I've mascara on, maybe a bit of concealer and, erm,' he sounded slightly embarrassed, 'oh, maybe just a touch of bronzer too.'

'I'd never have guessed,' Phoebe smiled encouragingly at him, 'that's so brilliant that you're now a proper working makeup artist, I'm really happy for you.' She leapt up to give Simon a congratulatory hug and in doing so knocked her glass of water all over him. He screamed a high pitched girly-style shriek and everyone in the café turned round to look.

Phoebe knew she was now a deep shade of red from the blush she could feel tingling and creeping up her body and

222

face. 'I'm so sorry, I'm so clumsy and I've a bit of a hangover today too.'

'Don't worry Phoebes it's only water, I'll live. I've had worse spilt over me.' Phoebe chose not to ask. Once they'd both mopped up all the water from both themselves and the table, they resumed their catch up.

'So… tell me more about what you're now working on.' Phoebe wanted to know everything about Simon's new career.

'I'm mostly living in London but travelling abroad for loads of magazine shoots. I'm leaving Paris tomorrow, to go onto Milan for the next season's runway fashion shows.'

'I'm so happy for you, how do you ever get to see Jake though?' Phoebe was feeling worried for their relationship.

'We speak a few times a week on the phone and that's really tough with the time difference between LA and London. I've only managed to see him twice so far this year, but it'll all change when we've both got some more money.' Simon still sounded positive and upbeat about his long-distance relationship, so immediately Phoebe felt less concerned about the outcome, when she remembered the pact they'd made back in the day at the Rainbow Rooms.

'Si, when I'm a famous stylist too, we could all work in LA together. Remember our pact we made? Did you hear what Joe said to me last night at the club?' The coke that Phoebe had snorted earlier was still very active on top of the current strong coffee; so her energy levels and enthusiasm for anything she said were more noticeably upbeat than normal.

'I did and it's what you've always wanted. I've always known that you'd be successful.' Simon was an intuitive young man and felt he knew Phoebe nearly as well as he knew himself. However, he wasn't quite buying into her exuberance being completely natural. He wondered what she'd been taking to be so chatty and confident; whether it could be slimming pills, speed or cocaine. He'd never touched drugs himself, apart from an occasional joint, but he recognised when someone did. Something wasn't quite right, of that he was sure and decided to keep an eagle eye on her when she was back in London. Even though she now appeared to be okay, he understood that the past self-harming and non-eating issues she'd had were each addictions that could evolve into new ones.

Simon was no psychiatrist or psychologist but he'd learned a lot when dealing with his own issues and now had a better understanding of how everyone dealt with their own personal issues. In Phoebe's case, maybe they were now constant self-sabotaging habits to cope with whatever the horrendous secret was she'd buried deep inside her psyche.

Chapter 18. Paula. Paris, 1975

Madjid had rented a small studio apartment in the Marais district for Paula to stay safely hidden away until he decided it was safe to venture out again. He visited her daily, bringing food and necessities, often staying over with her some evenings.

Paula understood that it was never going to become a proper real life relationship, although somewhere deep down inside she wished it could become one as she really enjoyed Madjid's company, he was the first man who'd actually seemed to care for her. However, she'd always been a realist and completely understood that there was an element of a mutual business transaction in their relationship; sexual for him and financial for her. Even so, she still nursed a small flicker of hope for the fairy tale ending that he'd really fallen in love with her and would leave his wife. Paula, being a pragmatist, knew that really this was never going to happen so she made the best of the situation, telling herself that one day a new opportunity would present itself again, it always did. Anyway she didn't need a man.

Weeks passed and one evening Madjid appeared at her door with a new spring in his step and a broad smile on his face;

'I've decided that enough time has passed now to feel safe enough for us to go out on the town. I've not ever seen anything written anywhere about Pierre's death in any of the papers.'

Paula was so excited that she could finally go out and even dress up, not just in the sexy underwear Madjid had regularly bought her, but in one of the designer dresses that she'd hardly worn since her date nights with him in Paris away from Pierre's.

'Tonight Paula, we're going to make it extra special. First we're dining at Maxim's and then going on to Regine's to show you how such a beautiful woman as you should be treated by your lover.'

Paula smiled, acknowledging his compliment, privately lapping up the word lover as opposed to mistress. 'That sounds wonderful.' She knew she mustn't read too much into his words, they were often empty ones, as she knew so well from all her past tricks when they'd told her they loved her, that was what she knew men did when they were in the "moment". For Paula, actions always spoke louder than words.

Dinner at Maxim's was everything and more that Paula had imagined, in fact it was incredible, she'd never been anywhere like it in her life. Her menu hadn't any prices written on it, so she had no idea whether she was choosing the most expensive or cheapest items, although she knew for sure that even the cheapest dish cost an arm and a leg. She was so pleased that she had taken the time to watch and learn from Phoebe all those years ago on how to use the multitude of knives and forks properly, working from the outside in. She could look like she really belonged in such a smart place as this, without letting Madjid down. No-one would ever think she'd once been a hooker - or even that she still was.

They continued on to Regine's, where Paula embraced every single second she was there, from the moment she walked in, so she would be able to remember it all and re-run it again later when she was once again alone her own in bed, which was most nights. She knew that Regine's was "the" place to be seen; there were mirrors covering most of the walls, making it easy to have a really good stare discreetly without doing a full three sixty degree head-swivel.

She'd been hiding away for so long, her only access to the outside world being TV and gossip magazines, she'd become adept at recognising anyone who was anyone in the public eye; international jet set, multi-millionaires, socialites and celebrities, so she was on a roll, it was like opening one of the gossip magazines and the pages coming alive. The place was full of one famous face after another. Paula tried to look as though she was used to places like this all the time, she knew it wouldn't matter to Madjid but she was very aware that she was undoubtedly on show now to everyone else.

They were shown to a special banquette table in the VIP area where as soon as they sat down together, Madjid pointed to the corner banquette.

'Paula, see over there, that's Regine herself. I'll take you over and introduce you, she'll love you as you're so beautiful.' As they walked over to Regine, Paula could feel all eyes on her. She relished the attention, aware that it wasn't just from men but from women too. That gave her even more satisfaction as it meant she was definitely looking good.

'Bonsoir Regine, this is a model friend of mine, Paula.' Madjid introduced her, brimming over with pride that such a beautiful woman should be at his side, and also well aware that Regine was always extraordinarily discreet when she knew one of her regular guests was not with their wife. Paula hadn't realised Madjid was going to say she was a model, although she wasn't going to grumble as it sounded perfect. She greeted Regine in her best French. 'Ravi de faire votre connaissance.'

Regine acknowledged Paula's excellent French with a smile. 'I would like to hear all about you, young lady. I can hear a slight accent but you speak French beautifully, are you English? Please, come and sit here with me for a little while. Two glasses of champagne please for my friends.'

Regine clicked her fingers and the champagne arrived just like that. Paula thought this was how life should be all the time. She suddenly realised that Regine had been saying something just to her, quiet enough so Madjid couldn't quite hear. Regine was looking at her intently with her green cat-like eyes as she spoke, 'You know life is what you make it Paula, if you're in the right place at the right time.'

Paula wasn't sure exactly what Regine might be implying by this and politely waited for her to say more. There was nothing though, she'd already changed the conversation back to being all about her.

'When I was a little girl, I'd tell everybody that one day I'd have a big nightclub and rule the world. I always knew I'd be a legend. It'll be New York next for me.' She tossed back her flaming red hair and laughed. Madjid and Paula both joined in the laughter, showing their agreement that she was indeed already a legend. Paula loved this woman's self-belief, if she could only just bottle a little of it.

There had been a constant flow of famous faces coming over to their corner banquette to pay homage to their Queen bee, Regine. Paula had been watching her closely and found her intriguing. How had this woman managed to remain continuously smiling, air kissing and pouring champagne? Her own celebrity was such that the constant stream of admirers who came over to pay homage to her was never ending. Paula felt she could learn a thing or two from her on how to make everyone believe they were special. In fact the more

228

Paula considered this, she realised that both she and Regine were quite similar in how they treated their clients; Regine, her guests and Paula, her men. They both always made sure that everyone who came in contact with them felt they were special.

Meanwhile, a tiny blonde, perfectly coiffed woman dressed in head-to-toe Chanel, appeared at their table and was air-kissing Regine. This same woman was now looking at Paula with intense and obvious interest whilst she was speaking to Regine. As she stared at her, Paula could hear her ask, 'So who is this beautiful young girl sitting at your table?' Paula didn't hear Regine's answer. However, Paula couldn't understand why Madjid should suddenly have become so fidgety, looking distinctly unhappy at this chic and tiny woman's arrival. By now he'd already stood up, greeted her too and was starting to introduce her.

'Paula, this is Madame Claude.'

Paula put out her hand to shake Madame Claude's but it seemed that she wasn't quick enough. The woman simply looked at her briefly again, voicing a short and almost a throw-away comment in her direction before she glided off to chat to another table. 'Cherie, I think we could have a lot to talk about together. Please take my card and come and see me when you're ready.'

Paula had absolutely no idea who Claude could be and why she should want to meet up with her, so she picked the woman's business card up off the table and put it in her purse. She knew to never waste an opportunity, whatever it might be. Madjid was now looking even more ill-at-ease. Paula had felt the whole mood of the evening change when this woman had appeared.

Madjid put his arm protectively around her and seemed poised to leave. Paula felt as though her happy bubble had just been pricked as he spoke, 'I think it's very late now and you're getting up early for a modelling job, aren't you?' Paula wondered where that idea had suddenly come from and why he was saying this in front of Regine, letting her know why they were leaving. He then continued to speak to Regine. 'Thank you so much for your hospitality.'

It seemed Regine's attention span was minimal as she'd already acknowledged Madjid's goodbye with just a brief, almost royal hand-wave and was now organising staff to prepare her best table, number one, for some new arrivals who seemed to be on their way.

'Nous attendons que le seigneur britannique, The Earl of Dudley et ses amis arrivent. Il y aura cinq d'entre eux, y compris le rock star Leon Jaks.'

Paula understood everything she'd just said; that a British Lord was about to arrive here with an entourage of all his friends, including the rock star Leon Jaks. She would have loved to have stayed on so she could have had a really good stare, especially at Leon himself. God, he was so sexy. She would have fucked him for nothing. She briefly wondered if he was as sexy in bed as he was on stage. She'd learnt after being paid to fuck so many men, that the quietest and most unlikely men were often the best under the sheets as they had to try harder. Still, she was with Madjid and they'd had a wonderful time until now. If he wanted to leave, it was his prerogative, he was paying after all, although she still didn't understand why it had needed to end so suddenly.

Paula stood by the coat check in the entrance to the club whilst Madjid was exchanging her cloakroom ticket for her coat which it seemed they couldn't find, she thought back to her days on the Kings Road with Phoebe and all the music they'd listened to in the record shops, and all the pop star posters that Phoebe had stuck up on the walls in her bedroom. She wondered whether Phoebe had ever liked Leon, she couldn't remember if they'd ever discussed him, maybe it had been much more about Bowie then. How she still missed her friend so much.

As she stood there waiting for her coat, the queue behind her was becoming longer and the waiting crowd bigger. She knew that Madjid was always so polite and never pushed so it was going to be a while. Outside the club she could just see a stretch black limo with tinted windows pulling up outside. The doormen were rushing forward. Paula wondered if this was the group of friends arriving that Regine had just been talking about. She hoped Madjid would keep on being really slow so she could have a proper look whilst she was standing there in her prime position.

She could just see outside and beyond the red roped entrance as the driver got out to open the back doors on both sides on the car. A pointy cowboy booted foot stepped out first. Paula strained to see more. A faded pair of jeans followed the boot and then the whole person; It was Leon Jaks. Paula tried to stay cool but she was feeling just a tiny frisson of excitement down in her girly bits – she would have to imagine it was Leon when she was fucking Madjid later – she was already feeling wet with anticipation. Her night had already improved again.

As she continued to stare, she could see that next person out was an extremely good looking very tall black man, dressed all in leather. Then another tall boy, this time blonde and very pretty, followed by a flamboyantly dressed quintessentially British man, this must be the Lord, Paula

231

thought to herself, he couldn't be anything else. Paula immediately made the judgement that they must all be gay, especially as there were no girls. Oh no, maybe Leon was a closet queen. She'd all but lost interest once she'd drawn that conclusion and turned back to Madjid to finally claim and put on her coat. By the time she'd turned back to him and he'd helped her on with her coat, then given her a long lingering kiss, as though to apologise that they were leaving, the car outside had already driven on having discharged its occupants. Paula supposed that the group had been whisked quickly and invisibly in through the crowded foyer; that's what happened with big celebrities.

How many people had Regine said there were to be in the group,- hadn't she said five? Paula realised she'd only seen four, so who had been the fifth? Maybe Leon wasn't gay after all and he'd been with some stunning girl who he'd wanted to hide, so she had come out last so as not be seen with him in case they were snapped by any paparazzi. Yes, that must have been it, she was glad she had just worked that out, at least she could now still fantasise about him later.

Once again outside the red roped entrance, the doormen called them a taxi.

'Madjid, why are we leaving, it's still so busy in there and we were having such a lovely time?' Paula didn't want to make it an issue, she just wanted to know if it was something she'd done. She was sure she'd been on her best behaviour.

'I think it's for the best. We just need to talk when we get back and I'll explain about the woman who gave you her card.' Madjid still sounded distinctly unhappy.

Fate though plays cruel games. If Paula had turned around a few minutes later when she was being handed her coat and then shut her eyes kissing Madjid, she would have been able

232

to see Phoebe together with George, Simon, Leon and Joe being whisked past her by security, ready to celebrate Phoebe's last night in Paris before returning to London.

The taxi took Madjid and Paula back to the tiny studio. Once inside they sat down together. It had been one of the best nights of her life and now when she looked at Madjid, she saw only sadness in his eyes, what was he going to say, was it over? She knew she'd had feelings for him but had always repressed them. She sat patiently and waited for him to speak.

'So Paula, Madame Claude, whom you met earlier is Fernande Grudet, Madame Claude is her working name. She's one of the most successful high class Madames in the world, well-known for honing the most beautiful girls to fit her very specific criteria; she made a bee-line for you as you're her perfect kind of girl.'

Paula listened carefully, astonished. She didn't quite understand where this conversation was going, Madjid still seemed so serious and upset.

'I care for you so much, but as you know I can never give you more than we have now, and I've always been completely honest with you that I can never leave my wife. I have always wanted the best for you and Madame Claude would undoubtedly change your life for the better. I've enjoyed every single moment we've shared together and I'm so happy that I've been able to help you in my own small way. So, Paula, you must go and meet Madame Claude and listen to what she has to say to you.'

Paula felt sad now that she understood what he was saying. She'd kept her emotions in check, although suddenly it was all too much for her. She never cried, especially in front of any man, now she was unable to hold back her tears.

'Madjid, I shall miss you so much, you've been there for me all the time since we first met.'

He touched her cheek, gently wiping away her tears with his finger tip.

'You've no idea how much I shall miss you too, Paula, but sometimes when you love someone you have to let them go and spread their wings, especially when they're like a beautiful butterfly. Please stay here in this studio as long as you like until you're ready to leave. I shall continue to pay the rent, but will not come round again as I will find it too hard to bear knowing that we can no longer be together.'

Paula couldn't believe he'd just said that he loved her and yet still he had to leave her. Why did life never turn out how she imagined? She'd always pretended she didn't care, of course she really did and she'd finally let her guard down with him. Now it was time for the walls to go up again. She had to get back to being the tough old Paula; the Paula who took no prisoners and let no one touch her heart.

Paula waited a few days before she checked Madame Claude's card once again. She'd been so scared that she might lose it that she'd also committed the address to memory, 18 Rue de Marignan. It had then taken her another week to conjure up the courage to phone and make an appointment and now that she'd actually made it, she realised that she needed to present herself in the best way possible. Madame Claude had already seen her, but that was in "sexy night-time glamour" mode, now she wanted to be chic and classy. Maybe it was all about wearing one of her Designer label outfits that Madjid had bought for her during their time together. She peered into her small wardrobe wondering which outfit would work best, maybe it was the understated Chanel. She tried on the pale pink silk boucle tweed jacket and skirt and checked herself in the mirror. It seemed to do the trick, elegant and refined, hopefully channelling Jackie O. Well, it had worked okay for the First Lady, so it would have to do for her too. Now she just needed a quick touch of mascara and lipstick and she was good to go; dressed and prepared for whatever the Madame offered.

Paula went outside onto the street and hailed a passing taxi as neither her high heels nor her pencil skirt lent themselves to walking any significant distance. Madame Claude lived in one of the most expensive areas of the French capital, the sixteenth arrondissement, just off the Champs Elysees. Her apartment was situated above a branch of the Rothschild bank. Paula took a deep breath and rang the bell knowing that this meeting could change her life for ever; she had to make a good impression. She didn't know quite what to expect, but felt fairly hopeful that the interview wasn't going to involve another blow job. By location alone, she knew everything would be on a different level; classy and discreet and she'd dressed accordingly.

The Madame herself answered the door. 'Thank you for coming, Paula.'

'Thank you, Madame, for inviting me.' Paula was pulling out all the stops of politeness and best behaviour.

'Come upstairs and we'll talk. Please call me Claude, everyone does.' Standing in front of Paula was a discreet, well-dressed woman wearing classic subdued beige and grey colours and minimal makeup. This daytime version of Claude was not what she'd expected at all. Claude indicated to Paula to follow her into the lounge. 'Would you like a drink, a whisky perhaps or a cognac?'

Paula smiled and refused, shaking her head. She'd been looking around as she followed Claude and hadn't noticed a maid or any extra help there, simply Claude on her own.

Claude indicated that Paula should sit down. Once she had seen Paula was settled, she started to speak.

'Paula, when I first started, I realised that there were two things in life that people would always pay for, food and sex and I wasn't any good at cooking.' Paula laughed as she realised that Claude had meant her opening sentence to be an ice-breaker. 'So Paula, I can give you a new start in a life and a lifestyle that could be measured in diamonds, furs, jet set travel and thousands in your bank account. Does this sound like something you'd be interested in? My girls, mes jeunes filles, go on to marry money, power and status.'

Paula was already all in but tried to keep poker-faced to suggest she was still considering everything.

'I like to first do a little makeover on all my girls so they're flawless in every way. You'll have access to Saint Laurent clothes, Cartier watches, Winston jewels, Vuitton luggage and even to plastic surgeons if I feel necessary, but we never change the breasts. These must always stay au naturel. I like my girls to look just like you Paula, they're usually tall, blonde and Scandinavian looking, so you're a perfect fit. Understand this though, once you've had your makeover, you'll be in debt to me as I'll have paid all your bills to Dior, to Vuitton, to the hairdressers, to the beauty salons, the doctors and everything that's been done as part of your transformation. So you'll be working for me to pay off the debts and I'll take thirty percent of your income. Is that all understood?'

This all seemed perfect to Paula, she couldn't wait to start this new life.

'And by the way, another little rule of mine to remember is to only wear white underwear as it never looks cheap. So if you're interested, I'd like you to come back tomorrow evening to meet my close friend Jacques Quiroez. He'll be reporting back to me about you.

Paula realised that this was likely to be an upmarket version of the Benjamin scenario, with Jacques being Claude's ratings expert. She hoped he wasn't going to be old and ugly even though she'd perfected making sex into an art form over the last few years with any man – young or old, handsome or ugly. She knew she'd be able to show him what she was capable of and pass this test with flying colours. She was confident in her looks, spoke English and French, had good manners, understood etiquette and anything she didn't yet know, she was sure Claude could teach her.

'Paula, my girls are world famous and in a class of their own and now that the Arabs are in Paris, I charge my girls out at more than five hundred dollars. You'll also find that eventually, you're not just being requested for hours at a time, but for whole weekends on yachts and private jets. You'll be flown to meet these men in the Caribbean and all over the world.

This was definitely the future that Paula had envisioned. Claude looked at Paula, waiting for her answer. Paula felt she could no longer sustain her poker-face and broke into a huge smile, her eyes sparkling with excitement.

'Oui Madame, merci. Je suis d'accord à demain soir.'

As she agreed, she wondered whether she'd just made a pact with the devil, or in this case the Madame Claude, as she became her latest recruit.

Chapter 19. Phoebe. London, 1975

George and Joe were true to their word. The following week Phoebe settled herself into George's extremely comfortable Chelsea studio, wondering what her future might hold. She couldn't understand why she felt permanently exhausted as she'd spent most of the last few days sleeping. She'd not bought any coke since she'd arrived back, maybe that's what she needed now to give her some energy. It was also lonely being on her own again but she was reluctant to contact any of her old friends, so she kept reminding herself that she was about to be living her dream in order to motivate herself. She was still sitting slumped on her unmade bed when she heard the phone ringing; she wasn't expecting anyone to be calling her. When the ringing finally stopped and then restarted again, she realised that she'd actually have to answer it, moving herself lethargically from the sofa-bed across the airy studio room to the phone on the kitchen worktop.

'Hello?' she asked, wondering who on earth could be so persistent in wanting to get hold of her.

'Hey, Phoebe, how are you settling in?' Phoebe suddenly wondered how she could have forgotten that Joe would be likely to call her today. He sounded way more upbeat than she was feeling. 'I'm about to go shopping for myself and I've decided I'd like you to help me, I'll be with you in thirty minutes.'

Phoebe knew she had to pull herself together both mentally and physically before he arrived and she didn't have much time. She tried her best and there he was, exactly thirty minutes later. As they started walking down the Kings Road towards World's End, Phoebe realised that her life had done a full circle, remembering that it was there at Mr Freedom on

238

the Worlds End, where she'd bought her first cool outfit. The boutique was no longer there now; the strangest shop she'd ever seen had taken its place.

'Joe, look!' Phoebe grabbed his arm to stop him walking on as she stared at a pale pink-fronted boutique with huge bright pink letters suspended outside spelling the word Sex. A girl was leaning against the entrance of the boutique, smoking a roll-up cigarette and exuding attitude. Her peroxided blonde hair was worn swept up and her only makeup was a heavy-handed application of black eyeliner ending in a perfect flick. She stared defiantly at Phoebe and Joe, who both stared back at her and beyond into the graffiti-walled shop. Phoebe was speechless at what she was seeing, she'd obviously been in Paris for too long. She continued standing where she was, clutching Joe's arm.

'Is this the strange place where you were taking me?'

'No, this is a punk shop owned by Malcolm McLaren and Vivienne Westwood.' He explained in a matter of fact way.

'Punk?' Phoebe had no clue who or what Joe was talking about, how could she have become so out of touch with what was happening in London's fashion scene?

'I'll tell you more another time, where we're heading for is a little further on.' Joe answered, patiently realising Phoebe had been immersed in Parisian life for a little too long. She needed to get back in the groove.

Phoebe couldn't believe the transformation of this small stretch of fashion shops that had happened so quickly whilst she'd been away, London had changed so much, although maybe she had too. She followed Joe as they turned around the bend on the road, where he stopped and pointed to the boutique on his right.

'Here we are, welcome to Granny Takes A Trip.'

There in front of her was the most incredible mural painted across the whole shop front, unlike any boutique she'd ever seen before.

'Come on, we're going in, you'll love it. I often style Leon in their fabulous embroidered velvet suits. You never know, we might see some other rock stars as they all shop here; Elton, Paul, David, Marc, Rod, Eric.' The names tripped easily off his tongue.

Phoebe suddenly realised that Joe must be on first name terms with all the hugest rock stars in the world like Elton John, David Bowie and Marc Bolan and this was who she was now working with, why on earth wasn't she filled full of enthusiasm and excitement today as this was what she'd always wanted. Maybe she was coming down with a flu virus or some other lurgy that was making her feel so low and lethargic.

The atmosphere in the interior was heady and intoxicating with patchouli and incense, reminding her of the Kensington Market. She blinked as she walked in from the bright sunlight through a heavy beaded curtain into the very dark interior, an exotic mysterious space with psychedelic music playing so loudly that Phoebe felt like covering her ears, although she knew she couldn't as that would have been so uncool. Out of the darkness a disembodied voice shouted over the blaring music.

'Hey man, how are you? Who's this with you?'

'Hey, I'm with Phoebe my new assistant stylist.' Joe shouted back to the invisible man.

Oh gosh, he'd just called her his assistant stylist. Hearing this endorsement helped rays of sunlight filter through the heavy fog cloud of Phoebe's mood, she'd been promoted before she'd even done a day's work. She peered through the

240

gloom and could just make out two guys sitting at the back of the boutique who looked completely spaced out smoking joints. She hadn't realised people were now able to do drugs so openly in London.

'Groovy, man. Good to meet you Phoebe.' Gene slurred his words as he dragged on the joint. Phoebe felt slightly disorientated, she was sure she was getting stoned just by standing there, however, after her time in Paris there was little now that phased her.

Gene passed Joe the joint who then passed it on to Phoebe. 'Here you go, girl.'

She pretended to inhale and passed it back. She preferred drugs that switched her mood up rather than brought it down and she most definitely needed "up"' at the moment. It was a shame it wasn't a line that she was being offered. She squinted in the gloom to see what the clothes in there looked like; she could hardly even see Joe as he'd disappeared into the darkness. She headed to where she could just make out his teeth and the whites of his eyes.

'Hey, Joe? Look, you just have to buy these.' Phoebe had spotted some velvet high heeled men's boots with stars printed all over them. 'You could wear them with your jeans tucked in them. What do you think?'

'Love them, great choice Phoebe.' As Joe was speaking Leon walked in.

Joe hadn't mentioned anything about meeting him there and Phoebe had forgotten how good-looking he was, her heart was now beating extra fast. This place was making everything feel unreal.

'Hey guys, great to see you again too, Phoebe.' Phoebe felt faint, he still remembered her and he'd only met her twice before. 'Have you picked any outfits for me yet?'

Joe immediately sprung into work-mode.

'Marty and Jean have put some choices aside which they're going to customise especially for your tour; they'll send them when they're ready over to your hotel. By the way, isn't young Phoebe clever, she chose these boots for you, don't you love them?' Phoebe couldn't believe that she was being included and even complimented. She realised how generous it was of Joe not to take any of the credit. It made her feel as though she could burst with pleasure after having felt so incredibly low and unmotivated earlier that day. Why, she wondered, should she now be having such severe mood swings that were affecting her so badly?

'Super cool, split now - what d'ya think? How about that pub over there, The Water Rat?' Leon had taken charge.

'Sure, let's split.' As Joe followed together with Phoebe, he threw her a quick aside.

'You should come in here whenever you like. Marty and Jean will make you up little mini-skirts or customize anything you want. You never know who you'll find in here too. It's always party time.'

They emerged from the darkness into the bright sunshine. Phoebe now felt lighter in her mood too. She decided she would try and see if she could survive in London without any coke after all.

Chapter 20. Phoebe. London, 1976

Joe had promised Phoebe that he would tell her more about the weird Punk shop she'd asked about on the New Kings Road, but instead he went one step further and they were now standing inside the Roundhouse waiting to see some Punk bands. It was so hot in there that Phoebe thought she was going to actually melt, it was bad enough outside, still 30C at night and now inside the building the temperature was off the scale. A new American punk band, The Ramones, hadn't come on yet, so she and Joe still had a chance to chat before the noise became deafening.

Phoebe looked around her, she wasn't sure yet if she was really into Punk and this place was very different to all the other venues and clubs she'd been with him before; it was an old industrial train shed. She'd never been anywhere quite so dilapidated, everything was so run down; tacky, dirty and basic. Suddenly, she thought of her mother, she had no idea why. Phoebe imagined how aghast she'd be that her daughter was now standing in such a revolting place with dirty people too. The thought made Phoebe smile as she looked around at the hard core fans that were slowly arriving to support the Punk band called The Flamin' Groovies, not the Ramones.

Phoebe suddenly felt she wanted to express how much she appreciated everything Joe had done for her so far.

'Joe, it's so amazing going to see all these new bands with you, especially tonight as it's the first time the Ramones have ever played in this country. I'm so grateful for every single opportunity you've given me.' Phoebe felt emotional as she spoke from her heart. However, a line of coke always added to her heightened sensitivity and she'd already done a couple before she'd left Chelsea for Camden.

'It's a pleasure, I've seen how hard you've worked helping to style Leon. I've loved watching you grow and one day I'm sure you'll be even more successful than I've ever been and you'll deserve it; I know you still don't realise how good you are. A word of warning though, don't let success ever go to your head, it's so easy to get carried away with all this seductive rock and roll life shit, it can suck you in and spit you out. I know, I've been there myself and I've watched so many friends die from drug overdoses, way too many.' As he spoke Phoebe realised, at that moment, Joe seemed the saddest she'd ever seen him. She wondered whether he'd had a hidden agenda mentioning the drugs and paused to consider before she replied. She was now questioning if Joe had ever noticed her doing a line or two, taken simply to help her get through really some long work days. No, she definitely didn't *need* the drug and quickly jumped to make sure that was very clear.

'Joe, I'd *never* do that. Both you and George have helped so much to get me to where I am today, so I'm not intending to throw it all away. Yes, I admit I have done an occasional line or two but never when I've been working with you.' Phoebe was extremely good at fibbing convincingly, after all, she'd first started practicing when she was still at school.

Joe was now looking at her so intently that she felt he was looking right into her soul. Maybe he did knew she wasn't telling him the complete truth, but she'd already convinced herself that it really was only an occasional line here and there, limiting herself to buying a maximum of a gram a week. Yes, she still always had her tiny made-up envelope of coke with her, that was just a social thing in case anyone else wanted some and then they'd do it together, usually in the loos. No, she categorically didn't have a problem and she could definitely stop when she needed to.

Joe nodded slowly and smiled his wide and very white-teethed smile at her, 'Good girl, keep it that way.'

Maybe she would need to be a little more circumspect where and when she did her lines? Suddenly, the band was on and the crowd roaring; Phoebe was used to loud music but nothing compared to the level now. She looked around her and wondered why this audience seemed so angry and aggressive, was it the Punk effect? She moved even closer to Joe, feeling protected by his additional height and broad shoulders.

She considered the band's styling as she wasn't sure she liked their music too much. Yes, the Beatles-style suits were definitely cool and wondered what Joe was thinking. The music was too loud now to even shout over, so she reached up and poked him in the shoulder, caught his eye and mimed "move?" Waving her arms and pointing away from the stage. It did the trick as he immediately took her hand, pushing purposely through the crowds up to a deserted bar area where a few guys were standing at the bar.

'Phoebe, this is Danny Fields, the Ramones Manager, a living legend. He's worked with everyone including Jim Morrison and the Doors too.'

Phoebe was impressed, 'I love the Doors, "Light my Fire" is one of my all-time favourite songs.' They were definitely more Phoebe's thing than this whole Punk scene.

'How's everything with you mate?' Danny asked Joe.

'Great man... Phoebe and I are both real excited to see your boys play their first gig here in London town. It must be so exciting for them, I reckon there's about two thousand people downstairs.'

'Yeah, this is the first time the boys have ever played outside of the small clubs and they're shitting themselves.' Danny had no qualms of saying it how it was.

'Me too, I'm so scared of the crowd down there.' Phoebe laughed.

Joe and Phoebe went back downstairs to watch The Stranglers, leaving the Ramones still by the bar waiting their turn. When the Ramones finally came on stage, Phoebe immediately decided they were the poor man's Doors, with more aggression, although they'd all seemed so quiet, humble and unassuming upstairs.

She once again considered the band's appearance with her critical stylist's hat on. They didn't look like any other band Phoebe had ever seen; she'd expected to see three "Fonzi-style" singers but these boys were properly rock and roll, they were wearing torn jeans and biker jackets with shaggy mop-style hairstyles. All they had on the stage was a single cheap blue guitar by a stack of speakers and although they were acting tough, the singer was a skinny, spindly guy with psychedelic glasses.

She could see that the audience were now going wild over this new band. It was still hard to speak over the music but Joe was shouting right into her ear. 'Phoebe, I think this just might be a moment to remember in music biz history.' It was too loud for Phoebe to be able to reply until they were on their way back upstairs to see Danny and the boys once again after their set.

Phoebe was now fully invested into the whole Punk scene after watching this band and loving them. 'So Joe, now that you've taken me to my first Punk gig, can we go back next week to that Punk shop Sex on the New Kings Road. I'd like to see what proper Punk clothes are.'

'Sure, I'll dig that.' Joe always embraced Phoebe's suggestions of places she'd like to check out.

'Did you know we're playing Dingwall's tomorrow night?' Danny was asking Joe.

'Are you going?' Phoebe looked at Joe hopefully, she wanted to go and see them again.

'Of course and so are you, as where I go when I'm in London, so do you.'

Phoebe beamed back at him.

They arrived early at Dingwall's whilst the sound check was happening. Outside, the crowds already seemed quite scary to Phoebe, who had started to cling onto Joe as though her life depended on it. She could feel way more tension in the air than at the Roundhouse the previous day, although she wondered whether it was all swagger and part of the whole Punk attitude. She was glad though, that she had a tall man looking after her. She wondered though, if push came to shove, whether he would be more likely to be running away with her than street fighting. As a gay man, street fashion seemed to be much more his thing.

As Phoebe clung even tighter onto Joe, she wondered what the Ramones themselves thought of the Sex Pistols and the Clash, as the two British punk bands were still sitting outside the venue on the bonnets of some parked cars.

'Do you think the Ramones expected anything like this? It's a bit like two gangs in West Side Story.' Phoebe was fascinated.

'Maybe they just want to appear like they're looking for trouble.' Joe confirmed her earlier thoughts.

They finally went into the venue and the first person they bumped into was Chrissie Hynde of the Pretenders. Just like George, Joe always knew everyone and they all knew him.

Phoebe was a huge fan of Chrissie and was even more awestruck when Chrissie stayed standing together with them to watch the band from the side of the stage. Phoebe loved this feeling of proper involvement with the musicians when she was with Joe; It felt more real, like living in a foreign country rather than being a tourist.

After the gig, whilst she stood there feeling slightly shell-shocked with her ears still ringing she, together with everyone else in there, was handed a mini baseball bat. Phoebe's was a black one with The Ramones written down the side of it. She knew she would keep it forever to remind herself of her first Punk gigs, although she jokingly thought to herself that if she kept it by her bed, she could use it to protect herself if she ever had any unwanted intruder.

Phoebe realised that her opportunities to style musicians were growing rapidly over the following months. She was meeting new people all the time as she hung out and worked together with Joe, and he seemed happy with what she was doing and gave her increasingly more chances to shine and show how creative she could be when left to her own devices. The coke was helping her be chatty and confident with clients too; she felt she could conquer the world when she'd had a line or two, just like the imaginary alter ego she'd created at school.

Chapter 21. Jake. Los Angeles, 1977

Jake was just about managing to survive financially in Hollywood. He'd rented a room in a tiny apartment in West Hollywood and waiting on tables, valet parking and the odd modelling job had kept him off the streets, fed and watered while he was studying at the acting academy. He went to as many auditions as he could afford to travel to, driving there in a very beaten up old car he'd bought, as it was impossible to live in LA without a car. No one walked anywhere, unless they were hiking in the canyons - he'd had to get used to that part of LA life as he'd always walked everywhere in London.

He'd eventually realised that sooner or later he may have to be willing to do anything legal to pay his bills. He knew so many aspiring actors and actresses, who'd resorted to all sorts of lifestyle choices that he'd never have considered before coming to live in the land of dreams. Everyone knew about the proverbial 'casting couch' but turned a blind eye. Jake knew he was now down to his last few hundred dollars, with no acting jobs on the horizon and he was getting worried.

He'd just been invited to the opening of The Hollywood Century Theatre on Hollywood Boulevard, to its incarnation as a "private" theatre by two *very* friendly guys he'd recently met whilst waiting tables at a West Hollywood café. The guys had chatted to him all evening and then left him a very large tip. He'd had no idea what they both did or what their relationship was, but he did remember that the older man was called Stu and the younger called Roman. They'd both seemed fun at the time and had suggested that he should join them the next time they were having a night out. Jake rarely went out any more as he couldn't afford to, this evening would be an exception though as he couldn't stay in every night, he was sure Simon wouldn't mind, it was simply a boys' night out. He wasn't sure what a "private" theatre was when the two men had invited him along, but he'd said yes as it had sounded harmless, what could be wrong with a simple theatre club?

Stu and Roman were already waiting outside when he turned up. They were dressed identically in tight tartan cowboy shirts, zipper bomber jackets, Levi jeans and Converse trainers. Jake appreciated they were both good looking boys, not as good looking as his Simon though. No one could turn his head, he was in love with Simon.

'Hey bud. Cool that you could come along tonight.' Stu and Roman both greeted him with simultaneous kisses on either sides of his cheeks. 'Just to let you know, when we go in it's ten dollars for membership and you'll get a membership card and reduced admission each time you come back.'

Simon was confused and rubbed his designer-stubbly chin, he'd thought it would be free and he was so short of money.

'So what sort of private members club is this? Somewhere we can meet bigwig talent agents and film producers?'

The two guys laughed and both spoke at the same time, 'You're so funny Jake, we love your British humour; this probably isn't really the place that agents and talent spotters come, maybe a different sort of talent spotter than the ones you might be thinking of… do you really not know what this place is?'

Jake shook his head, running his fingers through his dark hair as he did when he was worried, was he that dumb?

This time Roman was the one to fill him in, 'It's a gay movie theatre. Hadn't you noticed the posters outside whilst you were waiting for us?'

Jake considered this for a moment. No, he actually hadn't, although now that Roman had mentioned it, he wasn't sure how he'd missed the oversized pictures of the most un-attractive vacant-looking teen stud boys looking pensively into the distance. This confirmed that he wasn't always the most observant guy and had often been told by his friends and tutors that he needed to take more notice of what was going on around him. He'd heard them say;

"Jake, observing real life makes acting easier when you can relate to what you've seen." He really had tried but his concentration was rubbish.

Stu winked at him as he continued, 'So, Jake, as it's a private club we can all do anything we want to do in the auditorium whilst the movies are playing.' Jake suddenly wondered what he'd got himself into, especially as he knew that in acting circles he had to be seen to be straight if he was ever going to be a convincing leading man. He'd been so careful until now to keep his private life private.

He hesitantly tagged behind Stu, knowing what he now knew, into the movie theatre. This place was on another level from the Sombrero, which had always seemed quite decadent back in the day when he and Simon had hung out there with the smell of poppers, dirty dancing and snogging and quickie sex in the toilets, although he'd never engaged in any naughtiness as he'd always been with Simon, and little Phoebe had been so innocent then. Suddenly he wondered what had happened to her. He knew Simon had met up with her in Paris, but no more than that. He did miss his old life in London but there was no going back now, he was going to make a name for himself here in Hollywood, whatever it took. When he did, Simon would come out to join him as they'd always agreed.

He sat unaware of anything happening around him in the darkness of the auditorium and when the movie was over, and the lights came up just a little, Jake realised that Stu and Roman had already both disappeared and he'd also managed to sit through the whole movie with no-one hitting on him. He breathed a sigh of relief and decided maybe it was time to leave again whilst the going was still good.

As he stood up ready to leave and started walking in the darkness towards what he hoped was the exit, a voice came out of the darkness. 'Hey you...'

Jake had no idea where it was coming from but it sounded as though it was coming from behind the large screen. The voice came again:

'Hey, good looking, wanna come round the back for some action? I'd make it worth your while...'

Jake hesitated. Simon was the first and only man he'd ever had a relationship with. He'd been faithful to him all through acting school even though both the girls and guys had hit on him regularly. How did he feel now that he was being propositioned with a faceless fuck? Why had the guy said he would make it worth his while? Was he talking money or just a good time. Jake's head was spinning as he weighed up the pros and cons. There'd be no emotion attached; it was just sex and he definitely still had needs which hadn't been met for a while now since the last time Simon had flown over to see him. No one would ever need to know. Any hook ups that happened here surely would never be leaked beyond these four walls, as everyone had too much to lose.

He walked tentatively round towards the back room area and tried to acclimatise his eyes to the darkness seeing what appeared to be an older guy standing silhouetted against the screen. The guy watched Jake's hesitancy and spoke again;

252

'As I said I'll make it worth your while... so how would a hundred dollars be?'

Jake immediately calculated how many bills he would be able to pay with this sudden windfall. It seemed unlikely that he would ever get to meet or recognise this man ever again and the movie had somehow stirred his sexual fantasies, he'd never have thought that it could have such an effect on him. Maybe if he shut his eyes he could imagine this bloke was Simon, or maybe he wouldn't need to as it was so dark back there.

'Okay, you've got a deal.' Jake put out his hand for the cash and the guy handed him over a fistful of notes. Simon just shoved the dollars in his jeans back pocket without looking and swigged the rest of his plastic tumbler of cheap warm wine in one gulp and shut his eyes. The man immediately grabbed him in a clinch and undid Simon flies. It was all over quickly, with no emotional connection or an exchange of names.

Jake was already regretting what he'd just done and now it was too late. Hopefully no one would ever recognise him again and he'd never properly seen the other man's face either. He felt claustrophobic in this dark place and dumbstruck at how stupid he'd been. He could have jeopardized his whole career for a hundred dollars. He needed to get as far away as possible and as quickly as he could. It all felt so sordid and tacky now. As darkness fell over the Hollywood Hills, he walked briskly back to his car resolving that he would never ever succumb to such temptations ever again.

A few weeks passed and as he woke up every morning he lay in bed thankful he'd managed to get away with his stupid one-off indiscretion and tried to wipe it from his memory, never to take any risks like that ever again. Especially as today he'd been called, out of the blue, to meet a new agent who was one of the big cheeses in Hollywood. It seemed to have been through an introduction by a friend of a friend. Maybe with this new agent's help, he might be able to hit the big time and Simon could finally come out to LA and live with him.

Jake drew up outside the Beverly Hills Hotel, feeling embarrassed that the Valet Parking attendant should have to sit in, drive and park his beaten up old car. The Valet parking guy seemed to take it in his stride as he got in to drive it away and Jake breathed a sigh of relief. He tried to control his nerves with breathing techniques learnt in his acting classes, as he made his way to the famous Polo Bar. He'd never been to the Hotel or the bar before as it was so totally out of his league, both financially and socially although he knew it was "the" place to be seen for meeting anyone who was anyone in the movie biz.

He was shown through to the bar and taken straight over to a man already sitting in a booth. Jake took another deep breath, willing his actor self to appear the most confident version he could be. His facial muscles were already aching from the fixed smile he'd put on too soon. Don Buchwald, who was sitting there in front of him, was the man with the power to change Jake's life at the click of his fingers. Jake stood there waiting for Don to say anything, even good morning but the agent just gave him a firm but cursory handshake and then waved for him to come and join him in the booth. Jake quickly realised that Don didn't do chit-chat.

'So Jake, we finally meet. I've been watching you in all the small acting jobs you've done since drama school and can see that you have talent, charisma and that women will love you.

So here's the thing - I'm offering to represent you at my new agency, Don Buchwald & Associates, where there will be five associates and myself running it and we'll have offices in Los Angeles and New York. Are you interested?'

Was he interested? Was that actually a question? Jake wondered how quickly he could sign on the dotted line, like now? He had already noticed Don's expensive dark grey Brioni suite and his DHB initials embroidered on his cuffs. Jake knew that he had to be for real to be wearing clothes like that, maybe he even had a sense of humour too, as Jake spotted unlikely purple socks just peeping out between his trousers and lace-up traditional shoes.

Jake brought his focus quickly back to Don; 'Jake, please remember what I'm about to say; Hollywood is full of baloney and the truth can be quite a disarming thing. I never lie, I like to shoot from the hip so, young man, here's what you're going to do. You're going to leave your crappy little small time agent and come to me. I'm going to get you an audition for the lead in Marcus Lean's new movie that's being cast right now, as I know they want an "unknown" and you'd be perfect. Marcus is a very good friend of mine and owes me a favour too.' Don tapped his cigar on the ashtray to get rid of the ash that had been building up as he spoke. 'Sound good so far?' Don asked.

Jake nodded, stunned, unable to speak.

'Okay, we have the outline of a deal. Before we start, I want to make sure of one important thing, that your reputation is squeaky clean. When the PR machine goes into action there can be no dirty linen to air in public or anything that the Hollywood Reporter can find on you. So let's cut to the chase, I've heard you visited the Hollywood Century Theatre the other week...'

From his euphoria a few minutes ago, Jake now felt like Don had punched him straight in the guts. How on earth could Don have known this? He was sure he'd got away with it. Was he about to lose everything that Don had just talked about before it had even been handed to him?

'Listen Jake, I don't give a flying fuck what you do in private or who you shtup, but you need to keep it quiet. If you are that way inclined then you'll need a "beard" to hide your sexual orientation and we can find enough starlets who'd kill to be on your arm. So any future gossip and trust me, you're out. I've already sorted any issues from your little visit of the other night. Now look at me closely and read my lips; *A Leading Man Cannot Be Gay*. I don't care what anyone else says, it's a fact. I'm going to make you into a big star and I want my female movie-goers to be wetting their panties over you. If you're in a gay relationship, it will have to be hidden away... like... more top secret than the whereabouts of the Holy Grail, got it?'

Jake was nodding emphatically again, he wasn't losing this chance for anything. Don had now stood up and firmly clasped Jake's shoulders making solid and sustained eye contact with him before they ended the meeting. 'Jake, we're a team now and all my team players play the game according to my rules - *capisce*?'

Jake didn't know whether to laugh or cry; Don had said he was going to make him a star – except how was he now going to be able to keep his relationship with Simon a secret? As he went outside to wait for his car, he realised that it might be just possible by next year that he'd be able to hand over a car that he'd be proud to have valet parked. He just had to shine at the audition.

By the time he'd driven home again and walked into his small apartment, pages of script were already lying all over the floor spewed out from his fax machine. He tore them off and picked them up with trembling hands. It was actually a script from "the" Marcus Lean and the part to read through and learn was for the leading man. Don had believed in him enough to give him this chance and he wouldn't let him down.

It was still early in the morning in London and late at night in Los Angeles. Jake just couldn't wait any longer to tell Simon his news, he would have to wake him up. Jake dialled with shaking fingers and waited for the phone to be picked up. It took a while and he could hear a confused and sleepy Simon fumbling with phone before he spoke.

'Si, it's me. Don't panic, nothing's wrong for me to be calling so early. You remember I said you should come out here when I finally get a proper job? Well...'

Simon was now fully awake. 'Jakey, have you finally got a movie!'

'I have and not just any movie. I've just been cast in Marcus Lean's latest movie.'

Jake could hear Simon squealing at the other end of the transatlantic call. 'And wait for it... Si, I'm not just in a movie, I'm the lead!'

Simon was really screaming now and Jake could imagine he might even be jumping up and down on the bed. Jake held the phone further from his ear and Simon's exuberant screams.

Simon stopped screaming for a minute to speak normally, although he did now sound out of breath. 'I knew you'd get that break, so happy for you. I'll come out as soon as you've finished filming.'

Jake paused for a minute as he decided how he was going to phrase his next part of the news. 'So... that was my good news, there's some bad too though, my new hot shot agent has told me that under no circumstances can I be known to be queer. I can only ever be seen out with actresses, starlets, models, anyone, as long as they're female. My cover can't ever be blown so if you come out, we'll have to meet secretly.'

There was a long silence, filled with everything that both Jake and Simon didn't want to say. Things were better now in the seventies than they'd been for, say, Oscar Wilde, but there was still such a long way to go for acceptance. They both however understood the rules. Simon spoke first, 'Don't worry, I'll do whatever it takes to not blow your cover.'

Chapter 22. Phoebe, London, 1977

Working together with Joe was presenting Phoebe with amazing opportunities and meeting rock star royalty. She was aware that all good things had to come to an end and soon it would be time for her to venture out on her own, however the time came sooner than she was expecting.

'Hey, Phoebe, I'm returning to LA next week with Leon and I'm going to hand you over your first client before I go. You're going to be working together with Gerard Storm the designer. He dresses this singer and coordinates all of his looks and any of the models appearing with him in his video. I'll be at the end of the phone if you need any help.' Phoebe was reassured by the tone of his voice that Joe sounded confident she could pull this off successfully.

'Who's the client, Joe, you haven't said!' Phoebe realised he hadn't divulged the most important bit of information.

'Sorry,' Joe laughed as he apologised, 'it's Morgan Wells.

Phoebe couldn't believe her luck. Her first proper solo styling job was with "the" Morgan Wells. He was in the same league as Bowie -this was the big time. Wow, this was her moment to show exactly what she was made of. She was buzzing with excitement at the anticipation of such a huge job and not for one moment did she doubt that she could do it. Her professional confidence had grown incrementally over the months of working together with Joe, unlike her self-confidence and self-esteem which was still at rock bottom.

'Morgan's requested Simon to do all the makeup as he saw all the amazing high-fashion make-up looks Simon has recently created for the catwalk shows. So you'll be in the company of friends and don't panic, Morgan won't bite, he's actually quite shy. Gerard is lovely too but a little theatrical in his moods so you may need to tread more carefully with him. He's also very protective of Morgan whom he has collaborated with since their art college days together.'

Phoebe tried to process everything Joe had just told her. 'I'll do my absolute best for you Joe and… thank you so much for believing in me enough to give me this chance.'

'Phoebe, you just need to believe in yourself, you're super-talented, which is why I've given you this opportunity. Don't fuck up… or fuck him, as every other girl usually tries to.' Joe was once again giving her one of his warnings and she knew when he did, he should be taken seriously.

'Don't worry, I won't.' Phoebe didn't bother to add that any thoughts of sex were pretty low on her personal agenda nowadays, to the point of non-existent.

Still, Joe was determined to drive his point home. 'He's super charming and may try to charm you into bed, especially as you're just his type, he likes curvy petite girls. And no drugs either please, so you can keep a cool head; Simon will be my eyes and ears.'

Phoebe smiled, Joe was sounding like Big Brother now.

'It'll all be okay Joe, I won't let you down.' Phoebe meant it as she said it. She finally felt that she'd got her life under control, managing to compartmentalise the two sides of her life; work and personal, with the personal side having been shut down ages ago. It was a system that worked for her. Her internal dialogue and coping mechanism of feeling that she'd been responsible for being raped had shut off any desire for intimacy with anyone. The thought of sex filled her with horror. She didn't even know if she'd ever want to sleep with a man again, although she was sure all men couldn't be the same; she just didn't want to risk it. She'd discovered how much fun she could have with her gay men friends, first with

Simon and Jake in London and then with George in Paris. Working hard with Joe had also stopped her thoughts returning to that dark place she didn't want to go to. Cocaine was her other crutch, with a line or two she could conquer and climb any mountain she faced. What Phoebe didn't understand though, was that in suppressing all her feelings in this way, it would just take one person to unlock them and then the floodgates would open.

She arrived early to prep the Morgan Wells video shoot. Everyone involved was going to be there to discuss and coordinate the required "looks"; the video director, the producer, Simon on makeup and hair and of course Morgan and Gerard. She'd never been so nervous, it was ten times worse than her eleven year old self's first day back to school. She hadn't had a chance to speak properly to Simon again since she'd last seen him in Paris, as he'd been away working so much and had become such a big star in his own right now.

She'd made a huge effort with how she looked that day, scrutinising herself in the mirror just as she used to when she was a child. She preferred not to look in the mirror too often, as she didn't much like the reflection of the young woman she now saw. It wasn't simply her appearance, she quite liked her new slimmer body and her hair as it was now back to the long pre-Raphaelite curls which she regularly coloured with henna to a deeper red. It wasn't what she wore either, as she knew that she could always style herself the best way possible; living in Paris with Bettina's influence and then working with Joe had taught her that. It was how she still felt inside when she looked at her reflection. It was the buried feelings that she couldn't always keep suppressed, the same feelings which caused her to constantly question her judgement and even her sanity. She still blamed herself for being raped and that she was "dirty" or "damaged", with strangers judging her if they knew. So she kept herself constantly busy working, so she could shut out any resurfacing bad memories. What she didn't realise was that the alcohol and drugs that she was self-medicating with were emotionally numbing, making her depressed. In fact she had created a vicious circle that somehow would need to be broken, but this was not the time to think about all that. This was the biggest break of her career to date and she needed to put on her happy face, ready to face the world.

Simon was first to arrive. He instantly put down all his makeup kit at the door of the studio the moment he saw her and rushed over to hug her in a fiercely protective embrace.

'Phoebes, you look wonderful, better than in Paris. You look so pretty and you've got a little of your curves back.' He looked overjoyed to see her looking so healthy again and went on hugging her so tightly that Phoebe nearly felt all her air was about to be squeezed out of her lungs. 'I'm so happy that Joe's given you the chance to work on this video, I hope we can now work together much more.'

'I'd really love that Si, though I need to get through today as I'm so very nervous now. Will you tell me if you see me doing anything really wrong? I hear that Gerard can be quite scary and doesn't take any prisoners.' Phoebe was beginning to panic as she spoke her fears out loud.

'Phoebes, he's a pussycat and just wait till you meet Morgan, you'll die and go to heaven as he's so good looking.' Simon's blue eyes were twinkling as he endorsed Morgan's looks. He knew when a good looking man was a die-hard straight one and Morgan was definitely one of those, however, there was nothing wrong with admiring from afar, or close up in his case as a makeup artist.

'Wow, if you think he's good looking then he really must be.' Phoebe was now even more nervous to meet Morgan.

Simon and Phoebe both went off to organise their work station spaces and their kits, and then made themselves coffees and went to sit in the reception area of the studio to wait for the others. Suddenly, everyone appeared at the same time and Phoebe's eyes were instantly drawn to Morgan, he was one of those men you saw that made everyone else disappear into the background. Simon, as always, was right, Morgan was indeed astonishingly good looking but his looks created absolutely no internal flutters for Phoebe as she still felt dead inside. Now that Simon was going to be around and back in her life, could she bring herself to finally tell him the truth of what had happened? Keeping this secret over all the years was taking a toll on both her mental and physical well-being. She wondered if Simon would be supportive, empathetic or judgemental if he knew everything, she just didn't know, so she pushed away the thought as she scanned Morgan quickly from top to toe. She'd learnt to do this to assess her clients' style, then she could make a quick judgement on what look she'd give them to nail down the brief.

Morgan was tall, over six feet, blessed with an abundance of the thickest jet black hair. He constantly ran his fingers through it sweeping it back before it immediately fell forward again, it was his trademark look. Phoebe wondered if he knew how sexy his actions were, they reminded her how Paula had exhibited the same affectation of sweeping back her hair. Phoebe had understood that for Paula, this had been from shyness, so maybe Morgan's was too, she'd have to get to know him better.

Phoebe suddenly realised that she was still staring and broke her gaze. Morgan had already noticed and gave her a wink; she blushed, how embarrassing, she hadn't done that for a long time. She felt herself burning up and kept looking down at her cowboy boot clad feet as though they'd become the most interesting things in the world to her.

The promo director kicked off the meeting by showing the storyboard to the small group, detailing his vision with a series of cartoon-like pencil drawings in boxes. Phoebe watched completely captivated as he talked them through the story as he'd planned it; then handing over to Gerard to discuss costume ideas and on to Simon for makeup and hair.

Then it was Phoebe's turn. She wondered whether she was going to be able to carry this off as she stood up and felt all eyes on her, Simon willing her on. A few short years ago, she knew she would rather have died than stand up and give her creative thoughts to a small group of people she didn't know. Now she was not only going to do it but also show them what she was made of. She hadn't even had any coke today.

Phoebe had listened carefully to what everyone had been saying and could now see clearly what she needed to do to style up all the looks. She'd been busy sketching whilst everyone had been talking. Once she'd stood up, she paused, looked around and took a deep breath before she spoke. She explained each of her fashion sketches one by one, clearly and fluently illustrating her ideas. She was so focused and enthusiastic in her delivery that when she'd finally stopped she hadn't realised everyone was clapping her. Simon was beaming, mouthing 'well done.'

There was silence before Morgan finally spoke. His voice was soft and mellifluous with a distinctive Welsh lilt;

everything about him oozed sex appeal and Phoebe wondered if he knew the effect he had. She looked at Simon and he was transfixed too. Morgan looked round at the small group, acknowledging everyone who was working with him.

'Thank you all for today. I'm really looking forward to working with you on my new video, and I know that I couldn't be in better hands. I've known both David our director and Peter our producer and everyone here from my record label for a quite a few years now and I've recently worked with Simon, so I know how brilliant he is and Phoebe, both Gerard and I loved what you'd just suggested... well done you.'

Phoebe blushed for the second time that day, she could once again feel herself burning from the tips of her fingers to the top of her head, although she was actually bursting with pride at his words. Maybe she really could be a stylist to the stars one day. This was just the beginning.

Phoebe was finally having a well-deserved Saturday morning lie-in before the filming started on the Monday. She just didn't feel like answering the phone at all today, even though it had now rung three times. She reasoned whoever wanted her badly enough would try again, she was sure it wasn't a work call, so it was probably someone looking for George. She still felt slightly strange living in George's flat now she was back in London instead of returning home. Living there gave her a different life from before, one that was independent and away from all possible memory triggers- although she did miss Mrs Abbott and knew she owed it to her to call her and let her know she was okay. Phoebe felt bad that she hadn't got around to doing so yet; she'd definitely call her over the weekend.

However, she had absolutely no regrets about not contacting her parents as she'd realised, a long time ago, that they really didn't care about her like Mrs Abbott did. She sighed, why was that phone still ringing? Whoever it was, they clearly weren't giving up, maybe she'd have to answer it after all. She'd managed to move the phone from across the studio room to beside her bed since she'd arrived at the studio, so she could work from her bed some days. She stretched over and picked up the receiver.

'Who's speaking, please?'

'Bea… finally, thought you were never going to pick up. It's me, Caroline. George gave me your number since you didn't tell me you'd left Paris and you're now back in London, you naughty thing. How am I ever supposed to give you all my gossip and hear yours too if I don't know where you are? Remember, I'm stuck in the middle of Gloucestershire countryside up to my knees in horse muck and hay.'

Phoebe laughed as she could hear her friend's frustration; 'Hi Caro, I'm so sorry, life just took over. I've been working so hard and, you won't believe it - no try and guess first - who do you think I've been styling at the moment?'

'No idea at all! Go on, tell then.' Caroline wanted to hear straight away, she only had a window of opportunity to chat, as the horses were still waiting to be mucked out, the dogs to be walked and a husband to feed, in that order.

'Morgan Wells.' Phoebe savoured the sound of his name as she announced her news.

'Gosh, Bea, even I know who Morgan Wells is and I know more about horses than pop stars! He's really famous and gorgeous too. You lucky girl, you've hit the big time.'

'Not quite yet. I'm getting there slowly. I'm also working with Simon, so that makes it doubly fab.'

Caroline could hear how happy Phoebe sounded and was thrilled for her. 'That's fantastic. I always knew you and Simon were going to succeed at whatever you both decided to do, all I succeeded in was marrying the man I wanted but hey, I suppose all I ever really wanted to do, was live in the country with Charlie and have loads of horses and dogs and eventually a couple of kids... umm, so... would you like to hear my news?'

'Always.' Phoebe loved Caro like the sister she'd never had.

'Well, I'm preggers and... it's twins.'

Phoebe shouted with pleasure down the phone, 'Ohmygosh! I'm so thrilled for you both, that's so brilliant. When are they due?'

Well, I'm four months pregnant and couldn't understand why I was already looking so huge, so now I know and would you believe Charlie hadn't ever told me there were twins in his family? Suppose it gets it all over with as soon as possible though, doesn't it? I look like a beached whale.'

'Oh, I'm sure you don't, 'Phoebe was laughing, she could totally imagine Caroline standing there now looking down at her growing tummy; 'I'll see if I can find any fab maternity dresses on my travels, then you can wow all the county-set women.'

'That's so sweet, it's so hard to find anything that's half decent here in the middle of the Gloucestershire countryside, apart from a good Barbour jacket and wellies that is.'

'Well, I'll definitely find you some sexy dresses that don't look like tents, ones that'll get those Gloucestershire women chattering.'

'That'll be fun, always good to cause a bit of a stir at my bridge evenings.' Caroline was now giggling madly down the line, 'love you loads, Bea, and so miss not seeing you. Now before I forget what I was really calling about, do you remember that I once asked if you'd like to be god mummy? Well, Charlie and I would be thrilled if you'd like to be the god mummy to these twins.'

Phoebe gulped as tears pricked her eyes, 'Oh, I'd love to, I'd be honoured.'

'Brilliant! So please don't now disappear on us again or we'll have to come up with a way of keeping track of you.'

'Don't worry, I promise I'll call you once a week from now on and I'm in London for a while now. Please do try to come down soon so we can have a proper chin wag.'

'I'll try really hard, miss you.' Caroline made lots of kiss noises down the phone.

'Miss you more.' Phoebe responded, sending back a whole lot of kissing sounds too, Phoebe's close friendship group was becoming more and more important to her and she cherished every moment that she could see or speak to them. She'd spent so much of her childhood alone and now she knew she had a few real friends who'd always have her back, just as she would always have theirs. She did, however, wish that she could find Paula again one day.

Monday's shoot day had finally arrived. Phoebe had been on magazine shoots and videos before as Joe's assistant but this was the first time she'd ever been in charge. She'd turned up so early on set, that she was there before most of the crew and began to slowly and methodically set herself up in the wardrobe room. She systematically hung up each of the model's outfits on the rails, named, with all its accessories grouped together. On another rail on the other side of the room, she hung all of Morgan's suits and jackets that Gerard had designed for him. Now that she'd got to know Gerard better, she appreciated how clever and talented he was and how brilliant a professional relationship he had with Morgan, she wanted to have that too.

'Morning,' Simon greeted her breezily as he walked into the wardrobe room and gave her a huge morning hug. Phoebe always enjoyed the feeling of his arms round her, she felt safe and loved with him and now it brought up only happy memories. 'How are you today? I'm all set up in the makeup room next door, are you all good to go as well?'

Yup, I'm all ready and set up too.' Phoebe hoped her nervousness wasn't showing in her voice.

'You'll be fine, Phoebes. I know you. Actually, you won't just be fine, you'll be brilliant.' Simon hoped his positive words would help Phoebe's very obvious nerves.

Morgan's sudden appearance at the wardrobe room door stopped their chat. They both stared at him. They were always both blown away by his charismatic presence that immediately filled the room.

'Don't mind me both of you, I just came to say hi, ignore me and consider me part of the furniture.' Morgan smiled his enigmatic smile as he teased them before he turned round and walked off to his own dressing room. They all fell about laughing, he so clearly was anything but part of the furniture.

The models were now all turning up, one by one. Phoebe set to work dressing them and she breathed a sigh of relief as everything fitted perfectly. Gerard appeared briefly too, checking the fit of all Morgan's suits and giving them the thumbs up. Everything was finally under control.

By eight thirty that evening the last shot of the day was over. Simon had returned to his makeup room to clean his brushes and tidy everything away and Phoebe was suddenly alone with Morgan whilst she was sorting and hanging the costumes in her wardrobe room. She really didn't understand why she should feel so hot and bothered each time Morgan was in the room, she wasn't interested in men or in sex and then, of course, Joe had warned her off. Morgan was changing out of his final suit and so the door was shut affording him some privacy.

'Morgan, here, let me take your jacket and trousers from you so I can hang them up again for you.' Phoebe was trying very hard to not look directly at him as he was undressing. She felt so awkward.

'No problem, sweetie, here you are.'

She realised that taking his suit from him would require her to move closer. She had the feeling that if she did, it would be like being sucked into a vortex where she'd have no control over her actions, so she stood as far away as she could. As he handed her the suit, he brushed her hand and she felt a frisson of electricity between them and jumped at the shock. She hoped he hadn't noticed.

Maybe he had, as he immediately reacted with an invitation, 'Phoebe, come for a drink with me after the shoot later.'

Phoebe looked up at him. Everyone was always so much taller than her five foot two, especially when she only ever wore flat shoes when she was working so she could move around the set quietly and quickly.

She wondered what she should say as she needed to be super-tactful if she were to turn him down; 'Morgan I'd love to, but is that a good idea as we're working together? You know what they say; never mix business and pleasure.' She smiled both with her eyes and her voice, so that her rejection could be laughed off.

'Sweetie, the shoot's finished now and you did a wonderful job. I just want to say thank you with a drink, that's all. Maybe tomorrow evening's better? My driver will pick you up at seven and we'll go for cocktails.'

Phoebe realised he wasn't going to give up and what girl wouldn't be flattered by his invitation and it was only a drink, so she conceded, 'Morgan, thank you, I'd love to.'

It was extremely rare for Phoebe to ever have a fashion crisis. Now that she was getting ready to meet Morgan for a drink, she was having a serious one; she'd wanted to look as though she'd thrown together a stylish but casual outfit without looking too contrived. She scanned her wardrobe and it just didn't help that she didn't know where they were going. She finally decided on platform shoes to give herself some height, silky wide-legged trousers and a boob tube. Her boobs had shrunk enough with her weight loss to comfortably wear such a top. She lined her eyes with kohl and ran her fingers through her thick curls. She checked herself in the mirror, leaving all the discarded reject outfits still all over the floor. Yes, this final choice would have to now do as she'd run out of time, it was one of those do or die moments.

Morgan's driver was waiting outside as Phoebe rushed out, slamming the door behind her, hoping she didn't already have sweaty pits from her sartorial panic. The driver got out to open the back door of the Mercedes saloon for her to climb in and there was Morgan larger than life, sitting on the back seat hidden from the street by the car's tinted windows.

'Good evening pretty girl,' he smiled warmly at her and as he did, his eyes crinkled a little at the sides, causing Phoebe once again to feel some butterflies fluttering around in her tummy and knew she was starting to blush. She tried to calm her breathing; she'd never been called a pretty girl before. Morgan decided as he greeted her that she seemed so sweet and unspoilt, the very opposite of all the girls who constantly hit on him. He gave his driver directions, 'Trader Vic's please.' Phoebe had never been there but she'd heard all about the tropical rum-based Mai Tai cocktails served in huge sharing glasses.

There was no traffic that evening and they arrived quickly at the Hilton Hotel, immediately walking straight down the sweeping curved staircase to the basement and Trader Vic's, the Polynesian style Tiki bar where Phoebe felt they'd time-travelled from Chelsea to the Tropics. She loved the way this bar had been so cleverly styled and decorated with all the amazing bamboo, palms and carvings, creating the impression of a tropical oasis. Someone whom she assumed to be the manager rushed over to shake Morgan's hand.

'Good evening, Mr Wells, it's a pleasure to see you and of course, this lovely young lady.' Phoebe greeted the manager too with one of her confident and biggest smiles, no longer reluctant to show off her once-crowded childhood teeth. 'Your table is over here, it's a nice quiet table where you can be a little more private, we don't want autograph hunters coming over to bother you all the evening do we.'

'Always appreciated, thank you.' Morgan smiled and shook the manager's hand to express his gratitude. Phoebe always noticed how polite and unassuming Morgan was and she was beginning to relax in his company and enjoy herself. She was even enjoying the jealous glances she was getting from all the women who'd seen them come in.

The largest cocktail she'd ever seen arrived with rainbow-coloured tropical umbrellas and fruits on sticks poking out of it. Phoebe's jaw dropped.

'Don't worry it's not all for you, it's a sharing cocktail, sweetie.' Morgan chuckled as he'd noticed her look of astonishment. Phoebe now realised they would have to lean together to share the drink and this felt so awkward as it would be the first time she'd been up so close to any man since the night of the ball. She wasn't yet sure how she was feeling about it, maybe she'd have to drink quickly to calm her nerves or if she went to the ladies for a quick line of coke that might help. She still always carried her trusty little white packet in her handbag as her safety blanket. She decided that the coke would be the way forward.

'Will you excuse me while I quickly to go to the ladies.'

The few sips so far of the rum-based cocktail on an empty stomach and now the line of coke gave Phoebe a heady rush. Maybe she'd be able to cope better with these new feelings that the evening was throwing up. She knew Morgan had said it was just a friend date, but deep down she knew it wasn't and she was dealing with mixed emotions of fear and attraction. She returned from the loos and Morgan, ever the gentleman, stood up and pulled her chair out for her to sit down. Phoebe loved a man who acted like a gentleman. Perhaps some of her mother's values had rubbed off on her.

Morgan was hard to talk to as he was so shy. She felt she had to drive the conversation herself, but now she'd had a line of coke it was easier. She looked around again and realised that even though they were on a reasonably private table, most people were now staring at them - so this is what it was like to be super-famous. She wasn't sure she entirely liked it. Morgan too had noticed the attention they were now receiving. 'Sorry sweetie, but we just can't sit here any longer, our every movement is being scrutinised. I'd prefer to go somewhere a little more private.' Morgan was looking upset as he spoke and Phoebe realised that this obviously happened often.

'Of course, I completely understand, it's hard when you know all eyes are on you.' Phoebe hoped she sounded empathetic.

Morgan quickly paid the bill and they got up to leave. Just as they were about to walk up the entrance staircase, a beautiful blonde woman came down the stairs all on her own.

Phoebe and Morgan stopped in their tracks. The woman was so incredibly beautiful in an old-school style Hollywood glamorous way. Phoebe was awestruck. It seemed that so was Morgan. He kept on staring at the woman's back as she swept past them down the stairs. The woman seemed oblivious of anyone standing there as she neither turned her head to the left or right as she made her regal journey down to the bar. Phoebe wondered who she was. She'd never seen anyone so gorgeous, even the models she regularly styled. There was something different about her, not just the fact she was so tall. The woman left a waft of perfume in the air behind her. Phoebe recognised it, it was her favourite, the same one that she now wore, Opium by Yves Saint Laurent. It was the latest perfume to be launched and she'd never met anyone else yet who used it. Both she and the beautiful stranger obviously had the same good taste.

Morgan's driver was waiting for them outside.

'My apartment please, Frank.'

'Straight away, sir.'

Phoebe realised that Morgan was now holding her hand. How had that happened? Well, it was only a friendly hand hold, she needn't worry. Frank dropped them off behind Piccadilly in Burlington Gardens. Phoebe was now feeling confused about everything, not only was she actually enjoying him holding her hand but she also couldn't see anywhere that looked anything like a house or apartment building.

'We're here.' Morgan waited for Phoebe leading her towards a black door sandwiched between two shops. It was the least auspicious entrance Phoebe had ever seen, virtually invisible, where on earth was he taking her? She followed him into the building and then into his apartment, where she was struck by the high ceiling and old fashioned wood panelling, it seemed very much a bachelor pad, maybe somewhere an elderly university or college professor could have once lived.

'I can see you wondering about my apartment, you have that sort of look on your face.' Morgan seemed to be overly perceptive and immediately Phoebe wished her facial expressions wouldn't show so obviously what she was thinking.

Morgan had already launched enthusiastically into a quick potted history about his apartment building, pacing up and down his room like a tour guide as he spoke. 'The building was built in the eighteenth century, originally as a three storey mansion for Viscount Melbourne, then in the nineteenth century turned into sixty-nine bachelor apartments all accessed off common staircases without doors. The criteria to live here was that you had to be a single man over the age of fourteen, no families or children, so it works for me still.'

Phoebe was half listening as she considered what might happen next, did she want to be held in his arms and kissed if she now hated men. How could she be considering any sexual contact with Morgan, however famous and good looking he was? He was just another man, the same as all the rest.

'You don't have to stay at the door Phoebe you can come in, I'm not going to bite.' His eyes were twinkling once again as he smiled at her. She hadn't realised that she still hadn't moved from the threshold. 'Why don't you sit down on the sofa and I'll open a bottle.'

She obediently sat down, still with inner conflict bubbling and waited for him while he made himself busy sorting out drinks. He poured two glasses of champagne, offering her one and then tipped a small pile of cocaine onto the coffee table and chopped it with a credit card into four lines. 'Fancy some of this? If so, ladies first.' He handed her a rolled-up fifty pound note.

Phoebe's earlier line from in the bar was already wearing off and she was now back in familiar territory. Maybe it would get rid of the nerves that were slowly and relentlessly building again. Morgan was extremely close to her now and she could feel his breath on her neck. Everyone had warned her off, both Simon and Joe, she should listen to them and before the alcohol and coke could make her do anything she might regret.

She needed to say something, she tried to resist the magnetism of his eyes and kept looking down as she spoke, 'Morgan, maybe this isn't a good idea and I do love styling you, shouldn't we just stay friends?' She knew she'd be lost if she looked up now.

'Phoebe, of course we can still work together and I loved what you did together with Gerard, me and Simon for the video. We're already friends but maybe we could now be special friends...' Morgan didn't wait for her answer and dived in for a kiss. Phoebe was unprepared and tried to quickly swerve further away on the sofa. She gulped at her champagne, attempting to block out the painful emerging memories that had created her mind-body disconnect over the past few years.

'Really Morgan, I think it best if I go home now.' Phoebe now looked back him apologetically whilst he stared at her with surprise written all over his face. No one *ever* turned him down and this hot but innocent little red-haired chick was actually saying no. He agreed with her not wanting to sound too bothered as he agreed with her, 'Sure, if that's what you want.'

'Thanks Morgan. Sorry, I think it's for the best.' Phoebe spoke hesitantly and knew she didn't sound absolutely convinced as half of her still wanted to kiss him and more. Morgan leant over to gently attempt to kiss her once again and in doing so accidentally brushed her boob. Since that produced no adverse reaction, he pulled down her boob tube and cupped her breast. Still with no rebuttals, he hooked his fingers around her jeans' waist band and started to slide them down taking her panties down too.

Phoebe knew what was happening but somehow had managed to detach herself. She wondered how many other girls would dream to be in her shoes, although those girls hadn't been raped. Waves of panic and nausea suddenly washed over her as she heard Morgan softly saying, 'God, you're sexy Phoebe, such great tits.' Those few words were the trigger, the exact same words Giles had uttered before he'd raped her. Panic exploded within her: making it hard to breathe. She curled herself up into a foetal position, crying and shaking uncontrollably.

Morgan stared at her in alarm, he had no idea what had suddenly happened.

'Phoebe, what's the matter, what did I say, what did I do, what's the matter? I thought we both were on the same page, please talk to me?' He put his arms around her and gently rocked her like a baby. Phoebe let him, she couldn't speak. It was the first time she'd wanted to have sex with anyone, she'd suppressed her feelings for so many years that it had only taken one person to touch her and to trigger and resurrect the trauma memory which had turned into a panic attack and oh, why did it have to be with Morgan? She sobbed into his shoulder. Morgan gently stroked her back,

'There, it's okay,' he murmured sympathetically but not really understanding what had just happened, 'It's okay.'

Only when her sobs began to subside could she manage to get any words out. 'I was raped when I was seventeen, you're the first man I've let get near me since then. I just couldn't do it, when you leant over me to kiss me and touch me, all I could see was his face, not yours and all I wanted to see was yours. I've never told anybody this before, please don't tell anyone, especially Simon or Joe.'

Morgan was unsure what to say and wanted to say the right thing. He decided that maybe less was more. He was a playboy and rock star, he was a kind man and had no need to ever force himself on any girl.

'Phoebe, I'm so sorry, I would never have even suggested or brought you back to my apartment if I'd known. If you like you can stay the night and we simply cuddle, or I can call Frank and he can take you home now, if that's what you'd like to do, then promise you'll call me when you get home to let me know you're okay.'

Phoebe's sobs were gradually subsiding as Morgan held her. 'I'm so sorry, Morgan.'

She gulped down her sobs again feeling that she'd spent all the evening apologising to him and also embarrassed herself as well. Even worse, she knew some girls still managed to look pretty when they cried and she definitely wasn't one of them.

'Sweetie it's fine, friends first, maybe another time it'll be different. Come on, it's late, I'm calling Frank.' Morgan spoke gently but decisively and accompanied the still-dishevelled and tear-stained Phoebe to his chauffeured car outside where he hugged her tightly, kissing her gently on the lips. If anyone could have seen them together in the street at that moment they would have jumped to the wrong conclusion.

An opportunistic paparazzi photographer who just happened to be walking by on his way to pap celebrities that might be arriving later at Tramp night club, spotted Morgan with Phoebe across the road from him and immediately started snapping away. His camera was always ready and this photo was worth big bucks.

Chapter 23. Paula. St Tropez, 1977

'Paula, your next client is Prince Abdul, he will be sending his private jet for you to stay with him at the Dorchester Hotel and your fee for the weekend will be ten thousand dollars.' Paula tried not to let her sharp intake of breath be heard down the phone line, as she reeled from the shock of hearing how much money she was earning just to lie on her back and please a man. She had already adapted her mind set to living this new jet set life of luxury and travel by private jet. Most of her super-wealthy clients had the universal attitude that money could buy anybody and anything, so she was always prepared for their demands, however extraordinary, as they'd always be paying top dollar for the privilege of having sex with her. Madame Claude was fully aware of the value of each her girls.

She was already packed, ready to leave for London as she'd learnt to keep her Louis Vuitton carry-on bag permanently on stand-by with her travel essentials and beauty products. She'd found travelling with a small suitcase of clothes easiest as her punters usually liked to take her shopping, gifting her designer clothes, jewels, bags, furs and even underwear - although she always liked to have a selection of her own expensive sexy lingerie favourites with her.

'Has the Prince put in any special requests?' Forewarned was forearmed and Paula aimed to be as prepared and as professional as possible, it was a job after all and to stay at the top of her game required an element of preparation.

'No Cherie, just look beautiful and classy, he expects the best, money no object. He's in Europe for the summer and *fully* intends to enjoy himself.' Claude put emphasis on the fully as she always liked to give her girls a little insight into what could be expected from their next client.

The Prince's jet from Paris to London connected like clockwork with his limo, and Paula found herself standing with five minutes to spare, waiting in front of the Hotel's exclusive jewellery shop peering in past her own reflection at the dazzlingly beautiful diamonds sparkling away in the display window. She mused which pieces of bling she would most like to own. As she stood there considering the possibilities amongst the millions of pounds of jewellery in front of her, she did a quick three sixty scan of the hotel foyer to see if she could spot any other top class hookers. It didn't matter how chic or classy they were, she knew she could always sniff them out. She didn't believe that anyone could now rumble her though, she was now savvy and sophisticated, the epitome of glamour and class.

She wished Phoebe could see her now. She wasn't sure that Phoebe would be too impressed by how she actually earned her money, although she was sure that she'd be impressed by how she now behaved and carried herself. She still missed her so much, she missed their girly chats and silly jokes as she no longer had that with anyone; her life now was all about faking it.

'Paula?'

She turned round to find herself facing an extremely handsome man who looked a similar age to herself. He was exactly the same height as her, so she was now looking straight into his deep-set dark eyes, thick but tidy eyebrows, a Roman nose and generous lips. Paula immediately shone her most winning smile at him and swept her thick newly highlighted blonde hair back off her face, just as she'd always done since her teens. He smiled a gleaming white-teethed smile back at her and his dark eyes twinkled. She knew undoubtedly she was going to enjoy herself here. Claude had definitely underplayed how good-looking this Arab prince was who was now standing in front of her, the weekend was looking exceedingly promising already.

'Paula, thank you for coming over to London. I hope everything was satisfactory on your journey here and you were well looked after.'

Paula was surprised at how proper and British, Prince Abdul sounded. She'd forgotten that Claude had mentioned that he'd been educated at Eton.

'Yes, thank you, everyone couldn't have been more helpful.' She couldn't decide whether she should have called his cabin crew and drivers "staff" or not, so she left it as "everyone". She'd learnt when in doubt it was best to be vague.

'Come, we'll go straight up to my suite. Your suitcase is already up there. I'm sure you'd like to freshen up after your journey.' Paula followed alongside Abdul, quickly realising their weekend was going to be "plus two", his burly minders who were now following a few steps behind them. She acknowledged them quickly and then proceeded to ignore them, as she knew from past experiences with other high profile clients, these men would be discretely shadowing them from now on whenever they were out in public.

Abdul was looking pleased with himself as they reached the door of the suite they were being shown to. 'Here we are in the best and most beautiful suite in the hotel, the Oliver Messel, a beautiful suite for a beautiful girl.' Paula wondered whether she should know who this man Oliver Messel was. She'd find a moment to read up on him and the suite in the hotel brochure; she liked to learn everything she could at every given opportunity as she was aware that these rich and powerful men she escorted always appreciated she wasn't simply a pretty face, but could also hold a proper conversation as well as fuck like a demon.

Their personal butler opened the suite door and Paula felt as though she had walked onto a magical stage set with yellow silk walls and delicately painted panel walls. She could just see out to a terrace with views of the London skyline. As she stared at the beautiful room, she realised the overwhelmingly strong perfume of flowers wasn't from a single vase, but vases of all shapes and sizes everywhere, all full of varieties and shades of yellow roses, it looked as though the whole of Chelsea flower show had been transported there. Paula couldn't believe her eyes, she'd never seen so many stunning flower arrangements in one room.

'I hope the flowers are to your liking Paula? I asked for the room to be filled.' The Prince looked expectant, waiting for her reaction.

Paula wondered whether he was worrying there were too many or not enough, how could any girl not be impressed standing there in a suite overlooking Hyde Park filled full of roses. 'They're simply beautiful,' she exclaimed enthusiastically as she began to realise that this man was likely to be spoiling her with one grand gesture after another.

'It's the least I can do for such a beautiful woman.' Paula could feel him mentally undressing her as he stared at her long and hard from under his heavy brows. She shivered with anticipation.

The butler discretely disappeared again as did the prince's minders. Paula quickly leant forward to give him a quick kiss for the gesture of the flowers and found surprisingly soft lips on such a masculine man.

He kissed her back and savoured the moment before he broke away, 'Paula, first we should drink.' He walked over to the coffee table where there were bottles of champagne on ice waiting for them. He expertly popped a cork and poured them both a glass. 'Here's to a wonderful weekend together.'

Paula chinked the crystal glass of champagne with his and looked into his eyes. She saw the same glazed look of lust she'd always seen in all her punters' eyes, rich or poor. She embraced this power she had over men with no need of emotional ties or attachment. The loss of her baby daughter had been enough, she never wanted to feel that unbearable feeling of pain and loss ever again.

'Paula, this weekend I'm going to treat you as my Princess, your wish is my command. First, please take your glass of champagne and feel free to freshen up ready for our evening out.'

She gave him another lingering kiss on the lips, so he'd get a taste of what was to come, before she sashayed from the sitting room, knowing that his gaze hadn't left her for one minute as she exited the room. She opened the wardrobe in the bedroom where she found that a maid had already unpacked her bag. Her own clothes were all hung or neatly folded beside a complete rail of brand new designer outfits, each one ready accessorised with belts, bags and shoes. Paula couldn't believe her eyes - she was used to being bought an outfit or two but not a whole new wardrobe of them. A note was folded on the nearby table.

My beautiful Paula, I look forward to seeing you in one of these outfits tonight. It will be accessorised with a diamond necklace of your choice from the jewellers downstairs.
Yours Abdul.

Paula considered the diamonds she'd been looking at downstairs, each piece many thousands of pounds, some even more than the cost of a house, certainly more than the house she'd grown up in. She thought back to the times she'd slept with boys just for the hell of it and wondered why more girls hadn't turned to a life like hers now, what was not to like about it, she was using men rather than them using her. Yes, she was sure of that. If she could carry on like this and build up a collection of jewellery, designer clothes and bags and large amounts of cash, then one day she might have enough to pay lawyers to fight to get her baby back.

She stepped into the huge rainfall shower and turned it on, immediately enjoying the feel of the pinprick sensation of the powerful jets of water over her body. She picked up the soap and ran her hands, now covered with the slippery suds, all over her taut body and between her breasts and her legs. She shut her eyes and wasn't sure whether it was the thought of the prince himself or the promise of the imminent gifts making her pussy very wet and it wasn't just the soapy water.

She opened her eyes and called out, 'Abdul sir, your princess requests a *very* personal audience with you...' She liked to play games properly. She knew Abdul had been waiting patiently in the other room so she'd already left all the doors open from the sitting room through to the en-suite bedroom and bathroom so that he might just catch a glimpse of her as she'd walked around undressing. This sudden call to action in the shower was a spontaneous decision driven by

285

her increasingly wet pussy and sudden unusual and unexpected desire to fuck him. Abdul's head appeared round the slightly-ajar bathroom door and he looked expectantly at Paula like an obedient dog with the knowledge of an imminent treat. She knew he definitely hadn't been prepared to see her naked and ready for him in the shower, she always liked to surprise, it gave her the upper hand. Her long blonde hair was now wet and slicked back down her back and all she had left on was her Cartier love bracelets and a Tiffany gold and diamond necklace.

She heard his sharp intake of breath, as he processed what he was seeing and whispered half to himself, 'My beautiful Princess.' He tore off his clothes, leaving them strewn in a trail across the marble bathroom floor, to join Paula in the shower. She'd already noticed he was very obviously ready for her and she was going to enjoy every moment as much as he was. He pulled her warm and soapy body close to his own and the strong shower jets enveloped the two of them. She could feel his throbbing erection pressing urgently against her hip bones and pushed herself against him.

'It's my duty to help you bathe, my Princess,' and he ran his hand in a trail down her body across her breasts and past her tummy to where he paused, cupping his wet soapy palm up against her already pulsating pussy. Paula then knew for certain she wasn't going to have to fake a thing, she was more turned on than she'd ever been before with the sensations of the relentless pounding of the shower water, his muscular wet body rubbing up against her own slippery soapy one and his hard cock pressing urgently up against her, ready to slide effortlessly inside her. Paula never got dressed again that night, as they only moved from the bathroom to the bedroom and then stayed there all night – with their only interruption being a room service midnight feast of smoked salmon sandwiches, chocolate brownies and ice cream.

She woke up the next morning with his arms wrapped around her. She lay there luxuriating in the moment, thinking back to the previous night which had been one of the best nights ever of her life and she felt quite giddy with lust. She had been used to being paid to please and pleasure men but, a man who had only wanted to sexually please her all night was a brand new experience, even Madjid hadn't ever put that much effort in.

She'd never felt like this before; she'd been fond of Madjid as he'd cared for her; the teenage boys back home had simply been quick fucks like all her subsequent paid-for ones with Pierre as her pimp. Abdul was different, there was no doubt they actually had a real connection. She stretched out and stroked his face and he opened his eyes and smiled at her. She felt something stirring near her thigh and reached down under the sheets. It seemed foreplay wasn't on Abdul's mind this early in the morning and he deftly moved himself just enough to be able to slide his cock into her from the position they were in. Paula once again was already wet - she gave an involuntary gasp as he felt so good inside her. As they moved slowly and still drowsily together as one, Abdul whispered, 'Paula, I'm just warning you that I'm intending you to come a few more times before we even consider breakfast and that's how it's going to be for the rest of the weekend.'

Paula tried to say, 'It's supposed to be me saying that to you...' but was unable to finish her sentence as he suddenly thrust more deeply again and she felt yet another orgasm building ready to explode.

'Paula, it's my pleasure.' He smiled as he stared intently into her eyes, still focused on making sure that his efforts were eliciting the required result. When they both finally lay exhausted, stuck together in a sweaty embrace, Paula felt she needed to give herself a pinch to remind herself that she was being paid and to keep any personal feelings well in check.

By the time they'd both showered, breakfast had somehow already been laid out on their terrace. Paula lifted each of the silver covers off the platters and discovered two full English breakfasts there with scrambled eggs, crispy streaky bacon, tomatoes, mushrooms and hash browns - the complete works, and warm croissants, bread rolls, fresh orange juice, steaming pots of coffee and fresh fruit. Paula wrapped herself in a fluffy white bathrobe and joined Abdul at the table where the daily papers were also laid out.

'We don't need the papers at breakfast when we've got each other,' Abdul winked at Paula and threw all the newspapers in a pile on the floor next to Paula.

Paula nodded agreement as she tucked in to the delicious food. She'd realised how hungry she was as their late night snack had really been only a snack.

'So Princess, today we're going to actually get up, get dressed and go for lunch at the Cinquante Cinq. The maids have already packed your bag and we can buy anything else you need when we're there. Oh, and I haven't forgotten that I promised you that necklace, we'll choose it on the way out.'

Paula wondered how they could be having lunch at the place he'd mentioned. If she wasn't mistaken this was a beach restaurant in St Tropez and she and Abdul were definitely now in London, maybe it was another Cinquante Cinq. No, he'd just definitely said that the maid had packed her bag, they must be about to fly to the South of France, how her life had changed.

Abdul had just disappeared off to the bathroom and now that she was briefly sitting on her own, she took the opportunity to glance down at the discarded papers and picked up one of the red top tabloids, she always loved a bit of gossip, and stared at the newspaper's front page headline.

Is this Morgan Well's new love interest?

She examined with interest the large but grainy photo of Morgan standing in the street in a clinch with a dishevelled looking girl wearing a boob tube and silky wide trousers and wedge heels. Paula couldn't properly see the girl's face in the picture, just a mass of auburn pre-Raphaelite curls down her back. She was now intrigued and read on.

Morgan Wells was seen late last night with Miss Phoebe Clarke, the bright new young stylist to the stars who we've heard on the grapevine was styling Morgan's latest video for his latest single. Could Miss Clarke be the one girl to tame our Welsh playboy crooner?

Paula's heart was now beating so fast she thought it was going to burst through her ribs, she hadn't thought that she was ever going to see Phoebe again. How could she not have recognised Phoebe's hair straight away. Fate was a funny thing, if she hadn't been with Abdul in the hotel then she wouldn't have seen the paper. She was beyond excited with her newfound knowledge and it made her imminent hedonistic weekend pale temporarily into insignificance. However, things always fell into place when the timing was right and her focus at this moment was to make sure that Abdul was more than just happy.

They flew on his private jet into Nice airport, and from there they were helicoptered on to St Tropez and driven by a chauffeured car to the Club Cinquante Cinq, where Paula realised that she had never seen so many flashy cars lined up

289

at the car park entrance. The valet parking attendants had selected the sexiest cars, parking these in pole position to create impactful car-envy for arriving guests. Paparazzi were hanging around outside waiting for their moment to capture celebrity arrivals, or drunk and disorderly departures. The St Tropez hotspot offered an ostentatious spectacle of wealth and glamour.

The maître d' led Abdul to one of the best people-watching tables and Paula happily followed, letting him take complete control. She was perfectly happy to be in charge or dominant in the bedroom if and when required, she hadn't forgotten he was paying her. Now that Abdul had ordered, she realised she had absolutely no idea what dishes were coming as she'd been so engrossed in people-watching. Paula had never been star-struck but was over-awed at how many famous people she'd seen there. She'd tried very hard to give her full attention to Abdul but she'd already spotted Joan Collins eating there with her family and Michael Caine and his beautiful wife Shakira. She was relieved that she was with such a good looking young man as diners would just have assumed they were a happy, glamorous and very wealthy jet set couple. She could have bet a dollar or two though that there were a few other Madame Claude girls here as well. Huge super-yachts, some with heli-pads were moored out at sea in the deeper water. Tanned old men, with beautiful young girls all wearing very little, were regularly shuttled in on the club's tenders. It was like watching a fashion show catwalk as these yacht owners and their guests were discharged to walk up the beach to the restaurant. The girls were all now carrying their heels to manage any semblance of a dignified journey across the burning hot soft sand. Heels immediately put back on, once reaching the restaurant decking, for maximum arrival impact.

As the restaurant was so busy, service was extremely slow but as Paula was relishing every single moment of her time with Abdul, it didn't matter. Eventually a huge bowl of crudités arrived simultaneously with a bottle of the best Province Rose wine together with a huge platter overflowing with succulent and garlicky giant grilled prawns. They tucked in and Paula was feeling comfortable enough in his company to follow his lead and use her fingers to eat the prawns. She decided to lick each of her oily finger tips clean, one by one as he watched, holding his gaze as she sensually worked her way systematically across her eight fingers. She knew what it might be doing to him and put her hand, once she'd rinsed her fingers properly in the lemon water finger bowl on the table and wiped them dry on the napkin, straight under the table onto his crutch. Yes, there was certainly some stirring down there and she realised it might now be a little while before he could safely leave the table. She caught his eye as she removed her hand and they both laughed together at their private joke. Abdul ordered more wine as he waited for things to calm down.

Abdul then took her over to the beachside boutique where they both looked at the beautiful silk kaftans and sarongs on display that were blowing in the breeze. Paula picked up one of the most intricately beaded ones to study more closely and the sequins glittered in the sunlight; the workmanship was quite exquisite. Abdul saw her looking at it.

'Choose any ones you'd like to try on, those sequinned ones are truly beautiful.'

Paula took an armful to try on behind the makeshift curtained changing room. It reminded her of the very basic changing rooms she'd stood in when shopping with Phoebe. Momentarily she felt so sad as the last time they'd shopped together was when she hadn't yet realised she was pregnant.

She emerged on to the hot sand wearing the first bikini and then returned to behind the curtain to appear again, after a speedy change, wearing a second option, all the time watching Abdul's expression.

His eyes had lit up and he was grinning widely, almost clapping with the display he was being given. 'Beautiful,' was all he said. Paula wasn't sure whether he meant the bikini or her although it quickly became clear, 'I think you'll have to keep trying bikinis as each one looks more stunning on you than the last.' Paula was getting a buzz from coming out of the little curtained changing room at the edge of the beach wearing bikini after bikini knowing that it wasn't only Abdul who was lusting after her, but all the other men in the vicinity. Abdul proceeded to buy every single one that the shop assistant had brought out for Paula to try on. 'Yes, yes and yes!' he instructed.

Paula wondered whether the assistant was on commission as she handed the many bags of all the new beachwear over to her, now beautifully wrapped in tissue and tied with ribbons. Abdul's minders magically appeared again to carry all the bags and escort Paula and Abdul back to the car, everything seemed to happen so seamlessly, like a chauffeur-driven white convertible Bentley continental that had purred to a stop in the restaurant car park ready to collect them, as though orchestrated by an invisible puppeteer. Once they had climbed in the car to sit on the pristine white leather upholstery after all the bags had been loaded into the boot, Paula snuggled up to Abdul wondering where the next stop was on their magical mystery tour.

She found out as soon as the Bentley smoothly accelerated away from the dusty beach dirt track onto the main coast road into Saint Tropez. 'We're going to be staying for the rest of the weekend in a hotel in Saint Tropez as I'm not letting you leave me yet.' Abdul put his arm around her, pulling her closer as he spoke.

As they sat in the nearly stationary traffic to Saint Tropez town, Paula realised that Abdul's hand had now crept under her sarong and was working up her inner thigh closer and closer towards her pussy. The anticipation of where and what his fingers were about to do next was turning her on; God, he was good with his fingers, she let out an involuntary sigh of pleasure and briefly shut her eyes and tried as hard as she could to silently contain the orgasm she could already feel building. She knew Abdul was smiling, amusing himself the more he played with her, he knew exactly what he was doing and stared straight into her eyes as she came, fuck, he was so sexy.

She suddenly realised that the car's engine had purred to a stop outside a hotel.

'I hope you enjoyed the journey, we're here at the Byblos.' Abdul was completely poker-faced, 'I believe you may have just come as we arrived.' Paula wasn't sure what her response should be, she decided on demure as she stared up at the brightly coloured salmon, lemon and apricot stuccoed buildings in front of her, with the setting sun reflecting off the walls, giving everything a rosy hue. The rustic-tiled roofs and chimneys, together with the tallest palm trees she'd ever seen in a courtyard, were silhouetted against the reddening sky. It was just beautiful and so romantic, which wasn't a word often used in Paula's vocabulary. The doorman was opening the car doors and the next thing she knew, someone, possibly the manager, appeared together with a uniformed bellboy.

'Good evening and welcome to the Byblos Hotel. I hope you'll enjoy your stay with us, it's a pleasure to have you here Sir and Madam.' The manager was now leading them in the direction of their accommodation which Paula knew by now was never going to be just a room, more likely the best suite in the hotel.

The manager chatted on the way to their suite, 'Not sure if you knew this, but this is the hotel where Mick Jagger celebrated his wedding to Bianca six years ago.' Paula remembered seeing the wedding photos in magazines when she'd been in the unmarried mother's home; the pregnant girls had all pored over the pictures, their only escapism from the stark reality of their life. She'd also seen the iconic photo by Richard Avedon of Grace Coddington, Vogue magazine's creative director, wearing a black bikini and sunglasses at night by this hotel's pool, whilst others lounged around in the photo in evening wear. She'd never considered that she could be staying here herself one day.

So as she was now at such a stylish and stunning hotel, she wondered what was she going to wear that was appropriate; Abdul must have read her mind.

'I've just had some of the local boutiques send over a selection of outfits for you to choose from to wear tonight. I believe they're already unpacked and ready in our rooms here. However, before you try anything on, I'm going to make love to you all the rest of the evening and then, when it's cooler, we'll have a late dinner downstairs and end up at Les Caves du Roy nightclub which doesn't really come alive until the early hours, anyway.'

Paula was happy to go along with anything he suggested which was, on reaching the suite, being immediately thrown gently onto the bed. Abdul climbed onto the bed, stripped off her kaftan and bikini and knelt down between her legs, watching her react to every tiny flick of tongue he made. He moved from between her thighs, to up her body using his agile tongue to carefully explore every nook and cranny of her body. Paula lay back on the cool crisp Egyptian cotton sheets and shut her eyes, melting into the moment. It was a complete revelation for a man to be continuously giving her pleasure, she would reciprocate in a minute, after all she was being paid.

'Abdul, now it's my turn to do everything for you, you're not to lift a single finger, just lie there; lie on your front first as I'm starting with a massage.' Abdul obediently turned onto his front. 'Shut your eyes,' she commanded, 'this is all about you.' Paula dribbled suntan oil all the way down his back until it ran in rivulets into the crack between his taut bottom cheeks. She proceeded to massage with long slow firm strokes, systematically from the nape of his neck down to his feet, brushing the length of her body against his every time she reached up. She relished the idea that she was now in control of his pleasure as she let her fingers wander off course every so often, playing, teasing and lightly touching.

She ignored his responsive movements and attempts to turn over, keeping her long firm and rhythmic massaging strokes continuing up and down his body. Finally she decided she would let him turn over. 'Okay, you can turn over now, then shut your eyes again.' He tried to grab her as he turned to take back control, but Paula wasn't having any of it and continued on her oily massage journey, using a mix of her now oily body and hands. He once again tried to kiss her and pull her towards him but she didn't allow him to and pinned his hands behind his head. 'Stay like this and don't move - it's all about you now, lie back and enjoy it.' Paula knelt with her legs spread either side of him, her body open and exposed to him. She knew exactly what she was doing, he could look but he couldn't touch and once again she started to massage with long sweeping strokes and teasingly gently brushed between his legs, oily fingers just brushing his balls, giving a hint of what might be next. When she knew his arousal couldn't wait any longer, she manoeuvred herself so that he was finally inside her, he gasped, Paula knew exactly how to build up to a grand finale; one of her clients at Pierre's had wanted Tantric sex so she'd made it her business to learn all about it; if she was going to do something, she'd do it properly. Tantra was all about breath, slow sensual sensory touch, exchange of energy and delaying the orgasm and Abdul was getting the full works. She wanted his sex with her to be the best he'd ever had, she was confident it would be.

They lay wrapped round each other afterwards, oily, sweaty and spent. 'That was amazing, Princess.' Abdul contentedly kissed her with little butterfly kisses all over her face as they lay there. Paula smiled, acknowledging his compliment as she knew it was true.

They then showered together, ready for their late dinner, more champagne and a night of dancing at the Caves du Roi. The rest of the weekend passed in a blur, full of sensuous pleasures; all the S's – sun, sea, sex and sunset cocktails.

They sat on the terrace watching the sun go down, whilst having their early evening cocktail on the Sunday. Paula had been expecting Abdul to tell her that their weekend was now over and that she'd be going home in the morning but it seemed from an afternoon phone call with Madame Claude that the weekend was to stretch into the following week, and her bank balance was growing incrementally. Claude had left her a cryptic message at the Hotel reception to call her back privately when she had a chance. Paula had called the first opportunity she'd had that afternoon, hearing Claude sounding extraordinarily chirpy.

'Just to let you know that I believe Abdul may be quite smitten with you as he has booked you for another week going into the next weekend and he has deposited twenty thousand dollars into my account for you, Felicitations. You never know what might come of this little liaison. Do not let him know that you know any of this.'

Paula always listened carefully to every word of Claude's advice now.

'Merci, Claude. He's the best client I've ever had and I'm truly enjoying every moment. I'll keep in touch with you from wherever we are, don't worry.' Paula had slowly walked away from the reception desk phone trying to collate how many thousands of pounds she'd earned from Abdul against how many orgasms he'd given her.

Paula sat and sipped her cocktail, as she waited to hear this time from the horse's mouth where they were going for the next week. Abdul looked out to sea, then brought back his gaze to Paula's face noticing the small scattering of freckles that had appeared over her nose in the sun that day. 'Paula, I would like to share all my favourite places on the Riviera with you, so next on my list is the Hotel du Cap-Eden-Roc in Antibes.'

'I can't think of anything I'd like more, Abdul.' Paula meant it with all her body and soul and felt a warm fuzzy feeling come over her as in that moment, she was the happiest she'd been for a very long time.

The Eden Rock pool was unique. Paula loved the way it had been built on rocks, a level down from the main hotel and a level up from the sea. As she lay there listening to the waves lap at the rocks and chatting to Abdul, she almost began to feel like a real couple. Their first week together had now nearly ended and she was no longer playing any games or worrying she was going to slip up on any social etiquette, she was completely confident that no one would ever have suspected she'd been born on a council estate and spent a few years as a cheap hooker.

Life had definitely moved on. Paula was now only wearing designer labels, mixing with beautiful people and flying in private jets, experiencing the best of the best. Abdul leaned over from his lounger to give her a kiss.

'My beautiful Princess, we're still having way too wonderful a time, so I've decided that we're next going on to Monaco to a party on a yacht. We'll be travelling by helicopter, if that's okay with you. Of course, I've made all the necessary arrangements for your extended stay.'

Paula knew from the word "arrangements" that Abdul would already have contacted Claude to pay the extra. She needed to phone Claude again before they left, maybe she could find a moment to call from the Hotel Lobby. She smiled at him;

'I'm such a lucky girl,' and sealed her statement with a passionate kiss before she added as an after-thought, 'maybe I should just pop down to the hairdressers for a quick blow-dry before we get ready for dinner; I'll be back very quickly.'

'Anything you like Princess that makes you happy, just charge it to the room.'

She stopped off at the reception on the way. 'Please can you get me this phone number? I'll take the call here in the lobby and pay for it on my own credit card, not on the room bill, merci.' She leant on the corner of the reception desk and waited for the operator to connect her. 'Bonjour Claude, c'est Paula, comment allez-vous?'

'Trez bien, I gather you're still with Abdul. He's just deposited another twenty thousand dollars for you to stay another week until the next weekend for the Grand Prix, this is excellent news so congratulations, Cherie, he's one of the better men within his large family. He treats his women well but he doesn't usually keep them around for so long, this is all very unusual.'

Paula took on board what Claude was saying, 'Claude it's so easy to be with him and he's treating me so well, we will speak again soon.'

Chapter 24. Phoebe. Monte Carlo, 1977

It was one am and Phoebe was enjoying a late night drink in the dining room section of the Tramp night club. She could just hear the pulsating beat of the music from the disco in the other room. She'd started the evening together with the band she'd been styling that day, and now that they'd all left.

Glenn, an American Country and Western singer who'd been sitting on the next table, had invited himself to join her. She was high from all the coke she'd been doing throughout the shoot day, topping up her fixes regularly throughout the night. The effects of the coke made her crave sex with anyone. The Morgan episode seemed to have given her "a get out of jail free card". She'd gone from being locked up within herself to being compulsive and indiscriminate in her choice of sexual partners and every single one of them meant nothing to her, the sex was purely physical, although she still had one rule; no one could ever touch her breasts. She'd programmed herself to be disconnected during any foreplay and sometimes didn't even realise where she was being touched and when she was high, nothing mattered any more.

She repeatedly told herself she was "soiled and dirty" so why would anyone really want her for anything more than just a passing sexual encounter. Her self-esteem and self-worth were now based on being sexually desired and the multiple random partners made her feel that she had some control over this part of her life, if she ever felt anyone was getting too close she quickly moved on, tonight it was Glenn's turn.

'Wanna dance, babe?' he'd moved his chair even closer to her.

'Sure, is that Donna Summer playing? Let's do it.' Phoebe was ready to dance, the coke wasn't conducive to staying still for long.

'Fancy some of this first babe?' Glenn passed her a small white packet which she discreetly put it into her handbag under the table. Phoebe was already feeling a cocaine comedown from the earlier line she'd had - the more she had, the more it took to keep her high.

'I'll meet you in a minute outside the Ladies on the way to the dance floor.' She fought her way through all the throngs of people standing chatting around the dining tables, and through the middle seating area to the small ladies cloakroom. Here the cloakroom lady, who'd been a fixture of the ladies loos since time began, sat discretely in a corner, maybe seeing or hearing everything that went on in there, but never telling. She had her little secrets too.

Phoebe waited in line for the next one of the two cubicles to become free. Two girls emerged together giggling, sniffing and wiping their noses. Phoebe smiled knowingly at the girls and an unspoken code passed between them, bonding them invisibly together, although they'd never met before. She slipped into the loo and emptied enough powder for a small line along the back shelf of the cubicle. She rolled up a note and lowered her head to snort two lines. She felt the familiar unpleasant metallic taste trickle down the back of her throat but at the same time felt that buzz she loved when she'd just used. Now she was ready to hit the dance floor again.

'How are you this evening?' asked the cloakroom lady, now that she'd seen Phoebe here already three nights running this week.

'I'm good, thank you so much and you?' Phoebe quickly washed her hands but didn't wait to listen to the cloakroom lady's reply as she was now flying high and instead left her a generous tip in the tip tray - she could easily afford it now as she was so busy with all her starry music business clients who were all willing to pay top dollar for her exclusive styling services, with some of them also receiving additional one-to-one very personal service from Phoebe, after hours at no extra charge. She walked out amongst the heaving mass of sweaty people coming from the disco area. She'd already made sure there were no traces of white powder on her nose and that her makeup was still immaculate. She needed to keep it all together and keep up appearances if she was to keep on top of her game. She never knew who she might bump into as everyone now knew who she was, she was always being "papped" and written about; it had started with the picture of her and Morgan. When the newspaper headlines about her were positive and the cocaine was active, she believed she was invincible and still on an upward trajectory of fame and fortune.

'Phoebe Clarke is the girl who everyone wants to know.'

'Phoebe Clarke is the go-to stylist for anyone who is anyone.'

'When you're a celebrity, if Phoebe Clarke isn't your stylist, it means you're on the Z-list.'

Phoebe and Glenn danced, bodies pressed closely together in the middle of the crowded tiny dance floor. Phoebe had already lost herself in the continuing hypnotic beat of Donna Summer's "Love to love you baby". The song went on for ages and the longer she danced with Glenn, the sexier he became. She hoped he'd fuck as well as he danced, he was good; her now extensive sexual experiences had shown that the two were synonymous, so she was looking forward to partying all night.

She would have a full day to recover tomorrow before her weekend styling job. She had been booked to style a young Hollywood actress flying over to the South of France for a big party on a super yacht. Some Hollywood A-lister had hired the yacht, moored at Monte Carlo for his birthday and paid famous friends to fly out to party with him. This client was one of his guests and she'd booked Phoebe to bring a weekend's worth of designer clothes for her. Once Phoebe had checked out photos of the actress and been informed of her measurements and likes and dislikes, she'd called in all the day and evening looks which were now packed and ready to go. She'd been told that a chauffeured car would collect her from Nice and take her to Monte Carlo, where she'd be taken out to the yacht and as it was the Monaco Grand Prix weekend, she knew it would be fun. All expenses were paid as well as her fee, which had already been transferred in advance into her bank account. Life was looking good.

Now that she was back living in Chelsea, she'd finally managed to call and meet Mrs Abbott. Phoebe was surprised how emotional Mrs Abbott had seemed to be on hearing from her. Phoebe felt quite teary the first time they'd met up again, as she hadn't realised how much she'd actually meant to the housekeeper and also, how much Mrs Abbott had meant to her. So now she tried to meet up on Mrs Abbott's afternoons off once a month for a cup of tea, well away from the family home. Her parents obviously didn't miss her so she didn't even bother to contact them. She tried to fill Mrs Abbott in on stories about her celebrity styling life but the straight talking Yorkshire woman always brought her straight back down to earth and didn't stand for any airs and graces or name dropping. Phoebe realised that Mrs Abbott was simply proud of how far she'd come, but not of the superficiality in this transitory world of stardom. However, Phoebe's stories were always heavily edited as she knew that even if Mrs Abbott had understood she wouldn't have approved.

Her other grounding influence was Caroline whom she phoned once a week, when Caroline could get away from looking after her twins, the horses and dogs and her bridge evenings. George called her every so often too when he was back from partying late at night in Paris, he was happy for her to continue living at his flat and he liked to find out how she was getting on as he felt like a proud daddy, partially responsible for her success - and of course she saw Simon too as often as she could; she loved him so much, like a brother. There was still a gaping hole in her life for the friend she missed the most, Paula.

Phoebe looked out of the cabin window as the plane circled over the shimmering sea before landing at Nice airport - every time she now arrived at a new destination it felt like a new adventure. At the airport arrivals she found a clean shaven, tanned young man waiting for her, holding up a placard with her name: he was dressed in a crisp smart uniform of white Bermuda shorts and a short sleeved white shirt with 'Christina O' logo embroidered on the breast pocket. He greeted her, 'Bonjour, Mademoiselle Clarke, I'm here to take you to the Christina,' as he took over wheeling her trolley with all her bags on it.

'Bonjour,' Phoebe smiled back at him, thrilled for someone else to now take control of the luggage and trolley.

'I hope you had a good journey. We're off to Monte Carlo now, where one of the tenders will take us out to the yacht.'

'So, tell me a bit about this Christina yacht?' Phoebe felt full of goodwill as she now wasn't carrying any bags.

'The Christina O was owned by the late Aristotle Onassis and then loaned by his daughter to the Greek government for presidential use but this weekend it's been hired by someone for a party.'

'Who?' Phoebe's curiosity was now piqued.

'Sorry, I'm not allowed to say, all I can say is that it's a Hollywood celebrity who wishes to remain anonymous.'

Phoebe had no chance to ask any more questions as they had now managed to navigate around all Monaco's roadside barriers and security blocks ready for the Grand Prix and arrived at the harbour.

'There she is,' the young man announced proudly pointing out to sea.

'She's really beautiful.' Phoebe was impressed as the yacht was huge, Phoebe guessed maybe over three hundred feet long and that was bigger than most houses she'd been to.

'So, this is the tender for us to go out to the yacht, Miss Clarke. When you get on board, one of the crew will show you to your room. You might want to take your heels off now.' As they drew closer, the sheer scale of the yacht became ever more apparent to Phoebe. The increasing swell of the tide was also causing a significant gap between the lower level of the motor boat tender and the higher landing platform with the steps up to the yacht. Phoebe felt slightly panicked and held out her hands for the two crew guys to help her board the yacht steps, relieved once she was safely on board -she hoped she wasn't going to have to get on and off too often to go to shore.

The crew standing around on deck to greet her, all appeared to Phoebe to be model-like and super-fit, dressed in the same white shirt combo. It immediately crossed her mind they hadn't only been picked for their yachting skills. One of them stepped forward.

'Welcome Miss Clarke, let me take you to your stateroom. Your suitcases will be brought along soon and unpacked for you. I know that Saffron is expecting you.' So, it was Saffron she was dressing. She'd read so much about her but she knew most of it was speculation as she'd been told that the singer worked hard to keep her private life private.

Phoebe sat on her super-king sized bed in her state room as they'd called it, not cabin, and tried to regroup. Maybe a short nap would help before she felt ready to meet her client. No, that might make her feel worse and she needed to get herself back into work mode. Maybe if she showered and changed then she'd feel prepped and ready. The powerful shower jets helped revive her and within fifteen minutes she felt refreshed and was standing ready at Saffron's cabin door. When Saffron opened the door, Phoebe was blown away by how stunning she was, rather like a beautiful exotic bird.

'Hi, you're Phoebe? Thanks so much for coming to style me this weekend.'

Phoebe couldn't quite place her accent, it was South London mixed with Mid Atlantic and a hint of Jamaican lilt. She knew Saffron had an African-American father and a Norwegian mother and had been performing on the international music circuit since she was sixteen, so the mix of accents wasn't much of a surprise. However, her incredible looks were surprising and Phoebe couldn't take her eyes off her. Her afro hair had been dyed blonde and had been left to grow down to her shoulders like a huge lion's mane and her skin a warm coffee-colour.

Saffron tossed her mane of hair as she spoke. 'I had no time to sort out anything to wear as I came straight from recording an album in Jamaica. I rarely come to parties like this, but when I was told that no paparazzi or photographers would be allowed on the yacht I knew I could have fun and relax for a change.'

Phoebe immediately empathised, 'I know that feeling, Saffron, the paps get everywhere nowadays and manage to snap the most intrusive moments and at least you're safe here. I've brought a great selection of outfits from bikinis to evening dresses. The suitcases are just being unpacked by the yacht staff for us now.'

Saffron nodded, 'Cool, shall we go and sit up on deck and have a drink whilst we wait to for someone to come and tell us they're ready?'

Phoebe was happy to agree as a quick drink sounded perfect. The moment they were sitting down a crew member immediately appeared as though he was telepathic.

'What can I get you, ladies?'

The girls looked at each other to see what the other would order.

'I'll have a Mimosa please.' Saffron was quick to reply.

'What's that?' Phoebe asked Saffron, still staring at her, transfixed by how stunning she was.

'Champagne and orange juice.'

'Ah, a Bucks Fizz. Yes, I'd like one of those too, please.'

They sat together on one of the low white sofas on the deck which so far only had crew milling around. Saffron turned to face Phoebe with a small anxious frown wrinkling the wide space between her almond-shaped green eyes.

'Most of the guests are arriving later tonight for the drinks party and it's strange being here on my own...' she paused and looked a bit sheepish, 'my friend who was coming with me couldn't come at the last moment, would you hang out with me?'

'Happy to, I'm on my own as well.' Phoebe was only too happy to keep Saffron company, although surprised that she'd suddenly seemed shy as initially she'd seemed so ballsy and confident. The girls finished their drinks and returned to the cabin to look through Phoebe's now unpacked selections of outfits.

Saffron took a quick first look along the rail, 'They're perfect, Phoebe, great job. Here, let me take these to try,' she grabbed an armful of bikinis and dresses.

Phoebe continued sorting the rail of dresses. When she turned around again to speak to Saffron, she discovered that the girl was now standing completely naked the other side of the room holding, not wearing, a bikini - looking at Phoebe challengingly.

'You don't mind me getting naked in front of you like this, do you? Girls together and all that.'

'It's fine. I'm a stylist, nothing I've not seen before.' Phoebe wasn't sure how she suddenly felt at the sight of this stunning girl standing naked, almost defiantly. It wasn't the first time that a client had undressed in front of her but never before with so much "here I am" attitude. Phoebe had often wondered if she did fancy girls, she didn't think she did, although now that she was staring at Saffron, there might just be a possibility.

'So, do you think my body's okay?' Saffron stared challengingly at Phoebe, twisting her body from side to side from her naked stance of feet apart and hands on hips.

Phoebe suddenly wondered if she'd spoken her thoughts out loud by accident or had she been staring too hard. She could feel herself blushing.

'Hey, don't be shy, I like girls, Phoebe.' Naked and still clutching the bikini, Saffron walked slowly and purposefully back across the room towards Phoebe and stood right up close to her, not quite touching bodies. Phoebe was rooted to the spot like a statue and now that she was so close up to her, she could feel Saffron's sexual energy like a magnetic field drawing her in, their faces were so close now. Phoebe wanted to kiss Saffron more than she had ever wanted to kiss anyone, she threw caution to the wind and tentatively brought her lips to Saffron's full ones. The next thing she knew was that Saffron had taken control of the kiss and it had become a passionate full-on one with tongues.

Saffron then pulled back for a moment and paused before she spoke. 'I hired you Phoebe as I kept on reading about you in the papers and I wanted to find out more about the private Phoebe. I obviously know you're a brilliant stylist but I also wanted to know if all the stories about you were true...'

Phoebe looked at her, lost for words. She allowed Saffron to lead her over to the bed and to slowly untie her embroidered silk kimono. Phoebe liked the sensation of the softness of another girl's body against her own, it wasn't threatening. She realised that Saffron was now asking her something, 'Fancy a joint or some coke?'

'Both!' Phoebe laughed as she answered without hesitating. She was now fully committed to anything that Saffron was offering, she was committed to going with the flow. 'You roll, I'll chop.'

Saffron opened her Chanel bag that lay on the bedside table and took out a small silver cigarette case; out of which she extracted a small packet of coke and a tiny block of hash and some rolling papers. 'Here you go.'

The girls set to their respective drug-related tasks. Cocaine lines chopped and joint rolled, they were ready to party. Saffron began to kiss Phoebe again and her kisses were so gentle, even gentler than Simon's kisses had been.

Saffron paused again for breath, 'Have you ever been with a girl before?'

'Umm… no.' Phoebe was unsure whether to tell the truth or not as she wanted to appear cool.

'Then I'm going to make this especially memorable for you.'

'Saffron, trust me it will be, you'll never know how much…' Phoebe then decided that she'd said enough on this topic and shut up.

Saffron gazed deep into Phoebe's eyes and proceeded to wipe a finger over the powdery remains of the coke left on the table. She then rubbed the same finger over Phoebe's gums and left it there whilst she investigated Phoebe's mouth with her own tongue. Phoebe's gums had lost feeling from the numbing effects of the coke whereas her whole body was now tingling from drug-related heightened sensations of Saffron's actions.

She wanted to reciprocate as this felt so completely different from as any of her past random fucks. Saffron was still busy touching, feeling, probing, licking and rubbing. Phoebe felt lost in the depths of the waves of pleasure that were building within her, it was like a fairground rollercoaster ride, building and building slowly with its ultimate climb. She felt powerless now to do anything but pull Saffron closer to her before she felt her whole body shudder. Then she started to cry, she just couldn't help herself, until her whole body was racked with her sobs.

'What's the matter Phoebe?' Saffron was looking confused.

'Nothing at all,' Phoebe sobbed and smiled at the same time, 'they're happy tears, it was beautiful.'

The girls lay so close together that Phoebe could feel Saffron's breath on her cheek as she whispered, 'Shall we forget the drinks party this evening?'

With every single gentle and sensual touch from Saffron, Phoebe's demons were melting away in a candyfloss feeling of pleasure like she'd never experienced before.

Why had she waited so long to do this? Had styling celebrities unlocked and opened an unexpected previously hidden door to alternative sexual options?

Chapter 25. Paula. Monte Carlo, 1977

The bellboy was walking around the pool holding out a small blackboard with Abdul's name chalked up on it. *"Urgent message at reception"* Suddenly Abdul spotted him and leapt up from his sun lounger, 'Back in a minute Paula, I just have to find out why this message might be so urgent.'

Paula could see he looked worried, obviously wondering what could be so important. It was more than a minute, more like thirty minutes before he returned with his normally happy and outgoing personality transformed into a distinctly subdued and unhappy one, his low mood now permeating every fibre of his body. He stayed standing at the side of her pool lounger, casting a dark shadow over her.

'I'm so sorry Paula, I've just had a phone call from my father asking me to return home urgently to deal with family business matters. Not after this weekend but today, now, this minute. I would have loved for us to continue on as we'd planned but he's given me no choice. I've arranged for you to stay on in our suite for another week, that's if you'd like to, obviously everything is paid for. Charge anything you want to the room and just to warn you, I hate goodbyes, they remind me of leaving my family each term from the age of seven to go to my British boarding prep school.' Phoebe suddenly had insight into understanding more about Abdul's life and how controlled it had been and still was by his family.

Paula stared back realising how much she was going to miss him. She didn't trust herself to speak in case she cried and that certainly wouldn't be a Paula thing to do. Abdul sat back down on her sun lounger close to her and took both her hands in his.

'When you go back to our room later after I've left, you'll find a small gift from me to say thank you for all our time together. Also, all the clothes left behind at the Dorchester in London will be sent to any address you wish if you give it to one of my personal assistants. They will arrange that, together with my private plane to fly you back to the UK, or up to Paris, whenever you wish to leave.' He kissed her lingeringly on the lips and held her gaze for longer than he ever had before. 'You're an amazing, beautiful and very special girl, my Princess. I will always remember you and I hope you'll remember me too.'

Paula was overwhelmed by his words as she knew that he really meant them. Abdul had now stood up again ready to leave. Paula stood up off her sun lounger in one swift, elegant move.

'Thank you, I've had the most wonderful time with you and I too will never forget you.'

They hugged, both knowing it was likely that they may never meet again. Paula had enjoyed every single second of being in his company and it had taught her to value herself more. She lay back down on her sunbed feeling incredibly sad that this had ended so unexpectedly and abruptly. As she lay there, she considered how she was going to pass the time during this additional solitary week here. Maybe she'd amuse herself to start with by looking at all the menu prices as she'd never checked when she'd been with Madjid. She wasn't going to be paying still, but she was curious all the same as she knew she was staying in one of the most expensive hotels on the Cote D'Azur. The waiter bought her over a menu and she decided to do a quick check on a simple 'croque-monsieur' like the ones Phoebe and she had regularly ordered at the Kings Road Picasso in their school days, so here it was on the menu for around one hundred francs, the equivalent of ten pounds. Blimey, that was ridiculous. Paula hated rip-off prices and still liked to exercise some sensibility on the basics, so she didn't completely forget her roots. Still, this wasn't her money so she was going to enjoy every moment, savouring every mouthful of food that she chose to order. First though, she decided she should check in with Claude.

'Bonjour Paula. I gather that things went very well with Abdul. Your checking account has now had thirty thousand dollars placed in it, so where are you now?' Claude's voice was loud and clear down the line.

Paula realised that she hadn't misheard the amount of money mentioned now sitting in her bank account and felt slightly dizzy with shock at the sum mentioned, but continued on with no tremor in her voice.

'I'm still in the South of France. Abdul just paid for me to stay on another week here at the Eden Roc.'

'Well done, Paula, I think you might now be my most successful protégée. How would you like to leave the hotel just for one night and be collected by motor boat to go over to Monaco? A Hollywood film star has rented a yacht, the Christina, it used to belong to Onassis, for his birthday party during the Grand Prix weekend.'

Paula knew exactly who Onassis was and all about his yacht and his love affair with Maria Callas the Opera singer. She knew a lot about super-rich men, past and present, and their love lives now.

'There are a few of my girls going, you won't know who they are. The party host simply wants beautiful models and classy young women to decorate the yacht and make his party go with a swing. You won't be expected to do anything other than look beautiful, of course, it's your choice if you do.

Money is no object here as he only asked for the crème de la crème, you would be paid five thousand dollars for the night.'

'Claude, if it's just for a night, I'll go and return again here tomorrow. Please can you let the concierge here know what time I should be ready to be collected.'

'Bien sûr, au revoir Paula... amuses-toi bien.'

After ordering and sampling the Hotel's Croque Monsieur, which was indeed tastier than the Picasso one, Paula returned to her room. There she found a small box on the bed and inside was a gold Cartier love bangle; not a normal one but one heavy with diamonds. Engraved on its inner rim were the words... *always my Princess.* Paula was overcome with emotion, it wasn't the gift of the diamond bracelet that had moved her, she was used to being gifted diamonds now, it was the words he'd bothered to have engraved.

She dressed in one of the beautiful Dior gowns that Abdul had bought her and packed a tiny overnight bag with a bikini, a pair of her shortest shorts and a designer t-shirt and wedge heels for the next day - she always liked to be as tall as possible. She was collected by a beautiful Riva speed boat with a shiny teak deck and the same uniformed crew member, unbeknown to her, who had collected Phoebe earlier that day. The speed boat arrived very quickly into the Monte Carlo harbour and Paula could see the lights of the yacht reflecting and sparkling on the water as dusk turned to night.

'Are you British, Mademoiselle?' the good looking young crew member asked her, 'well, we've a lot of Brits on board tonight, together with both French and American guests and our own Princess Caroline of Monaco too, maybe you'll know some of the British guests.'

Paula sincerely hoped she wouldn't as they were likely to have been past clients if she did, so she said nothing and simply smiled her one hundred kilowatt smile at him. She climbed up onto the yacht, manoeuvring her way gracefully from the speed boat to the yacht steps. She looked around her and tried not to look too awestruck. After her short but intense time with Abdul, nothing much impressed her now but this yacht was something else. She decided that the bar would have to be her first port of call, she was already dressed for the party.

'A glass of champagne, please.' A glass of champagne was always a good start to anything in Paula's opinion. She perched elegantly on the edge of one of the white cushioned outside sofas and looked around her at the very beautiful girls all swanning around in barely-there evening dresses while the men, as usual, were less impressive on the looks front, many with bellies as fat as their wallets.

'In case you're wondering, the swimming pool turns into a dance floor.' The extremely deep Southern drawl was coming from another guest, not blessed with good looks either, who had appeared from nowhere. 'Hey, gorgeous, I'm Hank, one of our host's friends from LA. My instructions are to help look after any beautiful lady guests who might be looking a little lonesome.'

'Hi Hank, I've literally just arrived.' Paula quickly reminded herself that she was being paid to be there so she switched on the charm again, just as she'd watched Regine do with each person who'd approached her that night in her club.

'Hey, well, welcome on board, isn't this yacht a real beaut? Privacy guaranteed too as the paparazzi simply don't have lenses long enough if they're on the shore. Would you like me to show you around?'

'Yes please.' Paula was dying to have a proper look around the yacht and hear more about its history.

'So, the swimming pool with the minotaur mosaic floor that you were just sitting near to? Well, the floor can rise at a push of a button to become a dance floor and you'll see that happening later on tonight.'

'I shall look forward to that.' She responded politely, eager to do a whirlwind mini tour.

'This room here is Ari's... as in Aristotle Bar, the bar stools are quite unique, they still have the original upholstery made from whale foreskins.' Hank said this as though it was an everyday occurrence to be using such a body part as a furnishing material.

'From what, wait - you can't be serious!' Paula didn't know whether to laugh or look impressed at this information, and it was at this precise moment that she realised Hank was devoid of any humour. She then wondered who on earth would want to sit on whale foreskin? She'd sat on enough willies in her time and certainly didn't need to be sitting on a large mammalian one whilst having a cocktail.

'There's a master suite and eighteen passenger staterooms. Whilst we're walking around, I'm sure you noticed that the indoor and outdoor living spaces all connected by the spiral staircase we just went down.'

'Yes I did. Cleverly done.'

'Now we've nearly done a circuit I'll leave you here at the helipad deck. No, actually, let me find a crew member to show you the way back to your cabin again and if you'd like anything - anything at all – do come and see me. We have everything you could possibly want on board.' He smiled his wide white-toothed American smile at her.

Paula was absolutely sure that anything anyone wanted would immediately be found, however big or small the request was. A crew member appeared, everything happened so quickly in this privileged world of the super-rich and took her to her bedroom suite. It was huge, she'd be rattling around all on her own. She sat down at the dressing table for a minute to look at herself. Mmm, she looked passable, maybe her makeup could do with a little retouch. She powdered her nose, brushed more bronzing shading powder under her cheek bones and gave herself another coat of her pale pink iridescent lipstick, pursing her lips and rubbing them together to distribute the lipstick more evenly, yes, much better. She was now ready to face the world once again.

Just as she opened her cabin door, she heard drunken girly giggles coming from just down the corridor. Paula stepped further out into the passageway and peered down it, immediately recognising the girl nearest to her. It was the singer Saffron who was completely entwined around another girl whom she couldn't quite see. Curious now, she stared more and saw a short girl with long curly red hair. Hang on, had she seen long curly red hair just like Phoebe's? Was her imagination playing tricks again, how many girls had such amazing hair, it couldn't be that many surely? Paula looked once again, trying not to be too obvious. It couldn't be, could it?

She tried calling to see what would happen, 'Phee!'

The girl seemed to be struggling to pull herself together enough to stand up and look in her direction. Paula could see her trying to process the fact that someone had called her, but not the name that everyone knew her by, but her nickname.

'Paula?' Phoebe's voice came out as not much more than a whisper as though she was frightened to say the name out loud.

Paula just stood there and gazed at Phoebe in amazement. Saffron had now slid herself along the wall closer to them, watching them, not quite understanding what was going on. Paula wrapped her arms round Phoebe, wanting to feel that she was actually real. She was too overcome with happiness to be able to say a single word.

'Where did you disappear to?' Phoebe mumbled managing to stay upright as she was leaning against Paula.

This was not the moment to tell all, Paula thought to herself, so all she managed was, 'I missed you so much,' deflecting the question with her own question with all her emotions tumbling out in one short sentence. 'What the fuck are you doing here?'

Her thoughts were racing, how much could she tell Phoebe of her life so far and how much would Phoebe tell her of her own? That could all be for later, much later especially as right now, unlike Phoebe, she was completely sober. One look at the size of her friend's pupils told her everything she needed to know. She remembered the photo of a dishevelled Phoebe in the papers from a few weeks ago, but the close-up reality was worse. Paula had seen what drugs did when she'd lived with the other hookers and she'd seen Pierre die from an overdose and Phoebe was currently high and wired. She glanced at Saffron again who was still leaning against the wall watching them. Paula wondered why Phoebe should be coming out of her cabin and also be in such a state. This was clearly not the same innocent Phoebe that she'd known at school, but it was seven years now since they'd first met and this Phoebe was now a skinny, stoned girl who looked like

319

she'd just been having wild sex. If anyone could spot a post-sex look, Paula could.

She thought quickly. 'Why don't you both come into my room, I know there are no photographers here but I do think you both may need to tidy up a little bit before you are seen publicly. Paula suddenly felt protective as though she was Phoebe's big sister. Strange, she remembered feeling protective back in the day too when they'd been young teenagers and Phoebe had been so innocent. How was she going to get Phoebe away from this girl for the rest of the evening, maybe it needed a change of tactics.

'Hi, I'm Paula.' Although Paula knew exactly who the girl was, she decided to let her introduce herself.

'Saffron.' The girl just about managed to get her name out.

'So Saffron, why don't I take you back to your room and leave Phoebe here in mine with a strong black coffee and then we can both come back to get you, looking glamorous and together for the party.' Paula was still propping up Phoebe as she came up with her plan.

'You're welcome… to come back… to my room… any time.' Saffron slowly slurred to Paula as she still remained slumped against the wall. There was a crew member standing further down the corridor. Paula decided that she couldn't do everything on her own and she needed help now, she was sure that the crew had seen guests in worse states of repair than these two girls.

'Please can you help my friend here into my cabin please and then as quickly as you can, bring a very strong black coffee for her.

'Of course, Mademoiselle.'

She handed care of Phoebe temporarily over to the cabin boy and managed to get Saffron back to her own room. 'I think you should lie down for a bit, you'll be able to face everyone at the party better when the drugs have worn off some more. It's not a great idea for you to be seen in this state.'

'Couldn't give a flying fuck. Why don't you just stay in here with me for a while and we could get to know each other better?' Saffron tried to grab Paula round the neck to kiss her but Paula was too quick and manoeuvred Saffron onto the bed, ignoring everything she was saying.

'Here have a little rest. I'll be back soon to see you, don't worry.' And she left Saffron lying on her bed. She hoped that she would crash out and not wake up until the next morning, by which time she and Phoebe would have left again back to the Eden Rock. She and Phoebe just had to get through the next few hours of the party especially as she was being paid to be there.

She went back into her room and found Phoebe sitting on the edge of the bed, sobered up slightly after the coffee. 'How did you get here Paula, I want to know everything.'

'It's a long story, but let's save it for a quieter moment. We just need to sort everything out first and get off the yacht. Why are you here?'

'I was here to style Saffron who you just met, for the party. I'd brought her lots of outfits to choose from and to wear for the weekend.'

Paula realised that Phoebe was being slightly economical with her version of the story. She decided to let it go, there was time enough.

'Okay, so your job's done. Here's my plan, you're going to get yourself party ready and we're then going to go out together to face the guests for the next few hours and try to leave early not staying the night on the yacht. I've got a room in a hotel in Antibes we can take a taxi to once we're back on shore. I'm sure that Saffron can look after herself as she's a big girl and she's got all the dresses you brought her in her cabin.'

'Suppose.' Phoebe was still having a problem concentrating and focusing. She lost her balance and stumbled as she tried to stand up from the bed. 'Oops, I can't believe it's really you here, am I dreaming?' she smiled a glassy-eyed smile.

'No, it's definitely me. Here you can pinch me if you like?' Phoebe did.

'Ow, that hurt. See? I am actually here and now I'm going to help you get ready. It's so funny it used to be you helping me get ready and now I'm helping you.' They clutched onto each other giggling, then laughing so much that they collapsed in a tangled heap on the floor, holding each other so tightly, in fear of losing each other again.

Paula's plan worked like a dream. By two am they were off the yacht and back at the hotel. She still couldn't believe she and Phoebe were finally together again after all this time. There was so much to catch up on, but maybe it would be best to simply start by just enjoying each other's company, no questions. It felt to Paula like putting on an old favourite dress; like no time had passed at all, let alone seven years. She resolved they would never lose touch ever again.

They spent the first day just chilling out, neither knew how to start their story. Paula weighed up the options of going first as she possibly had more to tell. She also thought she'd have to tell Phoebe about the baby if she wasn't going to tell a colossal lie to her friend about why she disappeared, so maybe Phoebe needed to tell her story first - surely it couldn't be as shocking as hers. Clearly Phoebe was no longer the innocent sixteen year old she'd first met; she was sure that Phoebe's life had run a good deal more smoothly and conventionally than hers.

Getting really drunk first seemed to be the way forward to open up the conversations, so they started with champagne, moved on to a bottle of Rose and then a second bottle with a side order of food, a lobster sea food platter. 'Thank you, Abdul.' Paula toasted him with her glass of champagne, sending him an imaginary kiss into the air, as she sat with Phoebe outside on the terrace under the stars.

'To Abdul,' Phoebe echoed, with no clue as to who Abdul was, but happy to echo Paula's toast in her inebriated state. Paula still waited to see if Phoebe was going to open up first but nothing, what could she do to break the ice as alcohol hadn't. 'I know, let's toss a coin to decide who goes first, I've a franc coin in my pocket, heads or tails?'

'Heads.'

Paula looked down at the coin. 'Sorry it's tails, you first.' She looked at her friend expectantly, watching her sigh deeply before speaking.

Phoebe considered her words slowly and carefully as she started telling her story. 'Okay, where do I begin? I know, so when you suddenly disappeared I was beyond sad; my mother certainly didn't care about my feelings and definitely didn't want me around the house all the time, so she took it upon herself to basically find me a husband. I was invited to all these smart parties and met a whole new set of people and I ended up becoming friends with some of them. I helped them to dress differently, styling them to look funkier, less like their mothers, oh, I forgot, I met Simon who became my boyfriend and then Simon's boyfriend Jake.'

Paula was by now struggling to keep up. 'Whoa, hang on! You've lost me already. Simon was your boyfriend and Jake was then his boyfriend? That sounds well fucked up Phee.'

'Yup it does when I say it like that, doesn't it? Well, Simon was confused about his sexuality and he discovered he liked boys more than girls, he is very pretty you know, one day you'll meet him; he's a makeup artist now and I work with him all the time. Jake lives in LA and is an actor, not successful yet though I know he will be one day. There's so much more to tell and I'm having a really hard time to even think about it as it's why I left London and went to live in Paris with George, another friend and then ended up meeting Joe who was a stylist who helped me to be where I am now.' Phoebe tried to get the whole story out in the same breath.

Paula was completely lost now in the thread of the story as Phoebe's words were tumbling out at a hundred miles an hour, so she hugged Phoebe to let her know she was there for her, she could see Phoebe was becoming more and more emotional as she spoke.

'Phee, I'll tell you what, I'll start telling you my story and then you'll be so shocked by mine that you'll feel that yours isn't so bad and by the way, whatever's in your story, good or bad, it won't change how much I care for you. We're friends, whatever - end of.'

Phoebe gratefully smiled a teary smile back at her.

Paula started her story. 'When I never came back to school there was obviously a reason and it was a big, complicated reason...' she took a deep breath and drained her wine glass once again in one gulp. 'Do you remember when I couldn't understand why I didn't fit any of the clothes I was trying on that day with you in Carnaby Street?'

'Yes, you'd been eating too much.' Phoebe was quick to reply smiling.

'No Phee, I was pregnant.'

Paula watched Phoebe's expression change to shock. 'Oh Paula, I'm so sorry, that must have been really hard, what did you do?'

Paula looked down at her hands; she noticed they were shaking slightly. Briefly, she was back to being her teenage self, standing there once again facing her angry dad. 'Well, I had to tell my dad and he accused me of bringing shame on the family, immediately packing me off to have the baby secretly, in a draughty and bleak Dickensian mansion in the middle of nowhere, run by sadists and then, and then... when I couldn't manage...' Paula gulped, holding back a sob, 'to find work or anywhere to live, the baby was taken away from me and adopted.' Paula was trying to hold back her tears. She looked up and saw that Phoebe was, too.

Phoebe stretched out her hand and took tightly hold of one of Paula's hands, 'I'm so sorry, that's the worst ever outcome, so what happened then? Can you even bear to talk about it?'

'I've never talked about my baby girl to anyone ever before, her name was Phoebe, too.'

Phoebe's face lit up with pleasure, 'You called her after me, that's so lovely.'

'Yes, my friendship with you meant a lot. I wasn't given a choice in keeping her. The moral welfare officers at the unmarried mothers' home told me that keeping my daughter was selfish and that I was being immature and inconsiderate to her needs; my daughter needed to have a proper family. So there was just no way I was able to keep her. I tried so hard.

No room to rent would allow an unmarried mother with her baby. I tried so many and so... I signed the papers.'

Phoebe managed to find her voice again to speak, this time so softly that it was hardly audible. 'This is so beyond awful, Paula, and even worse that I never knew any of this.'

Paula was still trying to hold it together and knew that Phoebe's empathy was making her more emotional so she soldiered on, pulling herself back together.

'I was simply expected to get on with my life straight after as though nothing had happened. No one ever once asked me how I was.' Paula realised as she was speaking to Phoebe, that she'd never let any of this emotion out before. She wasn't sure whether she was feeling better or worse, but it was the first time she'd ever really thought back to the day she'd finally walked away from her child. 'Whilst the arrangements for little Phoebe's adoption were being finalised, I was given just six weeks grieving time; I used to hear the other new mothers crying themselves to sleep at night too. How could anyone ever get over the loss of her baby that quickly; I still think about baby Phoebe every day.'

'Oh Paula, I wish I'd known, I would have been there for you. Maybe we could have found a way to keep her? Lack of money has never been my problem, I could have helped.' Then a thought hit Phoebe, 'Maybe one day we could find her again?'

Paula looked at her friend through her tear-laden eyelashes, an overwhelming sadness and defeat showing through her normally feisty demeanour. 'I dream every day of finding her again, but if one could turn back time, you were so innocent then, you blushed if a boy even spoke to you and I knew you'd never been kissed yet. You didn't have to say, I could tell, you were all bravado and bullshit. Also you had absolutely no idea how badly I behaved. If you'd have known, you wouldn't have wanted to be my friend anymore and I was desperate not to lose you.'

'I think I may have changed somewhat since then.' Phoebe added quickly.

'Given what I read in the papers the other week and the state I just saw you in with Saffron, I think that may well be true.' Paula smiled as she said it, as she wanted to keep Phoebe continuing on with her story.

'So when I was doing all this stupid party stuff organised by my mother I went to a huge ball up in Yorkshire. It was all very smart and I was staying with Caroline, one of my new set of friends. There was a boy there who was her twin brother's friend and I got drunk and he gave me a pill when we were all at the ball, I think it was a Qualude, I don't remember exactly what happened, or maybe I don't want to, all I know is that it was all my fault that he raped me.'

Paula wasn't shocked that Phoebe had told her she'd been raped, but shocked at how Phoebe had expressed her feelings of guilt as no girl should ever feel like this. Now it was her turn to hold her friend's hand.

'No rape is ever your fault. How could you think that? He'd drugged you and you were drunk; you didn't agree and it was against your will. You weren't responsible and certainly didn't bring it on yourself.' Paula could sense a waiter hovering around them wondering if they wanted another drink. She caught his eye and shook her head at him, this wasn't the moment. Then she turned back to Phoebe who she could see was gradually becoming braver in the detail as she told her story.

'I've kept it hidden deep inside me until that day when I went back with Morgan after I'd been styling him.'

'Was that the night of the photo I saw of you in the newspaper?'

'Oh no, you saw that too?' Phoebe looked mortified.

'You were snogging,' Paula was laughing now, 'though I wouldn't blame you, he is so sexy.'

Phoebe tried to defend herself, 'We were definitely not snogging and it was the first time I'd ever gone back to any man's flat, apart from Simon's obviously, as I hadn't wanted to put myself into any situation where anything could happen again. The very thought had filled me with fear and horror. However, Morgan had already made me feel comfortable and safe and yes, I fancied him. Well who wouldn't, quite frankly.'

'Exactly.' Paula agreed.

'So, I went back with him and when he touched me it brought back the worst memories and I had a meltdown, so he called his driver who took me home and the photo you saw was Morgan giving me a kind hug and a friendly kiss before putting me in his car. No more than that, the newspapers always make everything up.'

'I know. So how on earth did you end up with Saffron and in such a state?' Phoebe now looked sheepish.

'It just all sort of spiralled. She'd undressed to try on the clothes I'd brought for her and one thing led to another, and if we're talking about everything, no holds barred, shall I tell you something else?'

Paula was agog, 'Please!'

'Do you know Saffron was the first person to ever give me an orgasm?'

Paula finally laughed - a proper belly laugh. She could absolutely identify with that. She thought back to Pierre and her first time there with Tracey. She decided she didn't need to include that story though.

'I say well done Saffron, a girl often knows better than any man what another girl likes.' Paula decided it was now an opportune moment to call the waiter over again. 'Another bottle of the same please,' and she resumed her story. 'Okay, so after what you've been through, I know you won't be so shocked at what I'm going to tell you about me. I wasn't going to but now maybe I can. I shall understand if you choose not to be my friend any more. I think we have to always tell each other the truth from now on, then we can always be there for each other, whatever happens, so let's agree to the truth and nothing but the truth. No secrets...' She looked at Phoebe with sad, pale eyes, linking her pinkie finger with Phoebe's as they made their pact.

'Paula, I'll always be friends with you whatever you tell me, don't be ridiculous.'

Paula silently and breathed a sigh of relief, she never wanted to lose Phoebe again. She could now tell the rest of her story with more of a safety net. 'I had to find a way to keep myself as I had no money, so when I saw an ad in the paper for working girls in Paris, I applied.'

Working girls?' Phoebe looked confused.

Paula decided not to mince her words. 'Hooker, prostitute, you know, not standing on street corners but living and working for a pimp, in this case a pimp called Pierre in Paris. He confiscated mine and the other girls' passports so we couldn't escape and we stayed there working for him for the next three years. He's dead now.'

Phoebe tried hard to remain expressionless even though she was inwardly shocked.

Paula continued, 'One of the men I'd been sleeping with helped me to escape and paid for me to stay in a tiny apartment in Paris; he was married but really kind to me and one day he introduced me to Madame-Claude who was a sort of female pimp or Madame, who only looked after a certain type of girl. Her clients were only the powerful, rich and famous and it was she who helped me to become the girl you now see today. My last client was an Arab Prince, Abdul, the one who paid for us to stay on here. When you and I met on the yacht, Claude had arranged for me to be paid to be there; not to sleep with anyone this time, just simply to look decorative.' Paula decided not to add if any wealthy man there had offered her enough she would have accepted, her body was an exclusive commodity that she sold - when the price was right. There, she'd told her story, nearly warts and all. She looked at Phoebe waiting for her reaction.

'We've both been through some serous shit, haven't we?'

Both girls now had tears streaming down their faces and Paula could see that Phoebe needed some kind of therapy if she wasn't to fall under the spell of the first man who told her he loved her. Although she was no longer little miss innocent, she still seemed naïve and vulnerable, hoping that somewhere out there her fairy tale handsome prince was waiting to rescue her, but Paula knew for certain that most men, even princes, spoke with their dicks not their hearts.

Another bottle of champagne arrived and as they toasted to their renewed friendship, Paula knew that there was still an elephant on the terrace with them – the question of drugs. She knew the signs and her best friend was showing them all. Whatever happened from now on, she knew she'd always be there for her.

Chapter 26. Marcus. Los Angeles, 1978

Marcus had read every single newspaper and gossip magazine headline and story about her. Rumour and speculation had been rife for a while in all the Hollywood gossip columns, although never before as prominent newspaper headlines.

"PHOEBE AND HER REBEL ROCK STARS"

"PHOEBE CLARKE, STYLIST TO THE STARS, SPOTTED IN NEW YORK WITH SID VICIOUS OF THE SEX PISTOLS"

"WHAT'S HAPPENED TO PHOEBE'S NOSE? WHITE POWDER OR MAKE UP MALFUNCTION?"

"CELEBRITY STYLIST PHOEBE CLARKE SEEN DRINKING IN LA WITH KEITH MOON OF THE WHO"

Now he'd found one more story about her, accompanied with a photograph of her tumbling out of some sleazy-looking London nightclub with yet another rock star. Marcus put down the newspaper and sat cradling his mug of specially milled extra strong Italian coffee, looking out of his floor-to-ceiling windows at his view over Laurel Canyon. There was no doubt about it, Ms Phoebe Clarke was looking decidedly worse for wear in that picture. Marcus fleetingly considered his own life, something he rarely did. He'd never married, he'd never needed to or wanted to, why would he? He was a movie producer for God's sake, with beautiful women constantly on tap, like hot and cold running water. They *all* opened their legs at the slightest whisper of the promise of a role in one of his movies. Why would he want to change anything?

He was a successful movie maker and he knew Hollywood loved a good love story especially where adversity had been overcome. It didn't matter whether it was drink and drugs, rags to riches, career or relationships; Hollywood loved success stories and America was the land of opportunity.

From his viewpoint, no one now deserved it more than Phoebe, the rising young star-stylist who was about to fall hard and fast if she carried on in her current ways. He absent-mindedly stroked the designer stubble on his strong jawline as he considered his strategy. Phoebe could be his ultimate prize; pretty, young and successful, a perfect wife for him. He would be seen as her knight in shining armour, rescuing her from a life spiralling so publicly out of control. The Hollywood gossip machine would go into overdrive, the press and all her fans would love the positive newspaper images of Phoebe looking lovingly into his eyes, instead of the shocking images of her falling out of nightclubs, glassy eyed and wrecked, propped up by her latest bad boy pop star client.

He'd first heard about her through the grapevine when he was casting his current movie as a fantastic new young British stylist who was likely to come to work in LA. He loved new girls in town, they were so full of hope and confident that Hollywood was going to be their golden ticket to stardom. It didn't take long for them to realise that their Hollywood dream might be just that; a dream, but Phoebe Clarke had made it. She was styling rock stars and movie stars and had become a star herself. He liked her chutzpa. She wasn't as pretty or in the same mould as the girls he usually fucked. Yes, the word was definitely fucked – usually once or twice before he moved on. The words dating and monogamy just weren't in his vocabulary. There was always a beautiful woman waiting somewhere for him, usually tall and blonde; a wannabe actress or model. It was a dog-eat-dog world out there and the most beautiful and ambitious always won.

He liked his women to be perfect in every way. Some people considered being a perfectionist was a bad thing, strange that, as it was one of his many qualities. Why wouldn't he embrace perfection when a smorgasbord of female perfection was regularly available, he only had to look at a girl and she'd be all over him like a rash. All these girls wanted to become stars and they thought if they slept with him, he'd be their stepping stone to stardom.

It was amazing what a bit of Hollywood power could do, he whole-heartedly embraced the concept of the casting couch. He hung out at the Dome Bar every evening with his movie biz friends; with Nicki Blair who knew everyone and his best friend the actor Tony Curtis. Tony was the opposite to Marcus when it came to matrimony, so far he'd had three wives with number four already on the cards. However they played it, these men all loved women and women loved them. The evidence from last night was somewhere in his jacket pocket, he remembered the exact moment she'd handed him her card.

'Hey, Marcus, I know just who you are, you're so famous and I just lurve your movies. I'm this month's centrefold in Playboy, here's my card call me, I'll be looking forward to getting to know you, sometime very soon.'

Marcus didn't like his women to be too available though, it bored him. He liked playing games as long as he was in control, his relationships were like a game of Jenga; he built them up gradually, then removing bricks one by one, slowly and systematically, until the tower tumbled down.

He knew he was confident, magnetic and charming and could easily attract any girl, usually an obedient admirer, not an equal partner, it was all about control and domination which made him feel strong and successful. He found it amusing when he could take control over someone who'd had a successful life, as he got off on causing their downfall. It was all one big game to him and a mind-fuck for them. Yes, Phoebe Clarke was perfect.

Damn, his coffee was now cold, where was his maid when he needed her. Would he actually have to make his own coffee now? 'Conchita!'

The Mexican housekeeper quickly appeared at his side with a fresh pot coffee. He'd trained her well and she'd been with him now for years. He'd learnt that the odd little threat to send her back over the border or report her and her family as illegal immigrants never hurt.

Now his coffee was replenished, he once again ran through his strategy to reel in Phoebe. He would show her only kindness and charm; she would only see this side of him until he'd wooed her just enough to make a marriage proposal. She would be different from all the others as all his past girls were flawed, never meeting his expectations. It was he who was always the victim anyway, not them, so why did no-one ever understand? He was a successful man in his fifties and he liked things a certain way, what could be wrong with that? Anyway, he was now in the middle of shooting his movie which was his priority and then he would kick-start his action plan to snare his future wife.

Chapter 27. Phoebe. The Bahamas, 1978

Phoebe was feeling anxious, even though she was sitting comfortably with her feet resting on her hand luggage, opposite Simon in the First Class lounge at Heathrow. She and Simon were so often together now working on celebrity fashion shoots on both sides of the Atlantic. People loved Phoebe's quirky Brit-style together with the creativity of Simon's makeup. The two friends had now both become as famous as the celebrity rock stars they were working with; they'd hit the big time with the pages of their Filofax diaries full of bookings for magazine photoshoots, ad campaigns, TV commercials, pop videos and red carpet jobs.

In spite of her success, when Phoebe was home alone, which was rare, she questioned her mental state as she veered between extremes of self-doubt and self-loathing to uber-confidence and can-do optimism helped with the drugs. She had a constant icy spine-chilling fear that her little packet of white powder would run out when she most needed it. Now she was sitting at the airport, the burning question uppermost in her mind was how could she manage for a week without it in the Bahamas. She knew that the world appeared to be at her feet with limitless opportunities of fame and fortune. At least, she told herself, her internal conflicts of anxiety weren't affecting her constant flow of work offers. She had magazine covers, articles on "how to get the look with Phoebe Clarke", her own fashion column, and TV appearances as a fashion guru. Now, she was on her way to a huge ad campaign with Ringo Starr, to be filmed in the Bahamas. She'd instantly accepted the job, especially as it was with Simon.

'This is the life.' Simon was talking to her. She willed herself to concentrate on what he was saying. 'Have you already met Ringo?'

'Yes, but I think he may have already been drinking that day and it was only mid-morning.' Phoebe liked to redirect attention to other people's excesses away from her own.

'Yes, I'd heard that he'd been on a bit of a self-destruct mode since his marriage broke up.'

Phoebe wondered if Simon was watching how she would react to what he'd just said. Was he testing her? She pulled a face.

'Poor guy, I don't blame him. Who wouldn't go on a bender if their marriage went pear-shaped?' Simon nodded in agreement, so maybe he hadn't been testing her. 'So my brief was to create various past-Beatles' looks for him. I was put in touch with his management and they suggested I should meet him at his house near Windsor. You know, Si, how I told you that I grew up listening to Beatles music and that their records were the first ones that I'd ever bought with my pocket money? Even collecting Beatles cigarette cards as a child, actually I think I also collected Monkees ones too, so although I'd liked Paul the most, it was beyond exciting to be going to meet Ringo at his house. Anyway, they sent a driver for me to go to his house at Tittenhurst Park in Sunningdale Ascot. The driver didn't talk to me at all until we were nearly there.'

'Was the house amazing?' Simon was impatient to know all the details before they got interrupted by the final call to board the plane.

'Wait and see, let me finish the story. When the driver finally decided to start chatting, he told me that the house had been John and Yoko's house with a recording studio in it where all the Beatles had met to work until they'd split up, nearly eleven years ago now. This was where John and Yoko had filmed the song Imagine in that white room with the white piano.'

'I know, I've seen that video, how amazing.' Simon was impressed.

'Anyway, apparently John left with Yoko for America and never came back and the house was sold to Ringo as part of an unpaid debt. Maybe the driver was being indiscreet telling me all this but I was listening to every single word. He then warned me that John and Ringo no longer spoke so it was probably best not to mention John to him. However, Ringo doesn't actually live there now he's divorced, but lives in Monte Carlo and the house is mostly used for bands to record and stay there too. Anyway, I waited in the back of the car whilst the driver pressed the intercom at the gates to enter the grounds of the estate. The house was a huge Georgian pile at the end of a winding driveway.'

'Bigger than George's house?' Simon was trying to picture the size.

'Yes, I think so; awesome and very grand with huge white pillars at the entrance. Ringo himself actually came out to greet me with his lovely Liverpudlian accent. Do you know I went completely dumb with the shock of actually meeting him and that's never happened to me before with any celebrity, except when I came across my long lost best school friend Paula in the South of France last month,' Phoebe paused for breath, 'maybe I was struck dumb because Ringo had been part of my Beatle school girl crushes.'

'Carry on, Phoebes.' Simon was desperate for Phoebe to get to the end of the story, he always knew all about her schoolgirl crushes, he'd heard about them often enough when they'd been dating.

'So, when I'd managed to speak again, I told him I needed to recreate some Beatles looks for him to wear in the commercial. "No problem, follow me", he said, so I did. I followed him down his beautiful manicured gardens to a sort of a temple building.'

'Temple?'

'Yes, a sort of hexagonal temple. I don't remember how many sides it actually had, so let's call it hexagonal anyway. I think it may have been something to do with the Hare Krishna who'd stayed at Tittenhurst before. Anyway, we went in and it was like a shrine full of old Beatles clothes.'

'Wow, Phoebes.' Simon actually felt quite jealous of Phoebe's experience just then, it must have felt like time-travelling.

'I know, it really was a definite "wow" moment and Ringo was so completely matter of fact, like it was a normal day to day occurrence for anyone to be looking through old Beatles clothes and accessories. "Help yourself to anything you need, just look after it and return it when you're done," he'd said. I suddenly had the same feeling then that I'd had when I was a child in my mother's dressing room, but ten times better. So there I was re-living my childhood standing with an actual Beatle, surrounded by Beatles clothes; patchwork boots with stars, embroidered mirrored shoes, Nehru jackets and Afghan waistcoats just like the ones we used to see in the Kensington Market, it felt like I was living a dream. And now all these clothes are packed together with some new tailored suits I'd had made for him too, all ready for the Bahamas.'

'Phoebes, that's so amazing, not many people can say they went through old Beatles clothes together with an actual

Beatle, well done. So, our last swig of champagne should be to toast our first big commercial abroad, working together and many more to come.' Simon held his glass in the air before they both gulped down the remainder of their champagne as their flight was finally called and they collected their hand luggage ready to board.

When they arrived at their location, they could have been anywhere in the world, as they spent every day shut away filming in an air conditioned studio, too tired to go out at night. Phoebe wished she'd had some coke with her and had to remind herself she'd promised Paula she was going to quit. She was beginning to feel quite ill though, it was the first time she'd been without any drugs for a long time and she hoped she could manage to get through the filming; she also hoped that Simon hadn't noticed anything odd. He kept asking if she was alright, she always said she was. Phoebe felt she could manage and vowed to change; she was finally facing up to the fact that her friends may have been correct when they'd suggested she was on the path to self-destruct. This would now be the new "no-drugs at all" Phoebe, she could do it.

The shoot finished and the crew held their Wrap party and said goodbye. There were a few throw away comments and winks from a couple of the crew to each other "What happens on location stays on location." Phoebe wasn't one of those who'd played away, so she just joined in the laughter and breathed a sigh of relief that she'd got through the week and everyone was still happy.

She and Simon flew out of the Bahamas straight after the shoot and into LAX airport, where Jake was waiting for Simon at the other side of customs. Simon did one of his girly shrieks of joy and both he and Phoebe rushed towards Jake to have a group hug, it felt just like old times again.

'How are we getting into LA?' Phoebe immediately asked Jake with childlike excitement.

'I've got a car, I'll go to the parking lot and bring it back,' and then Jake saw their bags, 'oh my god, you guys have so many bags.'

Phoebe surveyed the cases and trunks piled up all around them. 'Really, you think so?' she asked with a dead pan expression of British understatement.

Jake had to laugh, 'Don't worry, we'll still all fit.' He re-appeared a few minutes later behind the wheel of an enormous old open-top Chevy.

Phoebe patted its bonnet. 'Love it, Jake, it's so cool.'

Simon and Phoebe threw everything into the cavernous car boot and sat themselves between the overflow of the smaller bags that hadn't fitted. Phoebe looked out at the scenery as it whizzed past them on the freeway into Los Angeles. 'Everything here is so tidy and manicured looking, Jake, not at all like London.'

'Look, see that pink house with all the statues surrounding it?' Jake took one hand off the wheel and pointed to his right.

'Yes, it's huge. Why?' Simon and Phoebe chorused.

'Well, it belongs to one of the Arab sheiks who never stays. He has it on permanent stand-by just in case he decides to fly-in. The house is run like he's living there, even with all meals cooked daily.'

'That's mad, what a waste. Does he ever come?' Simon asked astonished, thinking that this Arab was living in a whole other parallel universe to him.

'Not as far as anyone knows, welcome to LA. So guys, we've arrived and this is my little house in West Hollywood.' They pulled up outside a pretty Spanish-style Hacienda with palm trees outside and a small front courtyard. 'The studio is renting this for me whilst we're filming.'

Phoebe got out of the car. 'It's so sweet and pretty, Jake.'

'I know, cute, isn't it? And it means we can all stay together although I have to be careful, Phoebes, about being seeing with Simon.'

'Simon told me,' Phoebe said sympathetically.

'We three together is no problem at all as you're simply my friends staying from back home.'

The three of them smiled at each other.

'Bliss.' Phoebe flopped down on a chair in his sitting room and for the first time in a while, she really meant it. She spent the next few days being shown around Los Angeles with the two boys and it was as if the three of them had never been apart. Jake pointed out all the cool boutiques on Melrose which were just her style, a mix of eclectic and vintage clothes, then drove them up and down Rodeo Drive, LA's most expensive designer shopping street. Each store had a valet parking guy who took Jake's huge car whilst they window-shopped and lusted after the Designer fashions. They went everywhere on their whirlwind tour. At Venice Beach they roller-bladed down the boardwalk past the muscle guys working out on the beach. They had drinks on the pier at Santa Monica and drove past all the Malibu beachside celebrities' houses.

Their final stop was the Malibu Pier café where they sat facing the ocean whilst sipping their B.52 cocktails, the café's must-have cocktail.

'You know, sitting here reminds me of an English seaside pier,' Phoebe mused as she gazed out to sea, 'I love piers, don't you? They have so much nostalgia about them and this pier has been featured in so many movies too, can you remember which ones? I can't. It feels so familiar as though I've been here before, like when you meet a movie star and you think you know him but you actually don't and it's only because you've seen the actor in so many movies. You know, I could happily live and work here, maybe I should set up my own business here too and then we could all hang out together again. What do you think guys?'

Simon looked thoughtful. 'Well, I was always intending to end up here with Jake when he'd finished his movie, so if you came to live with us, it would take the heat off our relationship, in fact it would be the perfect solution.'

The boys looked at each other in agreement and then at Phoebe.

'That's genius Si, what do you think Phoebes?' Jake sounded thrilled at the idea.

Phoebe nodded, as the thought of a fresh start was hugely appealing. 'To be honest, there's not much to keep me in London. I've got a few client projects to finish, then I could find and set up a style studio here as my base couldn't I? That could be so cool, what would I call it?'

'How about Phoebe's Style Bar,' Simon quickly threw his suggestion into the mix.

'Ooh yes,' Phoebe shrieked with pleasure, 'love that name, we could have a grand opening and get loads of my celebrity clients there and also press, I can imagine it already.' She grinned excitedly. A whole new chapter of her life was about to get underway.

Phoebe made it her business to spend the next few days meeting estate agents to look around vacant shop properties, and then one morning she knew she'd found the perfect one and immediately wanted Simon to come to see it. She phoned him straight from the viewing in a frenzy of excitement.

Simon answered the phone sounding sleepy, 'Morning, you were up and out early today.'

Phoebe was not feeling in the least bit chatty, she just wanted to tell him her news, 'Hi Si, you know I've been looking for somewhere to base my styling business? Well, I've found an empty store on Melrose, when can you come to see it? Please say today, please? I want you to be the first to see it.'

'I'll be there in an hour. What's the address again?'

Phoebe was beside herself with excitement now as she had already told the realtor she would take it, signed the papers and was ready for works to start immediately.

Simon was prompt as always and as Phoebe showed him around the empty shell of a building, he could totally imagine what she was envisioning as she described her plans.

'I want it to be a really cool place where my clients will enjoy the whole experience. It's got to have a back door too for any publicity-shy clients. There'll also be a separate room with all the designer sample dresses, shoes and accessories on display, oh and look books so clients can pre-select their options for the Oscars, Grammy's, music awards or any red carpet appearance or photo shoot. And I think there should also be a mini bar and coffee area where partners or husbands can chill whilst they're waiting. Ooh and Si, you could have a makeup corner or even your own makeup range that we could sell from there.'

'Hey, slow down one step at a time Phoebes, get it built and opened first. I can see that it's going to be so brilliant though. I'm so happy for you. You know you'll also need to find an assistant for when you're off travelling, one that's really creative and good and most importantly, not so ambitious that she wants to take your business over and

343

become you. How about a young guy you could train up, who loves fashion as much as me?'

'That's a brilliant idea maybe you could find him for me? We will be open very quickly. By the way, do you remember how I told you about my old friend Paula, the one I bumped into when I was in France? Well, we now speak most days, wherever we are in the world and she's going to be staying very soon at the Beverly Hills Hotel or the Chateau Marmont. So finally, you'll get to meet her; I know you'll love each other.'

Simon hadn't seen Phoebe look this happy for such a long time, everything seemed to be falling into place for her, 'I can't wait to meet her and I know I'll love her - any friend of yours is automatically a friend of mine.'

Their last night in LA arrived all too soon before Phoebe made a flying visit to London, and then come back before returning back that same week to start living at Jake's and working in LA full time at her just finished newly opened Style Bar.

'We've been invited to a cool party tonight at the house that was owned by Burt Ward, the original Robin, in the Batman TV series.' Jake was in charge of the trio's social diary.

'That sounds fun and a chance for us all to dress up, could you bear to do my make up for me please, Si?' Phoebe pleaded, 'it's my first party in LA, the girls here are all so tall and beautiful and I'm so not.'

'Don't be so silly, you don't have to be tall and blonde to be beautiful, it's all about what's within, and of course I'll do your makeup for you.'

'Your amazing makeup always gives me extra confidence.' Phoebe looked thrilled that he'd agreed, she didn't realise that Simon would have done absolutely anything for her - she just had ask.

They arrived at the party and waited while they watched Jake's car being driven off by a good looking, out-of-work actor/valet parking guy. Jake's was still the only car that wasn't a brand new "look-at-me" sort of car, but he didn't care, he was used to it being parked side by side to Bentleys, Ferraris and Porsches and it was a big improvement on the old banger he'd driven before. This car had character and one day he'd be able to afford a proper status symbol car.

'Golly, this house is left over from the sixties.' Phoebe couldn't believe her eyes,

'The carpet's not going to stay white for long, is it? Simon, the ever practical man, was staring at the white shag pile carpet that covered the whole of the huge living room area.

The three friends walked further into the already crowded room, glad they'd all gone to so much effort to dress up, with Phoebe being especially happy with Simon's makeup help.

'Shall we go over the bar area, at least we won't look like "Billy-no-mates" standing over there.' Phoebe and Simon followed Jake over to the bar area.

Phoebe was staring around her so intently as she was following behind Jake and Simon, that she didn't see a change of level in the room and tripped and fell flat on her face. She was momentarily shocked and then embarrassed that she should have made such a spectacle of herself.

'Are you okay?' The boys were peering down at her anxiously.

She looked back up at them and started laughing, and then laughing so much she couldn't answer.

'Yes, thank you... so silly.' Tears from laughter were now running down her face smudging Simon's perfect makeup and blurring her vision so much that she didn't notice a tall very good looking older man standing over her, offering to help her up; she thought she was still only talking to Simon and Jake. 'Why would anyone build a whole circular sunken area in this room?'

'It's called a conversation pit.' It wasn't Simon or Jake who'd responded to her question, it was the older man standing over her who'd given her the answer. This whole concept of a conversation pit started her off laughing again.

'Conversation pit, that's so funny, is that the only place we can go to chat?'

Simon and Jake started laughing too, when Phoebe realised that Jake had recognised the unknown man standing there and needed to introduce him.

'Umm... this is Marcus Lean, the producer of the movie I'm in. Marcus these are my friends from London; Phoebe, "the" best celebrity stylist and Simon, a brilliant celebrity makeup artist. They've just been working together in the Bahamas with Ringo Starr and came via LA on their way back to London to see me, we've all known each other for years now.'

Phoebe felt Marcus's eyes fixed on her and she caught his gaze just for a moment.

His eyes were a piercing blue and seemed even bluer against his slightly leathery perma-tanned skin. He resembled a cross between Clint Eastwood and George Hamilton, definitely a sexy silver fox, one that was extremely appealing to stare back at. He was probably even older than her father, making it seem even odder that she should be finding him so attractive, but there was no doubt in her mind that she was.

He acknowledged their group with a polite cursory and fleeting trace of smile, 'Good to meet you all and Jake I'll see you in the New Year on set,' and then switched to a full-on

Jack Nicholson smile, one that was so unsettling as his eyes didn't match his lips, it was a smile with menace attached;

'Phoebe I suggest you try not to fall into any more pits, conversation or other.' And he walked off, leaving the small group looking at the back view of his immaculately pressed pale blue Brooks Brothers button down shirt, chunky brown leather belt and Levi jeans.

His smile had had a strange effect on Phoebe. Her insides suddenly felt sort of mushy. 'Wow, he was good looking for an old man.' Phoebe was looking wistfully back at him as he disappeared into the party guests again.

'Phoebes forget him. Firstly, he's Jake's boss for the next year and secondly I've heard that he's a serial womaniser and not a very nice person.'

'Don't worry, Si, he's much too old for me.' However, Phoebe didn't say what she was really thinking, that the dangerous sexy glint in his steely blue eyes had already made a major impression on her, which wasn't going to go away anytime soon. She needed to gather her thoughts on her own for a moment.

'Guys, I'm just going to the loo, back in a minute, where shall I find you, here at the bar?'

'Sure, we'll wait for you.'

'Where's the loo, please?' Phoebe asked one of the beautiful Californian blonde girls.

'Loo?' she looked back blankly at Phoebe.

Phoebe tried again, 'The toilet?'

'Sorry?'

Phoebe realised that there was a completely different vocabulary going on here from the British one and started over again. 'The rest room, umm, the little girls' room, the powder room?'

'So sorry, didn't understand, are you Australian?'

'No, I'm British from London.'

'Oh gee, I'm sorry,' apologised the girl once again, 'I'll take you there.' Phoebe followed her. 'Here you are, there's a line though.'

Phoebe translated line to mean queue so she stood there patiently and waited. She realised that most of the girls weren't waiting in line for a pee though, they were all going in twos or threes, coming out sniffing or giving their noses a checking wipe, they'd been in there to do drugs. Phoebe really did need a pee and she'd made a pact with herself that she was no longer doing any coke.

'Hey, do you think the line will take long?' she asked the girl in front of her who smiled at her understandingly, waving her ahead.

'If you want to go in front of us...' Phoebe was really trying to be strong. She knew she'd only have to ask and one of the girls would immediately invite her into the loo to share a line. Could she hold her resolve, yes of course she could, so she went on in ahead of the girl.

Just as she was going to go inside the bathroom, one of the other girls asked her the million dollar question, 'Wanna line?'

Phoebe's inner demons wrestled with each other, which one was going to win the battle? She'd just told herself that she was never going to use again, maybe just one final one and then that would be it, never again, Simon and Jake wouldn't notice. She could hold it together if it was only one line.

'Maybe just one small one,' Phoebe answered hesitatingly. She sniffed the white powder from the girl's tiny silver spoon held out to her. It didn't take long for her to remember how

348

good she felt when the effects kicked in. When she finally emerged again, she found Simon and Jake waiting for her by the bar, although their happy demeanour and attitude towards her seemed to change as she re-joined them.

'Hey guys, finally back again. I was chatting to some of the girls in the line for the loo, it took forever as there were so many girls all waiting.' Phoebe was sure she was speaking convincingly but she could feel Simon looking at her closely before he answered her without any of his usual warmth in his voice.

'Phoebe, I know you only too well and I can see that you've just had a line or two. Please don't take me for stupid; come on now this has been going on too long, Jake and I think you've got a serious problem and need help.' Phoebe said nothing, but knew from the tone of his voice, and that he'd called her Phoebe not Phoebes, that she was in trouble. 'As your best friend, I'm telling you to sort yourself out and stop now before you ruin your life and everything that you've achieved. You know I love you and only want the best for you. Phoebe, you're not looking at me, are you even listening? Hey! Look at me!' Phoebe raised her eyes to look directly at him. 'Believe me when I tell you, I think you've got an addiction problem and if it stems back to whatever happened to you that night at the ball, you have to now face up to it.'

Phoebe tried to process what he was saying but the coke had made her feel defensive.

'Don't be stupid Simon, of course I don't have a problem, I may have just had one toot but I'm fine.'

'If you say so. Remember, I'm now watching you, this isn't the Phoebe I knew and loved that I now see before me.'

Phoebe was shocked at Simon's words, she decided they were unnecessarily harsh, he'd never spoken like this to her before ,or been this angry. Maybe she should go and hang out for a while on her own while he cooled down. She leant on the railings of the decked patio area overlooking the twinkling lights of Los Angeles city. Did she really have a problem? She was sure she could stop whenever she wanted, she'd managed when they were in the Bahamas hadn't she? Although, Paula too had told her she had a problem. Why were all her friends on at her all the time like this? She took a cigarette from the host's wooden cigarette box on the coffee table and looked around for a lighter or matches; she rarely smoked but she was now so annoyed by Simon that a cigarette was exactly what she needed.

'Here, let me.'

She looked around, oh God, it was that sexy older man again. He was standing very close, so close in fact that she could feel his breath on her neck. How had he appeared so quickly and silently from nowhere, like a predatory hunting cheetah, the fastest animal in the wild: She briefly wondered if she was his prey, and why was she suddenly comparing him to a cheetah? Cheetahs suffocated their prey and then hid the corpse so other animals wouldn't help themselves. Her brain was playing mad games, it must be the coke, or maybe it had been cut with something strange? She tried to clear her mind as she looked at him.

'Here, let me light it for you.'

Phoebe held the cigarette to her lips and as she did, she briefly looked into his eyes and then had to look away; his gaze was too intense to hold. He smiled at her with that same languid, sexy but scary smile of the hunter animal but this time with a show of teeth too, like he was about to devour his prize. He lit her cigarette; she inhaled and slowly exhaled the plume of smoke, once again turning her head away from his face playing for time.

'So, young lady, we can't go on meeting like this. I'm about to go off on location after this weekend, filming for the next six months. I'll call you when I'm back in town. That's a promise.' He bent over as he was so tall and Phoebe so short, kissing her full on the lips. 'Remember,' was all he said before he walked off again back inside without looking back.

Phoebe tracked his progress as he disappeared as quickly and silently as he'd appeared. Phoebe put her fingers to her lips where he'd just kissed them, she certainly wasn't going to forget Marcus Lean anytime soon.

Chapter 28. Phoebe. Los Angeles, 1979

Marcus had been regularly travelling back and forth between film locations and checking rushes in LA. All was going well, nearing the end and he was in a good mood. It had simply been a coincidence that Phoebe had been at the same parties and events as him over the last few weeks; LA wasn't really a very big place when it came to the social scene. Now, once again, they were at the same cocktail party and he decided it was time to make his move. He was filming the next day with a dawn start so it would need to be sooner in the evening rather than later. He walked straight up to her, ignoring the friends she was standing with.

'Hey again, Ms Phoebe Clarke top celebrity stylist in Hollywood and owner of the exclusive Style Bar. I believe I may have picked you up, literally, from the conversation pit you fell into at a party last year.' Phoebe stared at Marcus and blushed. Her friends had now all stopped talking to listen to what they could see unfolding in front of them. Marcus moved in even closer to Phoebe and spoke so quietly that only Phoebe could properly hear what he was saying;

'Phoebe, I've never said this before to any woman in my life, I fell in love with you at first sight. This is probably a strange thing for you to hear. It's the truth, so there it is.' With that, Marcus once again walked away, leaving her stunned and surprised in the centre of her friends. Simon, who had exceptional hearing, was the only one who overheard and was immediately deeply suspicious.

Marcus always liked to have the upper hand with any woman, with an element of surprise, it always worked, it worked in business and it worked in his private life. In business, he'd heard them call him controlling, but that's how he got successful movies made and in on budget and *all* his movies were always huge box office hits.

In his private life, he was adamant that all women liked men to be in control, just as animals did too. All the horses and dogs that he had on his ranch knew exactly who was boss and they always did what he asked of them. He also knew that his late mother had seen the bruises and cuts that his dad's leather belt and buckle had inflicted on him when he was a boy, although she had never said a word. Therefore he'd reasoned, as he grew up, that his father's actions must have been okay, yes, sure they were, they'd made him into the successful alpha man that he was today.

Animals needed a master, a boss to give them their orders and he was the equivalent of the leader of the pack, the top dog. He'd always watched how animals interacted with each other and considered the outcome from a specific repeated action. When he occasionally gave his dogs a new toy to play with, hidden treats inside, he'd noticed how enthusiastically they played at first, learning how to find the treats. Then, the moment the dogs managed to work out how to find their rewards they would quickly lose interest, eventually discarding or even destroying the toy. When life was all too easy with no challenges, everything became boring just as it did with women.

So Marcus lured them in, playing with them, then chewed them up and spat them out. There wasn't a single empathetic bone in his body, although every woman he had ever fucked would undoubtedly have confirmed how charming and solicitous he was, but only at the beginning. They would have then said that it had been too late by the time they'd discovered his dark side, they were already in lust, or maybe

353

even in love with him, and hoped for a ring on their finger more than just a "happy ending".

So Phoebe's relationship with Marcus went from nought to a hundred in no time at all He literally swept her off her feet and made her feel special. Every single day he sent huge bouquets of flowers to the Style Bar until her small studio began to resemble a florist. He sent envelopes containing tickets for surprise theatre visits or days out, often in a helicopter to fabulous locations. If he was away filming, he would send pre-paid indulgent spa treatments and pamper sessions for her to share with a girlfriend.

She was flattered, as any girl would obviously be, with such extravagant gifts. She was also impressed about the amount of time he wanted to spend with her as he was such a busy man. For the first time in her life she believed this man could love her and she was blown away by his financial generosity. She blinded herself however, to his complete lack of emotional richness.

Phoebe loved the novelty of being phoned by Marcus's PA to be given instructions of where to meet him that evening for the theatre or a restaurant, even though she chose to ignore that she was never asked if she had alternative plans. It was simply expected that she'd drop everything to be there. Phoebe remained on her fluffy cloud of happiness, playing along with his every whim and request. She'd known true love would appear again to her one day and now it had. Marcus was her soulmate, her shining knight on a white charger, or in his case a black Ferrari.

Although Phoebe was obviously filled with gratitude at everything he'd given her so far, the constant gifted surprises, each one more grandiose a gesture than the last, gradually started to feel slightly overwhelming and she wasn't sure why. She'd shown Simon some of these presents, but as they mostly arrived at the Style Bar, she kept them there. Oddly she felt slightly uncomfortable or even embarrassed at showing Simon, maybe it was because she knew deep down that Simon was deeply suspicious of Marcus's actions and he didn't actually like him.

Phoebe basked in all the attention Marcus was giving her. It was as though there was a sun now shining in her heart, bright and warming giving her an inner glow she had never had before. Marcus phoned her in the Style Bar throughout the day to ask how she was and even where she going out to next. At first, she would always stop her work to answer, even if she was with a client, to chat to him. As the weeks went on, she wondered why he should sound so put out or even offended if she couldn't find five minutes to speak when he called, or if she was too busy to answer – after all, she was working and had a business too. He then wouldn't answer if she tried to call him back, even if it was five minutes later, as though he was punishing her.

So Phoebe began to understand that everything would always be on Marcus's terms, even a simple phone call. She convinced herself that, as he was an older man, he was used to doing everything his way and that was what generally happened in a relationship if there was a thirty year age gap. He always had his reasons for everything he did, however, it did seem that he had now taken control of their social life. He made the movie and theatre bookings and chose the restaurants, they were always his choices. She'd initially liked that her *boyfriend*, she loved that word, had taken control, making all the decisions. However, she was a grown up woman of twenty-five years old, successful in her own right, so surely she should be able to have some say in their life together? She didn't say anything though as she didn't want to rock the boat.

Marcus gradually asked Phoebe about everything in her life, her lonely childhood, her distant parents and even her small but loyal circle of friends, and she was filled with joy that this powerful Hollywood man should now be investing so much time and effort in her. She willingly let him into her world and was available to him both emotionally and physically. She ignored the fact it was singularly one-sided as he never talked about himself, or had any physical interaction with her which seemed strange; Simon had warned her that Marcus was well-known as a player.

On their date nights, Marcus's driver would always collect her and return her back to Jake and Simon's house at the end of the night. Even on weekends, she would only spend the day with him, never the night. He had a never-ending store of seemingly valid reasons which he constantly produced before she could even query why she was once again going back to her own home.

'Sorry Phoebe, I'm filming tomorrow with a crack of dawn call,' or 'Phoebe, I know how busy you are this week with your clients and photo shoots; best if you go home tonight.' So Phoebe still hadn't done any more than have an occasional end of date kiss with Marcus and she was suddenly worried that he could be another Simon, unlikely though it seemed.

Even when they went away for weekends he'd booked them separate bedrooms. He defended the decision with, 'I don't want to take advantage of you Phoebe, the time has to be right.' Phoebe wondered when the time would be right as she would have been all too happy to be taken advantage of. She finally realised that she would have to summon up the courage to ask the question so she could remove all her doubts about his sexuality. She waited until they were having supper at one of his favourite restaurants and she could see he was in a good mood, with his filming having gone well that day. She'd taken extra care in what she'd chosen to wear and hoped it was one of the dresses he liked her most in. She braced herself and took a deep breath as she had no idea how he was going to react. She was already aware that his moods were unpredictable. She placed her hand on top of his on the table, and stroked his fingers gently as she spoke.

'Marcus, you say you love me and you know I love you too, I'm not sure how to ask this... umm, do you still fancy me as we've only ever kissed and it's been quite a few months now that I've been your girlfriend.' There she'd said it and she felt slightly sick as she waited for his reply.

He looked at her with slight annoyance showing in his expression, then immediately flashed a brief smile to make up for any visible loss of self-control and show his good intentions, 'Of course I do, Phoebe. You know how important our relationship is to me, and so special that I want to keep it pure like this until we're married. You know I love you and can't live without you now. When we're married everything will be different.'

Phoebe missed the forced fake smile and his annoyance. She was blinkered in her judgement and only saw what she wanted to see and believed what she wanted to believe. He'd said he loved her and that was surely enough.

So their life carried on. Marcus had now started to question her each day about all her Hollywood party invitations and red carpet events. Phoebe had loved how much he wanted to be involved in her life until he began to suggest what she could accept and decline and then bizarrely she thought, which dresses she should wear on their evenings out. She was a stylist for goodness sake, surely she should be able to make herself look her best, that was what her clients paid her to do for them, no one had ever complained before. However, no man had ever chosen and bought her designer dresses to wear before either, so maybe she should embrace this whole new experience of being looked after, like a pampered princess with Marcus, her prince.

Simon was not at all happy about the situation as he'd been watching Marcus from his very first meeting with Phoebe, and he was now becoming increasingly worried about how quickly Phoebe was being sucked into what Simon believed was emotional coercion. Marcus was such a powerful Hollywood player and with power, came silence from any who wished to continue working with him, or else to be blacklisted. Simon knew how it worked in this town. He could see that Phoebe had already fallen head over heels in love and could only see this man through rose-tinted glasses. Therefore, nothing he could say would ever make any difference, he knew she wouldn't choose to believe it.

As Phoebe felt discussing Marcus with Simon was becoming an off-limits subject, she began to discuss everything instead with Paula in their daily phone calls.

'Paula, I really want you to meet him, I know you'll see why I love him so much.' Paula, who could run a masterclass on men, doubted it, although she didn't have the heart to burst her best friend's love bubble.

No charm offensive could last forever and Marcus's was no exception. Phoebe didn't notice as the change was so subtle. 'You look so pretty in that dress,' Marcus would say when he'd first greeted Phoebe on their date nights. Now he looked at her asking. 'What *are* you wearing? Have you put on weight?' Phoebe would then spend the evening wishing she'd had time to change and worrying if she'd got fat again.

He was particular about everything she did, although she accepted it as one his character traits, why shouldn't he like everything to be perfect, his way. For example, his inflexibility on meal times, 'Phoebe, you're late. Dinner was on the table for eight O'clock. Conchita will be so upset that her beautiful food is now cold.' Phoebe had already apologised that she might be late as she'd been at the Style Bar finishing with a tricky client and had called to say she was on her way. She excused it as maybe he'd forgotten after all, he was a busy man.

She had liked it when he'd first ordered for her on their restaurant dates, enjoying his authority with staff and of how he took control of the situation, although she gradually realised each time he ordered for her, he'd never given her the chance to choose as he only ever ordered what he wanted her to eat.

Even all the small gestures that she'd done so willingly for him at the beginning, when she was over at his house, had gradually become an expectation or something to be grumbled at. 'Phoebe, you know I like my coffee with more milk.' 'Why is there a slice of lemon not lime in my vodka and soda?' Phoebe chose to ignore all this as well. She was in love and had had years of practice in denial.

When Marcus suggested that he should be able to see her diary too, she hesitated before she replied. It had seemed to her that everything had been working quite well until then.

'Phoebe, it's getting very hard to see you now, I've decided to collate our social diaries so we can plan our evenings more efficiently.'

'Marcus, darling, if you think that will work better. Although, you know how hard I try to juggle everything, you first of course above everything.' She knew she had to mention him first, above the Style Bar and her celebrity clients, 'Maybe I really do have to find an assistant now.' She knew immediately she shouldn't have spoken her thoughts out loud as the very next day he had taken control of finding her new assistant.

'You'll be thrilled to know I've already found you a lovely girl called Chloe, who I will add to my own payroll, see how much I help you? You only have to ask and it will be done, just like that.'

Phoebe felt that she should be pleased and grateful However, she was quite upset that she'd had no say in the hiring of her own assistant. She wondered who exactly this Chloe was and where he'd found her. This girl was going to have to be really good and up to speed as many of Phoebe's celebrity clients were extraordinarily demanding and difficult.

Chloe took control of Phoebe's diary and reported back to Marcus, so Phoebe suddenly found her own social arrangements crossed out with notes for her to reschedule. She ignored the warning bells for this too. She repeatedly reminded herself that she loved him as he'd told her he loved her. She'd never been happier, had she?

One morning they were having breakfast together, one of the rare times she'd started to stay over at his Laurel Canyon house in the Hollywood Hills. It had been Conchita's night off so they'd had the house to themselves. No sex had still had been forthcoming, just a kiss before he retired to his own master suite and she to the guest bedroom suite. He had already made the coffee and laid the breakfast table before she'd come down. He uncharacteristically offered her a warm cinnamon roll, Phoebe was surprised at this new turn of events and took the roll gratefully as he also poured her coffee.

'Thanks Marcus, this is lovely.' She looked at him, smiling, wondering what all this was about as this wasn't normal behaviour. He was looking pleased with himself.

'Phoebe, I've a lovely surprise for you. We're getting married secretly tomorrow afternoon on the front lawn, no paparazzi or photographers, just us, so it can be a special occasion for us to enjoy together without sharing it with anyone else.'

Phoebe wasn't sure whether to laugh or cry. This wasn't a surprise, it was a disaster. Of course she'd always wanted to marry him. She'd imagined Paula to be maid of honour, and Caroline and Charlie there too with her goddaughters, the twins, as her bridesmaids. Also Simon and Jake and even George and Joe too. These were all her closest friends who'd supported her. Then there was of course Mrs Abbott who'd be so upset to miss her wedding. Maybe though, Mrs Abbott wouldn't have approved of Marcus, thinking he was too old. Would her parents care? No, she was sure they wouldn't, well certainly her mother wouldn't as Marcus was just a wealthy American without a title, they wouldn't have taken on board that he was also a successful film producer.

Phoebe knew not to show how upset she was, or verbalise any of her emotions as it would start a fight and she knew she couldn't deal with that at the moment. So she went for the non-confrontational option. 'That's so sweet Marcus, I haven't got anything to wear though.'

'Don't worry, darling, that's all taken care of. Your dress will be arriving at lunchtime and so is a hairdresser and makeup artist.' He looked smug that he'd thought of everything.

She was now really shocked, 'Marcus, you know Simon who's my best friend in the whole world, is a makeup artist. He would have been thrilled to have done this for us.' Phoebe was careful to say *us* not *me.*

As usual Marcus had his own spin on everything. 'I wanted it to be a wonderful surprise Phoebe, so I couldn't risk him telling you. Don't tell me you're not happy. Everything I do is always for you, you do understand that, don't you?'

Phoebe turned away so he couldn't see her tears. This wasn't how she'd envisaged her wedding day to be; the day she'd dreamt of all her life – to be held with no guests.

She reminded herself that he loved her and how lucky she was. What other husband-to-be would arrange everything so perfectly and with such attention to detail, even the dress. She knew undoubtedly it would be beautiful.

'Of course I want to marry you,' Phoebe blinked away her tears as she turned back to Marcus, 'I love you so much.'

Marcus's petulant scowl turned back into one of his dead-eye smiles. 'You had me worried there for a moment. Chloe's on her way round to bring your dress, and she'll be our witness.'

Phoebe tried to not let the horror of this suggestion show on her face, but her new assistant Chloe as witness, really? She didn't even like the girl much. Phoebe hardly trusted herself to speak.

'We could have a small party next week.' Marcus added, cajolingly.

Phoebe smiled weakly. She was about to become Mrs Marcus Lean, why was she feeling so apprehensive - she was being silly. She'd have to learn not to overthink everything.

Tomorrow would be the best day of her life and the first day of her new life as Mrs Marcus Lean. She was a lucky girl.

Chapter 29. Paula. Los Angeles, 1979

Paula had not stopped working ever since she and Phoebe had parted company in the South of France. Claude was so thrilled at her success with Abdul, that she had started sending her to all her VIP clients over the last few months. As a result, Paula had travelled all over the world to meet them. Her bank account had subsequently swelled to such an extent, that she'd had to discretely ask one of her past clients where and how to invest. She absolutely knew she just couldn't leave all those thousands of dollars and pounds just sitting languishing in her various foreign, American, British and French bank accounts. Her diamonds were already safely in her safety deposit box in the Harrods bank vault together with substantial cash in case of an emergency.

Paula had learned that however many contingency plans she made, there could always be more as life had unexpected twists and turns. A girl always needed to look after herself, just in case. Paula was happy though for men to be her major benefactors. Yes, she liked the word benefactor, it sounded classier.

So she invested in property. It was good that she had so many helpful clients who could advise in all areas. One of her New York benefactors found her a Manhattan loft apartment and a London client found her a studio just up the road from where Phoebe had lived with her parents. Even with these two properties bought outright, Paula still had money left over. Maybe one day she could fight hard and dirty, throwing unlimited money at top lawyers to find her daughter and get her back.

She had just returned from a job in Hong Kong and was feeling badly jet-lagged. She already had another job booked tomorrow to fly to Washington. She imagined it was likely to be someone high up in politics but obviously wasn't going to be President Carter, he was a happily married man.

She lay stretched out along her sofa, perfectly pedicured feet up on the arm and out of her Manolo sandals. She was exhausted, maybe she just needed a holiday on her own, or even another girls holiday with Phoebe. That would be such fun, they could go to Barbados to the Sandy Lane Hotel. Yes she would call her to suggest it, she loved that idea. She wasn't sure how she was going to get hold of Phoebe though. If Paula called her at Jake and Simon's home, she only ever got the answer phone, so she left messages. If she left messages at the Style Bar where she knew Phoebe was most likely to be, that rude Chloe girl usually answered and she was sure that she never gave Phoebe her messages. She didn't have the phone number of Marcus's house although she was sure she could find his office number, although she was also sure no messages were going to get to Phoebe from there either. She would have to make a trip to LA straight from Washington and literally sit and wait for Phoebe outside her home or work.

She switched on the TV and channel hopped. She realised she so much preferred British TV, the American channels seemed to always be full of adverts. She stayed on All My Children, it was one of the best soaps as TV soaps went. She shut her eyes for a moment and dozed off. The phone was ringing, was it the TV or her phone? The only people who had her number were Claude and Phoebe. This was her private sacrosanct space, as was London too, never for entertaining clients.

'Hi, who's speaking please?' Paula thought she'd better ask just in case, even though there were only two people it could have been.

'You sound so proper and polite, Paula. Who do you think it could be, it's me Phoebe, except I'm no longer Phoebe Clarke, I'm now Phoebe Lean.' Phoebe rolled this information down the telephone line in a very matter of fact way. Almost as though she was telling Paula it was going to be raining tomorrow.

Paula sat up so quickly from her supine position that she had a head rush. 'You're what?' she screamed down the phone so loudly that she was sure that everyone else in her building could have heard her. 'What the fuck? How could you have got married without me there? You know I'd have cancelled everything and flown half way round the world the same day to be with you, and it would have been as I was in Hong Kong.' Paula felt sick from the sudden shock and unbelievably sad that she had missed her best friend's most important day.

Phoebe replied quickly, 'Well, it would have been the same day. Marcus sprung it on me yesterday as a surprise. He's gone away now. Listen, I'm literally only on my own for the next forty eight hours. Can you fly up to LA?'

Paula knew she would say yes even if it meant a black mark in Madame Claude's book, she needed to be there for her friend as soon as she could. There was no way that Phoebe would ever have wanted to marry so suddenly like this, she guessed it was that manipulative bully Marcus who had forced her into it. She knew she should have tried to warn her friend away, but she couldn't see how she would have managed it as Phoebe was so besotted with him. She also knew that as Phoebe had been living with Jake and

Simon until then, neither of whom Paula had yet met, she was sure they would both have had a view and maybe tried to stop the relationship before it progressed too far. So no one would have been able to do anything except maybe Mrs Abbott, but she was on the wrong continent to be able to help. Paula didn't know what to say, she was so upset for her friend.

'What about the perfect wedding dress? And everything else you'd always wanted, and all your friends being there? Oh Phee.' Paula was feeling Phoebe's pain.

'He'd said he'd wanted it to be special, just for us.' Phoebe was holding back her sobs now as she was realising the enormity of what had happened. She didn't want to cry though as she did love him.

Paula could hear so many warning bells, but she didn't want to rain on her best friend's parade who'd just married the man she said she loved. She wasn't sure what to do now, to warn her to be wary of him or to be happy for her, so she held her tongue.

Phoebe sounded like she had gathered herself together again. 'Paula, listen I'll be fine and we're happy. Marcus just wanted everything to be absolutely perfect for the two of us on our very own.'

Paula quickly changed tack. She still didn't trust herself to say too much. 'So where's the honeymoon?'

There was a long silence. Paula could sense the hesitation in Phoebe's voice. 'Umm. We don't seem to have scheduled one as we're both so busy.'

Paula digested that information. 'Well, I hope at the very least you've got a huge rock on your finger,' she said with a smile in her voice.

'Trust you, Paula! Yes, I've got a huge fuck-off diamond. It's weighing my hand down as we speak. In fact, I have to hold the phone with the other hand.' The girls laughed together. It seemed to ease the tension between them.

'Phee, I'm out of here on the next flight. I'll be with you as quickly as I can. Love you.' Paula just couldn't bring herself to say congratulations. She had such a bad feeling about all this. Phoebe was good at lots of things, but judging men wasn't one of them, especially as she was far too naïve and romantic.

Paula's viewpoint was that all men should be appraised with an unemotional detachment, more like a business transaction. There was no point in telling that to her best friend now, it was too late and she'd gone and married the guy. So the next best thing she could do was to cancel or postpone the Washington job and immediately get on the next plane to LA and support her.

Phoebe worried about Marcus finding out that Paula was now staying in the house whilst he was away, but if the worse came to the worst, she knew that Paula could always quickly move to a Hotel. She was also worried about the situation with Simon and Jake as it meant suddenly there was no girl in the house as a buffer for the whole gay-living-together situation. At least at the moment Jake was mostly on location and Simon travelling all the time for work. Worst of all though, was that they still didn't know she was now married and had moved out all in the last twenty four hours.

She needed to urgently let everyone know her news before the press got wind of it, and get the rest of her clothes and belongings from her room in Jake's house. Maybe she could do that together with Paula as soon as she arrived. Phoebe kept on wondering what was really bothering her as the only change in her life was that she was now a married woman, it wasn't as though she was a prisoner or anything. She really had to sort out how she felt about her sudden change of circumstances, after all, it was what she had always wanted. Maybe having her best friend to stay with her soon would help clear her current anxiety.

Phoebe received the same shocked reaction from every friend that she phoned. Simon seemed the most upset and Phoebe completely understood why, as they'd always talked about how he would make her look her most beautiful on her wedding day and would be there to support her together with Jake. Phoebe could hear his voice breaking with emotion as he struggled to say what he knew she wanted to hear. She knew in her heart it wasn't how he'd imagined being supportive, but she quickly tried to push these thoughts away.

'Phoebes, I'm so happy for you but you know I would have wished it to have happened all differently. I'll tell Jake when he next phones me as he's in the middle of nowhere filming at the moment, but I'm sure he would be as thrilled for you as I am.' Phoebe somehow sensed a flatness in Simon's congratulations, as though he was delivering them mechanically before he continued to say, 'Just remember, I'm always there for you when you need me.' Simon hoped that he sounded happy for her and decided not to mention any of his worries about Marcus, and definitely not his whole living situation. It wasn't the moment.

Caroline at first sounded equally surprised at the news. She immediately wondered why Marcus had been so keen to marry her friend so quickly and then in such a selfish manner. Surely a girl's wedding day was one of the biggest and most important days of her life, it certainly had been for her with Charlie. So to deprive Phoebe of all that and also of not being with all her friends and even family, well Mrs Abbott anyway. Caroline was so upset and worried for her friend that she nearly forgot to congratulate her, although once she had, she decided to lighten the mood with a joke.

'Well, purely on a selfish note, I've now missed out on a new wedding outfit, so it'll be back to that sexy old country Barbour and wellies for me. Maybe as a treat for Charlie tonight I can just wear the two together with nothing underneath.' Good that had made Phoebe laugh. It sounded more to Caroline that she wanted to cry.

After all the negative response, Phoebe just couldn't face calling Mrs Abbott and hearing her disappointment and even disapproval. The possibility of any more disapproval, even unsaid would be too much; she'd already heard it in the poignant silences in the other phone calls. Maybe she'd quickly write and send Mrs Abbott a letter. No, a telegram would be the best way to tell her. Maybe that was a coward's way out, but for the best.

Phoebe still continued ignoring all the noise of the chattering voices in her head, telling her everything wasn't as it should be and that she shouldn't have allowed herself to be swept off her feet by Marcus. Everything was going to be alright and she was happy. Yes… she was happy. Yes… definitely very happy. She repeated it again and again to herself to help a positive mind set. Paula was about to come to stay with her too and her best friend always said it as it was, but Phoebe wasn't sure she wanted to say to Paula how it all actually was.

Paula's sudden arrival in the house seemed to set Conchita in a bit of a spin, although she quickly made up one of the guest suites for her boss's new young wife. Paula immediately understood from the expression on the Mexican housekeeper's face that she was very much in Marcus's employ and would be reporting back to him straight away. Paula's sixth sense was telling her that Conchita was Marcus's silent eyes and ears on everything that always happened in the house, and anything else that that she'd ever seen happening in Marcus Lean's home stayed firmly within the confines of his four walls and her well-paid loyalty to her boss.

The girls lay and sunbathed in the garden, swam in the pool and went out for their meals. Phoebe didn't want to ask Conchita to cook anything for them: She felt awkward, as though she shouldn't even be already living in the house. Although she was of course now Mrs Lean and fully entitled to be there and give Conchita orders. Oh gosh why did she overthink everything?

As the girls lay by the pool, they each waited for the other to say something but the conversation always seemed to veer away from the sensitive topic of Marcus. Paula could see that Phoebe was on edge the whole time and didn't know how to address this new elephant in the room. Her gut told her that there were definitely issues with Marcus, but no hard evidence of anything untoward apart from organising a surprise wedding and was that so different from marrying on the spur of the moment in Vegas? Unusually for Paula, she was at a loss what to do. She'd just have to wait for Phoebe to open up and take it gently. She'd start with sex chat, that was always a good girly ice breaker between them.

'So how was your wedding night? Did Marcus deliver on all counts? Was it all worth waiting for? Come on details, please.' Paula was sure that Phoebe would tell her everything after having heard all about her past sexual encounters. They were now sitting at Café Figaro on Melrose, where Paula had suggested as she knew Phoebe would love it there; it was very Parisian, bohemian and cool; very Phoebe.

Phoebe answered as though she was deliberating just how much to tell, 'Well, he was very passionate and definitely sexy and we made up for all those months of nothing, just as a wedding night should be.' Phoebe couldn't bear to look Paula in the eye as she spoke, and she continued to tuck into her hot fudge sundae as though her life depended on it. She'd had no expectations of how a wedding night should be, but she knew hers wasn't it. They'd had the evening ceremony on the lawn with just the priest and Chloe and Conchita standing there. Marcus then opened a bottle of champagne which they drank before Chloe left and Conchita disappeared to make them dinner.

Phoebe had tried hard to warm to Chloe as they all celebrated over their glasses of champagne, she even tried to view her in a different light away from their work environment of the Style Bar, but Chloe seemed colder and even more distant. If anything, she seemed jealous that Phoebe appeared to have everything now; a fabulous house, a good looking rich and successful husband and a thriving styling business.

Phoebe and Marcus then dined on the perfect romantic combination of lobster, strawberries and more champagne on the candlelit terrace. Phoebe was gradually having high hopes of the night continuing in this way until they reached the bedroom. To start with everything was gentle and sensual and beautiful, just how any foreplay should have been with a new partner, getting to know their bodies, after all, it was the first time she and Marcus had done anything more than kissed. Phoebe was losing herself in the moment and knew she really did love him so much and would do anything for him as they continued caressing. Then, it was though a demon had suddenly taken over his whole being as he'd entered her. All his gentleness turned to fucking her so hard that she cried out. He no longer held any eye contact with her as he rammed his rock hard cock repeatedly deep inside her until she felt her very ovaries bruising. After only a few thrusts he came. Quickly removed his now flaccid member without even a kiss for his new wife and took himself off to the bathroom. Phoebe had had no chance to come and she knew she now could, after her time with Saffron. Marcus had taken no interest in any of her needs, only his own. Phoebe had lain there looking at the ceiling, shocked, whilst Marcus had already got back into bed, given her a cursory kiss and fallen asleep, leaving her lonely and frustrated as he snored.

Phoebe knew she didn't want to tell Paula any of this as maybe this was just as it was a first night thing and Marcus had been tired and drunk. The following morning Marcus had been exactly as she would have hoped, greeting her with his early morning hard-on poking into her back before they had leisurely languid sex as new husband and wife. Yes, she really did love Marcus and all her doubts from the previous night were to be forgotten.

She didn't need to tell Paula how Marcus had seemed to take control of her life gradually over the last months and she couldn't see how Paula would be able to do anything to help. When it came to Paula leaving, she looked closely at Phoebe again.

'Are you sure you're alright? You know we agreed we would always tell each other the truth now. Well, I still feel that you're holding something back. Although you look happy enough your eyes are sad. Phee, I know you so well, I know that something's not right. I'll not be back in LA for a while so please tell me now so I can help you whilst I'm still here.'

Phoebe looked at her friend and at that moment wanted so much to tell her everything. How could she begin to tell Paula how Marcus had slowly changed from appearing to be a doting caring boyfriend and now husband to the outside world, whereas he was actually critical and controlling. Phoebe simply said nothing as the two friends hugged and Paula left for the airport and Phoebe returned to wait for Marcus's return.

No post-wedding party ever materialised again in any conversations and in the subsequent months, Phoebe decided it was best not to bring the subject up as Marcus's volatility and moods changed like the British weather. When he lost his temper and became anything other than the loving man she thought she knew and loved, he immediately reigned back and switched on the full throttle charm offensive again. His extremes of behaviour confused Phoebe, but she chose to believe it must have been something that she'd done wrong each time.

She gradually realised that Marcus didn't like being criticised about anything he did, however small and inconsequential, quickly becoming angry and defensive. Phoebe was beginning to feel that she was walking on eggshells all the time. She learnt to say as little as possible and bite her tongue rather than any of her words being misconstrued. She'd learnt how to live like that years ago growing up with her mother, so this was her default mode and she'd returned to her childhood settings.

Everything he did, she believed stemmed from his love for her and wanting to be with her twenty-four-seven.

'Why don't I get you a personal trainer, then you don't have to drive over each day to the Jane Fonda studio. I'll hire one of the instructors from there for us, then we can exercise together at home. That would be so much easier for you, especially during your busy awards season.'

'That's so sweet of you Marcus, but I do quite like going to the studio and having coffee or a juice after the classes with all the girls.' She stood firm and she was surprised he didn't fight it. So she continued to go to her aerobics classes at the Jane Fonda Studio on South Robertson Boulevard. It seemed to be one of the few things left that she was still able to do with her Beverly Hills housewife friends. She'd started going when it had first opened that year. Paula had gone with her too when she was in town. Jane Fonda herself had even taught some of the morning classes. "Go for the burn!" Jane had shouted at them as they all sweated away in their headbands, leotards and leg warmers.

After classes all the girls stayed around to have a healthy juice and gossip in the studio café. They were all so open and honest with each other about what went on in their lives, but she always held back on her personal disclosures. She wondered what they'd think. Sometimes, Jane joined them too.

'Do you know, girls, that my dad Henry Fonda told me as I was growing up that unless I looked perfect I was never going to be loved.'

'That's so wicked, a parent should never say something like that to a daughter. To be honest, my father wasn't too kind either.' Paula sympathised.

This also resonated with Phoebe. 'That's strange, Jane, that was exactly what my mother said to me too.'

The other girls in the class, chimed in as well with their stories. It felt a bit like group therapy, although Phoebe always remained more of an onlooker than a participant. It seemed all the women there had had family members who'd made a negative impact on their lives. It was so interesting always hearing others' stories. She learnt something new every time. Phoebe's chances to go to the classes and then stay and chat with the group didn't last for very long. It seemed coincidental, but Marcus started finding reasons to come past to take her off out to lunch with him, reasons why she needed to come home, there and then, to change and get ready. Her gym buddy friends sighed and thought how lucky she was that she had a husband that wanted to be with her so much, but Phoebe knew she wouldn't be going anywhere but to inside her own gated home.

Marcus then began to look in her diary and see when she'd arranged an evening out with Simon and Jake. He'd always come up with some obscure alternative plan that would mean she had to cancel them. She realised that somehow Marcus had gradually whitewashed all of her circle of friends out of her life; it was subtle and anyone looking in from the outside would only see her perfect life.

Although Marcus professed to want her to be with him all the time, she rarely saw him except for dinner as he was always shut away in his office, away working on the final cuts of his movie or having business meetings. Occasionally Phoebe was invited along to some of the business dinners but she knew she was not expected to say much, just be decorative. None of the executives ever asked her about her own business, they only saw her as Marcus's new young wife. The Style Bar was busy, although Marcus only allowed her to work with her clients there for a few hours a day, always with his driver taking and collecting her to and from there. It seemed that Chloe had been instructed by Marcus to take over all her client red carpet events and gradually all her own invites dried up or coincided with one of Marcus's dinners which he required her to be attending with him. Often those dinners seemed to get cancelled at the last minute, leaving Phoebe sitting on her own at home whilst he went off to the Dome with his all-male drinking buddies. Phoebe knew that's where he'd gone, although he always denied it.

'Why would I do that, Phoebe, when I have a beautiful wife, whom I love, waiting for me at home. Don't you trust me? It would seem that you don't.' Phoebe wasn't sure any more of anything. It seemed that when he climbed into their bed late at night, he smelt of other women's perfume.

Phoebe was beginning to wonder how it could have happened so gradually that she hadn't noticed; this transition from super-successful celebrity stylist to the stars and owner of the Style Bar, to Beverley Hills power couple wife, to Beverley Hills housewife, to Beverley Hills princess locked up in her ivory tower.

Chapter 30. Forbes. Los Angeles, 1979

'Hello, may I speak to Mrs Lean please. No, she's out? Okay, please tell her that Paula called again.'

'Si, si,' the voice at the other end of the line assured her.

Paula frowned before she remembered not to, wrinkles, and replaced the receiver.

She was becoming increasingly worried about Phoebe. She was finding it impossible to reach her friend on the phone or to see her in person. It was so unlike Phoebe not to call back and however many messages Paula left with the Mexican housekeeper, she still heard nothing back.

Paula stood up and crossed the lounge of her Beverley Wilshire Hotel suite to look out at the busy LA rush hour traffic several storeys below. The Hotel was perfectly situated at the intersection of Wilshire Boulevard and her favourite shopping street Rodeo Drive. A shopping spree was paling into insignificance as her bad feelings about Marcus grew.

What if he was distancing Phoebe from everyone, from all the friends who cared about her? Paula decided she'd have to find an alternative way to see Phoebe, perhaps a way that could include Marcus and gave Paula a chance to get to know him a little better. She was momentarily distracted by the sight of a police car, siren flashing, speeding down the wide boulevard below. That was it, she'd include a man in the mix, so Marcus could have someone to talk business with and she could also catch up with her best friend. She'd ask Forbes, the new man in her life. He'd been another of Claude's introductions. He wasn't exactly the sort of man she'd imagined she would end up with but he was kind and generous and cared about her. He was also very, very rich.

Marshall Forbes the Second was a seventy year old Texan oil millionaire who seemed to be a stayer and Paula was determined to keep him. He liked her to be around regularly in his life, so she'd phased out all the other men. She had already mentioned him in passing when she'd flown to see Phoebe straight after her wedding day, however the subject had somehow paled into insignificance after the shock announcement of the marriage.

So Paula had then suggested a meeting, 'I want you to meet my new man, so shall we meet next time he's in LA on business?'

'Paula, I'd love to meet him. That would be so brilliant, give me a date and I'll put it in Marcus and my joint diary.'

'Great, I'll sort it with Forbes and let you know.'

However that date had yet to be set as each time Phoebe wrote it in their diary Marcus found another excuse to postpone. So Paula decided that maybe if the invite came directly from Forbes himself with Marcus, it could be more likely to happen.

Nobody in the film industry ever passed up a chance to meet a potential investor as wealthy as Forbes. It would also be interesting to hear what his opinion might be of Marcus as she totally trusted Forbes. Hopefully, the men would get on well enough and they could do their men's business chat, giving Phoebe and herself time for their girls' catch up.

Paula picked up the phone to call Forbes in his office; he always answered the phone to her, however busy he was. He immediately made the arrangements and booked Chasens, one the oldest and best restaurants in Hollywood for dinner the following week. Occasionally, Paula wondered if there was anything he couldn't fix and then immediately dismissed the idea as laughable; power and money spoke everywhere.

Chasens, she knew, was an excellent choice, everyone in the movie business went there and getting a table at short notice meant you were a big cheese. She also knew Phoebe would enjoy it.

Phoebe took extra care in getting ready and was careful to keep out of Marcus's way so that they could arrive free of any conflict. It was going to be fun to finally double date with her best friend. How could she have reached the ripe old age of twenty five years old and never yet double dated with any girls. This was going to be an interesting night and hopefully a successful one. She hoped that Marcus would be welcoming her friends with his public persona of full-on charm.

If he did she would be able to relax and enjoy the evening.

Marcus did indeed turn up with all his charismatic charming side fully operational and on full-throttle, so far so good. They'd already got through the starters and onto the main course now and all seemed to still be running smoothly. Phoebe had been half watching and listening to him whilst managing to chat to Paula and could overhear him talking business to Forbes.

'I've nearly finished tying up all the loose ends of my new movie, ready for release. Have you ever dabbled in movie investment, Forbes?'

'Indeed-y, I have and this current movie sounds mighty interesting, Marcus. I know all your movies and they've always been big box office successes. Why don't we talk again when we're on our own. I never like to mix business and pleasure, don't you agree? Especially whilst we're in the company of these two beautiful women.' Forbes wasn't one that anyone ever argued with or even contradicted, so both girls were keenly watching how this conversation may unfold. They both were holding their breath as they could feel the palpable tension suddenly that was hovering over their very prominent and visible table in the restaurant.

Phoebe glanced at Paula, who had actually blushed, Phoebe had never seen her do that before, this was a new side of Paula; a new softer, feminine side. These two made a really sweet couple together. Yes, he was a bit old but then so was Marcus. Forbes obviously cared a lot for Paula by the way he was looking at her adoringly, the same way she remembered that Marcus had first looked at her.

'Let's reconvene tomorrow in my office.' Forbes closed down the conversation, giving Marcus a friendly slap on the back as though he'd already sealed the deal and Marcus was now looking irritated. Phoebe noticed every nuance of change of his mood nowadays and began to worry how the rest of the evening was going to go. She had a bad feeling as she could sense that Marcus had suddenly become a ticking time bomb. She was sure she hadn't done anything wrong. The tension in the air over the dinner table had gradually become more pronounced and uncomfortable with Marcus progressively monosyllabic and offhand. No one wanted to be the one to break the silence. Then Marcus abruptly told her it was time to leave, just like that. Phoebe had at least thought they might be able to finish their dinner. It was the first time he'd ever sat with any of her friends and she was utterly mortified.

'Maybe just a little bit longer Marcus? It's been so lovely to spend time with Forbes and Paula.' That seemed to be the nail in the coffin. She could feel the pressure of his hand on her thigh squeezing his nails into her flesh.

'Phoebe, you know I've an early start. We're leaving *now.*' And with that, he stood up and shook hands formally with Forbes, 'I've settled the bill.'

Phoebe could see Forbes looked surprised as he had expected to pay but, magnanimous as ever, he thanked him with a second Presidential style pat on Marcus's back adding, 'My secretary will call your office tomorrow to confirm a time for our meeting.'

Phoebe wondered why Marcus had felt the need to completely ignore Paula as he was saying goodbye. Phoebe tried to catch Paula's eye but didn't manage as she was whispering something at that moment to Forbes. Marcus had put his hand firmly on Phoebe's back and swiftly propelled her out of the restaurant before she'd even managed to kiss Paula goodbye, it had all been so sudden. She tried to look back but it was too late as they were already out of sight and they got into the car in silence.

Phoebe knew Marcus was holding back as they were now with his driver. She could feel the atmosphere, weighing down on her like a heavy cloak. She realised that Marcus was quite drunk and this did not bode well; cold icy fingers of fear were creeping up her body at the thought of being alone with him in the house. She shivered and felt herself shrink into a metaphorical ball, bracing herself for what was to come. She knew she must have said or done something to displease him, but still had no idea what.

They arrived back at the house and she undressed and got into bed. Her sleep was restless and disturbed as she was on high alert to hear the bedroom door opening during the night but he never came so Phoebe realised, her punishment this time was the silent treatment. When she came down to breakfast she found he was already getting ready to leave and didn't look at her or acknowledge her on his way to the front door.

The moment she heard his car engine start, she grabbed the kitchen phone to call Paula; that was strange there was no dial tone. She tried another phone in the sitting room, nothing there either. She desperately wanted to speak to Paula to apologise and hear her feedback about the evening; they'd always held post-mortems after their nights out. Maybe she could go to an exercise class instead to meet her.

She went back to her bedroom to change into her exercise kit and went back downstairs to go to the front door. They always kept it locked from the inside when anyone was in the house, leaving the key hanging on a hook by the side of the door. Phoebe looked but the key wasn't there. Maybe it had fallen off its hook? It wasn't anywhere at all, how strange.

Phoebe walked all the way around the house checking for doors open onto the garden. They were all locked too, but that was normal unless they were having guests round and opened all the French windows to the terrace. She tried round the back door which led off the kitchen where she found Conchita busy working away in the kitchen. The back doors from the kitchen to the garden was open, Phoebe breathed a sigh of relief – maybe Marcus had just locked all the doors carefully last night and not had time to re-open them all for the morning as he'd rushed off so quickly.

'Morning Conchita, how are you today? Just to let you know I'm going out and won't need lunch, thank you. I'm off to the gym now and then to the Style Bar.'

'Muy bien, Senora Phoebe but Senor Marcus, he say that you stay in house all day today and that I must to look after you as you tired from last night. He say you no go out today.' Conchita had been leaning with one hand on the marble worktop, the other holding a large whisk with which she'd just been mixing a cake mixture.

Phoebe was confused, she felt fine. 'I'd really like to go out, Conchita, I'm fine, really.' What was going on here?

Conchita stopped leaning on the counter, and stood up tall to her full height which was only about the same as Phoebe's; she then folded her arms defensively across her bird-like petite body, whilst still holding the whisk, unaware she was letting the cake mixture drip to the floor.

'He say... no... I must tell you, lo siento, Senora Phoebe.' Conchita's stance was firm both in her body language and tone of voice.

Phoebe wondered why the housekeeper should be telling her what she could do and not do and finishing her sentence with an apology. Why were all the doors shut too and only the kitchen door open and, why no phones working? This was just all too bizarre.

Conchita and Phoebe stood there staring at each other. Phoebe puzzled and Conchita defiant, although slightly ashamed that she couldn't let this young woman, who actually didn't seem to be ill at all out of the house. However, these had been Marcus's instructions this morning.

Then it occurred to Phoebe, if all the house doors were locked it was likely that the security gates to the property would also be locked. Why should Marcus have done this today, had he locked her in today to teach her lesson for something she was unaware she may have done last night?

How could Marcus have taken over such control of her life, and if today's actions were anything to go by, then she was likely to be fighting a losing battle that Marcus was going to win. Okay, today she'd let it go and tomorrow was another day. He loved her, he told her that daily and she absolutely loved him still. She'd make it up to him tonight, wearing his favourite dress, the way he liked her hair and make-up and ask Conchita to cook his favourite dinner. Then she would take him to bed, submitting to any of his increasingly perverted sexual demands with no boundaries, that he now regularly pressurised her into performing. Then everything would be okay again tomorrow, he always seemed sorry for his behaviour and usually apologised afterwards when she cried.

Chapter 31. Phoebe. Los Angeles, 1980

The fortress-like electronic gates of their house swung open, they were on their way back from an extremely rare evening out together. Phoebe wasn't sure what had prompted Marcus's suggestion, however she'd leapt at the chance of finally leaving the house again and seeing the outside world.

Over the last three months, she'd had intermittent stretches of time imprisoned in her own house. Marcus's mood swings had dictated how he had controlled her hourly passes to freedom, with his lows and highs influenced by Phoebe's abilities to confirm his doubts that he was the centre of her universe. When he felt she was everything a perfect wife should be, then he opened that door, just a tiny chink, to the free world that she'd always known before.

However, with this came new non-negotiable caveats firmly in place; limited, once-weekly or sometimes fortnightly, chauffeured journeys with one of his rota of drivers to the Style Bar, to a gym class, to a morning coffee with gym ladies, to a lunch with the Beverley Hills wives of his business partners and a very occasional and very quick coffee with Simon or Jake but never with Paula, and always with the driver sitting waiting in the limo overseeing her every movement.

To the outsider it simply looked as though Marcus was a kind, thoughtful and caring husband who liked his wife to always have his driver available for her own personal use. To Phoebe, it was a complete loss of her personal freedom and possibility to spend time with her true friends.

All chances of any social engagements were so limited that Phoebe found herself having to decline most invitations, always blaming it on her husband's busy forward social planning. The wives all gazed enviously at Phoebe's lifestyle, believing it to be perfect with a generous and omnipresent husband; their older husbands were likely to be off somewhere sleeping with their young secretaries or starlets, or preparing to jettison the wife for another newer younger version.

Paula appeared to be Marcus's main bugbear and Phoebe was absolutely sure that Paula had phoned numerous times to the house with all these messages never passed on to her.

The Style Bar phone was as normal, as it was obviously used daily by Chloe for their clients, although Phoebe was sure that on her rare visits there, Chloe tried to listen in to her calls, even taped them on an extension or reported back to Marcus. Maybe even the phone was tapped, she was now sure that Marcus could be capable of such a thing.

When Phoebe occasionally succeeded in speaking to Caroline, Paula, Simon or even Mrs Abbott, she was careful to be monosyllabic and superficial in her chat. Everything appeared to be rosy in her married life with limited personal information offered. Any questions asked were swerved around or ignored just as politicians did. In fact, Phoebe realised that she was now as tactical as one, under Marcus's restricted and regimented regime ; she was only able to speak Marcus's version of the truth, not her actual reality.

Marcus and Phoebe were on their way back from Morton's, a restaurant owned by one of Marcus's business friends, Peter Morton, who also owned the Hard Rock restaurants. It was super-trendy and the hub of the Hollywood TV and Film industry on a Monday night. Phoebe had realised that Marcus was going there to talk up his new movie and she would sit in the background and be happy to do so. It was so exciting to actually be out to see people.

Marcus never left her side during the short time they were there and they were home again before it was dark.

Phoebe looked up at their palatial home as they drove up the long drive, still awed at the size of the mansion they lived in. The surrounding lawns were manicured and tended to within an inch of their immaculate roots by a small army of gardeners, just like her glam squad army that had worked on perfecting the looks of her celebrity clients. That now seemed to be another life, an alternative reality and a long time since it had happened, as it was mostly Chloe that worked with her clients on shoot days.

Phoebe was confused now by days and time. In her new normal, each day blended into another, they were all the same until the occasional hours of supervised freedom.

'I think you should go to your room to lie down and have a rest. I'll tell Conchita not to disturb you.'

'Marcus, I would prefer not to spend the rest of the evening alone in my room.' She tried to say it in the least provocative way she knew, so as not to incite any anger. It had been a calm night so far as she was becoming more and more adept at reading his moods and how to play them, until he lost control.

Marcus appeared to be briefly considering her comment before he dismissed it, staring back at her with cold and un-empathetic eyes and a small curl of a lip promising a smile that never materialised.

'You know I love you and only want what's best for you, so I'll bring you up a cup of tea myself, and how about I give you a massage before I leave again? It will help you relax properly so you can sleep tonight? It seems to be so difficult now for you to sleep.' It was true, Phoebe had been having problems sleeping with recurring nightmares too. Marcus had told her he would give her something called barbiturates to help. She didn't know what a barbiturate was, but the tiny purple pill seemed to be helping at night, even if it made her feel drowsy and disorientated in the daytime.

However, she didn't actually want to go to bed yet, she wasn't ready, but it was easier to acquiesce. Marcus led her up the wide marble staircase to the galleried second floor overlooking the high-dome ceiling entrance hall, shutting the bedroom door firmly behind him.

'Lie down darling and get undressed. I'll be back in a minute with your tea.'

Phoebe wondered what other busy film mogul husband would be so thoughtful to bring his wife tea in bed when she's not feeling well and then to offer to give her a massage? She was a lucky girl, he was excellent at massages, except when he reached her shoulders, digging too hard into her tension knots. Sometimes she then wondered whether his hands were about to travel around her neck and close over her throat, but they'd always stopped at the back of her neck.

She undressed and lay down onto their crisp white Egyptian cotton sheets. Their super-king size bed's freshly ironed sheets were changed daily, it was one of Marcus's rules. Admittedly there was nothing like getting into a bed with cool crisp sheets, especially when it was so humid outside.

Phoebe lay there and obediently waited for him. She put her hand between her legs, she still fancied Marcus as much as she had on the first day she'd met him, she could feel herself getting wet in anticipation. She might just get out her vibrator whilst she was waiting, although Marcus hated her using a vibrator, so she'd had to hide it. She didn't really understand why it should have upset him so much, did it make him feel inadequate; not enough for her? Of course he was enough, it was just something that girls liked as well sometimes, a quick moment of pleasure, what could be wrong with that?

Yes, it might take a little while for him to come back with the tea, she still had time. She focused on being in the moment and turned the reality of the vibrating pink plastic wand into an imaginary lover going down on her, it wouldn't take long as she was wet already; she turned the controls to the highest speed setting. The buzzing of the vibrator was quite loud and as her eyes were shut so she didn't see or hear Marcus coming back in the room. Suddenly she heard him screaming at her.

'What the fuck are you doing, can't you even wait a few minutes for me?'

The next thing she knew was that Marcus had thrown the tea at her. She was so surprised that she didn't feel the pain of the hot liquid trickling down her bare body. He stood there white with anger, palpably shaking.

'You're an ungrateful bitch, I go to make you tea and I come back and find you like this.' He grabbed the vibrator from her hand and threw it across the room at the same time as undoing his flies, 'Is this what you really want?' He was holding his hardening penis out like a menacing weapon as he approached her angrily. 'Tell me my cock's better than the vibrator, go on say it!'

He threw himself on top of her and rammed himself in with no preamble. The shock of his sudden assault returned her to a flashback of her teenage rape. She tried to disassociate her body and her mind, it was difficult. She'd already been wet in a state of arousal from the vibrator which had allowed him to slide in with no pain, but now her body was shutting off with shock. He relentlessly drove his cock into her, pumping faster and faster. It hurt, why didn't he stop? Marcus braced himself onto his forearms as he pushed harder and deeper inside her. She tried to look away and not see the icy cold anger in his eyes; they were the eyes of someone she'd loved, still loved but no longer knew.

'Look at me Phoebe, you've had your moment of pleasure. Shame you just couldn't wait for me and it's my turn now.' He ignored her tiny whimpers of pain as he drove himself deeper and deeper inside her. 'Why aren't you screaming with pleasure, you little slut. Do you only get off on your vibrator? Tell me you like my cock better.'

She didn't know what she liked anymore and couldn't bring herself to answer. She no longer knew what was right and what was wrong. What was normal, what did other girls do? She no longer knew . She needed to speak to Paula. She'd thought she'd enjoyed sex with Marcus until now and she'd always wanted to please him. She'd agreed to all his warped sexual requests even though she didn't enjoy them, did other husbands behave like this? She knew in her heart they didn't - she'd had enough experience of random fucks over the past few years. Why was she allowing herself to be treated this way by a husband she loved so deeply and who professed to love her. The only answer she could come up with was that if he loved her too, then she must deserve whatever he chose to inflict on her.

It must be her fault.

Chapter 32. Phoebe. Los Angeles, May 1980

Two weeks before Marcus's Film Premiere

'My wife's so beautiful and talented, I simply don't know how she finds the time to have such a successful styling career and still be able to look after me so well, aren't I just the lucky one? Let's have a toast to Phoebe, for throwing such a fabulous dinner party tonight,' Marcus held up his champagne flute, 'here's to Phoebe.' And everyone joined him in his toast to his wife.

Phoebe blushed, 'Thank you all so much for coming, it was my pleasure.' She looked around at their table of dinner guests, some who'd flown in especially from Europe. She'd tried her best to put together the perfect stylish dinner party for him, as a stylist she knew she could always make anything look beautiful, making an evening successful was much harder, especially when she felt so constantly tired and disorientated. She was taking two little purple pills a night now instead of the initial single one, to help her disturbed sleep and nightmares. Now, she felt zombie-like though and it was so hard to collect her thoughts.

Marcus had hired caterers for the dinner, as that's what everyone did in Los Angeles. Everything still needed overseeing and he liked perfection, so she'd tried to make sure nothing went wrong or was left to chance, but it was so tricky to remember everything or indeed anything at all through her brain fog and she so wanted to please him. She'd talked or had she mumbled, she didn't remember, to the guests on either side of her and opposite her, just as she had been brought up to do. She'd had a glass or two of wine, surely she couldn't be drunk on only two glasses of wine, since when had she become such a lightweight? She was doing her best to be a good wife and dinner party hostess.

Try to focus, Phoebe, she reprimanded herself, as the dinner was for some of the business partners and financial backers of her husband's new movie, "The girl next door" which was launching at the Cannes Film Festival in two weeks with Jake starring in it. She was so proud of her friends, they'd all become so successful. What had happened to her, she'd once been so successful too, when and how had it slipped away?

The guests were still looking at her expectantly after Marcus's toast. She attempted to smile back at them, but she felt tears welling up in her eyes. Why was she so emotional all the time now, she no longer felt like the same girl who'd been stylist to the stars and business owner. She desperately tried to stop her tears as she knew they'd be noticed by Marcus.

'Thank you, Marcus, that's sweet of you, darling. Can you please excuse me for a moment as I've just got to make sure everything's okay with Conchita in the kitchen and that desserts and coffee are nearly ready.' The guests all smiled back at her as she excused herself from the table.

She tried to walk as silently as she could across the marble floor in her stilettos, it was hard to do in the high heels that Marcus demanded she should wear. Why was she stumbling so badly, she'd always found walking in heels easy, even in her highest Manolos, they were the perfectly designed and crafted shoe. She progressed slowly from the dining area on one side of their eighty foot drawing room to the kitchen. She'd walked across this room hundreds of times, now it felt like she'd succeeded in climbing Everest. She stopped to take a moment to look at the amazing view from their house down across the twinkling lights of the houses in the Canyon. Yes, she was a lucky girl, most people would dream of living the life they thought she led when they read about her in the magazines and newspapers, but they didn't know that Marcus had now succeeded in cutting her off from every one of her friends and celebrity clients.

She felt so confused all the time. She forgot where she'd put things and then they'd then turn up again somewhere else, how could she misplace everything? That was really strange as she'd always had a brilliant memory; she'd always managed to remember everything she needed to when she was styling. What was wrong with her, was she losing her mind? It wasn't like she was doing drugs any more, she'd stopped all that when she'd opened the Style Bar after Simon and Paula had both been so vocal about her drug using.

Phoebe stumbled on into their secondary kitchen, holding onto work surface tops to help her round the room. This kitchen had banks of ovens and equipment that looked like a scientific laboratory; it was only ever used by caterers for entertaining Hollywood-style. The other small kitchen was the one they used daily for breakfast and light meals, where Conchita cooked for them. Conchita was with the caterers in the midst of a hive of activity. Phoebe acknowledged all her hard work with a big smile and Conchita returned a smile in a motherly caring sort of way. Phoebe attempted to pull herself together, stand unsupported and to sound business-like, 'How's everything going, Conchita?'

'Muy bien, Senora Phoebe, Gracias a Dios! Senor Marcus is happy?'

'Thanks Conchita, yes, the food is delicious and the guests seem to be enjoying themselves too.' Phoebe liked Conchita and she wanted her to become a Mexican version of Mrs Abbott for her, but Phoebe knew if push came to shove,

Conchita would always take Marcus's side. He had given her the possibility of living illegally in Los Angeles with her daughter - never to return to a life of poverty again in Mexico. Phoebe was sure Conchita saw everything and said nothing.

Phoebe attempted to focus on the hive of activity in the kitchen and at what remained of the beautifully prepared and presented food that had been served for their dinner. It seemed that there was as much left as they'd eaten, Los Angeles women only ate the odd lettuce leaf as they all wanted to keep young, slim and attractive for their powerful rich older husbands, oh how could she have forgotten, she was one of them now too.

'Senora Phoebe, I worry about you, me preocupo por ti.' Conchita walked over to Phoebe to pat her in a caring way on her shoulder.

'I'm fine, really Conchita, just a bit tired. It's been a long day.' Maybe what she needed now was to be on her own just for a moment. 'Gracias Conchita. I'm going to go to the bathroom and then back to join my guests, please tell Marcus I'll be back at the table very soon. Actually, whilst you're there, please could you ask our guests if they'd like coffee or umm, herbal teas with their dessert? Oh, and whether they'd like to move out to the terrace or stay in the dining room?' She tailed off as she wasn't sure she was making sense to Conchita.

'Si, Senora, will do.'

Phoebe knew Conchita was staring after her with concern as she left the busy kitchen on her way to their main guest cloakroom, why did they live in such a big house, even the cloakroom was about three times the size of most normal people's bathrooms, it was where Marcus kept all his film awards, without looking like he was bragging or saying "look at what I've done", as it was after all, only the loo. Phoebe had always admired that understated side of him, as for a really super-successful film producer whose movies had won so many Oscars, he was actually very modest.

She slumped down on the toilet, just managing to remember to lift the lid up first and wondered how long she could get away with staying in there. She stared at the walls covered with signed photos of him together with all the famous actors and actresses who'd starred in his movies. She shut her eyes for a moment, she mustn't stay in there for too long.

The walk back to the dining table seemed to be even more daunting now. She tried to pull herself together before she faced Marcus and took a deep breath before she visualised walking down a red carpet to face banks of cameramen instead of Marcus and their guests. Somehow, that felt easier as she was experiencing so much anxiety at the moment.

'Darling, I'm sorry I was a bit longer than I said, I just had to freshen up.'

'Sure, honey pie.' Marcus didn't even bother to look up at her. He took her hand lovingly, in full view, so that his guests could see his devotion, then he squeezed it so hard that she felt her knuckles crack, no one saw that - it was so subtle, everything always was. Even in her de-sensitised state she felt the pain. Phoebe convinced herself that he hadn't meant to squeeze so hard that it hurt. She was being tired and over-sensitive, it must have been a mistake.

She decided to do a lovely return toast for him, that would be nice thing to do, she was proud of her husband, could she manage to articulate what she wanted to say though? She tapped her wine glass with a knife to gain the guests' attention. They all looked up. This was taking so much courage. She clenched her fists as she spoke and tried to stand up as straight as she could. 'Here's to a successful Cannes and to my clever husband winning another Palme D'Or,' was she mumbling, she hoped not. 'Don't I tell you how clever and wonderful you are darling, every day?' All she felt was coldness exuding from him as she drew close enough to kiss him, while the guests simply saw a happy and successful Hollywood power couple and chose to clap at their visible signs of affection and of course, success.

All the guests left early by ten pm, as was the Hollywood way, as they all needed their beauty sleep. However, Phoebe wanted the success of the dinner to continue on a little longer and then maybe their night could end on a good note. She spoke tentatively.

'Another drink, Marcus darling, maybe out on the terrace?'

'No, Phoebe, I've another early start tomorrow, I'll see you in our bedroom in a minute.'

At least she'd tried. She managed to crawl slowly up the stairs to her bedroom, holding onto the bannisters all the way. She fell onto the bed, half in and half out of her evening dress, still wearing her heels when Marcus came in. He was smiling but the smile didn't reach his eyes. Even in her sedated state, Phoebe knew to brace herself as she recognised the glint in his eyes as he spoke.

'You looked so beautiful tonight, darling, and you know I love you and you tell me you love me so why would you flirt with my guest who was sitting next to you?'

She didn't remember flirting with anyone, why would he say that?

'I love you too, you know I do. I wasn't flirting with anyone, just chatting to all our guests, especially those on either side of me.' She tried to defend herself as what he said felt so unjust, she'd tried so hard to be a good hostess.

Suddenly she found herself pushed up against the bedroom wall with her hands pinned hands behind her so she was unable to move. He didn't bother to finish unzipping the five thousand dollar designer dress he'd bought her that was already half off, he ripped it fully off and Phoebe's body went rigid with fear. Suddenly he let go of her hands and unexpectedly grabbed her hair so hard that she cried out.

'You bitch! How can you flirt so blatantly like that right in front of me? I know what you were like before I met you two years ago, you fucked anything that moved, are you trying to fuck my business partners now too?'

He pulled handfuls of her thick curls harder and harder with every increasingly aggressive thrust inside her. She went limp allowing him to do whatever he was going to do. She now knew better than to struggle or fight, it was always over quicker when she was submissive. She slid down the wall onto the floor.

As quickly as his anger had arisen, it disappeared and he crouched down and held her tightly. Phoebe's own tears from the shock of his assault were now streaming down her face and she felt empty, alone and used, although she couldn't imagine life without him. How could someone who regularly professed his love for her be so abusive? Then she felt guilty for questioning his motives.

'Phoebe, I don't believe you love me anymore, not from your constant disrespectful actions.' Marcus spoke coldly to her, physically present - emotionally distanced, as her tears caused a damp mascara trail over the shoulder of his Brooks Brothers white shirt.

Everything was all about his own gratification as he deserved it. An apology to never hurt her again was simply self-serving and offered to reel her back in. He took absolutely no responsibility for his actions as it was all Phoebe's fault; she was flawed, just like all his other women.

He needed to teach her a lesson and move on to pastures new.

Chapter 33. Lily Rose. Los Angeles, 1980

Six nights before The Premiere

Chloe was standing in the reception of Phoebe's Style Salon on Melrose Avenue, reflecting on what a fabulous life she now had, this was truly her dream job. She was meeting and working with major celebrities every day and earning huge money for doing it; travelling first class to see all the Designer runway collections in Europe with access to the most fabulous designer clothes to wear. Phoebe hadn't been around at all for the last few weeks so Chloe was now charge of everything. This was what she'd always wanted, her own personal clients and her own business. Marcus had told her earlier that week that Phoebe still wasn't very well and needed to rest. So finally the title she'd always lusted after, "Stylist to the stars" was nearly within her grasp.

'Well, times are a-changing, get ready to rock and roll Chloe babe,' she liked to regularly give herself positive pep talks.

'Roxy, do you know who this next client is?' she peered with the Style Bar's new young receptionist at the appointments book lying open on the front desk. 'Who's this Lily Rose? I don't know any celebrities called Lily Rose, maybe she's some new wannabe star.' She stopped mid-sentence as the doorbell chimed and opened.

There in the reception was the most beautiful girl she'd seen in Hollywood for a very long time. She decided there and then that this new client was going to be exclusively hers; with the photos of her wearing Chloe's dress choice seen on every magazine cover, this would be her golden ticket to fame and fortune.

Chloe put on her biggest, sexiest, most-welcoming Hollywood-perfect smile. 'Hiya, welcome to Phoebe's Style Bar, I'm Chloe.' Lily Rose looked at both girls, pausing thoughtfully before she spoke or acknowledging either of them. She was so perfectly poised in the way she was standing, one leg in front of the other, hip jutting out, almost seemed to Chloe that this tall stunning girl had been practicing her perfect posing stance in a mirror.

'I've an appointment booked for a red carpet styling session with Phoebe.' Lily Rose spoke softly with a husky sexy voice.

Chloe quickly jumped in confident she could close the deal. 'Phoebe isn't here today so I'm sure I can help you instead. I do work super-closely with her.'

'I'm so sorry but I'd really wanted Phoebe.' Lily Rose answered so abruptly and decisively, that Chloe realised her offer had already been discounted. However, she was mesmerised by this girl's beauty and couldn't stop staring. Lily Rose was way taller than her own five foot nine inches, maybe she was even six foot. How could anyone look so perfect with such amazing long blonde straight hair, delicate facial features and the best legs she'd ever seen, they just went on and on.

Chloe was suddenly feeling an unusual mix of emotions, she felt jealous of the girl's beauty but also attracted to her. Girls hadn't ever been her thing, men with money were more her bag, but this girl was so stunning she found that she was imagining what Lily Rose would look like naked and what she'd like to do to her; to make her come over and over again as they rubbed their naked bodies together. She tried to pull herself together and focus back to the question she was being asked. What was she being asked? She now had no idea.

'I'm so sorry, what did you just say?' Chloe needed Lily Rose to repeat the question.

Lily Rose obliged, 'Where is Phoebe, please?' she was beginning to look irritated. Chloe could see that Lily Rose might be the sort to stamp her foot with a hissy fit.

'I'm so sorry, she's not very well at the moment. Marcus called in saying she was still ill and had to stay at home to recuperate.'

Chloe saw a brief look of concern pass across Lily Rose's perfect features, 'That's such a shame, I was really expecting to see her, especially as I've just flown in from London. Maybe I'll just have a quick look at the red carpet dresses you have here today and then make another appointment to come back. When could that be please?'

'Roxy, can we fit in any appointments at the beginning of next week for Lily Rose with Phoebe?' Chloe asked, knowing full well that it was very unlikely that Phoebe would be there.

'Sorry, not possible, We're all booked up with pre-Cannes appointments.'

Chloe could see that Lily Rose was now looking distinctly unhappy at this information.

'You know I'd really like to see Phoebe for some "Brits together" nostalgic gossip with her, you know, what we both miss most about London when we're here in LA? Silly things like the weather, Christmas pudding, Marmite. Chloe honey, I'm sure you'll see what you can do, please? I'll be back tomorrow, same time.' Lily Rose threw Chloe a megawatt smile and sashayed out of the shop.

Chloe stared after her. She could and would do anything to see her again; she really needed Phoebe to come in. She went into the back office and dialled Marcus's home office number. He picked up immediately, 'Yes what is it? I'm real busy.'

'Marcus, it's me, Chloe. Sorry to bother you, I wouldn't call you unless it was super urgent. I've just had a beautiful starlet with me at the Style Bar who only wants Phoebe to style her.'

'Don't you *ever* listen, Chloe? I've told you Phoebe's ill and can't leave the house.'

'Yes, I do always listen Marcus, but a stunning new client has just now left the shop saying that she's coming back again tomorrow to see Phoebe and she didn't leave a phone number to contact her, so what shall I now do?' She waited whilst there was a long silence.

'I really don't understand why you can't deal with this yourself, Phoebe is completely exhausted.' Marcus sounded on edge and about to blow a fuse.

'I'm sorry, Marcus, but she was really persistent.' Chloe felt she really needed to say it as it was and waited for a tsunami of abuse to come back at her down the phone line. She could feel Marcus's rage filling the silence down the phone line before he spoke again. She held the receiver away from her ear as though it was now scalding hot.

'Chloe, don't let this ever happen again. I'll see to it that Phoebe will be in very briefly tomorrow at midday. I'll bring her in myself.'

'Thanks Marcus, I'm very sorry to have bothered you. It won't happen again.' Chloe apologised, as she knew Marcus's type and she wasn't scared by him, but she was deeply fascinated with this unknown girl and couldn't wait for her to come back tomorrow. She'd still make sure she took all the credit for her styling once Phoebe had returned home again, why shouldn't she? After all, what had Phoebe ever done for her? Chloe wasn't one who had ever believed in such a thing as 'girl code'.

Lily Rose came back the next day as she'd said she would and once again Chloe was blown away by her beauty. Today Lily Rose seemed more tense, agitated and fidgety. Chloe couldn't think why, maybe if she offered her a drink it might help. 'Can I offer you a glass of Prosecco or coffee, or anything at all whilst you're waiting?'

'No thanks, Chloe, I'm fine.'

Chloe hoped Marcus would hurry up and arrive with Phoebe as she was feeling increasingly awkward waiting there helplessly with Lily Rose. After what seemed an eternity, Marcus's car pulled up and Phoebe got out. Chloe hadn't seen her for a few weeks and she was really surprised at Phoebe's pale and gaunt appearance. Marcus was holding Phoebe tightly, his arm around her back, as though he was helping her stay standing.

'How are you today, Chloe?' Marcus asked as a cursory throwaway pleasantry, as he stared briefly at her with his piercingly blue eyes. Chloe knew he didn't really care, it was all for show.

All good, thank you, Marcus. This is the client I mentioned, Lily Rose. She'd specially requested only Phoebe to style her.'

Marcus didn't bother to engage or even look at Chloe again or cast a single glance at Lily Rose, he seemed more interested at removing both himself and Phoebe away and out from the salon as quickly as possible. He propelled Phoebe forward, still with his arm around her. "A crazy little thing called love" happened to be playing at that moment in the Style Bar and Chloe noticed Phoebe's face briefly light up and some life flicker in her eyes at hearing the song, before her expression fell back into being unreadable, with dead eyes and a sadness that seemed to have taken over her whole being.

Chloe intuitively wondered what this Queen tune had reminded Phoebe of. Had Phoebe simply liked it or had she'd styled one of the band, Chloe's brain was now ticking away like a time-bomb with all the unanswered questions now whizzing around in her head.

'Hi, Lovely to meet you.' Phoebe directed a lifeless monotone greeting at Lily Rose, as though she was on auto-pilot, body and mind disconnected. Chloe observed how Lily Rose's expression changed at seeing Phoebe. Chloe wasn't sure whether it was from surprise or shock, however, Lily Rose seemed to compose herself as she spoke, speaking even lower than her earlier tones and very softly as though she was only meant for Phoebe to hear. 'Thank you for coming in especially to style me.'

Chloe closely watched the scenario unfolding between the two of them, finding the whole atmosphere really strange. She felt Phoebe was finding it hard to remain focused and present in the room and it appeared as though she was struggling to speak. Then it was as if someone had suddenly replaced Phoebe's batteries and she'd become temporarily operational again. She was staring intently at Lily Rose and slurred a bit as she spoke. 'Do I know you, have we ever met?'

'I live in London sometimes, so that's probably where.' Lily Rose looked uncomfortable and closed down the conversation by quickly laughing it off.

Phoebe nodded and spoke very slowly as though she was having trouble processing this information, 'Yes, that... must... be... it.' She then continued to stare at Lily Rose silently, whilst Lily Rose stared back at her.

Chloe felt she was missing an important piece of the jigsaw puzzle and her gut was telling her there was something going on here that was being left unsaid, and also that Phoebe was definitely not herself. It was as if all the vibrancy, life and colour had been sucked out of her; she was simply a shadow of her former self. A lot of things were really not stacking up.

Chloe looked from Phoebe to Lily Rose and to Marcus. Why had Lily Rose been so keen to be styled by Phoebe and not by her, it shouldn't be that big a deal for God's sake, it was just one dress to find.

Marcus pulled Phoebe closer to him, as though he was the puppet master and needed closer contact with his marionette.

'Phoebe, you're looking even paler than you were when we left home. In fact, you really don't look well at all so I really do think we're going to have to hand this lovely young lady over to Chloe to style after all. You're definitely not well enough to work today; in fact I'm not going to let you.'

He finally bothered to look back fleetingly into the studio as he walked out of the door holding Phoebe firmly.

'My sincere apologies in taking Phoebe away from you, but I guarantee you'll be well looked after in Chloe's capable hands.'

Chloe stood motionless, watching all of this play out. Marcus turned back briefly to have a quick appraisal of the beautiful girl that had caused all these problems. An "I want to fuck her" look appeared briefly in his steely blue eyes. Chloe, fully alert now to every nuance of emotion that was ping-ponging around the place, noticed Lily Rose's newly self-congratulatory expression that she too had observed Marcus's flicker of lust as he'd steered Phoebe out of the shop.

Yes steer was the correct word, as Phoebe seemed to be unaware of what was happening. Chloe had spotted tears in Phoebe's eyes too, but put it down to the fact that Marcus had just told her that she couldn't work. Why though was Lily Rose now looking so upset at what had just happened. This girl's moods seemed to be so changeable as the British weather. How could not being styled by Phoebe just for one dress have upset her so much?

Chloe sprung back into action the moment Marcus and Phoebe left as she was impatient to get started. 'Okay, shall we firm up on the dress you'd like to wear for your event? How about looking at the Valentino rail, possibly the Gucci and even the Versace?'

Lily Rose seemed to still be distracted and not respond to her question. Chloe knew she'd better pull all the stops out to humour her and get her on side.

Chapter 34. Phoebe. Los Angeles, 1980

Five nights before the Premiere

'Phoebe, we're going straight home. You're really not in the right state to be able to style anyone.' Phoebe could tell Marcus was holding back his anger as his voice was low and threatening although his words were not. She decided she would try to reason gently with him, with the little strength she had left.

'I only wanted to be able to stay and style Lily Rose, she was so beautiful. I miss going to my studio and seeing my clients, Marcus.' Phoebe whispered, without daring to look at him.

'It's for the best, Phoebe, you should be resting in bed, I've told you, I'm taking you to the South of France after this weekend for the premiere and you know perfectly well that Chloe's doing a great job with your clients.' Marcus always made everything sound so convincing in his reasoning.

Phoebe tried to gather her thoughts and think rationally but as soon as any thoughts came into her mind, they vanished again into this strange brain fog. She knew she'd felt a familiar frisson of excitement on walking back into the Style Bar, although she couldn't manage to remember the last time she'd been in there with a client. She had obviously had a client today who'd only wanted to see her and there must still be lots of others, having noticed all the rails of designer dresses hanging ready for them. So, it was now Chloe who had taken over all her clients and her business.

Phoebe sat quietly; sad, pale, small and lonely in the back of their SUV on the way back home, just as she had done as a small child when she sat in the back of her father's Bentley. However, now she was sitting as far away as she could from a monster who she still loved. Once again she tried to force her brain to function through this fog and overwhelming tiredness, to be able to think back over the last few days, or was it a week, she still had no idea, days ran into weeks, since the night of the dinner party.

Marcus had become successively more abusive since then. She wasn't sure she could manage to carry on living like this any longer; maybe ending it all was the only answer. To be able do that though, she'd have to find the bottle of those little purple pills and swallow the whole lot in one go.

Phoebe had only ever wanted to see the perfect Marcus in the beginning and she was still in denial that he hadn't turned out to be that man, although every so often she had rare moments of clarity when she questioned everything, whether she was going mad, or was Marcus manipulating the situation so she felt she was going mad? Her extreme anxiety had returned with a vengeance, slightly suppressed by the barbiturate pills she knew Marcus was administering with increasing doses, which did indeed help, but now she wondered whether she'd turned into a pill-addicted zombie.

When she'd met Marcus, it was an instant attraction and he'd swept her off her feet and all her friends had all warned her, although she hadn't wanted to believe them. How could one man have so many personalities; when she saw a particular look in his eyes, she knew that he was going to turn on her and it only took one tiny thing to push him over the edge into a man she was truly fearful of. She wanted more than anything to believe he loved her in the way she loved him, in the way they had at the beginning.

However, his abuse had become her normal and he was now so often angry with her, making her sit down and listen to him whilst he ranted. 'I hope you know how awful and disgusting you are, Phoebe - you're a slut and a whore.'

She tried to zone out when he started and not hear his hurtful words. Then the physical abuse slowly built up. It had first started when he threw a shoe. It had been such a shock, so Phoebe thought it must have been a mistake as he immediately apologised.

'I'm so sorry. It won't happen again.' He had been so humble and effusive in his apologies that she believed him and gave him the benefit of the doubt that he wouldn't do it again. She always did but he did it again and again.

Phoebe hoped and believed each time anything ever happened it was just a bad patch and tried to find an excuse or reason, this time she blamed it on the stress of his movie launch the following week. In each episode, when Marcus the controlling and jealous bully appeared out of the blue, it was with a vicious cycle of mental and physical abuse. He'd belittle her and build her up again ready to knock her down once more.

She still couldn't imagine life without him; he was her life.

She'd blinded herself to the reality of the truth until yesterday, or was it the day before? She couldn't remember, or maybe she'd tried to forget, when he'd nearly strangled her to death. His eyes had been scarier than usual and she'd been petrified; when he was really angry he turned into a stranger.

Marcus hadn't just pulled her hair this time, but ripped clumps of it out by the root. When his hands had been tight around her throat, instead of struggling she'd tried turning it around by saying 'I love you,' but he was deaf to anything she said and they'd tightened even more, stopping her ability to breathe.

As she gasped for air, in desperation she then tried, 'Please don't kill me.' In her extreme terror of this assault by her husband who she loved, who had suddenly turned into a psychopath, she wet herself. She'd never done that since she'd had night-time terrors as a small child. It was a strange feeling to know that she might die at the hands of someone she loved.

Then he'd suddenly stopped, like a switch had been flicked; removing his hands from her throat and leaving the house as he had done so many times before without another word. She'd lain in the dark shaking with fear for all the rest of the night in case he came back. She wondered if he ever felt guilt or shame, possibly shame as that was more manageable than guilt and he always told her afterwards it was her fault.

'You made me do this, if you hadn't then I wouldn't have got so angry; *you're* the problem, Phoebe, everyone agrees with me. Let's face it, that's why no one calls you anymore.'

Was that really true? Was that why she no longer heard or saw from any of her friends? It must be, so she reverted to doubting everything she'd achieved and believed positively about herself over the last few years, to now believing everything negative that Marcus convincingly and repeatedly instilled in her pill-befuddled consciousness.

Chapter 35. Caroline. Cannes, May 1980

Three nights before the Premiere, Mougins

'I'm just nipping out to the village boulangerie whilst you're getting up, do you think the children might like croissants today?' Caroline was still upstairs with the twins and Charlie was trying to be a helpful husband.

'Definitely darling, it's holiday treat time. We can be healthy, can't we, when we're home again.' Caroline believed life was for living and that meant eating everything and anything, especially when on holiday. She knew Charlie loved her, so a bit of extra holiday flesh wouldn't make too much difference. Anyway, they were staying in a villa on their own as a family, so no comparison anxiety was likely. She added, 'Supermarket croissants eaten on a farm in Gloucestershire aren't really the same as eating yummy fresh warm French croissants, are they?'

'True, darling. Shall we all walk down to the café together then and have the croissants there for a change?'

Caroline hurried downstairs and hugged the man she'd loved since she was eighteen, when she'd first clapped eyes on him at her friend Mary's dance. They say you can fall in love at first sight and she knew she had and it had been the happiest eight years of her life.

'Come on Marisa and Charlotte,' she shouted for her daughters whilst enjoying the familiarity and warmth of Charlie's bear-like hug.

'Coming, mummy.' her three year old twins echoed in unison.

The family finally all trooped out, Charlie good looking and so properly British in his Englishman-abroad clothes; straw trilby, Polo shirt with collar turned up, chinos and loafers. The girls were wearing quite random outfits, having dressed themselves independently. Caroline liked to leave them to dress themselves as she felt it expressed their individual personalities; she hoped that in doing this, maybe they'd become as stylish as their god-mummy Phoebe when they grew up. She pretended it was fun for them, although it was actually because she had no idea about fashion or how to put her clothes together with any sort of style. She'd first met Charlie the evening when Phoebe had helped her get ready for the ball they'd both gone to and Phoebe had been brilliant at styling then. Caroline could see exactly why she was such a famous stylist now. To think, all those years ago she'd been styled by her and met her husband-to-be all in the same night.

She spoke to Phoebe as regularly as she could and occasionally discussed sartorial issues. Their lives were so different though, that it was difficult to find a good time of day to phone as LA was eight hours behind. Caroline always went to bed early in order to be able to get through her daily routine of children, horses and dogs from early in the morning.

Caroline suddenly realised that they hadn't spoken for a while now and that was so unlike Phoebe to not to stay in touch. She hoped she was okay, maybe she'd try to call later when the children were in bed. She wondered what Charlie thought.

'Charlie, I know you don't read celebrity gossip magazines, but you know I told you that Phoebe became a really successful celebrity stylist living in LA, recently married to a hot shot film producer? Well, there were *always* photos of her in magazines with the various rock stars she'd dressed. Oh, and where she looked so skinny too, sorry, nothing to do with anything - anyway, since she got married, she's spoken to me less and less and now not at all for the last few weeks. Nor have I seen any pictures of her recently in any magazines which is all very unusual.'

'I did think that at the girls' christening how she'd changed from the shy teenager she was when I first met her. She certainly stood out from your twin set and pearls country ladies.' Charlie always said it as it was.

Caroline chortled with laughter. 'She certainly did, but she always stood out even when she was a deb as she loved to dress differently from everyone. I do think our vicar was a bit shocked to see that a variation from the Laura Ashley and pearls look actually existed in any of his congregation's wardrobe and Mummy was so pleased to see her again. I do hope we can catch up again with her soon, Charlie. You know I hope she's alright.'

'Why wouldn't she be? Didn't you just say that she recently get married?' Charlie looked confused at his wife's female logic.

'Yes, it was a bit cloak and dagger, all very odd. I just hope she's happy, that's all. There was always something a bit fragile about Phoebe and bad things seemed to happen to her.'

Charlie listened patiently to his wife's musings as they walked through the village. He loved the way she always discussed everything so openly with him.

'What do you think of the little I've told you about Marcus after Phoebe married him so quickly, Charlie?'

'Difficult to say as I've never met him, although Phoebe was always a bit of a romantic, wasn't she? I think you're right about her though, appearing to be strong, capable and successful doesn't mean you're actually strong and confident inside. She did always have a certain vulnerability about her.'

They'd arrived quickly at the bakery. They twins ran inside and each immediately chose chocolate pastries. The homely-looking bakery owner proudly handed her home-made pastries over the counter, beaming a dentist's nightmare of a smile at the two little English girls. 'Voilà, deux pains au chocolats.'

'Go on girls,' Caroline directed, 'go and sit at that little window table in the corner and start eating your pastries. We'll be there in a second when we've got the rest of our order.' She stood with Charlie waiting at the counter whilst they ordered their coffees. She kept an eye on the girls, while chatting away to her husband at the same time.

'You always talk such sense Charlie, Phoebe was always quite vulnerable. I know for certain something awful happened to her at Mary's dance and she's never quite got over it.'

'Why, what do you think happened, Caro? You eventually got to see her after that call from her housekeeper, what was her name, Mrs Bott?' Caroline laughed at Charlie, who could never remember anyone's names.

'You're so funny Charlie, I love you so much. No, not Mrs Bott, that was Violet-Elizabeth Bott's mother in the Just William books; Mrs *Ab*-bott, such a lovely caring woman. A better mother to Phoebe than her actual mother, who, I have to say, was an absolute bitch. You know, I'm never mean about anyone but she really was. You know what I think happened?'

'No?'

'I think Phoebe got so drunk that she didn't know what was going on and some boy took advantage of her. She wouldn't tell me and still never has, but from the amount of trauma I saw her going through after, it must have been something quite significant that actually happened.'

Charlie looked appalled. He spoke even more quietly, not wanting his daughters to hear any of this. 'Do you think she was raped?'

'I think very possibly and maybe that's why she went into shock afterwards and retreated into herself. You remember I told you she wouldn't leave her room at all and had been self-harming.'

'Oh Caroline, you never told me that, that's so sad. That would be why the first man who came along after all these years, who managed to convince her to trust him, would turn her head so quickly. Why though, would Marcus have chosen Phoebe when he could have the pick of any Hollywood starlet?'

Caroline glared indignantly at her husband. 'That's a bit harsh, Charlie. She's British, pretty and very successful. You know how those American men like British girls, especially posh classy ones.'

'True and I know Phoebe's a catch. What I meant was why did he choose Phoebe and then want to marry her so quickly; he's a successful man in in fifties and never been married. He's even known as a serial womaniser, so why would he bother getting married?'

'Maybe he fell in love with her?' Caroline was a glass half-full sort of girl.

Charlie shook his head slowly.

'No, sorry. I think it's strange. I'd love to meet them both together and then I'll tell you what I really think.'

Caroline kissed her husband on the lips. 'You're very perceptive for a stuffy old Etonian,' she liked to tease him affectionately. 'Okay, I'll try calling her in Los Angeles tonight and see if I can track her down. I did read that Marcus has a movie premiering at the Cannes Film Festival next week, maybe we could drive down there and meet up. I'm sure we could find a babysitter for the night - we could even invite my mother out for a few days to help look after the girls, I'm sure she'd love that if she was free.'

'That's a brilliant idea. The girls love their Yorkshire gangan.'

'Et voila, deux grands cafés au lait, deux chocolats chauds pour les petites filles et deux croissants.' The café owner proudly handed over the tray with a grand Gallic flourish.

Caro inhaled the yummy mix of warm pastries, fresh coffee and hot chocolate smells. She was salivating just with the deliciousness of it all.

'Ooh,' she mumbled to herself under her breath, 'this is better than sex,' hoping that neither her husband nor her daughters would overhear the first part and then, 'oh my god - complete bliss.'

Charlie hadn't actually heard a word as he was already outside with the tray.

She grabbed the twins' hands. 'Come on girls, let's all go and sit outside in the sunshine.'

Chapter 36. Paula. Cannes, May 1980

The night of The Premiere

'What shall I wear tonight, Forbesy-poo?' Paula was standing in front of an enormous walk-in wardrobe, surveying the hanging rail with her designer evening dresses, all still wrapped pristinely in their protective dress covers. She and Forbes had just moved temporarily into a suite at the Martinez from their rented villa up in the hills. Forbes had suggested the Martinez just for a couple of nights, so they could simply fall back into bed after the movie premiere and party.

'As little as possible,' Forbes chuckled and winked at her, gazing admiringly from where he was lying on the bed. 'Whatever you like honey-bun, you always look gorgeous in anything you wear... you know I can't keep my hands off you, especially when you're standing there like that in front of me.'

Paula adjusted her stance, pulled in her non-existent tummy and rolled back her shoulders so her tits would look their perkiest best. She was realistic that her lovely, devoted Forbes might only be devoted to her until it was time to move on to a younger model, as that's what she knew all really rich men did. She understood how it worked, so she really had to keep on top of her game. It was funny that what Forbes lacked in stature and good looks, he made up for in dynamism and confidence. In fact, when she thought about it, all the super-rich men she'd had the fortune to have dalliances with so far, had always exuded power which in Paula's book had equalled sexiness.

She focused back to her wardrobe choices. 'So Forbesy-poo, which dress should it be?' she went on standing there provocatively in her tiny lace thong and heels, fully aware of the effect it was having. She always considered the outcome when she did anything; she'd learnt by now that she had to look after number one and that was herself.

'I think you should stop looking for a dress and come back over here.' Forbes cajoled.

Paula posed there just a little longer for full effect, sometimes a girl just had to do what she had to do and often it wasn't very much as most men were led by their dicks.

Since Paula's first introduction to Forbes by Madame Claude, now more than a year ago, she'd met up with him on his "business" trips all around the world, always travelling on his private jet; she'd forgotten what it was like to fly on a regular plane, even first class. He'd set her up in a fabulous mews house in Mayfair, London where he met her after flying in from his marital home in Dallas, Texas at least a few times a month. The rest of the time she could do whatever she wanted to do.

Forbes was short, balding and over double Paula's age, but he was funny and kind and he looked after her. In return for her availability at any time and as much sex as he could manage, he gave her a generous allowance, paid all her bills and paid for all her designer clothes and jewellery as he liked her to always look glamorous and chic, no expense spared; a win-win situation for both of them. To Paula, it had never been a big deal using her body and looks to get what she wanted and even though she didn't want to admit it, she really was very fond of this kind and generous man.

Suddenly she started wondering what had happened to Phoebe. Why though, should she be randomly thinking about Phoebe whilst standing there with no clothes on, that was odd, she should be concentrating on Forbes. Maybe it was because she'd been asking him what to wear and she'd always loved Phoebe's style advice. What was even odder was that she hadn't heard anything at all from Phoebe in the last few weeks, or even managed to speak to her at the Style Bar. She'd left so many messages with that unhelpful bitch Chloe. The last time they'd seen each other was at the dinner with Marcus a while ago and that had been a really strange night. Even Forbes had commented how rude and controlling he'd found Marcus to be.

Could Marcus have actually stopped Phoebe seeing her, did he consider her a bad influence, she was sure he didn't know anything about her background. Or did he see her as a threat to his relationship with Phoebe, aware that she could see through his fake charm. She knew his sort; men like him weren't to be trusted and certainly shouldn't be together with a vulnerable young woman like Phoebe. In fact, men like him weren't ever the sort to get involved with – for anyone. She was definitely worried about her best friend and nothing added up.

She realised that Forbes was becoming impatient, 'Paula, hunny, look who's waiting for you.'

Paula looked across the room at her Texan millionaire's member standing proudly to attention. It was likely Forbes had taken some Viagra earlier so it wasn't going down any time soon. She decided to voice her worries, whilst she still had some time.

'Forbesy, do you remember my best friend Phoebe?'

'Of course, honeybun, but at this moment I'm much more interested in you.'

'I know, Forbesy, I can see you are.' Paula was now sitting at the top of the bed, absent-mindedly fiddling with his chest hairs, 'but you know I'm really worried about her. I haven't

420

heard from her for the last few weeks now and she's completely disappeared from everywhere she was always seen at.'

'Could we discuss this later, sugar pie, maybe Marcus has taken her on a belated honeymoon, I'm sure there's some reason. Come on over here to Daddy, you're far too delicious to resist.' Forbes was lying back in his full five foot six naked glory.

Although he was seventy, he was in good shape and really fit for his age, and Paula found his curly grey hairs on his chest really quite cute. She walked over to lie on top of him with all her taut, slim five foot ten inch body with his toes poking at her shins. As Paula reminded herself, there was a saying that height didn't matter when you're lying down. She pulled down her thong in one adept practiced movement, managing to slide it off over her stilettos, which she'd purposely kept on. She licked her fingers and trickled them slowly down Forbes's body ending up at his sparse grey pubes. She gently stroked past his erection with her wet fingers and cupped his balls, she liked his cock, as cocks went it was one of the better looking ones. She'd seen so many over the last few years, she appreciated one that was reasonably attractive. It was the perfect size; not too big, not too small and also circumcised. She started to stroke it and manoeuvred herself so he slid inside her. He groaned with pleasure as did she, with genuine enjoyment and satisfaction; power and money had always turned her on. She closed her long legs tight and squeezed her pussy muscles around his rock hard cock. She adjusted herself so she could jiggle her full bosoms against his hairy chest then further up towards his face so he could suck her nipples, she knew what he liked.

Forbes sighed again with pleasure and managed to speak quickly before his face was smothered with Paula's generous bosoms. 'Hey honeybun, you're so good.'

'You too sweetie,' she faked her orgasm as she felt him about to come, she'd always been good at that, she was a good actress. Sometimes it was necessary to shorten their fuck time. She occasionally had unexpected orgasms with Forbes, never the intense ones she'd once experienced with Abdul, however she could live with that as she could do them for herself when she was on her own.

Sex over, she returned to the two burning questions: what to wear and what to do about Phoebe. 'So shall I wear that Armani dress you chose last week for me, or this Gucci?'

'Honeybun, you look stunning in anything. Although maybe the Gucci tonight, it makes those puppies of yours look so darn good.' Forbes stood up, flaccid penis now hanging spent between his short muscular legs. He walked over to his jacket which was hung over the back of a chair and pulled out a little blue box from one of the inside pockets. 'Here's a little something to show how much I appreciate you, honeybun.'

Lying in the box was the most beautiful Tiffany platinum and diamond necklace, which would work beautifully with the simple lines of the plunging necked Gucci dress she was going to wear. Paula loved it and it was another stunning trinket to add to her ever-growing collection of serious jewellery. 'I think you should put it on me now whilst I'm still naked, so that you can visualise me like this for the rest of the evening; wearing nothing but diamonds and heels.'

Forbes's eyes lit up, he loved playing Paula's games, 'That's my gal.' He swept back her heavy straight blonde hair off her neck and deftly did up the beautiful necklace. He stood back to admire it on her. 'Pretty darn good, eh Paula?'

'Love you Forbesy, you're so wonderful to me.'

'Love you too, sweetie pie, we're going to have a good week here in Cannes baby, aren't we.'

In reply, Paula knelt down and put his now sleepy penis in her mouth. She wasn't sure if she could manage to get it fully hard again so quickly after he'd just come, but even if nothing happened he would still appreciate her efforts. That's what every girl did after she'd been given a diamond necklace, wasn't it?

Forbes broke his concentration for a minute, 'Honey bun, a limo will be picking us up at seven. I think that'll give us enough time to finish off what we're doing here and then for your hair and makeup people to get you ready for the party.'

Paula paused, looked up, nodded and went back to business. If he got hard, she was ready for him always; any time, any place, anywhere. Wasn't that a Martini ad slogan?

Maybe it would be better to revisit the subject of Phoebe at a more opportune moment.

Chapter 37. Simon. Cannes, May 1980

The night of The Premiere

Simon surveyed his bedroom suite, it was doubling up as the pre-screening make-up and hair room for any celebrities who were booked in to see him. He had so much to do over the next few hours, including making sure Jake looked his best for the red carpet.

Simon had always used subtle make-up; concealer, a touch of bronzer and even some mascara for his leading men. He'd managed to organise the large bathroom to now have a stool in front of each of the twin basin mirrors for the celebrities to sit at and his makeup kit was all laid out systematically along the marble bathroom surfaces. Foundations, blushers, eyeshadows, lipsticks, concealers, brushes all ready to go at the first knock on the door, he was always a perfectionist and consummate professional.

Clothes rails and shoes and accessories were lined up in the sitting area, for celebrities to get dressed in their red carpet gowns once their hair and makeup was done. A French stylist had been brought in to help dress them, although Simon wished he could have been working with Phoebe as they would have been such a brilliant team together. He had a makeup and hair assistant on standby waiting in the sitting room too, in case he became overwhelmed with celebrities who might unexpectedly appear, this had happened before to him at these junkets. He was super-organised and it was still early and he and his team were now ready for a long afternoon and evening ahead. First he needed to nip upstairs to attend to Jake's make-up in the suite that he'd been given. Jake was already dressed and ready.

'You look fabulous in your tux, darling.' Simon checked Jake out from top to toe; Simon's chest full of pride and joy at how far his boyfriend had come from when he'd first met him.

'You, too,' Jake replied as Simon straightened his bow tie and brushed a bit of fluff off his shoulder, then standing back to admire the finished result.

'It was so lucky that Phoebe managed to fit us both for our tuxes a few months ago once we knew the film was premiering in Cannes. A custom-made designer tux looks so different from one bought on the high street. So, who are you going to walk down the red carpet with?' Simon was finding it difficult to keep his hands off Jake now as he looked so handsome.

Jake snorted dismissively. 'Some starlet I think, management arranged it. She walks with me and we both benefit; you know how it works, it helps her career move up the ladder and she makes me look butch.' Simon and Jake both fell about laughing. 'Little do they know what I'm like behind closed doors, or maybe they do.' They started laughing again until they both had tears running down their faces.

Then Simon looked serious for a moment as a thought struck him, he'd remembered that Jake had also been with girls in his teens, 'Really, a starlet? Do you think your head could be turned?' Simon looked searchingly at Jake and was interested in how long he waited before he answered back.

Jake's reply was immediate, 'Don't be silly, Si, I'm all yours and I love you. I just wish we could be open about our relationship and I'm so sorry that management made us have individual suites in our own names. I suppose no-one will notice if we spend tonight together as long as we appeared to actually have stayed in our own rooms. It might be okay for you as a makeup artist to come out, but as a leading man I have to be so careful, especially after that initial agent warning chat I was given. Look at all those past movie stars who were rumoured to be gay, some even married multiple times to keep up the pretence.'

'Some names please.' Simon jokingly tried testing him.

'Okay, here's a few: Cary Grant, Rock Hudson, Lawrence Olivier and umm… Dirk Bogarde. All rumours but a rumour is always founded on some truth, isn't it?'

'Hmm,' Simon answered distractedly as he'd thought of something else, 'so whilst you pose on the red carpet with your date, Marcus will be schmoosing the press and media. What do you think Phoebe will be doing and who will she be going with? I haven't heard a whisper from her for weeks now, which is really strange - absolutely nothing.'

'Given that you two are nearly joined at the hip, that is really odd. Have you spoken to George or Caroline, or her friend Paula at all? Has anyone actually seen her?'

Simon looked worriedly at Jake. 'No, no-one and I'm becoming more and more concerned - I never liked Marcus anyway. Maybe he just didn't like me as I was too camp for him.' Simon demonstrated the campest mince, hand on hip, up and down the room as he was speaking.

'No, I don't think he minds camp, after all he works in the film industry so he must be used to camp from some of his actors - not me, obviously - I'm as butch as I can be when I'm around him.' Jake had now joined Simon mincing in synchronisation with him like two models down the catwalk, posing at the end of the room with a flick and a flourish before they turned.

Simon was still worrying about Phoebe though, so from his brief moment of joking around, he quickly resumed his train of thought.

'So, what shall we do about Phoebe?'

'You're really worried about her, aren't you, Si?'

'Seriously, yes. I've dropped into the Style Bar a few times and that opportunistic bitch Chloe has always been unhelpful and monosyllabic. I've phoned the house with no reply. I've left messages and no returned calls. My intuition is telling me all is not well.'

Jake looked at Simon and waited for him to continue.

'I saw her so much more than anyone else, especially as I was working so often with her, now it's like someone pulled the plug and nothing.'

'So, if there's something wrong, what can we do?' Jake felt at a loss and was feeling Simon's pain.

'Do you know, I've actually no idea at the moment, although I'm sure I'll be able to think of something very soon,' Simon tried to sound more confident than he felt, 'between you and me, Jake, I think Marcus is a controlling bully and she's frightened of him.'

'He was always so charming to everyone on set though. No hang on, I saw him lose his temper once with a camera man. In fact, I thought he was going to hit him he was so angry. I'd never seen anyone lose their cool and turn into someone else so quickly. The set went dead quiet and it was really awkward, we didn't know where to look. Maybe there is another side of him that we don't know about. I'm sure Phoebe will be with Marcus this evening, so there has to be a moment when we'll be able to get her on her own to have a proper chat.' Jake was starting to feel as worried as Simon now he'd thought back to the incident on set, he'd forgotten all about it.

'Hey, the phone is ringing, shall I get it? Oh no, I forgot I'm not supposed to be in here with you.' Simon remembered just in time stopping himself grabbing the phone.

Jake reached over instead.

'Hi, Jake speaking.'

'Hi Jake, this is Sacha from your management team. Do you remember that we'd agreed you were going to walk the red carpet with an up-and-coming beautiful young actress? Well, unfortunately she called a little while ago to cancel and we still don't know why. So, when we told Marcus he eventually agreed for Phoebe to be your date. That was the only solution that we could all come up with at the last minute and Marcus didn't seem very happy about it but he understood that it would absolutely get column inches. However, there's a caveat, he's instructed us that she's not allowed to speak to any press and that we have to keep an eye on her at all times as she's been so unwell.'

'Okay, thanks Sacha for letting me know.'

'By the way, the limo will come to collect you first and then will be picking up Marcus and Phoebe.'

'All understood, see you later.' Jake replaced the phone back on its base and tried to look poker-faced as he decided to spin a new story for Simon, he wanted to cheer him up, 'Si, I've been stood up by my starlet, I obviously wasn't her type.'

Jake knew this would work and Simon started laughing again until they were clutching each other to stay upright as they were laughing so much.

Simon finally managed to speak again, 'Well, at least you're my type and, the really good news is you're now going to be with Phoebe. See if you can find out what's going on in her life. Listen I've now got to rush back to my make-up room suite, love you so much Jake and lots and lots of good luck.' Simon blew Jake loads of kisses which he sent on their way gently blowing on his upturned palm.

'Love you too and I'll do what I can, although it may be difficult as we'll be surrounded by management and you know, a whole entourage. I promise I'll try and between the two of us I'm sure we can see what we can find out and a way to help her. Maybe it's a "Rescue Phoebe from the clutches of the evil Marcus" kind of night.'

Little did Simon know that Jake had never spoken a truer word.

Chapter 37. Caroline. Mougins, May 1980

The night of The Premiere, Mougins

It was one of those days that seemed to be full of strange twists and turns that were never expected on a normal family holiday.

Caroline wasn't sure how everything had happened so quickly. It had all started earlier that afternoon when she'd stood on her tiptoes and leant over the hibiscus covered boundary wall of the adjacent villa to apologise for her noisy children, and there in the neighbouring garden had been a surprisingly friendly woman.

'Mais j'assure, ce n'est pas de tout une problème, we have small children too. It's normal, non? They are content, how you say, 'appy playing enjoying les vacances. Mais dis donc, why don't you come over to our home and have a glass of Champagne together with your husband and les enfants to play all together at our pool? Ce sera un plaisir de faire votre connaissance, to get to know you.'

So there they now were, lying on the sun loungers with their French neighbour friends, Natalie and Frederic. Both families' children were playing happily together in the pool, language seemingly no barrier. Caroline was feeling decidedly "less than" her French neighbour in every way. She felt so very British, patchily sunburnt rather than beautifully tanned, with a mummy tummy, cellulite bum and an unflattering old Marks and Spencer bikini that hadn't been intended for public scrutiny. She'd only bought it at the time as it had had a 'lift and sculpt' swing label. Today she felt it wasn't delivering what it had promised or, maybe it was and her body had deteriorated after all her holiday indulgences. Life was to be lived though and she would start when she was home again, maybe try a boiled egg and grapefruit diet or something hard-core like that. If she'd known that she was going to be joining her French neighbours, then she would at least have showered, washed her hair, done a quick leg and bikini shave and changed into a better swimsuit and sarong, but everything had all happened so quickly. It would have looked rude for them not to accept their neighbour's hospitality.

Her French neighbour's body, even after three children, was a very different story from her own; legs without a glimpse of cellulite anywhere, a toned tummy, hip bones that jutted beyond her stomach whilst she was lying down and no stretch marks on her upper thighs, how could Natalie look that good? She had to be around the same age as her, with two kids too and her tiny-weeny bikini, a few strips of expensive fabric, barely contained those pert French breasts.

Caroline's own boobs, that she considered looked like two saggy poached eggs, needed padding and scaffolding to keep them supported to anywhere near where they'd once been. She pondered why all French women seemed to look so effortlessly chic, did they spend more on their clothes and beauty regimes? She was sure that her French neighbour's tiny triangles of bikini fabric had probably cost quadruple what she'd paid for her M&S cozzy, even though all three triangles together were about the same size of her bikini bottom's gusset. Whilst she was considering this financial equation, she'd also have wagered that Natalie didn't have a single hair left anywhere on her body and probably did her pelvic floor or kegel exercises three times a day to make sure her vagina was as tight as it'd been before she'd had her two perfect little French girls.

Caroline was certain that the women in her village bridge club group, back in her Gloucestershire, never pruned or trimmed their personal bushes, or even considered making them look pretty. Caroline parked her musings to pay better attention to her new French friend.

'This is so lovely, to spend the afternoon all together, Caroline.'

'Un autre coup de champagne pour nos voisins Anglais, our lovely new friends,' Frederic got up from his sun lounger to pour more champagne for everyone.

'That would be lovely, merci.' Charlie and Caroline held out their champagne glasses for Frederic.

'Écoutez, listen, why don't you both come with us to the big party tonight after Marcus Lean's movie screening. I am one of his business partners in this movie, so we have a couple of spare tickets. Our nanny could babysit your girls here too and she speaks good English. We're trying to raise our children bilingual.'

Caroline suddenly was on full alert when she heard the name and instantly sat right up on her sun-lounger forgetting it was the worst position for stomach rolls.

'Marcus Lean, the American film producer, married to the celebrity stylist?' she couldn't believe this serendipitous luck and joined in the conversation with more enthusiasm and invested interest than she'd shown all the afternoon. She suddenly could forgive the French woman's perfect bikini body.

'Yes, we were both at a business dinner with them in Los Angeles two weeks ago.'

'And with his wife, Phoebe?' Caroline was nearly panting with excitement at all this news that was unfolding.

'Mais oui, why?' Natalie looked confused as to why Caroline should suddenly be showing so much interest.

'I knew her when I was a teenager eight years ago and she's our twins' god-mummy and I haven't seen her for yonks.'

'Yonks?'

'Sorry, it means for ages, for a long time, Natalie. So how was she?' Caroline was desperate now to hear as much as Natalie could tell her.

'Phoebe was very quiet and, how do you say, timide.'

'Frightened?'

'No, timide is shy, not really shy, maybe sad? It's difficult to describe exactly how she was as she was genial, friendly but withdrawn and I don't know whether I should say this, even a little scared maybe.'

Caroline's heart was now racing at this new knowledge, 'Scared, why should she be scared?'

'I don't know, it was just an impression. Marcus is my husband's business associate and I've only met Marcus a few times. I've heard he's very controlling in business and also very successful, sometimes the two go together, non?'

Caroline noticed Frederic suddenly give his wife a subtle sideways look as if to say "stop now" and she swiftly changed the subject.

'Caroline, why don't you come inside and help me bring out some canapés and we can make arrangements for later at the same time.'

Natalie linked arms with Caroline and they walked inside into the welcome coolness of the villa.

The moment they were out of view, Natalie whispered to Caroline, 'I couldn't say more in front of my husband, I was worried for the girl as she seemed really scared of Marcus. I've heard before from my husband that Marcus has a terrible temper and bad reputation, but his PR people are paid to make sure that everything written is always positive so it doesn't damage his movie brand. I have my own thoughts about him.'

Caroline suddenly felt her skin get goose-bumps as she listened to Natalie. Her worst fears were being confirmed.

'Natalie, Phoebe's completely disappeared from the public eye and she hasn't called me for a few weeks now, nor has she called another British friend of ours George, who lives in Paris. This is totally out of character for Phoebe, she's always called us. She likes to know her friends are all there for her, as she's had some difficult times.'

Caroline watched Natalie process this before she spoke, 'When we were at the dinner in Los Angeles I read many rumours in magazines that she was never seen out any more. Why should une célèbre styliste de celebrites, a famous celebrity stylist always seen on the red carpet, suddenly disappear? I cannot say more in front of my husband but I can understand why you might be worried for her.' Natalie was looking more and more concerned as she'd voiced her thoughts to Caroline.

'Thank you so much for telling me, maybe tonight when we're all at the party we can both go and find her to ask her what's going on.'

Caroline looked gratefully at the French woman. Natalie was back to being briskly efficient ready to go back outside to her husband. 'Come, vas-y, let's go out again with the food, no word now please, I trust you.'

'Of course.' Caroline gave Natalie a reassuring smile and the two women walked out to the pool again; new friends bonded by a secret.

Chapter 38. Phoebe. Cannes, May 1980

The night of The Premiere

Marcus's sense of superiority was like a balloon that had gradually lost air without the steady stream of applause and recognition from his wife to keep it inflated. He had an obsessive craving for affirmation and she was no longer feeding his needs. Everything had changed since his wife had become more and more addicted to the drugs he'd given her for anxiety, depression and insomnia. As the doses he had given her had incrementally increased over the last months, she'd stopped defying him but still not complying with his every wish and whim. So she deserved anything he did as it was all her fault.

She'd been so successful when he'd married her and he'd liked that as he could play his game and knock her down, that was how he rolled, it made him feel good about himself. Insults, bullying and threats had all been necessary, especially as she'd become more and more argumentative, until the barbiturates he gave her stopped all that. Sometimes he'd apologized to her, but only to get her back into line and he felt no remorse or shame. He always rewrote the story in his head until he knew he hadn't done anything wrong. She was the problem and he always sorted problems out, sooner rather than later. The Phoebe problem would somehow soon be resolved. It was a shame it hadn't been yet as it was the night of his film premiere and party.

'Can I just straighten this? There you go, much better.' Phoebe adjusted Marcus's bow tie and stood back to look at the whole effect. 'You look so suave and handsome tonight, I love a man in a tux, especially you, you do know that I love you so much, don't you?' Phoebe, with her metaphorical stylist hat on, was giving Marcus some final checks, then she would try to sort out her own hair, makeup and dress, although she felt that it was inside her head that needed the most help. She just couldn't manage to muster up any energy and break through the fog in her brain to think straight. She'd tried downing a few cups of the strongest black coffee but they hadn't made the slightest difference. She felt so woozy and detached from the world, as though her contact lenses were blurry, maybe that's what was wrong it was the lenses, no, it couldn't be, she'd had the same mist in front of her eyes when she was wearing her specs.

She suddenly realised that Marcus hadn't been listening to anything she'd just said; he'd been lost in thought.

'Phoebe, I've just been watching you and I can see you're still not nearly well enough to come tonight to either the screening or the party this evening.'

Even in her current fuzzy world, Phoebe could sense Marcus's growing irritation and impatience with her. She wanted to muster the mental and physical strength to stand her ground and put across a valid argument of why she should be at his side for the whole night, but it was so hard to think or even speak. She tried to collect her thoughts and make some sense.

'Marcus, this is your big night and I've just flown over with you from LA to be here at your side as I am your wife and people will wonder why I'm not with you.' Phoebe was now concentrating extraordinarily hard to get the rest of her thoughts out there before she lost the thread again of what she'd started to say. 'Maybe people are already wondering what's going on, I can see burning questions in people's eyes if anyone sees me out anywhere now. It's so rare that you allow me out at all and I just don't understand why.'

There she'd managed to get it all out and she now felt completely drained. It had taken everything she had left in her tank to even manage those few sentences, what on earth was wrong with her? Surely those pills she was taking each day couldn't be affecting her that much, could they?

'Of course, I don't stop you Phoebe, it's all in your imagination. You know I love you and only want what's best for you. You've obviously been working way too hard and you're burnt out. See, that's the reason I put Chloe in charge of The Style Bar, so you could rest and get better.' Marcus spoke as though he were trying to reason with a child.

Phoebe wondered why he had to have that tone of voice and looked back at him with glazed eyes, feeling more confused than ever. He always seemed so genuine with his concerns and his explanations when she challenged him. At this moment, she wasn't sure whether she loved or hated him, then sometimes both love and hate were such close emotions they could be confused. She no longer knew what to do, she needed to have one more go at changing his mind and mustered all her mental resources to sound confident as she spoke;

'Marcus, I'm going to my room now to get ready as you know people will really start to ask questions in the press if I'm not seen with you tonight.'

All her efforts seemed futile as Marcus was now looking at her as though he hated the very sight of her. 'I don't understand why you question my actions all the time, I've made my decision and it's final.' He virtually spat his words out at her.

Phoebe felt herself visibly sag with disappointment. She'd tried so hard to fight and now she had no more energy. Why was he looking at her as though she was a piece of shit on the sole of his shoe? She wished she knew what she'd done to turn him into this monster. There must have been something - maybe it was the nightmares she'd started having a few months ago that had left her waking up screaming every night.

'Marcus I'll go to my room for a little while, maybe you'll change your mind.' Phoebe felt physically defeated as though she'd just been punched in the head and body during several rounds of a boxing match. She dragged her feet slowly to her bedroom in the suite and lay down on the bed. When she shut her eyes tears slowly trickled down the side of her face and onto the pillow. She wasn't sure she could go on like this any longer, this wasn't a life worth living. Would she be better dead? Maybe she could take the whole bottle of pills at once if she could just find where Marcus kept them or could she manage to escape, maybe here in the South of France it would be easier. How could she do that, she needed her friends to help and they knew nothing of what was going on. They must all be there in Cannes somewhere. Phoebe knew that Jake was the lead in the movie, Simon was obviously with him and maybe doing some makeup for celebrities and Paula and Forbes too, as Forbes had invested in the movie. These thoughts were just too overwhelming and tiring to compute and she fell asleep exhausted.

She didn't know how long she'd dozed for, it could have been minutes or hours, time had no meaning for her any longer and most of her days were like this now, alternating between half-awake and half-asleep. Back in Los Angeles in her half-awake constantly twilight-like days, she'd sat watching but not seeing, one daytime soap after another. The storylines she'd loved and been addicted to, had been replaced by her new addiction to the little purple pills that

Marcus was prescribing her with ever-increasing doses over the last few months. It seemed that with regular usage, the tolerance to their effects developed quickly and she had absolutely no idea how many she was now taking.

She could just hear Marcus talking in a low voice on the phone from the adjoining room, 'Dropped out last minute? Who the fuck then can he walk with, he's suggesting my wife, really? She's not well. He's insisting? You think the press will love them together? Okay, just for the red carpet then. I'll bring her with me and we'll all walk together as a threesome.'

Phoebe wished she could have heard the whole conversation, although it still wouldn't have made much sense to her as her brain just wouldn't fire into action. She went on lying there, eyes still shut. The world was much better shut out at the moment as she didn't really have a proper world anymore, hers was now simply confined to whatever room Marcus left her in and no more than that.

Suddenly she heard his voice now close up; he must be close to her in the bedroom. She tried to open her eyes and squinted against the bright sunlight streaming into the room. He was standing silhouetted against the doorway. She braced herself for what he was going to do or say next. In this drugged and sluggish state she was even less able to anticipate and pre-empt his volatile and now scary unpredictability.

'Phoebe, against my better judgement you're now walking the red carpet before the movie screening so you'd better not let me down.' Marcus did not sound happy to be imparting this news to her, in fact he sounded even more stressed than before. There seemed to be one problem arising after another and the biggest one currently was his wife.

439

Phoebe had no idea what had made him change his mind but she suddenly felt a tiny flicker of hope, at least she was now getting out for a few hours and surely something good could be made to come of that.

Marcus couldn't bear to stay too long near his zombie-like wife and quickly left the room again to concentrate on his big night. Everything should now finally be in place; Simon and his team were in the suite he'd organised, doing the makeup and hair for any of his celebrity guests who didn't have their own glam squad with them and Jake was in his own suite. In fact, everything was under control except for Phoebe.

Why on earth had he married the girl, he'd thought she'd be different from all the others. Surely she'd appreciated everything he'd done for her and had paid for too. His wife shouldn't have been working or gallivanting around the world with her celebrity clients, she should have been staying at home looking after her husband's needs. So he'd stopped her working but then she'd become disobedient. When he'd upped the dosage of the barbiturates to stop her petulance, she'd become a zombie. He just couldn't win.

Marcus wanted this night to be perfect as everything in his life always had to be. Maybe it was fortuitous that the starlet had just baled on Jake and now that he, Jake and Phoebe were all going together, all the speculative gossip might stop. He'd need to keep a close eye on her though and to control her behaviour whilst they were out.

Maybe the press would let up on writing about his wife if he manipulated this occasion enough, their interest in her was still relentless. They had championed her meteoric rise to fame giving her a high profile and now even higher as part of a celebrity couple. She was still headline news, this time with questions about her disappearance from the public eye.

Marcus gave his mental check list one more run-through. The guest lists for the movie screening, the after party, the international press and media and photographers, all tick. The party planners in the South of France hadn't been as efficient as in LA, it had all been very frustrating as he'd had to chase them up the whole time; why couldn't everyone do everything exactly how he wanted things to be done? He felt as though he'd done it all himself in the end. He could feel his stress levels rising with all these additional worries. He'd have to remember to take his heart pills out with him as he kept on feeling extra flutters. He had to stop worrying about how his movie was going to be received, and then the Phoebe problem too. He wondered if she was even ready yet?

'Phoebe,' he shouted loudly and angrily at the bedroom door.

'Yes darling, here and ready.' Marcus was surprised that she was actually standing at the bedroom door. 'The dress you got me looks beautiful, thank you.' Marcus looked at her. The dress was hanging off her; how had Chloe got the size so wrong, she was supposed to be good at this styling job, that's why he'd employed her. Why was Phoebe so thin now, he liked slim but not this skinny, she'd always had curves. How could he ever have found her attractive? Yes, it was definitely time for someone new in his bed.

'Phoebe, the chauffeur is waiting outside in the limo and I'm warning you, don't you dare do anything that'll ruin my night. You're going to be walking the red carpet with Jake and me, and I'll hold your hand. Don't embarrass me or let me down, this is my night and also Jake's, it's not yours.'

Phoebe didn't reply. Marcus could see her processing what he'd said. God she was so slow now. What the fuck was wrong with the woman?

441

Suddenly she spoke up, 'Marcus, you know those pills you give me to take to help me to sleep, they're making me feel so groggy. Have you got anything that could help me get through this evening with you, so I don't let you down?' Phoebe looked pleadingly, almost child-like at him.

However, Marcus simply looked back at her with utter disgust. 'Phoebe, I can see that nothing ever changes with you, once an addict always an addict. I should have left you in the gutter where you belonged with your junkie music clients. Here, have some alcohol, that'll help, God, how could I have married you, you're such a loser.'

He handed her a large neat whisky and watched her swallow it down it one gulp. That would wake the silly bitch up as he was sure she hadn't eaten anything. They walked out to the limo and she saw Jake sitting in the back as the driver opened the door for her.

The whisky seemed to have given Phoebe a sudden burst of clarity and energy. It was the first time she'd felt even slightly alive again and she wondered how long this new feeling might last? The sleeping pills he'd been giving her may have helped her nightmares, but daily hallucinations had become her new nightmare. Everything was so messed up, how could she ever manage to tell any of her friends that she'd become a prisoner in her own home? If she could just write a tiny note, maybe she could then slip it to Jake.

'I just need to go to the loo again quickly Marcus, it must be nerves. Sorry I'll be with you in a minute.'

Marcus scowled at her. 'Really? You've had all the time in the world to go earlier. Hurry up, we can't be late.'

Phoebe ran back to the bathroom and locked the door. She rummaged in her bag and found a lip liner pencil. She pulled off a piece of the toilet paper and tried to write on it but the pencil dragged on the paper, tearing it. She tried again and with a lighter touch on the paper- managed to write a single word. She flushed the toilet and checked her face in the mirror. Her cheeks felt strangely hot and flushed, maybe she was coming down with something. She tried to pull herself together and get ready to face not only Marcus but the stress of walking the red carpet again. She concealed the tiny scrap of paper in her palm of her hand under her evening purse and walked outside.

Marcus was pacing up and down like a caged lion; she wondered whether he was going to roar at her. 'Get in,' he snarled close to her face as she leant forward to get in the car, 'I'm watching you, remember.'

She noticed that Marcus then immediately switched over to his fake-smile public face, acknowledging Jake who was already seated in the car in the back. Marcus strategically placed himself next to her in the middle row of seats, leaving her no possibility to speak to Jake although he saw Jake briefly glance at Phoebe with an unreadable expression on his face. Yes, he definitely needed to keep the two of them apart.

As soon as their limo drew up outside the Palais and they stepped out onto the red carpet, the paparazzi went wild. Phoebe was blinded by the flashes and deafened by the shouting of the photographers and crowds.

'Jake over here please.'

'Phoebe and Marcus, one of you both together please.'

'Phoebe, look this way please.'

'Jake and Phoebe... thank you!'

She knew Marcus was watching her every move. Jake suddenly took her hand as they posed together on the red carpet. Phoebe knew she was shaking and wondered if Jake felt it. She was feeling dizzy too, maybe what she needed was

443

more water. She'd always felt confident before posing together with her celebrities on the red carpet, it had been her job and she and her clients had been there for each other.

Tonight she was inexplicably terrified. She felt Jake squeeze her hand, this had to be her moment to pass over the note. She'd had years of practice at passing small envelopes of coke subtly in public, so a scrap of paper should be a breeze as long as he didn't drop it. She managed to hand it over and he stroked her fingers to acknowledge it. Phoebe breathed a sigh of relief, mission accomplished. Marcus had definitely not noticed anything.

The girls in the crowds all around them were screaming for Jake. Phoebe was so happy for him, he deserved every bit of success that was coming to him, he'd worked hard enough and she'd always known that the public would love him. She suddenly found herself being steered by Marcus into the building, his hand firmly in the small of her back, leaving her no chance to linger any longer. Jake remained outside for the crowds to sign autographs and then went in surrounded by his management team, with the scrap of paper now safely tucked into the pocket of his tux.

Chapter 39. Jake. The Martinez Hotel

The Premiere after-party

Phoebe walked into the party together with Marcus, she could see that the room was already full of anyone who was anyone in the film world. The guests instantly stopped chatting and began clapping, as the couple stood at the entrance, there was no doubt the movie had been a huge success.

The select few photographers who'd been allowed up to the suite were all capturing the moment, snapping the famous film producer with his equally famous wife; the couple were the epitome of Hollywood royalty. Phoebe felt all eyes on them. She was really trying to look happy and vibrant but she was feeling so strange, the dizziness she'd experienced earlier had been increasing as the evening had progressed. She'd tried a sip of the champagne she'd been handed as she walked in, but the room was beginning to spin and there was a loud buzzing in her ears. She held Marcus's arm tighter, clutching onto him for dear life, then she suddenly felt like she was drowning, sinking into the deeper darker depths of the ocean.

The sea of faces in the room was turning into a blur and she tried to focus and gripped even harder onto Marcus's arm. The last thing she saw as she fell was his cold angry eyes filled full of hate, she didn't see the look of horror and shock on the guests' faces. As she collapsed, Phoebe knew, without any shadow of doubt, Marcus would never forgive her for this. Her life would never be worth living again. In fact she might as well be dead. She'd ruined his night and it was now captured on film.

The photographers' camera flashes had gone crazy capturing the exact moment that Phoebe Clarke, stylist to the stars had collapsed at her film producer husband's party, and everyone at the party had seen, except for Simon and Jake.

Simon had just been finishing yet another celebrity guest's makeup back in his suite and Jake had finally managed to find a window of opportunity to go the men's room, not just for a pee but to look at the scrap of paper that had been burning a hole in his pocket. He'd stayed longer at the Palais before leaving there as there had been so many well-wishers afterwards.

The movie had received a standing ovation and he, together with Marcus and the other lead actors, had all proudly stood up in the auditorium to take their bows. Jake hadn't been in the right frame of mind to appreciate the applause at all as he had been worrying all the time about Phoebe. He'd been watching her body language whilst she was sitting with Marcus and Jake knew all about body language from his acting classes; Marcus and Phoebe's awkward and distant body language spoke volumes.

When Jake had stood outside the foyer of the Palais waiting for his limo, he'd realised he could hear Marcus telling Phoebe exactly what she was going to do.

'Phoebe, you're coming to the party with me only to publicly show your support for me, then I'm taking you straight back to our suite. I've already told you that you're not well enough to stay the whole evening.' Jake had been shocked at Marcus's assertive tone, it was though he'd been speaking to a particularly troublesome child. He'd never seen Marcus behave in such a bullying manner before.

He straightened the tiny crumpled bit of paper as he stood in one of the locked stalls. The writing was smudged but he could just make it out, *"Help!"* He simply had to find and speak to Simon as quickly as he could. He rushed back to the party and found Marcus, just inside the entrance, crouching over Phoebe who was lying in a heap on the floor. He could see that Marcus was making a big song and dance of how attentive and caring he was before he stood up again, so that his stunned and silent party guests could see and hear him better,

'Apologies to you all, my wife's been quite ill recently and I'm sure she simply fainted, it's so hot tonight so if you can just give us some space, I'll get security to carry her up to our suite straight away. Please, please do all carry on and enjoy the party.' He made sweeping gestures with his hands to demonstrate all that was on offer. 'There's champagne and caviar, ask away for anything else you want. The night has only just begun... enjoy... I'll be back very soon.'

Marcus didn't want any doctors coming forward to check her. If they ran health checks on her they'd find large amounts of the drugs in her system that he'd been administering to her for weeks now, but it had been Phoebe who'd asked for them; she'd liked those little 'purple heart' pills and had repeatedly asked for more and as they had become more and more ineffectual, she had become more and more addicted.

One of the security guards came over to carry Phoebe.

'To our suite, please,' directed Marcus. The guard carried the unconscious Phoebe, who was as limp as a corpse in his arms, out of the room as quickly as he could. As they went up in the lift, she started stirring.

'Where am I... what happened?' she mumbled.

Marcus put on a show of charm and caring in front of the guard. 'Darling, you fainted, so this kind security man is taking you to our suite and I'll make sure that he stays outside the room to make sure you're okay.'

Phoebe's eyelids flickered as she was just conscious of Marcus directing his commands to the security guard.

'Please make sure my wife doesn't leave the room under any circumstances. I'll tell reception not to put any calls through to our room and also a "do not disturb" sign on the door, she's been very poorly recently and sleep will be the answer. I'll come back to check on her myself later.'

Marcus opened the door and helped the guard place Phoebe on the bed. He made the pretence of leaning in to kiss her again for the benefit of the guard, but it wasn't a kiss - it was a threat.

'You'll regret this Phoebe and I'll *never* forget what you did tonight; you ruined everything.' His face was twisted with hate and his words filled with vitriol as he clenched his fists trying to contain his anger.

He then made sure he added another crumbled sleeping pill to the water he left beside her bed, he wasn't going to leave anything to chance. He swiftly left the room and temporarily closed the door on that part of his life, leaving the guard seated outside the door of the suite. He returned to the party vowing to put his bitch of a wife completely out of his mind.

On his return, he was instantly surrounded by well-wishers all asking how Phoebe was, why would they care? He wanted to forget her now for the rest of the night and not be questioned about her. He was becoming increasingly angry. It was his night not hers and she'd made it all about her. They should be talking about his movie not his wife, how fucking dare she.

He tried to compartmentalise everything and put on his full-on charming public-face reassuring them and thanking them all for their concern. Maybe a glass of champagne or three would help his stress, even some cocaine. One of his team would be able to access some immediately, they'd know a local dealer. It was now time to enjoy his party as Phoebe couldn't ruin it any more. She was safe, locked away in their room, dosed with a sleeping pill that should have already taken effect. He'd deal with her again later. However, he hadn't yet decided what her punishment would be but she deserved everything she had coming.

There were so many women at the party and every woman there was beautiful. He was the host and therefore he could have the pick of the bunch, screw Phoebe, what a bitch. He'd show her what happened when she ruined his night, and the night was still young. The terrace of the Suite des Oliviers at the Martinez Hotel was the perfect place to throw a party. The promenade lights of the Croisette had now come on and the final glow of the setting sun was reflecting on the sea and the marble surface of the roof terrace.

The unfortunate incident had already been forgotten by his guests who'd reverted to party mode, making the most of everything on offer. The waiters and waitresses were standing around holding silver platters of extravagant canapés and champagne. Ice buckets with magnums of champagne were also on the tables, next to bowls of caviar.

Marcus had intended that this was to be The Party of the Cannes Film Festival week and nothing was going to spoil his night now. It would be the ultimate party that everyone would be talking about for weeks after.

Chapter 40. Circle of Friends, Cannes

The Premiere after-party

Jake was frustrated as he was constantly surrounded by his PR team who wanted him to network and meet all the film-world bigwigs at the party.

Normally he would have been thrilled at all the attention, but the pressing problem of Phoebe was foremost on his mind. So many girls wanted to meet him too and were constantly circling like vultures to their prey, but they'd been held back by his minders. He understood that this was all part of the job description, but he desperately needed to be on his own to speak to Simon. The specially invited top photographers were still snapping away whilst the paparazzi outside the hotel were photographing guests as they arrived; there was anticipation and excitement everywhere.

Jake had still not seen Simon yet. He hoped Simon had seen Phoebe collapse and would understand the severity of what was happening. No one wrote notes saying "help", unless something was really wrong. Where could Simon have gone and why was he still not here? Another celebrity must have asked him to refresh her makeup before she arrived at the party. Jake persevered with his search, scanning all corners of the terrace and suite during his interviews. It was really hard to focus on anything anyone was asking him. The excitement of being at his own first big premiere had been eradicated as his friends were more important to him, especially when they were in trouble.

As he looked around the room once again, he saw a face he thought looked familiar; it looked very much like Caroline from Phoebe's debutante days. That was a strange coincidence if it was her, how had she ended up at this party?

'I'm just going to say hi to some friends of mine, I'll be back in a sec.' Jake politely extracted himself from his agent and PR people and approached her. 'Caroline?'

'Jake!' she greeted him warmly and kissed him on both his cheeks in the Gallic way, 'You were so fab in the film, congratulations.'

'This is so lovely to see you here for my movie and especially after so long.' Jake was thrilled to see one of their old circle of friends again.

'Jake, I have to say that you're even better looking now than you were when we first met and you were drop dead handsome then! Oops, sorry Charlie, I forgot to introduce you – do you remember Charlie? My now-husband, whom I met at the ball in Yorkshire that you all came to. Oh and how rude of me, this is Natalie and Frederic, they were the ones who kindly invited us here, Frederic works with Marcus.' Caroline didn't get to finish her introduction properly before there was a shriek behind her and Simon appeared. Jake breathed a sigh of relief, finally.

'Hey guys, I had to go and do some make up touch ups just now for Sharon and now I have to go back again for a few others, so I've left the team in charge for the moment. Jake, you were wonderful in the film, I'm so proud of you.' He moved closer and whispered in Jake's ear, 'I'd give you a kiss if I could but I really can't in here can I.' Jake acknowledged his whisper with a brief brush of finger tips across Simon's hand.

Jake continued the introductions, 'So do you remember Caroline and Charlie from the Yorkshire ball all those years ago? They've come tonight with Marcus's French business partner Frederic and his wife Natalie. There we are, everyone knows everyone now.' Jake just wanted to get Simon on his own, but it wasn't looking possible.

Simon returned to normal volume of speaking. 'What's up? Why is everyone looking like someone's died?'

'Feels a bit like it Simon, we're so worried about Phoebe.' Caroline spoke for everyone.

'Why, what's happened? I've only just arrived.' Simon's voice had become shrill as he looked at his friends' solemn faces and heard the anxiety in Caroline's voice.

Jake took up the story; he'd been waiting for what seemed an eternity to tell it to Simon and now he had a whole audience.

'Phoebe arrived together with Marcus and me at the screening. He wouldn't let her talk to me and sat very firmly between us. We all walked the red carpet together but again she wasn't able to speak. Then, apparently she arrived here at the party but immediately fainted before she'd hardly put a foot in the door. I wasn't here yet when she fainted, although by the time I'd arrived I could see the anger all over his face. Everyone else would have mistaken it for worry, but believe me I knew it was real anger, remember I've just spent the last year working with him and look, read this - it's what Phoebe secretly handed me on the red carpet.' Jake bought the tiny note out again.

They all huddled together and peered down at scrap of paper with *"help"* scribbled on it. Simon looked pale with shock. His voice shook as he spoke. 'My poor little Phoebes, what's that man been doing to her? I knew something had to be very wrong when I hadn't seen or heard from her over the last few weeks. Oh my god, I knew I never liked him.' Simon was looking close to tears.

'I hadn't heard from her either for the last few months and we used to speak at least once a week,' Caroline added her view, 'I just assumed she'd been busy especially as I'm in England and she's in LA. I'd literally just been saying yesterday to Charlie that I wondered what had happened to her. I thought she looked so ill and frightened on the red carpet, just not herself, sort of spaced out weird. Not like she looked when she was doing drugs and we all know she used to do those, not that sort of look in her eyes, more like zoned out.'

They all stood together in their huddle, trying to decide what to do next, when Jake heard a booming Texan voice. 'Paula honeybun, come over here and look at the view. It's even better than the view from our own suite.'

Then he heard a well-spoken English female voice with a touch of Mid-Atlantic accent, 'Forbesy, I'm so happy wherever we are as long as I'm with you.'

They all looked round to see the owners of the two voices. They belonged to an unassuming short, elderly man with a bald head and a big belly together with a tall, beautiful Nordic-looking blonde. She was dripping with diamonds that were sparkling in the last rays of the sun and she was wearing the most beautiful but simplistic evening dress.

The Texan man wrapped his elderly lips around the fattest cigar Jake had ever seen, savouring a long and pleasurable cigar moment before he spoke to the group of friends.

'May we come and join you? We've just arrived and can't see anyone we know here. I think I may have invested some money into tonight's little movie, but it's my beautiful girlfriend who knows Marcus and his wife Phoebe better than me. Phoebe and Paula were at school together, weren't you honeybun?'

Paula smiled with a one hundred and eighty degree sweep, immediately including everyone in their little huddle. 'Hi, yes I was at school with Phoebe but we lost touch for years until recently. Then we spoke every day from wherever we were in the world. This is my boyfriend, Forbes.' She looked back at Forbes as if she needed him to confirm her statement, and kissed him tenderly on his cheek and he immediately returned the kiss on her neck.

Jake watched everything unfolding, still hoping for Simon to come up with a plan. Instead Simon seemed more interested in the fact that he'd finally actually met Paula.

'How fantastic, you're *that* Paula, her-best-friend-Paula, the one who disappeared for years and then re-appeared again. So, you and I have never actually met and I'm her other best friend Simon, the gay makeup artist best friend. Well, you're even more beautiful than Phoebe described.' Simon was impressed by how stunning she was.

'Isn't that the truth Simon, she is gorgeous... and all mine!' Forbes put his arm proudly and protectively around Paula's waist and kissed her again, and this time she kissed him back full on the lips, she really was very fond of him.

Caroline did a little cough, 'Ahem... and I'm Phoebe's other best friend from Gloucestershire,' and laughed as she joined in the Paula admiration society; 'I've heard a lot about you too and we've never met either, so here we all are together now worrying about Phoebe. So just to fill you in Paula, not only did she collapse as she arrived at the party but passed this very worrying note earlier to Jake.'

Paula peered quickly over at the note, then, with a tremor in her voice read the one word to Forbes.

'Gee Paula, I know you think I don't always listen to what you say and you did mention earlier that you were worried about not hearing from her, but I was just a little pre-occupied at that point.' Forbes gave Paula a gentle friendly slap on her bottom and winked. Paula didn't react at all as she was now so focused on what to do after seeing this note.

'So what can we do? Marcus has obviously taken Phoebe back to their suite. I don't know where it is but I'm sure it can't be that hard to find out.' Simon was first to start coming up with a plan, just as Jake had known he would.

'But we can't just break into the room and smuggle her out in a blanket. This is real life not a movie,' Jake quite reasonably pointed out, 'there has to be a plan.'

Caroline, always the logical one interrupted, in the same tone as she probably used to focus her children. 'Come on chaps, put on your thinking hats before the champagne takes hold, we've a small window of opportunity whilst the party's in full swing. Paula, perhaps you should chat up Marcus and see what you can find out, he likes a beautiful woman.'

'Hey, not too much chat, honey bun.' Forbes was very possessive when it came to his women.

Paula squeezed Forbes's hand to assure him she wouldn't, and then continued thoughtfully, 'Forbes and I met Marcus and Phoebe a little while ago for dinner and Marcus was really off that night, so unbelievably rude and they left early. I only ever went to their house once to meet Phoebe when Marcus wasn't there, straight after their wedding. From then on, it was always easier to meet her out for a coffee, at the gym or at the Style Bar as Marcus didn't like her having visiting friends; all very strange. So we're agreed, my role is to chat up Marcus but don't worry Forbes, I have eyes for no man but you.'

'What shall we all do?' Jake, Caroline and Charlie all asked at the same time.

Simon, who'd been silent again suddenly spoke before anyone else could answer.

'Listen, guys, I'm sorry I've got to go as I'm really late for the makeup suite, I just can't keep a celebrity waiting. I'll think of a plan whilst I'm in there. We'll sort this out and at least we know what we're dealing with now. We all love Phoebe and we can't let this monster of a man hurt her, a single second longer. I knew there was something fishy about Marcus from the first time I heard about him. Why does Phoebe always pick the wrong men, all she wants is to be loved. It's sad that so many bad things keep happening to her; first she went out with me, a gay man - not an auspicious start to any girl's love life is it?' Simon did a jokey expression of camp horror, 'then something bad happened to her at that ball in Yorkshire.'

'Yes, she was raped, I'm the only one she ever told the whole story to.' Paula said it so quietly that they only just heard her over the noise of the party chatter. They all looked at her with shock. 'That's why she left London and went to Paris to live with George, in fact, where is George tonight? I'm surprised he's not here. They still speak all the time, or did until she went missing. She always stayed at his London studio flat when she was working in London.'

'So I know this doesn't have anything to do with how we're going to get Phoebe away tonight but, who was it who raped her and why wouldn't she ever tell me? Mrs Abbott called me in desperation when Phoebe had gone into meltdown to ask me to come and help her.' Caroline was looking increasingly upset as she spoke and Charlie was hugging her tightly as he could see she was about to cry. 'This is just all so horrid. Poor, poor Bea.' Caroline was still bravely holding back her tears.

Frederic, meanwhile, had been cornered by some of the other film backers, who'd taken him away to talk business. Natalie was still there though, listening compassionately to what was unfolding. She reached out for Caroline's hand empathising with her; she was more worried for Phoebe's wellbeing than Phoebe's longstanding friends, she'd seen first-hand the subtle but intimidating manner of how Marcus had treated Phoebe at the Los Angeles dinner. She wanted to help now too, although she'd have to be discreet as she couldn't jeopardize her marriage or her husband's business relationship with Marcus. She'd never been taken in by Marcus's charisma or charm, even when he'd chosen to switch it on.

Paula also saw how upset Caroline was becoming. 'She didn't want to tell you Caroline, in case it upset your family. It was your brother's friend who raped her, the one who was staying with you. I'm so sorry.'

'Oh my God that was Giles. Oh no, I knew it was going to be someone I knew and that makes it all even worse. I now understand even more why Phoebe was so reluctant to tell me anything, and Giles was acting so strangely when I saw him later at the party. My brother has never spoken to him since as Giles was so rude to our family and my mother said she'd never have him in the house again. When all this is over and we've rescued Phoebe, I'm going to have to tell my brother. Even though it's all these years on, Giles could still be raping other girls and needs to be stopped.'

'This is all just so terrible that none of us knew exactly what was happening in Phoebe's life. She was always so good at keeping secrets. No wonder Marcus found it so easy to reel her in, making her believe he was her shining knight.' Jake said exactly what they were all thinking and now, how they were all feeling equally bad that not one of them had managed to be there for her.

'I'll do everything I can to help too. I thought Phoebe was a lovely girl when I met her at dinner, that once. My jet is on standby at Nice Airport whilst I'm here in case I have to fly back suddenly to Texas for urgent business, but I'm sure we can come up with a plan. Anyone who upsets a friend of my Paula will always have me to reckon with.' He paused for thought. He was used to making snap decisions for his multi-million dollar oil deals. 'Paula, I'm just going down to the lobby for a moment and I'll be back soon. Love you, baby.'

'Love you too, Forbes. I'm sure I'll still be here and if I'm not, then I'll be back at our room waiting for you.'

Caroline and Charlie looked at each other, with Caroline asking the question, 'So what shall we do?'

Natalie answered for them, 'Why don't you stay here and enjoy the party for a little while, while I go and see what I can find out from my husband or even from Marcus; he knows me and always chats to me, as my husband works so closely with him.'

'Well, that just leaves me and it's really difficult for me to disappear with all the PRs and management team on my case, so maybe I'll hold the fort here for a while and be the central intelligence person so to speak.' Jake felt bad he couldn't do more, but at least he could keep his eyes and ears open.

Caroline still felt helpless, 'Charlie, what do you think we should do? I so want to be able to help; Bea's my oldest best friend.'

Charlie always thought carefully before he answered anything. He raked his fingers back through his hair; Caroline knew he did this when he was under pressure. 'I think we should leave now to go back to our villa, giving our address and house phone number to Paula. I just saw Forbes leave and she looks like she is about to go too. They're staying here at the Hotel, so it will be easier for them to keep us posted and then we can see what we can do to help from our home base.'

'Okay, I'm going over to her now, have you got a biro to write our contact details?'

'Yup, here we are, already done.' He tore a page out of his pocket diary and handed it to his wife.

Caroline rushed over to Paula, 'Paula, I know we hardly know each other but will you promise to keep Charlie and I in the loop with any developments with Phoebe? We need go back to our villa now as we've two small children being looked after by a babysitter, but we'll do anything we can to help.'

Paula took the piece of paper with their phone number and leant forward to give her a "keep your chin up" hug.

'Of course I will and I know Forbes is already on it. If anyone can do anything, it will be him.' Paula made herself sound confident, hoping that it would sound reassuring to Caroline.

'Thank you so much, Phoebe means the world to me.'

'I know and to me, too.'

The two women embraced and held each other for a short time, taking comfort in the physical closeness and their mutual worry over their closest friend before the last of the small group of Phoebe's loyal friends disbanded, all armed with their personal rescue-strategy mission.

Chapter 41. Lily Rose, Cannes

The Premiere after-party

Lily Rose was in a bit of a panic as she was surrounded by makeup and still not nearly ready. It was so lucky that she'd cancelled walking the red carpet with Jake and that his management had been okay with it.

There was no way she would ever have been able to get ready in time as she still had so much to do, but she would definitely be ready for the after-party. She just needed some more time and as all girls knew, it didn't take five minutes to create an evening version of natural beauty.

The suite was full of everything she needed to become the glamorous red-carpet-ready version of Lily Rose; and once she'd transformed herself to perfection, she'd make her entrance at the party like Cinderella to the ball, especially as she was so late. She could be that beautiful unknown girl that everyone noticed, and who then disappeared into the night as mysteriously as she'd arrived, never to be seen again.

Maybe she could even leave one of her shoes behind too and that would confuse everyone as her feet weren't really very small and dainty. She smiled to herself with a glint of excitement in her eyes, before she decided that she needed to check in the mirror and see how she looked when she smiled. She pouted and practised her enigmatic mysterious girl smile, yes that was good, or was coquettish and flirty better? She stared at her reflection wondering which smile worked better for her perfectly symmetrical facial features, hmm, she wasn't sure.

Was there anything else now that she'd omitted to consider? She paced up and down the hotel bedroom as she thought about this. She knew what she was going to be wearing so that was sorted, she knew how her hair and makeup was going to be and she'd just practised her seductive smile, she checked back in the mirror again, had she been smiling with her eyes like they told the models in photo shoots? She lowered her head and gazed back at herself seductively through her extra-long fake lashes, yes, that was definitely working. Lily Rose's whole public image was nearly perfect and ready to be tested.

She just had to look incredible tonight though as it was now even more important that she made an optimal impact. She had always been a perfectionist but now there was even more reason to be the whole fabulous package and she couldn't slip up. Chloe at the Style Bar had done an adequate job of selecting a designer sample dress for this Cannes debut, but Lily Rose had decided to return it unworn before leaving LA as she'd found a better dress instead in a tiny vintage boutique. The dress was forties Hollywood style, a sexy silk slip of an evening dress that fitted like a glove and created the best body shape and sexy silhouette just as she'd learnt suited her, all by trial and error. She'd chosen everything with the utmost attention to detail, even down to her unbelievably expensive Italian lingerie which sculpted, shaped, and created cleavage where there really wasn't any.

She looked once again in the bathroom mirror. She would never tire of seeing this glamorised version of herself, it was how she would really like to have dressed all the time, but unfortunately life just wasn't like that and you couldn't always have what you wanted, just as the Rolling Stones song went:

"you can't always get what you want,
you can't always get what you want,
but if you try sometimes, well, you might just find

You get what you need."

She checked for the very last time in the different light of the bedroom suite mirror. Yes, all those hours spent perfecting her makeup, the longer lashes that she'd just practised fluttering and the more accentuated eyeliner flick was all working. She'd also had a chance earlier that day to shave her legs and other bits that needed attention, moisturise and fake tan and generally groom herself to perfection.

She was now ready to hit the party. She wasn't sure if she was nervous or excited about making the entrance on her own, but as she drew closer she could practically hear her heart beating so loudly. She felt her confidence building, holding her head high, talking care not to trip on her heels or her evening dress as she elegantly navigated the few flights of stairs down to the first floor suite where the party was taking place. She could hear the chill-out Ibiza style music coming from the terrace as she approached. She kept her eyes down as she walked in, missing the admiring glances from another tall blonde who was just leaving. The security man also gave her lingering and approving looks from head to toe as she stepped onto the terrace.

It was after midnight and the party seemed already to be winding down with waiters and waitresses, no longer so attentive after a long night, now standing around in the shadows, waiting for the last guests to go so they could clear as much of the party glasses and debris that they could. Lily Rose could see that the party had obviously been a success as empty champagne bottles now stood upturned in their ice buckets and the caviar bowls scraped clean, just a remnant of the shiny fish balls glistening around the edges; it was such a shame she couldn't have managed an earlier entrance.

The good looking young waiter handed her a glass of champagne and Lily Rose was aware of him boldly checking her out from head to toe with appreciation; and with that additional male reassurance, she sashayed with attitude and sass further into the central hub of the party. The few remaining guests unfortunately were by now too stoned or drunk to take much notice of this new arrival. However Marcus had immediately.

Lily Rose was now completely confident that she looked not just good but fabulous, she'd checked enough times before she left the room, in all the mirrors and from all angles. She absolutely knew she would pass as she'd practiced enough.

Marcus came rushing over, like an eager puppy, stumbling slightly in his haste. He wasn't just stumbling over his own feet, but also over his words and sentences which were tumbling out on top of each other at double speed. It was obvious to Lily Rose that he had been partying hard for the last few hours, as she could see from his dilated pupils and bloodshot eyes that he'd been on a cocaine binge. This was the man she had her sights set on, whether or not he was now on an alcohol and cocaine-fuelled high.

'Hi, I don't believe we know each other. I'm your host Marcus Lean and you are?'

'Lily Rose.' She immediately put her eyelash flutter into action as she needed to use all her tools in her newly found mastery of the art of seduction.

'That name rings a bell I think, I don't know why.' Marcus looked puzzled for an instant as though some memory had briefly raced across his mind, disappearing again as quickly as it had arrived. Lily Rose didn't feel this needed a response.

'So Ms Lily Rose, the most beautiful woman in the whole room, how would you feel about being monopolised by your host for a while? Do you think we could just sit down over in that corner away from everyone and get to know each other better?'

Lily Rose flashed agreement with a seductive smile that showed her perfect teeth, before following him over to a secluded corner sofa by the edge of the terrace where they sat down together under a glorious bougainvillea-covered arbour, offering a view over the twinkling masthead lights of bobbing yachts moored out at sea. It was the most stunningly beautiful setting, the perfect place for most couples to start their love story from, but it wasn't romance that either Lily Rose or Marcus were looking for that night.

Marcus held her hand, curling his fingers round her long, delicate and perfectly manicured ones as he looked searchingly into her eyes.

'So Lily, may I call you that, how come you arrived so late? Didn't you come to my movie showing?'

She knew she could answer that question completely truthfully, 'No, I'm afraid I couldn't as I was just so busy. You know how life gets during the festival, maybe you could give me a personal viewing – just the two of us – I would enjoy that so much more.' Her voice as she answered was too low to be called a purr, it was like Eartha Kitt's voice; provocative, earthy and bewitching.

Lily Rose was working hard to entice and become dangerously alluring with the promise of what could come, just like one of the ancient Greek mythology Sirens whose beauty and sexuality lured sailors to their deaths.

Marcus was already in thrall to this beautiful enchantress who embodied temptation, desire and risk, 'Maybe we could

464

do just that; the guests will all be gone soon and then we can be all on our own.'

'What an unexpected treat, a private showing from the famous Marcus Lean just for me.' She smiled flirtatiously and once again ran her tongue over her perfectly applied pink lipstick cupid bow lips making them appear even more moist, glossy and kissable.

'It'll be my pleasure,' and Marcus quickly leant in to kiss the lips he could no longer resist.

She gently placed her fingers on his lips and pushed him away. 'Let's wait a little, there are still so many guests here, there's time later. We've a whole night left to party together. I prefer to be a little discreet, don't you?' Lily Rose was really getting into this whole seduction routine now.

'True,' Marcus reluctantly agreed and pulled back from her, 'a woman as beautiful as you, will always be worth waiting for.'

Lily Rose could see that Marcus was already in lust, her game of push and pull was working on this emotionally unavailable man; she held his gaze and smiled tantalisingly back at him.

Chapter 42. Forbes, Cannes

After the after-party

Forbes was a strategic and rapid problem solver, it wasn't by chance he'd made so many millions.

'Honey-bun, if I don't return to the party within the next half an hour, I'll see you back in our room as I can dial directly from there without having to wait for the operator to connect me. I've a feeling that we may need to move quickly to find Phoebe.'

Paula replied with a lingering kiss on his lips. Forbes loved the touch of her soft sensual lips; he really was going to have to consider what to do very soon with his second wife back in Texas. How would he feel about making Paula his third one, he really was very fond of this young woman. This was a thought for future consideration, for now he was going to do everything in his power to help her friend.

'See you very soon, sugar plum.' He reluctantly left his beautiful mistress and walked briskly downstairs to the lobby to the concierge. The night concierge was a temporary replacement who was a nervous young man, standing in for the usual one, and he was still trying to get to grips with the job; he'd hoped it was going to be a quiet night.

'Good evening Sir, how can I help?'

Forbes had already formulated his plan and considered what he was going to say. 'I'm very worried about my young friend, Mrs Lean, who fainted earlier at her husband's party tonight. Her husband asked me to go check on her in their room as it's difficult for him to leave his own party and he was worrying about her. I can't remember the suite number Marcus told me they're staying in, you know I forget everything as I'm so old now.'

Forbes knew the young concierge would have no clue what happened when people got old. His own memory and brain was still as sharp as a pin, but it was a completely feasible story and he was also simultaneously discreetly sliding a five hundred franc note over the desk; money always talked.

The young concierge had no hesitation in wrapping his hand over the note and sliding it quickly towards his side of the desk.

'Of course, Sir, as you know room numbers are not something we would normally give out but, in the circumstances, maybe I can help you, write it down for you so you don't forget it.'

'Thank you very much young man, I'll let the manager know how helpful you've been; he's a personal friend of mine. Of course, I won't be mentioning this particular moment specifically.'

The young concierge puffed up with mistaken pride, 'Merci Monsieur, c'est très gentil.'

Satisfied with the first part of his plan executed successfully , Forbes set off back up to his suite to continue on with the second part.

Paula hated staying at the party without Forbes, she felt as though she had lost a limb, so she decided to leave and meet Forbes back at their room. She absolutely knew he would already have come up with some sort of plan. She hadn't been able to say goodbye to Jake as he was still surrounded by his PR and management people, and Simon had already left. She could just spot Caroline's French friend Natalie walking toward the small admiring crowd surrounding Marcus. It was definitely time to go to find out how Forbes was getting on. It was late and the party was already winding down anyway.

As she walked up the stairs again, she passed a stunning looking woman who was even taller than she was, that was unusual. She stared back at her again, she was just gorgeous, maybe she was also one of Claude's girls? She looked just the type; blonde, classy, elegant and beautiful. Well, good luck to her, there were certainly still enough pickings of uber-wealthy men left at the party.

Paula decided to continue walking up to their suite, instead of taking the lift, she always liked to take the opportunity to keep fit and in the best shape possible, even when it was late at night. She found Forbes already sitting there in the bedroom on the phone. He quickly put his fingers to his lips motioning to Paula to stay silent. She looked at him, briefly raising one eyebrow expectantly, trying not to wrinkle her forehead, wondering who he was talking to. She sat close to him on the edge of the bed, leaning in as she listened.

Forbes seemed to be speaking with less of a Texan drawl. In fact, he sounded completely different, she'd never heard him speaking this way.

'So, Danny, you do understand that my business partner Forbes will be coming up in a minute to check on my wife. I can't come myself as I can't leave the party, please let him in.'

She could just hear a man's voice at the other end of the phone.

Forbes continued, 'Yes, Danny, I do understand that I told you not to let anyone in under any circumstances. I've changed my mind and now I want you to let him in,' Forbes looked over to Paula conspiratorially, from under his bushy grey eyebrows as he continued speaking, 'He'll be with my wife's best friend.'

Paula could hear the voice at the other end getting louder, whereas Forbes remained calm and authoritative. 'Yes, I do hear you very clearly Danny and I know you're carrying out your orders, however your security team are working for *me* and *I've* changed my mind. Am I making myself clear or do I actually have to leave my own party and come up myself to tell you in person? No, I thought not. Glad you finally came round to my way of thinking. They'll be with you within the next ten minutes.'

Chapter 43. The Martinez Hotel, Cannes

After the after-party

Dawn was breaking over the bay. A "Do Not Disturb" sign was hanging on the bedroom suite door. The guests had left and Marcus and Lily Rose had partied on, she'd known just how to play him, like a musical instrument, from high to low and slow to fast until he didn't know whether he was coming or going, but he'd found it hard to breathe as his heart had been racing so fast. They'd done so much coke, or had it only been him doing the coke, he didn't remember. Whatever she'd been doing to him had obliterated all thoughts of hate towards his bitch of a wife, replacing hate with lust or, could it even be love for this amazing new young woman?

No one had ever made him come like her, why wouldn't she let him touch her, he'd wanted to. Every time he'd gone to fondle her breasts or touch her anywhere she hadn't let him, she'd pulled away. Maybe that was how she liked it, especially as she'd kept her lace basque and panties on, maybe she only liked to *give* pleasure, after all it had been his party. Maybe she'd seen herself as his party favour, his end-of-party gift. She was certainly all of that - and more. He'd never known a night like it and he'd had a lot of women. She was just incredible.

'Here,' she was telling him to sniff something that she was now putting under his nose, he couldn't see as she'd blindfolded him. He'd sniffed and it had smelt like old socks. Whatever it was, it took effect immediately and he felt his heart racing and he couldn't breathe. He felt his orgasm building but he couldn't get enough oxygen to take another breath at the same time. He felt himself starting to black out. Was he having a heart attack, a stroke or an-out-of-this-world orgasm like he'd never experienced before, he cried out in pain.

'My heart pills... they're on the table next to the bed.'

Marcus never got to finish his sentence as his heart finally gave out on his ultimate orgasm. Lily Rose was now looking at him, wondering what people looked like if they were actually dead should she take his blindfold off to see if his eyes were now open or shut. She'd watched movies where someone actually closed the eyes of the dead person, did she need to do that, or should she feel his wrist to see if there was still a pulse, she wanted to be sure so she placed her fingers on his wrist. No, there seemed to be nothing. She climbed off the bed and stood considering everything for a moment. Then she leaned right back over him again.

'I hope you enjoyed your final moments of pleasure,' she spat the words out venomously right into his lifeless face. She stood up again, stretched her sinewy body and surveyed the bedroom scene. It would be easy to conclude that death was from an overdose of alcohol and drugs, especially if Marcus had a weak heart. His bottle of heart pills still lay unopened on his bedside table. She was sure she'd not left any identifying traces of her presence.

She now needed to gather together her evening dress, shoes and bag and leave as quickly as she could before any of the hotel's morning staff came in to clean the suite. She was sure she'd put a "Do Not Disturb" sign on the bedroom door in the early hours. She stripped off the lace basque that had so cleverly sculpted and shaped her body and then grabbed a handful of plastic laundry bags. She systematically threw the lingerie into one of the bags, the dress into another and her evening bag and shoes into a third. She grabbed one of the luxurious large bath towels and bundled all the laundry bags into the folds of the towel and finally wound a hand towel round her head as a turban.

She retrieved her oversized Sophia Loren-style sunglasses from the bottom of her discarded handbag and put those on; there, she was now ready to leave the suite. She definitely looked like some rich bitch hotel guest up early for a quick dip in the sea. She was completely unrecognisable, swathed in white towelling from head to toe.

She checked behind her one more time and opened the door with the sleeve of her towelling robe - always better to be safe than sorry. Once out in the corridor she needed to make a quick decision as to whether she was going to walk down the one flight of stairs to the lobby or turn the opposite direction and go down by way of the back staff stairs. She wasn't sure where the staff stairs might lead to, so maybe it would be best to brazen it out and go straight down the beautiful curving art-deco staircase she'd navigated the night before. She could then walk purposefully through the lobby and past the swimming pool at the front of the hotel and she was sure she wouldn't be the only guest who chose to have an early morning swim.

The young night porter didn't notice her as she walked through the lobby as he was busy in the back office, ready for the change-over to daytime staff. He was richer by five hundred francs and was considering all the ways he could spend his lucky windfall. Lily Rose decided to stroll straight across the main road and down to the beach. As she crossed the road, she saw an early morning dustcart heading in her direction, doing the daily collections. She quickly knotted each of the plastic laundry bags and threw them down randomly, scattering them amongst the piles of roadside rubbish bags. She walked down onto the beach and sat on the stone steps waiting for the bin men to come past. She wanted to make sure everything was properly gone. The rubbish truck was progressing extremely slowly and watching it was like watching a kettle boil. She suddenly remembered her mother's saying, "A watched kettle never boils". She wasn't sure whether to laugh or cry at the memory; it reminded her of home and at this moment, home felt a million miles away.

The truck was moving agonisingly slowly. She realised that she still had some time to add the remaining vestiges of what had been Lily Rose into other random rubbish bags without the bin collection men seeing her. She pulled off the towelling turban and with it, the wig. She walked back to the roadside piles of rubbish and secreted the wig into another bin bag. The bin men were nearly there. She quickly retraced her steps back to the beach. Once everything had been collected all traces of Lily Rose would be crushed and eradicated for ever amongst the Cote d'Azur refuse.

The beach was completely deserted. No one noticed the early morning naked swimmer modestly drop their towelling robe as close to the water as possible and plunge quickly into the sea for a short dip. The swimmer then walked back to shore, wrapped up once again in the towelling robe, with damp blonde hair now slicked back and make-up washed off - Lily-Rose wasn't real, no one would ever meet her again.

One day, he could dress up and pass once more as a beautiful woman. He knew now that he could get away with it, even with people who knew him well. His guilty pleasure though would always remain a secret one, he had too much to lose and he wasn't sure those closest to him would ever really understand.

He let the early morning sun warm his body and dry his hair as he lay on one of the beach beds on the deserted beach. He dozed for a short while, he was exhausted. When he woke up again, he slowly sat up from the beach bed, pulling the dressing gown tightly around him and made his way back to the Martinez. He walked back through the lobby.

'Bonjour monsieur,' the daytime reception staff newly arrived on duty, greeted him warmly, 'did you have a lovely swim, it's the best time of day, isn't it, sir?'

'Yes, perfect when it's quiet, the best start to the day before breakfast.' He smiled at them as he waited for the lift and went up to the third floor and knocked on the door.

Jake opened the door and stood there hung over and sleep-deprived but looking even more designer-stubbly handsome than ever. He looked at his early morning visitor with confusion.

'What's going on, what's the time?' he wiped the sleep from his bleary eyes and focused, now seeing Simon's damp hair and dressing gown. 'You can't have already been for a swim, it's so early. I did wonder what had happened to you. You never came back to the party before we all left.'

'So sorry, Jake, I just wasn't able to let you know. I went back to my make-up room suite and whilst I was in there more celebrities came and knocked on the door who wanted me to redo their makeup before they went onto other parties. When I'd finished I sat on the bed for what was supposed to be a minute and the next thing I knew it was morning. I was so exhausted that I'd fallen asleep where I was sitting, so I decided to go for a quick swim to clear my brain before I came to see you.'

Simon couldn't look Jake in the eye as he hated lying to him, but this time he had no choice, he wanted to protect Jake from the knowledge of what had really happened. He also wanted to quickly change the subject so he kissed him.

'Come on. let's go back to bed, I'll just go to the bathroom to shower and dry myself properly so I don't make the bed all sandy.' He didn't want Jake to notice he had no swim shorts on. If questioned, he would have said he'd left them to dry back in his own room, the same place he'd also left his dinner suit the night before when he'd embarked upon his transformation into Lily Rose.

As he stood in the shower, he thought back over the last twelve hours. It had been easy to do all the celebrities' red carpet makeup earlier in the afternoon and then go do Jake's makeup and grooming in Jake's own bedroom suite; managing to arrive at the party in time to see everyone although it was so much later than he'd anticipated. He'd even missed the drama of Phoebe's fainting episode and her rapid removal from the party.

The stories from Paula, Jake and the group of friends had confirmed his worst fears about the situation with Phoebe and Marcus, and the "help me" note had been the final straw. That was when he'd realised that if anyone could bring down Marcus, it was Lily Rose. He'd always intended going to the after-party as Lily Rose, it had been going to be her swansong and then he'd had his eureka moment. Lily Rose would be the one to demean Marcus, to make him do something likely to be so abhorrent to him, creating conflict with how he felt about himself so that he would feel degraded and what could make Marcus feel more conflicted or *played* than to be seduced by a beautiful woman who would then reveal herself to be a man.

Simon knew that this scenario could be many macho-straight men's worst nightmare, it would also make them question their sexuality, especially if they'd enjoyed the sex. Marcus had always undoubtedly been a player and what better punishment could Simon as Lily Rose dish out; it had to be to play a player.

Hopefully whilst Lily Rose had been working her charms on Marcus, Jake and everyone would have had time to come up with a rescue plan for Phoebe. It had all seemed the perfect plan at the time, but Simon didn't even like killing a fly. He was sure he hadn't murdered him though, or had he? Marcus had simply had a heart attack, hadn't he? He'd even had his heart pills by the bed. Surely no one could ever suspect Simon, or even connect him with being Lily Rose as he'd been so careful to cover Lily Rose's tracks.

No one had ever seen her go into the bedroom with Marcus as everyone had already left the party. No had ever talked to or got to know Lily Rose either, except Chloe briefly in the Style Bar in LA and a very dead Marcus. No... everything would be alright.

Simon tried to breathe out all his stress and worry as he stood there in the shower. No one was going to find Marcus's body for at least the next few hours as the room had the "Do Not Disturb" sign on the door and heart attacks could happen at any time, to anyone. Phoebe was now safe from that monster of a man and hopefully Forbes had managed to find her somewhere in the hotel.

He felt emotionally and physically drained. He climbed into bed and felt the welcoming warmth of Jake's body. Simon shivered, it must be delayed shock. He held Jake closer. He wanted to feel the reassuring touch of the man he loved, he also desperately wanted to know if Jake knew any more about Phoebe. 'So what happened after I left last night?'

Before he answered, Jake ran a hand through Simon's hair and gently stroked his face and then went back to holding him tightly; he could feel that he needed the closeness, although he didn't know why. 'I was just about to tell you but I was worried what had happened to you as you never came to my room last night.' Jake gently chastised him.

'I'm truly sorry Jake, however, I'm back now.' Simon shut his eyes as he lay there with him, he just couldn't keep them open any longer.

'I miss you so much when you're not with me.' Jake kissed Simon again and then on both his closed eyes and then he continued with his story. 'So Paula's boyfriend Forbes left before everyone else, he said to make phone calls, I don't know more than that – and then he phoned me in my room, here in the middle of the night, to say that everyone should check out as soon as possible and to meet them at a villa he's rented up in the hills in a few hours' time. I have the address, apparently all is well now, I know no more than that.'

Simon felt himself breathe a sigh of relief, before he started worrying if everyone checked out, would that not make them all look guilty by association when the news of the death came out. He just wanted Phoebe to be alright again and he opened his eyes for a moment and pulled Jake towards him. In fact he just wanted to wind the clock back; days, weeks, even months, and for everything to be alright again. He looked deep into Jake's eyes, he spoke from his heart,

'I love you, Jake, never forget it, in case anything ever happens to take me away from you.' Jake looked strangely at Simon wondering why he should suddenly say that.

'I love you too, Si.'

Simon was now beyond tired and his extreme exhaustion finally took over and he promptly fell asleep lying in Jake's arms.

477

Chapter 44. Somewhere in Cannes

The morning-after the party

Paula was so proud of Forbes, she couldn't stop hugging him. She knew from what she'd just seen him do that if she was ever in trouble again he would be there for her too. She couldn't wait for their group of friends to arrive to tell them what had happened. She could hear the sound of a car bumping along the cobblestones of the driveway to their villa and then the diesel ticking of a taxi. She rushed out into the bright sunlight to see Simon and Jake alighting from the taxi, and Caroline and Charlie just parking their car with two small identical girls sitting excitedly on the back seat.

'Come in, come in! Come through to the terrace where Jean-Marie, our housekeeper has laid out breakfast for us.'

The four friends followed Paula from the bright sunlight through to the shaded terrace which had the most incredible view overlooking the whole of the Bay of Cannes.

'Wow,' they all instantly chorused, it was quite breath-taking.

'Yes, I'm a lucky girl.' Paula acknowledged, feeling blessed with her current life.

'She looks so happy, something must have gone right,' Paula could hear Caroline's loud whispering to Charlie, 'do you think she's got Phoebe here with her now?'

Paula smirked knowingly to herself. 'Come and sit down, Forbes will be out in a minute and I'm bursting to tell you what happened, especially as you must all be wondering why you're here.' She knew she wasn't managing to be her normal ice-cool, reserved self at all. She could also see that they were all far too interested in hearing the outcome of the previous night to tuck into any of the breakfast laid out there, even those warm, flaky croissants that smelled so delicious. She could finally hear footsteps, more than just a pair, approaching from inside the house and across the marble floors.

They all turned round to see who was coming and there was Forbes walking slowly toward them supporting a very pale-faced and wobbly Phoebe. They cheered - they couldn't help themselves - it was a spontaneous reaction of joy. Paula watched Phoebe slowly smile, her face momentarily lighting up, even in her confused state she was aware enough to be able to acknowledge all her closest friends sitting there around the terrace table.

Her eyes were still dead from her long-standing barbiturate dependency. It was almost as though she was now in a drunken daze with occasional tremors coursing down her skinny body as she was supported by Forbes. She tried to speak very slowly, slurring her words between laboured breaths.

'You'll never know... how much it means... to me... to be here... with you all again.' She succeeded in getting the sentence out and Forbes started helping her toward a nearby sunbed by their table in the shade so she could lie down again.

The group just couldn't contain themselves any longer and all rushed as one towards Forbes and Phoebe to have a group hug. Paula felt like a proud mother hen.

Once they had all had their group hug and he had settled Phoebe, Forbes started speaking. 'Hey gang, let's all sit down again, Phoebe is still very fragile and weak and then I can tell you how we got her out. Please help yourselves to the croissants and coffee. It's all for you, not me, Paula keeps a beady eye on what I eat. She likes me to maintain my six-pack.' He kept a straight face as he patted his portly tum. Paula laughed together with everyone as he clearly no longer had anything remotely resembling a six-pack. Forbes affectionately took her hand as she sat down next to him at the table, a fleeting thought suddenly came and went that maybe she really was in love with Forbes.

'If you're all sitting comfortably now, I'll begin.' All eyes were on Forbes and you could have heard a pin drop. 'So, I knew we had to get poor Phoebe away from Marcus and the hotel. We first had to find out where she was and I knew the front desk wouldn't tell me which suite Marcus and she were staying in, without a little added – let's call it incentive. Once I had this information, I dialled direct to the suite. One of Marcus's security team answered and it appeared that Marcus had ordered him not let anyone in or out of the suite, so I pretended to be Marcus sending myself and Paula up to check on Phoebe's wellbeing.'

Paula interrupted, looking at Forbes with such pride, 'And he was so brilliant at impersonating Marcus, taking no prisoners.'

'Thanks, sweetie, it was nothing really. Anyway, Paula and I were able to go up to the suite where the guard reluctantly let us in. Phoebe was asleep on the bed, still wearing her evening dress. Once the guard had let us in, he seemed to not be very interested in us as he was glued to a baseball game on the TV set in the lounge area. I knew that we absolutely needed to get her out of there as quickly as possible together with her passport too. In all my years of staying in hotels, I realised that most people have always chosen the easiest safe lock code to remember. So I tried 0000; nothing then, 1234 and that sweet-ass safe door opened for me just like that. God was looking down on us, wasn't he honeybun? This beautiful girlfriend of mine,' he patted Paula's hand lovingly, 'had by now put a few of Phoebe's belongings into a small suitcase and then we were ready to go but was the guard going to let us out? That was the million dollar question.

Paula picked up Phoebe, who as you can see weighs very little now and we walked together to the door. The guard did try to stop us but determination is the key and I could see that words weren't going to help. The man was under orders, so I decided to revert to brute force. When I was a kid I'd had to learn to be a good fighter as I was the short fat nerdy boy needing to hold my own with the neighbourhood kids, so the guard wasn't expecting a surprise punch from a short fat elderly American and lost his balance. Paula and I together, quickly carried Phoebe past him and out as quickly as we could manage, and back to our own suite with no one seeing us.

So gang, here we are all safely gathered here. Simon and Jake, I believe you've both checked out of the hotel too? It shouldn't look too strange that everyone has suddenly checked out as the film awards week is coming to an end and most people would have been checking out anyway. My private plane is waiting at Nice airport ready for us to all leave this afternoon. I've found and rented a country house in Gloucestershire for Phoebe to stay in together with Paula, where medical experts, nutritionists and psychiatrists will be on hand to help her get back on track.'

Forbes finished his long monologue and stretched out to tear off a corner of a croissant. Paula decided to let it go as he completely deserved anything he wanted after what he'd managed to do.

'Gloucestershire, that's so perfect. It also means that I can easily drive over to visit Bea every day from our home.'

481

Caroline exclaimed excitedly, beaming with joy that her friend was now away from Marcus's evil and manipulative clutches.

Forbes had forgotten to add an important footnote, this time directing his words to Phoebe, 'And Phoebe, when you're feeling a bit stronger, then we'll send for the famous Mrs Abbott to come to see you as much as she can, as well. We aren't telling George at the moment, as we don't want the possibility of any drug influences near you and we do know his reputation.'

'That is just so lovely what you've done for Phoebe, we're so grateful.' Simon had tears in his eyes as he spoke and Jake pulled him in close to him to demonstrate his own similar sentiment.

A phone was ringing somewhere inside the villa.

'So that just about sums it up everyone and just so you all know, I will never ever let Marcus near Phoebe ever again, nor will a single cent of mine ever go into any one of his movies.'

The phone was still ringing. 'Shall I get the phone?' Paula wondered

'No, it's okay I'll get it, it may be my London office.' Forbes walked back into the house to take the call. They all waited silently and expectantly for him to come back before they spoke again. When he walked back out again, he had an expression that Paula just couldn't read.

He seemed to struggle for a moment before he spoke again, looking now quite shocked. 'It seems that Marcus has been found dead in the bedroom of his party suite with a suspected heart attack.'

Everyone round the table looked at each other in stunned silence. Paula looked at her friends, shocked as they were and with their emotions all over the place; finally, her friend had now been set free for ever. Simon though, seemed to have suddenly gone pale, maybe it was the shock of everything together with a hangover from the party.

'Phoebe you're free now – forever - you'll never need to worry again.' Paula had rushed over to hug Phoebe so tightly that she nearly squashed the breath out of her.

Phoebe suddenly started crying and slid even further down on her sunbed. Paula couldn't be sure if Phoebe was now crying from the shock news of her husband's death, a husband whom she had loved in spite of his abuse, or from the relief that she was now free. She was sure though, that Phoebe would never again let herself believe empty promises that may be offered to her by any future men.

This was the new beginning for all of them. The friends all looked at each other vowing silently to always be there, whatever, for each other.

Paula knew that they all felt, deep down, as guilty as her that they'd failed Phoebe so badly. None of the friends would ever again believe what anyone chose to tell them or what they only wished them to see. There would never be any secrets any more as there were always three sides to every story - his, hers and the truth.

~ ~ ~ ~

Also by Ceril Campbell:

Discover the New You takes you on a personal journey with celebrity stylist Ceril Campbell as she shows you how you can feel special and look your best, regardless of age, shape or size.

Ceril's expertise, perfected over 30 years of styling celebrities such as Jane Seymour, Darcey Bussell CBE, Katherine Jenkins and Zara Phillips, will enable you to... Discover the Inner You Transform the Outer You Become the Best You This book offers simple but brilliantly effective advice on style and self-confidence, based on Ceril's red carpet beauty secrets.